Copyright © 20

The right of Samuel Randall to be identified as the author of this work has been asserted in accordance with sections 77 and 78 of the Copyright Designs and Patents Act 1988.

In this work of fiction, the characters, places, and events are either the product of the author's imagination or they are used entirely fictitiously.

No part of this book may be reproduced, or stored in a retrieval system, or transmitted in any form or by any means, electronic, mechanical, photocopying, recording, or otherwise, without express written permission of the publisher.

ISBN-13: 978-1-0683554-0-0

First Edition

Cover design by: Samuel Randall

*To everyone who helped make this a reality.
I couldn't pick just one*

SET IN STONE

A Luke Knight Adventure

Sam L. Randall

'It is in truth not for glory, nor riches, nor honours that we are fighting, but for freedom – for that alone, which no honest man gives up but with life itself.'

– DECLARATION OF ARBROATH, 1320

PROLOGUE

1296, Scone Abbey, Perthshire, Scotland – 35 miles North of Edinburgh

Rain thundered down on the cold hewn stones of the Abbey. Raindrops hammering on the high roof sounded like war drums echoing through the cavernous space below, threatening to drown out the chanting intonement of the black-clad monks knelt before the cloth-covered alter.

Footsteps echoed off the flagstones as a hooded figure quickened their pace down the length of the nave towards the kneeling monks. Forgetting the peace and sanctity of the building he grasped one of the monks by the shoulder, cutting off his prayer mid word, and stooped to whisper in his ear. The kneeling monk rose to his feet before hurrying from the yawning space trailed closely by the hooded man. The haunting song faded behind them as they moved out of the church and into the cloister outside. Rain splashed off the flagstones forming small rippling pools that reflected and distorted the ornate stone building around. The two men hurried into the sacristy off the cloister, a heavy wooden door closing them off from the world.

'Father Thomas,' said the hooded man, 'I am glad to see you in good health, but I fear the good days shall be few.'

The abbot inclined his head to the man, his arm rose from his side and a ringed hand extended towards him. He took the abbot's hand and knelt kissing the ring that lay upon his finger. The abbot's hand moved to his shoulder and guided the shadowed figure back to his feet.

'My child, we have heard of the tyrant's victory at Dunbar, even now we pray to the father for our salvation from the hands of the English.'

The man flicked back the thick woollen hood of his cloak, bathing his face in light from a small stained-glass window that cast his features in a strange shadow. He was young, a short way into his twentieth year but his face showed the weariness caused only by the weight of responsibility and a body honed and carved by war.

'Father, it is a greater matter that brings me here. As we speak Edward's men ride on the abbey.'

The abbot's face twisted from peace into a bitter pain. 'They come for the stone?'

'Yes Father.' The man moved to the door easing

it open and peering into the dark cloister beyond. Satisfied that no one could overhear he closed the door and turned towards the abbot. 'Edward means to take the stone to Westminster, as spoils of war!' he spat.

The abbot thought for several moments. 'The stone must not fall into Edward's hands. Robert, my child, you must take it from this place for safety.'

The man looked at the abbot with sadness in his eyes. 'I cannot Father. Now the English have taken Dunbar, soon King John will be deposed and I will be made to swear fealty to Edward.' The words came with a venom. The man slammed his fist into the rough stone wall before him, the pain on his face only partly the result of his knuckles splitting and blood dripping down his hand. 'I must go south, but I have made arrangements for the stone's safe keeping. Bishop Wishart will take the stone into his care.'

'Wishart protect the stone?' questioned the abbot.

'Bishop Wishart is a great supporter of the cause and does not wish to see Edward take the stone.'

The man placed his hand on the abbot's shoulder, locking eyes with the older man.

'Fear not Father, Bishop Wishart will not fail us.'

Lightning flashed, pouring light into the sacristy. The rain grew louder, sounding like the beating hooves of a hundred horses clattering on the stones of the cloister.

The abbot let out a long breath and muttered a small prayer.

'What do you need to pass the stone to Wishart?'

The man moved slowly to look the abbot in the eye, the importance of his next words conveyed without a sound. 'Wishart has arranged for the stone to be moved; the arrangements are all here.' He handed the abbot a folded letter, held closed with the Bishop's wax seal.

The abbot took the letter. The seal was already broken, no doubt read by the young man who handed it to him. The abbot read the message on the parchment. 'Thursday next before St Botulph's day?' said the abbot, worry breaking his voice. 'Robert, if time is of the essence, surely, we should take the stone now, two brothers in a boat, down the coast and to the Forth to…'

'No!' the younger man cut him off. 'The English have taken the castles at Edinburgh and Stirling. Wishart's plan will work, trust in him.'

'God deliver us,' the abbot muttered.

'Father, I leave this in your trust. No King of England will ever truly have Scotland,' said the man, fixing the old man with a look of iron. 'For the cause.'

'For the cause,' the abbot replied heavily.

* * *

The rain did not relent as hoofbeats pounded the wet soil, carrying the young, hooded man into the night. Mere minutes passed before two monks clad in black struggled with a rectangular load, wrapped not in the fine cloths it was once housed in but plain linen and leather wrapping. They struggled into an outbuilding, a door clattering behind them. Minutes later the wooden wheels of a cart pulled by two horses, dark as jet, creaked past the abbot, rain dripping down his face, watching the kingdom's future fade from view.

CHAPTER 1

*Lawrence Lecture Theatre,
University of the South of England,
Wiltshire, England – 77 Miles
Southwest of London*

Present Day

Six sets of equally cold and disinterested glares were fixed on the front of the lecture theatre, rows of curved seating empty all for the panel of dusty academics occupying the plush, red fabric covered chairs front and centre. Luke Knight shuffled a stack of notes on the lectern. Flustered, he turned to address the panel. A dusty cadre of old men, all comfortably in the latter halves of their lives with varying degrees of receding hairlines and a shared expression that lay somewhere between bored and outright contemptuous.

'Mr Knight I'm afraid we really must bring this…' the professor on the right of the group paused trying to find the words while pushing the glasses that were barely holding onto his face back to the bridge of his long nose, '...circus you have presented us with, to a conclusion.'

A short rumble of harsh, derisive laughs rose from the other scholars.

'Please, professors. If I could just explain—'

The scholar on the far left of the panel cut him off.

'Luke, my boy, we are interested in real historical research not chasing these... fairytales of yours.' He sat back in his chair to a muttering of agreement amongst the other scholars.

Luke ran a hand across the curve of his head, frustration twisting the soft lines of his face into a hard frown.

'With respect, Professor Jameson, my research is no more chasing fairytales than Howard Carter's was accidentally stumbling across Pharaohs' tombs. Countless sites and artefacts have been lost to history and are just waiting to be found, the crown jewels of King John, the Lochan of the Lost Sword, the...'

'Mr Knight,' a soft but stern voice cut in from the far side of the room.

Luke's head snapped to the man sat on the very end of the panel. Unlike the others, he was not in the flowing academic dress but instead the simple black robes of a Catholic priest. He was the youngest of the group of men by far, hair still a deep black not yet peppered by grey strands. His eyes were a piercing blue and projected a disapproving look only achievable by a member of the clergy. 'It is not within the interests of this university to fund uninformed treasure hunting with no real academic value. To ask us to consider further is ridiculous.'

Luke pinched the bridge of his nose, frustration quickly kindling to anger.

'Father Keir, my research is no more ridiculous than chasing holy relics around the Middle East at the university's expense.' Luke's eyes locked with the priest's icy glare. 'At least I'm basing my investigations on historical fact and not, what was it you called it professor?' said Luke turning to look at Professor Jameson, 'fairy tales?'

'That is enough Mr Knight!' Boomed a voice from the centre of the panel.

Dr John Aubry, Head of the Department of Archaeology and History, had not spoken up to that moment but only watched with a weary expression. He was one of the few at the university that had allowed Luke to present his proposal without interruption. Luke watched as Aubry stroked the short, ash-white beard that hung from his protruding chin.

'Mr Knight, we have been patient with you, indulged your... unorthodox approach, but I'm afraid this can go on no longer. Your outburst here is only another example of the lack of professionalism that we have endured from you.' He fixed Luke with a hard, pointed stare. 'I advise you return to your office and come up with a new research proposal before our patience for you expires entirely.'

Luke bit back a retort, he had gone too far with Father Keir and letting his tongue loose now wouldn't improve matters. He stood searching for words and failing. Grabbing his notes from the lectern he strode into the centre of the room, the hem of his robes fluttering in his wake.

'Thank you for your time professors.'

He spun on one foot and stalked to the door in the corner of the room, footsteps echoing in the uncomfortable silence he was leaving behind.

The quiet of the lecture theatre was met by the bustle and chaos of the hallways outside where students roved in hordes around the building, attempting to navigate the labyrinthine corridors in search of the room housing their next lecture. Scholars and professors in a variety of smart, expensive suits and occasionally the traditional billowing robes and coloured hoods that Luke himself wore, waded through the sea of students.

The crowds in the hallway thinned as the clock moved closer to the hour. Luke found the way to his office unobstructed not many people came to this end of the building anyway. His office was barely more than the storage cupboards that flanked it on the dead-end corridor, hidden behind a bleak, featureless door and identical to every other on that floor of the history building. Luke flung the door open and stepped into his office, kicking it closed behind him. A single window occupied the opposite wall, made up of dozens of smaller panes of glass held together with strips of mottled grey tarnished lead. A simple wooden desk marked and scarred by years of use sat underneath the window and was watched over on either wall by towering shelves holding row upon row of books, maps, and other odds and ends.

'Chasing fairy tales,' Luke muttered before flinging himself into the rickety office chair with a sigh. He looked at the papers littering his desk: copies of medieval manuscripts, chronicles and saga's, newspaper clippings about mysterious lumps in fields or recounts of legends of treasures passed down through generations.

'Useless!' exclaimed Luke, sweeping his arm across the desk and sending a flurry of sheets cascading to the floor in a torrent of black and white pages. His head thumped down on the desk, a groan escaping his mouth, muffled by the wood pressed against his face.

A gentle knock sounded outside the door: three short taps in quick succession. Probably some fresh first year, lost on their way to the anthropology labs.

'What?' ground out Luke, head still on the desk.

Three more knocks, louder this time and more noticeably impatient.

Luke picked himself up off the desk and turned towards the door.

'What do you want?' he shouted.

The door creaked open; a shock of deep garnet red hair appeared around the frame, shortly followed by a delicate face graced with a pair of inexplicably blue eyes, and a full, red-lipped smile.

'I'm not sure if I'm in the right place,' the woman said as she glanced down at some scrawled writing on the paper in her hand. 'I'm looking for Luke Knight. The man at reception gave me this room number.'

Luke stood and crossed the room to open the door, allowing the woman to step over the threshold.

'You have the right room. I'm Luke.'

'Ah perfect. I've gone to the wrong room three times now. All these doors look the same,' she chuckled half-heartedly.

Luke studied the woman stood in the doorway. She was short, having to tilt her head to look Luke in the eye. Despite her lack of stature and cheery demeanor she was an intimidating presence. A graceful, athletic frame that hid the strength in the honed muscles and those icy blue eyes that burnt with either passion or aggression, Luke couldn't quite tell.

'You aren't the first to get lost in this place.' Luke extended his hand. 'How can I help you Mrs....?'

'Crawford, Evelyn Crawford,' she said, shaking his hand, 'and it's Miss.'

'My apologies *Miss* Crawford. What can I do for you?'

Luke stepped back into the room. He moved to a battered chair in the corner of the room that was presently being used to house yet another mountain of paperwork.

'Please take a seat,' he said, clearing the papers onto the floor, one of the few remaining surfaces largely clear of clutter.

Evelyn took the chair, watching as Luke perched on the edge of his desk.

'I will get straight to the point. What do you know about the Stone of Scone?'

'The Stone of Destiny? It was taken from Scone Abbey in 1296 and then sat in Westminster Abbey in the coronation chair for the next 700 years,' Luke smirked slightly, 'give or take a year or so when some students took it on a magical mystery tour and left it in a pub in Glasgow.'

'And it's now in Edinburgh Castle,' Evelyn finished.

'Unless you believe one of the stories of the stone being replaced, that is.'

Evelyn leant forward in her chair, her expression becoming serious.

'I was led to believe that if anyone were to be of

the opinion that those stories were true it would be you Dr Knight.'

Luke let out an exasperated sigh, rubbing his forehead.

'Mr.'

'Excuse me?'

'*Mr* Knight,' he said pushing himself off the desk and staring at the shelves of books, his back to Evelyn. 'It's believing in stories like those that means I can't put PhD after my name on the door,' he said bitterly.

'It doesn't say anything on the door, that's why it took me so long to find...' Evelyn's voice trailed off.

Luke shot her a glare over his shoulder.

'Sorry,' she muttered, 'but what if the stone in Edinburgh is a fake? There's evidence, historical record.' Evelyn's voice became more impassioned.

'There are historical documents chronicling the life of King Arthur, that doesn't mean Geoffrey of Monmouth wasn't full of it.'

Evelyn stood and snapped.

'What happened to you?'

'Excuse me?'

Evelyn huffed, walking to the bookshelf. She stopped before the towering mass of books before her. She ran her hand along the spines of the shelf at her eye level. The authors reading in alphabetical order, her fingers brushed across the cracked spines...*Jones, Jury, Kristiansen, Kenyon.*

She stopped and spun on Luke.

'Where is it?' she demanded.

'Where's what?' asked Luke, tipping his chair back on its hind legs and kicking his feet onto the table.

'You're telling me you don't have a copy of your own book?'

'Oh that,' Luke groaned. He lifted his feet off the desk, letting all four of the legs of his chair fall back to the floor and pushing it back from the edge of the desk.

He reached under the desk, lifting one side, and retrieving a battered hardback book from beneath the foot of a leg. Luke tossed the book onto the, now lopsided, desk beside Evelyn, the scratched cover faded and dusty.

Hidden Histories: The Lost Treasures of Britain.

'You used your book to level a desk?' asked Evelyn in confusion.

'Seemed like the best use for it,' said Luke bitterly.

Evelyn carefully flipped open the battered book, leafing through the pages with a distant look.

'My brother, John, loved your book. It inspired him to protect the history we had and find what had been lost.' She turned to Luke and smiled. 'He would never shut up about it.'

'I can't believe someone actually read my book,' Luke said surprised.

'Your book was the reason I came to you for

help. The way John told it you were so passionate, nothing would stop you from finding the past.'

Luke slumped back into his chair.

'I was, but there's only so many times you can be told your work is a dead end before you start to give up.'

He looked again at the book in his hands. Years of work, struggles and pushback from every member of the university. His eyes trailed up to her face and he frowned at the sadness that had consumed the fire she had exuded.

'Miss Crawford, what exactly is it you want from me?'

Evelyn took a deep breath and gently closed the book.

'Your help, Mr Knight.' She fished in her pocket withdrawing a small rectangle of card and put it on the desk in front of Luke.

It was a business card.

Luke reached out and took it from the desk. The card was a heavy, textured paper that felt expensive. The parliamentary portcullis and coronet of the House of Commons was embossed in green foil. Simple black text below read: John Crawford, Under-Secretary of State for Arts, Heritage and Tourism.

'He took the position because of you Mr Knight,' said Evelyn quickly. 'He was researching the stone. As an important symbol of Anglo-Scottish relations, if the stone in Edinburgh is a fake, he wanted the original found and returned to its rightful place.'

'Spoken like a true politician,' said Luke. 'Your brother is responsible for all the heritage, culture and museums in the UK, if he wants to find the real stone then he could have a team of people at the top of their field to work for him, not,' said Luke pointedly, 'a nobody who's own university doesn't take him seriously. So I ask you again Miss Crawford, what do you want from me?'

Evelyn didn't speak for several moments, instead she walked over to the office door where it still hung open and gently pushed it closed, leaning against the solid door as the latch clicked into place.

'You know Mr Knight, you remind me of John.' She pushed off the door frame and turned to Luke. 'He was convinced the stone was a fake but no one took him seriously either, so he went looking for it himself. He did what you would do.'

'I'm flattered Miss Crawford but that doesn't answer my question. Even if your brother wanted me specifically why not contact me through official channels?'

Evelyn ignored his question. 'When John started looking into the stone, he warned me that he had gotten an anonymous letter telling him that some stones are best left unturned.'

Luke snorted, 'No pun intended, I assume?'

'This isn't funny Mr Knight,' Evelyn snapped.

'John seemed worried that someone didn't want the stone to be a fake, didn't want the real one to be found.'

Her shoulders slumped, the fire from her brief anger escaping.

'All that threat did was convince John that he was right, and the real stone was out there somewhere to be found.'

'Miss Crawford,' Luke said gently, 'you keep referring to him in the past tense. Why hasn't your brother contacted me himself?'

Evelyn's head dropped, tears burning in the corners of her eyes.

'John went to Edinburgh. He said he had found something, proof the stone was a fake.' She wiped her eyes and took a deep breath to steady her shaking voice. 'He told me that he knew where to find the real one and would call me that evening to explain… that was two days ago.'

'You think something happened to him in Edinburgh?'

Evelyn sniffed. 'The police told me they couldn't do anything because he's a "low risk case" and since he had taken leave from work, they had no reason to believe he was missing just because he was out of contact.'

Evelyn took Luke's hand gripping it in her own and stared deep into his eyes, as if trying to reach his soul itself.

'Please Mr Knight, if we can find what John had

found, maybe we can find him too. There's no one else he would have trusted to find it.'

Luke sighed and carefully took his hand back from her grip.

'I wish I could help Miss Crawford but even if John disappearing is linked to the stone...' he paused, trying to find the words, 'there is no way of knowing where to begin the search for the real one.'

Evelyn smiled through her tears and pulled another scrap of paper from her pocket.

'I think my brother might have learnt more from your book than you think.' She unfolded it and handed the crumpled sheet to Luke. 'In Edinburgh, he told me he was heading to the museum...that he had found the key.'

Luke took the paper and read the single word scrawled in the centre of the page.

Wishart

Luke's eyes widened as he read the word. He launched himself at one of the stacks of books, almost sending the precarious pile flying in his excitement. He cast aside half the stack before pulling out a thin, leatherbound book and flipping through the pages.

'I'm very much beginning to like your brother,' said Luke, continuing to flip through the thick dusty pages. 'He definitely said he was going to the museum, not the castle?'

'Does it matter?'

Luke found the page he was looking for. His fingers brushed over the page, feeling the subtle ridges of the old print beneath. He cast an eye at his own book where it lay on the table and then at the expectant face of the woman opposite him. She was right, what had happened to the Luke that wrote that book? Luke slammed closed the book in his hand, the heavy board covers making an audible *snap.*

'The stone is held in Edinburgh Castle Miss Crawford, not the museum. If you brother was investigating the stone why would be going to the museum unless he thought a clue was there?'

'So what does it mean, Wishart?'

Luke looked up from the book and smiled, his eyes meeting Evelyn's.

'It means Miss Crawford,' he paused, 'that we have a train to catch.'

CHAPTER 2

10:15 service from London Euston to Edinburgh Waverley, 20 miles south of the Scottish Border somewhere west of Bamburgh.

The dark stone towers and rocky crag of Bamburgh Castle were no more than a speck in the distance as the train hurtled though the fields of lush green farmland, disturbing the peace and tranquility of the Northumbrian countryside. Luke sat watching the world flitting by the train window, absentmindedly spinning a coin on the table, letting it whirl until it began to tumble but stopping its turn before it clattered onto the hard surface. Minutes passed and the grass on the horizon began to give way to the blue-grey waters home to the island of Lindisfarne.

The carriage was almost empty. Only a handful of passengers took seats at the last station and most that had started in London had departed by York. Luke studied the other passengers. Who were they? Where were they going? Not likely commuters at this time of day and not many people would be taking a holiday in the middle of the work week. The door opposite him hissed open and Luke looked away from the carriage's occupants to see Evelyn walking down the aisle, a steaming cup of tea in each hand. A dark-haired man in a suit that was too large for him shuffled awkwardly past her as they crossed in the confined aisle. He muttered a brusque apology before disappearing through the door Evelyn had entered. She slid into the seat on the opposite side of the table to Luke and put one of the paper cups in front of him, raising the other to her mouth to take a sip but stopping short when the still scalding liquid hit her tongue. She put the cup down on the table and crossed her hands in her lap. She looked out of the window as Luke had moments before.

'From its tall rock look grimly down, and on the swelling ocean frown; then from the coast they bore away...'

'And reached the Holy Island's Bay.' Luke looked at the woman sat across from him, still gazing wistfully at the island with its ruined priory passing by.

'Walter Scott,' said Luke, the intonation of his voice rising in question. 'Not one of his more famous poems.'

Evelyn dragged her eyes from the view outside the train.

'My father was a politician too. He didn't have much time with us — my brother and me—growing up but he used to take us to visit places like that.' She smiled, but Luke saw the sadness behind her eyes.

'He thought holidays should be educational. Lindisfarne was always his favourite and we lived in Dalkeith, so it wasn't far to come.'

'You don't have the accent anymore.'

'Boarding school since I was eleven,' she said simply, 'then four years at university.'

'Let me guess, politics at Oxford?'

Evelyn gave him a sarcastic glare.

'Poetry at Winchester.'

Luke smiled. 'That explains the Scott.'

Evelyn took a sip from the cup in front of her and looked back out of the window. Several moments passed in comfortable silence as the world swept by.

'You know,' said Evelyn, 'you still haven't told me what you think my brother found.'

Luke looked out the window one last time as the Holy Island faded into the distance and the view from the train was filled with a short stretch of land before the blue-grey expanse of the North Sea.

Wordlessly he reached across to the battered leather satchel on the seat next to him, loosening the dull brass buckles holding it closed. He rummaged in the bag, pulling out a stack of papers and dropped them onto the table.

'I actually started to research the Stone of Scone when I was a postgrad,' he flipped through the first few pages, pulling several from the stack. 'Your brother got much further than I ever did, Professor Aubry gently advised me to pick a more *academic* topic.'

The man in the poorly fitting suit came back thorough the far door, briefly catching Luke's attention. He could have sworn the man was watching them as he walked down the aisle and took a seat four rows from where they sat.

'Mr Knight?'

'Sorry, I just... never mind.'

Luke shook his head, focusing back on the papers in his hand.

'The early history of the stone is a bit sketchy. Some say it's the same stone as Lia Fáil, the coronation stone of Ireland and one of the four treasures of the Tuatha Dé Danann, which would support the legend that it was brought from Ireland by Fergus of Dál Riata sometime around 500 AD.'

Luke put one of the pages down on the table. It was a scan of a book page mostly occupied by a woodcut of a man in a fur collared cloak and bonnet.

'The stone stayed where Fergus left it on the island of Iona until 841 AD when this man,' Luke tapped his finger on the picture, 'Kenneth

MacAlpin, the current king of Dál Riata and later the first king of Alba, moved it, among other religious treasures, to Scone Priory, just north of Perth, to protect it from Viking raids. Hence, the name Stone of Scone.'

Luke looked up at Evelyn. Most people would have stopped listening to him by now, but Evelyn was leaning forward in her chair, her face set in concentration. Encouraged by her interest he laid the next sheet of paper down.

'The stone sat happily at Scone for the next half a millennium until 1296.'

'The War of Scottish independence.'

Luke couldn't stop the surprise on his face.

'I thought you were a poet?' he said.

'And that means I can't like history?' she smiled, 'and anyway there are poems about it too.'

'Bannockburn by Robert Burns.'

It was Evelyn's turn to hide surprise.

'I thought you were a historian, Mr Knight?' she mocked.

Luke turned his head towards the window, trying to hide the reddening in his cheeks.

'Archaeologist actually,' he corrected her, feigning offence. 'And call me Luke, only disapproving academics call me Mr knight.'

Evelyn stifled a laugh.

'It's a deal *Luke*,' she said deliberately, 'as long as you call me Evelyn, I'm only 25 and *Miss Crawford* makes me sound like an older spinster from a Jane

Austin novel.'

The pair both broke out into fits of laughter, garnering odd looks from the few passengers they shared the train with.

Evelyn broke off her laughter, her face becoming solemn remembering the reason for their journey: her brother that would have made the same one only days ago.

Sensing the change in mood, Luke put down another sheet of paper next to the first. Together they showed a wooden throne with a large, rectangular block of stone set into a shelf beneath the seat.

'After Edward I's victory at Dunbar the early rebellion was quashed, and the stone was taken as spoils of war to Westminster Abbey where it was built into the coronation throne used by almost every monarch since. Despite petition, argument, riots, and theft by both sides, it stayed more or less in Westminster until 1996, the 700th anniversary of its theft from Scone.'

Evelyn chewed her lip, processing all the information she had just heard.

'But what's any of that got to do with what John told me? What is Wishart?'

Luke went back to the satchel and pulled out the book he had taken from his office, flipping it open to the page he had found earlier.

'Not what, who.'

He dropped the open book on top of the sheets

of paper occupying the table. Evelyn leant over the book, the whole page was occupied by a black and white engraving of a seal showing a man in cassock and miter, holding a crosier in his left hand.

'The Bishop Wishart of Glasgow.'

Evelyn stared blankly at Luke, waiting for him to elaborate.

'The stones authenticity isn't a new debate; geologists have proven the one in Edinburgh Castle was quarried not far from Scone.'

'So, it is a fake?' Evelyn interjected.

'That depends on how you define fake. There are two possibilities: Either the stone was lost sometime before it supposedly left Iona and the one at Scone was and always has been a fake or...'

'Or my brother was right, and it was swapped before King Edward took it to Westminster.'

'Exactly,' said Luke, 'and it seems your brother thinks old Bishop Wishart knew something about that.'

Evelyn opened her mouth to say something more but was interrupted by an announcement crackling thorough the overhead speakers—the strange not quite human voice announcing the next and final stop as Edinburgh.

'You were going to ask me what Wishart has to do with the stone,' Luke said, a statement not a question.

Evelyn said nothing but nodded, the gesture

a mix of sadness and frustration impossible to miss.

'In truth I have no idea,' Luke sighed and leant back into the soft padding of the train seat. 'Wishart was a supporter of independence, a friend to William Wallace and Robert the Bruce, but beyond that...' he trailed off.

'I do know where to start though.' Luke pushed the book towards Evelyn, 'it just so happens that the seal in that book is the only object related to Wishart in the National Museum of Scotland. I'm guessing your brother thought it was significant enough to go and see it.'

'You think he found some sort of clue on it?'

'Maybe,' Luke said, gathering the mess of papers back into a single, slightly less erratic, pile. 'I'm hoping in a little over an hour, we'll find out.'

Silence fell between the pair as the train wound its way along the tall rocky cliffs passing from England to Scotland. The rare northern sunshine did nothing to help dismiss the rising sense of dread at what would be found once the train made its final stop.

CHAPTER 3

National Museum of Scotland, Chambers Street, Edinburgh.

The imposing, windowed façade of Scotland's national museum loomed in front of Luke and Evelyn as they approached along the busy Chambers Street. The once creamy-white stone had taken on a darker shade from the decades of soot and Scottish weather. The grand wooden doors of the Victorian building stood firmly closed to the world and instead, a steady stream of people moved in and out of a set of square portal doors set lower in the side of the building than the original entrance, so that patrons entered into the basement and ascended into the wonders of the museum. The pair tucked into the trail of visitors and wound their way past a colossal bronze statue of a man in Georgian dress. Caught in the flow of the crowd they moved through the open portals and into a corridor of low vaulted ceilings. Evelyn snagged a folded pamphlet from a stand as they passed before pulling Luke out of the tide of tourists to take cover beside a stone sarcophagus gracing the entrance hall.

'Where is the Wishart seal?' she asked, unfolding the pamphlet into a small but surprisingly colourful map of the museum.

'There's no point looking at the map. If there was something easily visible on the seal itself someone would have seen it already.'

'You said John saw something on it. That's the reason we came!' Snapped Evelyn.

'I said the Wishart seal was here and since it was the last place he visited before calling you, it stands to reason he found something.'

Luke could see Evelyn's temper was wearing thin.

'Your brother's job gave him more access than most. The museum has an archive, documents and material that aren't put on display,' he said quickly, seeing Evelyn's patience was hanging on by a thread. 'Your brother might have found something about the seal in there.'

'Ok, how do we get into the archives?'

Luke paused, debating his options.

'We ask very nicely?' he shrugged, then strode towards the wood clad information desk leaving Evelyn looking after him, at a loss for words.

She watched as he spoke to the short, grey-haired man behind the desk with the complete self-confidence of someone who was used to talking themselves into getting what they wanted, or Evelyn suspected, out of whatever situation they put themselves in.

She realised how little she knew about Luke Knight. Her brother talked about his work like it was the stuff of legend, but the man himself... She studied him as he spoke. Like Evelyn, he wasn't tall but he had a wiry muscle that came naturally from repeated manual labour. It was difficult to judge his age: the lack of hair covering his head and his eyes, one a deep moss green and the other a strange fractal of green and brown, made him seem older than she guessed he really was. He couldn't have been more than his late twenties, no older than Evelyn herself, but he had the aura and presence of someone who had seen the world and lived more lives than should be possible.

Luke spoke and Evelyn realised she had been staring at him and not heard a word.

'Sorry, what did you say?'

'I said we've hit a dead end,' he said chewing the edge of his lip, frustration clear in his voice.

'What did he say?'

'He said if we were interested in Wishart we could go and see the seal on display like everyone else.'

'What about the archive?' asked Evelyn.

'The archive is only open to research by advance request. We can't just go looking through it.'

Evelyn could see the muscle in Luke's jaw twitch as he ground his teeth, irked by the refusal. Definitely used to getting his own way.

Without warning, Luke marched towards the stairs leading up into the main hall of the museum, forcing Evelyn to half run after him.

'Where are you going?' Evelyn called.

'I'm doing what I was told; I'm going to see the seal like everyone else.'

'We have been looking at this thing for half an hour.' Evelyn had her head in her hands. 'Do you think if you stare at it for long enough Bishop Wishart himself will magically appear and tell you where the stone is?'

He was inches from the glass, his translucent reflection gazing back at him as he studied the small, sulphur-brown seal sat in its display case.

'This seal is the only thing on display in the entire museum to do with Robert Wishart,' said Luke, his eyes still locked intently on the seal. 'If your brother said he found something after leaving the museum then this is the only place we are going to find it.'

Evelyn walked away from the case. She admired Luke's persistence, but this was a lost cause. John was still missing: no trace, no clues and now no more ideas. They would have more luck standing on the High Street with a photo and asking passersby if they'd seen him. Voices echoed down the cavernous corridor, followed by the syncopated footsteps of a small crowd walking along the stone floors.

'Everyone keep together! We are moving into the *Kingdom of the Scots* gallery. Prepare yourselves for a journey from 1100 to 1707.' A bespectacled guide ushered the group into the far end of the hall, not bothering to wait for the bored looking children straggling at the rear of the convoy before launching into his speech.

'Prepare yourselves for the tales from the bloody wars of independence to the creation of the United Kingdom and see some of the greatest treasures of Scotland. Who here has heard of the Lewis Chessmen?' A smattering of hands raised at the guide's question. Seeming pleased with the response he carried on with the tour, walking the group further down the hall towards the case Luke and Evelyn stood by. Evelyn left Luke to his obsessive inspection and loitered at the back of the tour group. The guide was mid flow and doing his best to keep the attention of the crowd.

'You will encounter legends of Scottish history, the great leaders like Robert the Bruce and William Wallace. Now, Robert the Bruce may be the true hero of Scotland, but William Wallace is the man in one of my favourite stories.'

Evelyn glanced back at Luke to see he had moved to the other side of the case, tilting his head at odd angles, attempting to see the back of the seal.

'Before he became the folk hero and was unfortunately immortalised on the big screen in Braveheart, William Wallace made his name as a character worthy of legend with a daring robbery.' The guide paused and clearly not getting the *ooohhh* he expected from the crowd he hurried to finish his story and move on. 'In 1296, William Wallace and a young priest stole 36 gallons of beer from Christiana of St John in Perth just one day before Edward I arrived.'

Luke's head popped up from behind the glass case. He walked to stand beside Evelyn, suddenly interested in what the guide was saying.

'Just a year later, Wallace would graduate from this petty act of rebellion to rekindling the rebellion of a country by attacking Lanark and killing its English sheriff, likely with his iconic claymore which looked like some examples we have through here,' the guide said, gesturing through an ornate doorway to a room with three gigantic swords displayed in the centre.

'Excuse me, sorry!' Luke pushed his way through the crowd of tourists to their guide.

The guide seemed surprised by Luke's interruption. 'Is there something I can help you with sir?' said the guide, conscious some of the tour were beginning to wander away from the group collected by the swords.

'Just one question,' said Luke intently, 'who gave the order to Wallace to steal the beer?'

The tour guide looked at Luke with curiosity and suspicion in equal measure.

'Young man, you are the second person to ask me

that this week.'

Evelyn's entire body stiffened. 'John,' she whispered.

'In any case,' the guide hurried, keen to get back to his tour, 'it was rumoured that the Bishop of Glasgow, Robert Wishart gave the order to Wallace.'

Luke broke into a grin. 'Thank you,' he said quickly.

The tour guide nodded welcome before hurrying off after his group before they got too far ahead of his practised story of Scottish history.

'Why would John ask the same question you did?'

Luke walked back over to the case displaying Robert Wishart's seal.

'Your brother is smarter than the average politician,' he said still grinning. 'Did you hear what day the guide said the beer was stolen?'

'He just said 1296?' said Evelyn, confused. 'So what? It was the same year the stone was taken?'

'Not just the same year,' said Luke. 'He said 1296, one day before Edward I arrived in Perth.'

'Wallace took the stone when he took the beer,' Said Evelyn, picking up the trail Luke had been laying.

'Exactly! I would wager there was more than beer in those barrels and that's what John must have thought too.'

Luke started moving back down the hallway of

cases, passing fragments of pottery, silver goblets, coins, and rusted daggers.

'But we still don't know where Wallace took the stone.'

Luke stopped abruptly next to another case of silver goblets.

'No, we don't, but I think the better question is how did your brother know to look for Wishart in the first place?' he said, raising his eyebrow.

'And where did John go after finding out about Wallace.'

Luke stared past Evelyn, into the long empty hall they had just come from.

'What's wrong?'

He ignored her. At the end of the hall a man walked slowly to the display case holding the Wishart seal. He had black hair slicked back with so much wax it took on the iridescent sheen of an oil slick under the spotlights that illuminated the museum galleries from the ceilings. He stooped to be level with the seal, his suit jacket hanging loose around his shoulders.

Luke grabbed Evelyn, pulling her behind the case of silver goblets so the board they were mounted to shielded them from the rest of the gallery.

Evelyn made a disgruntled noise and opened her mouth to demand to know what had gotten into him but was hushed by Luke raising a finger to his lips in a shushing motion.

He leant around the case to see where the man

in the badly fitting suit had gone. He was still looking at the seal, studying its every surface just as Luke had done.

Luke moved back behind the case.

'The guy looking at the seal, he was on the train,' said Luke, keeping his voice low.

Evelyn looked around the case at the man.

'Coincidence?' she said hopefully.

'That a complete stranger on the same train as us just happened to be taking an interest in the exact obscure historical object that we, and John came here to see.'

'When you put it like that.'

Evelyn unfolded her map of the museum.

'The exit is back down the hall; we have to go past him to get out.'

Luke fished in his pocket and pulled out a copper coin of the kind that hadn't been used in at least half a century.

'What's that?'

'A distraction.' Luke threw the coin down the gallery past the man in the suit, it clattered to the floor, the sound echoing in the empty room. The man in the suit spun away from the case holding the seal and his hand went to his hip, pushing back the hem of his jacket to reveal a holstered pistol. The man's hand hovered above the wood and black steel grip of the Colt 1911.

The moment the coin hit the floor Luke grabbed Evelyn's hand.

'Run!' he said in a loud whisper, pulling Evelyn from behind the case and taking off in a sprint towards the stone archway leading to the exit.

Just as they cleared the final display case before the archway, the man in the suit turned back towards them and began to follow with barely a moment's hesitation. Luke and Evelyn barrelled through the museum, pushing past groups of tourists milling around in the grand, bright, atrium.

The man in the suit was not far behind, pushing carelessly through the same crowds, leaving a wake of disgruntled muttering.

'This way!' said Evelyn, heading for the stairs leading back to the vaulted basement where they came in. They burst out of the museum's door onto the wide road of Chambers Street. The sun was barely peeking above the buildings as Luke and Evelyn sprinted down the road towards the statue of Greyfriars Bobby and through the iron gate between two buildings, to the churchyard beyond. The churchyard was near empty as the sun began to drop behind the buildings that surrounded it, the last of the sightseers leaving the sea of graves in favour of the city's vibrant nightlife. Luke stopped and pulled Evelyn behind a wall that jutted out in into the churchyard. The view from the gates was obscured by cracked and moss-covered grave markers. Evelyn looked around at the engravings of skulls and crossbones that sat above their heads, adorning the wall like macabre murals to the dead.

Luke lay flat on his stomach, inching his way along a stone slab beneath them, buried in places by a thin layer of turf and sodden leaves, to get a look at the churchyard beyond the wall.

'I think we lost him,' said Luke, crawling back to slump against the wall, chest rising and falling rapidly trying to catch his breath.

'Who was he though?' Evelyn's voice shook as the adrenaline that had been coursing through her veins began to dissipate.

'I don't know, but I'm glad we didn't stick around for a chat and find out.' He flicked his hand, sending the mud and leaves stuck to it onto the ground. 'Anyone who carries a gun like that is bad news.'

'We can't stay here; we need to find out what John knew about Wallace and the Stone.' Evelyn got to her feet and stepped over Luke, still sitting on the cold stone. She stepped out onto the trail that led around the churchyard and disappeared with a yelp. Luke jumped to his feet but stopped dead. The man in the suit was staring back at Luke, gun no longer in the holster but in his hand and pointed at Evelyn, his finger hovering over the trigger.

'You can stop right there Mr Knight.' Said the man. His voice was like gravel, harsh and raw with a thick northern accent: Manchester maybe, thought Luke.

'Let her go. If you're looking for the stone, I'm more use to you.' Luke's voice didn't waver as he kept eye contact with the man, ignoring the pistols yawning barrel.

'Very noble of you Mr Knight, but it's not you I'm here for.' The man waved the gun, ushering Luke back. 'Turn around and get on the ground, then no one has to get hurt.'

Evelyn shifted her feet; the man caught the movement in the corner of his eye and swung the gun back to her.

'No funny business Miss Crawford, don't be a fool like your brother.'

Fury filled Evelyn eyes. 'What have you done with John?' she spat.

The man smiled, the look filled with venom.

'You'll see him again Miss Crawford don't worry,' he said turning the gun back on Luke.

'What do you want?'

The man pulled a folded letter out of his pocket.

'Miss Crawford's brother led us to believe the key to finding the stone was in this.' He tapped the note with his finger. 'Unfortunately, he wasn't very forthcoming with what he knew.'

Luke went to snatch the letter from the man's hand.

'Nice try Mr Knight.' The man whisked the letter out of Luke's reach, the page falling open in the motion. The paper was old, heavy, and checked on the edges from age. Luke scanned the letter. It wasn't signed and the writing unclear from the distance, but his eyes lingered on the wax seal that once held the letter closed, Wishart's seal.

'This is what John found, why he went to the museum?'

The man in the suit inclined his head in a half nod.

'My employer wants to know what Mr Crawford passed on to you, what he found out after he stole the letter.' The man raised his eyebrow.

'If John stole the letter, how do you have it?' asked Evelyn, already knowing the answer.

'You killed him for it,' said Luke. It wasn't a question.

'Mr Crawford was very keen the letter was not returned to my employer. Unfortunately he gave me no choice.'

Evelyn hissed, 'You said if we helped you, I would see him.'

'And you will Miss Crawford, I am a man of my word.' The man's arm tensed, his finger closing around the trigger of his gun. Luke moved to stop him, but he was too slow. Before Luke could move Evelyn lunged for the man, tackling him to the ground. The man's hand tensed around the gun as they both hit the floor, firing a bullet into the top of a nearby headstone and spraying Luke with a shower of razor-sharp marble. The man lost his grip on the pistol, sending it skittering across the ground. He threw Evelyn off and got to his feet, pulling a knife from his belt. Luke lunged at the man, grabbing his arm and twisting it to a painful, unnatural angle behind his back, forcing the knife from his grip. A sharp kick to the back of the man's knee made him bark out in pain and drop to one knee before Luke put a hand on the back of his neck and slammed his forehead into the solid stone skull and crossbones on the wall with a sickening crack. The man's body slumped to the floor. Evelyn stood and moved slowly to Luke's side, her eyes still full of fire, burning holes into the motionless man. Luke dusted off his hands and squatted next to the man feeling for a pulse in his neck.

'He's alive, just.'

'That's a shame,' said Evelyn coldly.

She walked to the unconscious man and pulled the letter from his hand.

'Someone will have heard that gunshot,' said Luke. He pushed off his knee to stand up and grabbed the man's ankles. 'Help me with his arms.'

'What are you doing?' asked Evelyn.

'It might have been in self-defence, but we still just nearly killed this guy. We need to move before the police arrive.' Luke grunted under the man's weight.

'What's the point?" Evelyn snapped, 'you heard him, John's dead.'

They dropped the man next to a strange iron cage set into the ground next to the path.

'John was killed because he wanted to find the stone. He died for it. If we give up he died for nothing.' Luke cringed slightly, the words coming out harsher than he had meant them. He forced his voice to soften. Fighting off the last of the adrenaline from the brawl. 'And whoever had him killed clearly wants something with the stone. If we find the stone we have a good chance of finding them.'

'You're right,' she breathed. 'Next time you should try getting more information from the bad guy before braining him with a wall.'

Luke stopped and smiled at Evelyn.

'Next time? You almost sound like you want more gun-toting psychopaths to come after us?'

Evelyn couldn't suppress a smile. 'If you fight like that again it won't be a problem.' She paused, 'Where did you learn to fight like that anyway?'

'I ran into some trouble once researching the missing treasures mentioned in the Dead Sea Scrolls. Some soldiers weren't too happy with my snooping and it was a tight escape I would rather avoid happening again.'

Luke searched the man's jacket pulling another knife from a sheath hidden inside the lining but finding little else. He went to the strange iron cage and yanked on the rusted latch. After a few attempts it gave way with a piercing shriek.

'What are you doing?' asked Evelyn, giving him a sideways look.

'This is a mortsafe,' said Luke, giving the iron bars a tap with his foot. 'They used them in the 1800's to stop resurrectionists digging up bodies.'

'Resurrectionists?'

'They dug up bodies to sell to the schools of anatomy. I figured it'll do just as good a job stopping this guy from rising up before the police get here.'

They hefted the man into the mortsafe and Evelyn slammed the lid shut and threw the latch back across sealing the suited man inside.

Evelyn picked up the gun. 'What do we do with this?' she asked. 'It could be useful if anyone else comes after us.'

'Leave it for the police,' said Luke. 'I don't do guns; give me a sword any day.'

She put the gun far enough away from the mortsafe that the man in the suit wouldn't be able to reach it if he woke up but still easy enough for any officers to spot.

Right on cue, sirens began to wail in the distance, blue lights reflecting off mist that had begun to settle as dusk fell.

'We need to move,' said Luke.

The pair ran along the lines of gravestones of military leaders and churchmen, noble houses, and the mundane alike that were resting under the ground. They slipped out of the gates at the rear of the churchyard into the descending darkness of the city. Edinburgh Castle glowed on the horizon, floodlights illuminating the magnificent structure and the rocky crag it sat on. Luke gazed at the castle as they ran, all the treasures that it housed, art, crown jewels and now he was sure, one completely fake Stone of Destiny.

CHAPTER 4

*Northwest Corner of George Square
Gardens, Edinburgh.*

Luke and Evelyn's shoes clicked along the horonised pavement that ran along the edge of the green expanse that was George Square Gardens. The houses that lined the western side of the square once housed the great and good; surgeons, architects, and writers. Now, they mercifully sat empty. The university staff that worked in the buildings having returned home after the day's work allowed Luke and Evelyn to slip unseen past the low iron fence trimmed with red, white, and blue bunting that cut off the gardens from the rest of the square.

'We should be safe enough in here,' said Evelyn, easing a gate closed behind them.

They walked a short distance through the dimly lit park, the green Baillie lamps that stood sentry shedding an eerie glow across the grass. Evelyn guided them to a corner of the park, to a mosaic labyrinth made of thousands of tiny yellow pebbles bordered by grey stone cobbles that occupied an area nestled within a horseshoe of bushes. The pair took up a bench set into the bushes, comforted by the foliage high enough to hide them from the world beyond.

'Lucky you knew this was here.' Luke panted still trying to regain his breath.

'My father used to bring us here,' said Evelyn wistfully. 'He liked to point out which house was Walter Scott's, and which was Conan Doyle's.'

Her face fell as she recalled the memories that felt like another life.

'I was seven when they built the labyrinth. John took me to see it….' she trailed off, tears burning in the corners of her eyes and threatening to spill over.

'Look at me,' said Luke, taking her hand. 'We will find whoever's responsible for John, you have my word.'

'We already did,' Evelyn sniffed, wiping her eyes with the back of her hand. 'He's lying in an iron cage in Greyfriars.'

Luke traced the winding circles of the labyrinth with his eyes, the twisting paths leading to the centre. It's not so hard to solve a maze when you can see all the turns and dead ends before you choose which path to take.

'He didn't kill John, he just pulled the trigger.' He looked away from the labyrinth and back at Evelyn. 'Whoever aimed the gun is still out there.'

Evelyn sniffed again and gave him a weak

smile. She reached inside her pocket, retrieving the folded letter with the seal of Robert Wishart clinging to the edge of the page.

'And now we have somewhere to start.' She unfolded the letter to reveal a thick, black, scrawling text across the page.

'What language is that?' asked Luke.

Evelyn scanned the page. 'It's Gaelic,' she said, continuing to read the words. 'Give me a second.'

Luke rubbed his hands together, the chill of the night starting to set in.

'Do you have a pen and paper?' asked Evelyn.

Luke reached into his bag and pulled out a battered notepad with a pen slotted into the spine. He gave it a cursory dust with his hand, clearing off the worst of the dried mud and grime, then handed it to Evelyn.

Several minutes passed with Evelyn scribbling down lines on the notepad while Luke watched intently, trying to ignore the cold that was getting more bitter and caused them both to shiver on the bench. The pen hung above the page as Evelyn finished translating. She tore the sheet out of the notebook and handed it to Luke. He took it, reading the words she had written.

Robert,

I fear my time on this earth is growing short. You left the stone in my care those many years ago and now I entrust its fate to you once again.

I must ask that you make the journey he did to deliver me the stone and take the waters from the traitor's well, as he did, to help you on your journey.

I trust you will keep it safe and know it must stay hidden. The power can never fall into the hands of the English. They must believe they have the stone.

God be with you.

'So that's what John found,' said Luke, looking up from the page.

'John saw the seal on the letter and went to the museum where he heard the tour guide's story about William Wallace,' said Evelyn. 'That's what he meant when he called me, but how do we know what happened to the stone from this?'

'We already know Wallace took the stone on Wishart's orders,' said Luke. 'We now know he delivered the stone to Wishart.'

'But he doesn't say what he did with it in the letter?'

'Oh, but he did.' Luke grinned and jumped to his feet, striding towards the gap in the hedge that led out of the labyrinth's liminal space and back into the wide-open park.

Evelyn hurried to catch up with Luke, stopping him in the centre of the labyrinth.

'Wishart said to take the waters as he did,' said Luke as he turned to look her in the eye.

'*He* being William Wallace,' said Evelyn. 'So, we

need to find what? The well William Wallace drank from.'

Luke nodded excitedly. 'Exactly that, but the question is which one?'

'There's a Wallace's Well at Elcho castle.' said Evelyn excitedly. 'It's not far from where Wallace got the stone in Perth.'

'Maybe,' said Luke, 'or there's Wallace's Well in Robroyston. Wishart was Bishop of Glasgow and the story goes that Wallace often stopped there before visiting Wishart during the war.'

Evelyn went still, a bulb exploding into light in her mind. She grabbed the page with the translated letter from Luke and read it over.

'The traitor's well!' she exclaimed.

Luke gave her a sideways look, not following her revelation.

'William Wallace was captured in Robroyston!' Evelyn was practically vibrating with excitement.

Luke thought for a moment, 'but John Menteith turned Wallace over to....'

Evelyn cut him off, 'Yes, but in *The Wallace*, Blind Harry tells us that Rab Rae owned the farm where Wallace was captured, Rab Rae tipped off Menteith.'

'Rab Rae's well in Rab Rae's town: The Traitor's Well,' Luke smiled. 'Who knew poetry could show up a historian?'

Evelyn blushed, her cheeks nearly matching the

cherry red of her hair.

'Would John have figured out the clue?' Luke asked her.

'Our father liked to read us the folk tales and poetry about Scotland,' she said. 'I don't know how much John listened, but he heard the same stories I did.'

Luke nodded, thinking.

'We have to assume whoever killed him won't be far behind,' he said, worry lines creasing his forehead.

'Then we should go to the station and get to Glasgow tonight before they do!' Evelyn said, enthusiastically.

'You're right,' Luke replied, once again walking towards the gap in the hedge encircling the labyrinth, Evelyn following close behind. 'But we can't risk public transport. The police will have found our friend in the mortsafe by now and if they check CCTV, we will be numbers one and two on their list of people to have a chat with.'

The pair walked through the grove of trees at the centre of the gardens, away from the Georgian houses and towards the modern university buildings. The gnarled, twisting branches of the trees they passed seemed to reach towards them like fleshless, skeletal hands in the moonlight.

Luke helped Evelyn over the locked gate on the eastern edge of the gardens and together they made for the pavement leading past the illuminated library sign.

'How do we get to Glasgow without public transport?' asked Evelyn as they turned the corner onto the empty road leading to the dark meadows beyond. 'We don't have a car.'

Luke's face was set with determination.

'Easy,' he said, matter of factly. 'We steal one.'

Luke walked down the line of cars parked on the secluded road by the side of The Meadows. The cars were all too new, thought Luke. He carried on walking down the row, Evelyn timidly following behind, doing her best not to look too conspicuous but succeeding only in looking like a cartoon thief sneaking between lampposts.

'Can you just pick one already!' she hissed, looking nervously around the dark street.

Luke looked over his shoulder at her. 'Stop trying to hide your face,' he said, ignoring her request. 'You look like you're trying not to get caught.'

'I am trying not to get caught!'

Luke walked a few paces back to Evelyn and looped his arm through hers.

'If you act like you're supposed to be somewhere people usually assume you are.' He started walking down the line of cars again, Evelyn in tow. 'As far as anyone else knows, we're not here to steal a car, we're just walking home.'

Luke peered through the window of another car as they passed.

'Could have fooled me,' muttered Evelyn.

A little way down the road Luke spotted what he was looking for. Tucked away at the side of the road was an old, cherry-red Vauxhall Corsa. Luke let go of Evelyn's arm and moved to the driver's door of the car.

'Why this one?' asked Evelyn.

Luke knelt and started to untie the long lace on his Converse.

'Older cars are easier to steal,' he said matter-of-factly. 'No computers or microchipped keys.'

He stood up, shoelace in hand and tied a simple slipknot in the middle before feeding it behind the top corner of the door and working it down behind the window.

'Also,' he said concentrating on the string behind the window, repositioning it with the ends still outside the door. 'I needed a car I could do this with.'

Luke positioned the slipknot, tightening it over locking knob that sat behind the glass. With a swift pull the knob popped up, unlocking the car with a muffled clunk.

Evelyn stood open mouthed as Luke opened the door and pulled the plastic cover under the steering wheel off.

'Do I want to know how you learned to do that?' asked Evelyn in mock disapproval.

Luke pulled out a set of wires, undoing the connector that ran to the back of the ignition.

'You wouldn't believe me if I told you,' he said, stripping the wires out of the connector.

'Try me?'

Luke looked back at Evelyn. 'My mother taught me.'

Evelyn stopped, visibly taken aback.

Luke connected two sets of the wires, making the lights on the dashboard flicker into life, and held another in his hand.

Evelyn shook her head, snapping back to the present.

'Where did she learn to steal cars?'

Luke looked up at her from the car's footwell and smiled. 'Probably best if I don't tell you that one.'

Evelyn laughed as Luke put the final wire to the power supply. The car shuddered, the engine roaring into life.

'What sort of historian can fight and hotwire cars?' asked Evelyn, curiously.

Luke stood up and brushed himself off. 'I told you,' he said, 'I'm an archaeologist, not a historian.'

Evelyn gave him an exasperated look but didn't push her question further. She brushed past him and got in the driver's seat.

'That car's not going anywhere yet,' said Luke.

'Why not?'

He grabbed hold of the steering wheel and threw his weight into turning it, a metallic crack echoing as the steering lock broke.

'That's why,' said Luke.

He walked around the car to the passenger door. Evelyn unlocked it for him and he slid into the seat.

'Glasgow?' Evelyn asked.

Luke pulled the door shut and agreed.

'Glasgow.'

CHAPTER 5

Wallace's Well, Langmuirhead Road, Robroyston, Glasgow.

The sun had not yet risen over the fields to start the new day, but neither was it fully dark. A wolf-grey light leached the colour out of the landscape around the lay-by where the cherry-red car sat, morning dew misting its windows. Luke and Evelyn had decided not to look for the well in the dark but instead to sleep and start the search at first light. Although it was more a reality than a decision, the pair having driven straight past the well in the dark and ending up lost down the twisting country lanes, before they decided to wait for morning.

Luke stretched as he got out of the car, his shoulders cracking like gunshots with the movement.

Evelyn stood looking across the rolling green fields towards the edges of the sprawling city.

'We should leave the car here,' said Luke, moving around the car to talk to Evelyn. 'It's probably been reported as stolen by now.'

'So, we're walking from now on?' asked Evelyn.
'Could be worse.'

She raised an eyebrow at him.

'We could be on the run from the police, being chased by gun-toting psychopaths working for a shadowy, murderous employer,' Luke said with a sarcastic smile.

Evelyn rolled her eyes and shut the car door behind her.

'Which way is the well?'

Evelyn pointed towards the rows of grey-rooved houses on the horizon. 'Only about half a mile down the road. We didn't go too far wrong,' she said. 'It should be quiet. Not many people know it's there.'

Luke nodded and swung his leather satchel over his shoulder.

'Let's hope you're right.'

Light was just beginning to break over the horizon as they made the final turn that led onto the very outskirts of Robroyston. Despite its proximity to the outer reaches of the suburban sprawl, the whole road was surprisingly quiet with nothing more than the dawn chorus of birds and the gentle bubbling of water in the nearby stream disturbed the peace.

'What exactly are we looking for?' asked Evelyn, 'the letter didn't tell us much?'

'I don't know, I thought we could just wing it.'

Luke flashed her a smile.

'Seriously?'

Luke stopped and turned to Evelyn.

'Wishart said to go to the well. He must have left a clue there for whoever came for the stone.'

'So, we're looking for a clue that may or may not be there and we have no idea what it is?' said Evelyn, her voice tinged with sarcasm.

'Exactly,' said Luke, still smiling. 'Should be easy.'

A stone wall wound its way around the bend in the road. The blocks were old, covered in moss and soot, and dulled by age, except for one spot about the width of a car where the mortar was gleaming and new, the old stones having been rebuilt.

Luke and Evelyn crossed the road and slipped through the break in the wall that led to a concrete bridge with a low iron railing. The bridge spanned the shallow stream to a paved forecourt at the base of a grassy bank. The well itself was a stone opening, set half into the bank that was retained by a wall made from the same stone that cut the area off from the road.

Luke squatted in front of the well's opening, dropping his bag by the wall. A pinkish stone lintel sat above the opening and simply read *Wallace's Well*.

'Can you see anything?' asked Evelyn.

Luke put his head into the opening of the well, the air inside was damp and stale, the earthy scent of wet stone filling his nostrils. Evelyn watched Luke's headless body twist as he looked around inside the well.

'There's a torch in my bag,' echoed Luke's disembodied voice, his hand pointing towards the leather satchel slumped against the wall. 'Can you pass it here?'

He opened his hand palm-up waiting to receive the torch, head still inside the well.

Evelyn flipped open the bag and rummaged through the assortment of papers, tools, maps of Scotland, and what looked disturbingly like a human bone carved with an assortment of symbols, that occupied Luke's bag. Finding the torch stuffed into a side pocket with a jumble of broken pot, she walked back to the well mouth and dropped it into Luke's hand which promptly joined his head inside the opening.

'See anything yet?' called Evelyn.

Luke flipped on the torch, blinking against the harsh white light that it threw against the walls of the well. The space looked even smaller with the darkness banished. It wasn't so much a well as a low stone roof built over a natural spring. The rough stone faces around Luke's head showed no sign of a clue; they were as the day they were dressed and laid in place, if a little dirtier and greener with algae. Luke rolled onto his stomach to look down into the well but came almost immediately face to face with a shallow muddy depression covered by a thin film of water, barely a few inches deep and gently bubbling up from the ground.

'Nothing,' said Luke, pushing himself back from the well and taking a deep breath of the fresh morning air. 'It has to be somewhere else.'

Evelyn helped him to his feet.

'Check around the well for anything that might be a clue,' said Luke, frustrated. He jumped up to the grassy bank behind the well and scrambled along a second low stone wall sat a few feet beyond. Evelyn watched him begin to comb every inch of the wall. Interrogating every section of the rough, cracked stone that he could access. She looked away and walked towards the steps on the opposite side of the forecourt that led to a short path heading back toward the road. She scanned the wall that ran along the path for... she wasn't sure, whatever Wishart's clue was she could have walked past without knowing it was what they were looking for. Her eyes fell on a weather faded sign near the end of the path, the centre of the sign was dominated by a sepia portrait of the bearded man in armour.

'William Wallace,' mused Evelyn.

Her eyes roamed over the sign, the story of Wallace's betrayal and capture laid out over its face. A small black and white photograph in the top right corner of the sign; a simple shot of two men sitting by a spring trickling from a grassy bank and flowing into a passing stream. Her heart sank as she read the caption of the picture.

'Luke,' she called across to him, 'you won't find anything.'

Luke walked along the top of the bank and hopped down over the wall next to Evelyn.

'It has to be somewhe...'

'No, look,' Evelyn cut him off and pointed at the picture on the sign.

Luke followed Evelyn's hand to the sign and took in the photograph of the well as it stood only a hundred years ago. He looked back at the well in the present and cursed loudly.

'How could I miss that.' He cursed again, kicking a loose pebble into the stream. 'None of this was here when Wishart left his clue.'

Evelyn put a hand on his shoulder. 'We don't know Wishart's clue was in the well,' she said. 'Look at the picture, before there was nothing but a spring here.'

Luke thought for a moment. 'If there was nowhere to leave a clue on the well...'

'Then the clue must be on something else,' Evelyn finished for him.

The two of them stood motionless for several moments, looking around for anything that could possibly be unchanged since the old bishop left his message.

'What exactly did Wishart's letter say?' asked Luke, breaking the silence.

'make the journey he did to deliver me the stone and take the waters from the traitor's well, as he did, to help you on your journey,' recited Evelyn from memory.

Luke went back to the well entrance, the muddy pool still trickling into the stone-lined space.

'I really hope he didn't mean drink the water,' said Evelyn in disgust, joining Luke by the well and turning up her nose at the murky pool.

'Take the waters to help you on your journey,' whispered Luke, still transfixed on the well.

He scanned his eyes across the opening. There was little difference inside the well to the outside, the damp allowing the growth of mosses, lichens and algae to form in a pallet of muted green. The same damp seeped into the stone itself picking out the seams of glinting minerals that ran through them. The stones!

'Evelyn,' said Luke. 'I need the letter.'

'What is it?' she asked, reaching into her pocket, and pulling out the folded letter.

Luke took the letter from her and unfolded it.

'The stones!' he said almost hysterically.

'What do you mean *the stones*?' asked Evelyn.

Luke took her by the shoulders and positioned her where he had stood.

'Look at the stones.'

'You're not making any sense!' said Evelyn. 'The clue isn't in the stones; they weren't here eight hundred years ago.'

Luke took a breath, steadying his thoughts.

'No but the clue isn't in the stones, they just gave me the key to Wishart's clue.'

'I'm not following,' said Evelyn, confusion clear on her face. 'The clue can't be in the stones, but the stones helped you find the clue?'

'Look,' said Luke, gesturing at the damp stones around the opening to the well. 'Those crystals that make up the stones, you can only see them when they're wet.'

'Ok,' said Evelyn slowly, 'what's that got to do with Wishart's letter.'

'If I'm right,' said Luke, 'then it's the key to finding the clue.'

'And if you're wrong?'

Luke shrugged. 'Then I'm about to destroy a very old and probably priceless piece of history.'

He walked up to the mouth of the well and knelt by the opening.

'Take the waters to help you on your journey,' Luke said under his breath, running his hand over the blank space of parchment below Wishart's message. 'I really hope I'm right about this.'

Evelyn watched in abject horror as Luke plunged the bottom of Wishart's Letter into the waters of Wallace's Well. The old parchment disappeared into the cloudy pool, soaking the fibres entirely. Luke waited a few painful seconds before pulling the letter out of the well and letting water drip off the page onto the stone slabs at his feet.

'What are you doing?' shouted Evelyn.

She lunged forward to rescue the letter but stopped in her tracks, open-mouthed. The water soaking into the parchment in Luke's hand had darkened the page like it had the stones around the well. Except it hadn't, not all of it anyway. A series of flowing lines ran across the page, almost glinting against the darkened parchment like the crystals in the stone. 'How?' asked Evelyn, stunned.

'I suspect,' said Luke, with a wide, full-toothed smile on his face, 'that a sheep helped.'

'A sheep?'

'Lanolin,' said Luke, before Evelyn accused him of making no sense again. 'It's a wax extracted from sheep's wool.'

Evelyn took the letter from Luke's hand.

'It's waterproof,' she said. 'Wishart wrote the clue in plain sight, but no one could see it unless it got wet.'

She smiled excitedly back at Luke. 'It's like Medieval invisible ink!'

Luke grinned back at her, her face was the brightest he had seen it since they'd met. Whatever cloud had been hanging over her cleared for that brief moment in the morning light. Luke caught himself staring and quickly decided to admire the stream instead.

'Genius really,' said Luke, still studying the scenery. 'Although maybe not since Scotland is one of the wettest places in Europe. What does it say?'

'What?' said Evelyn, cheeks suddenly flushing a light shade of pink.

'Wishart's letter,' said Luke. 'The mark left by the water, it's another message.'

'Oh right.' Evelyn scanned the words picked out by the dry patches on the page.

'I think it's a riddle,' she said after a few seconds.

'Why does it always have to be a riddle?' sighed Luke. 'The message was already hidden. Why can't it just say *three paces north and it's under the big rock?*'

Evelyn chuckled at him.

'That would make more sense than this,' she said, walking over to Luke's bag and taking out a paper and pen.

She scribbled the short translation onto a page and handed it to Luke.

He looked at the page, brows creasing.

'Stand where the waters burn?' he said, questioningly.

'Where does water burn?'

'A hot spring?' asked Evelyn.

Luke thought for a moment. 'There aren't any in Scotland. The closest ones are in Derbyshire.'

'Wishart wouldn't have hidden the stone in England,' said Evelyn.

Luke swung his legs over the iron railing that cut the stream off from the well forecourt and sat on the top rail, reading the line of text over and over. Evelyn leant against the railing by his side, arms crossed in front of her and resting her head on her hands. The stream trickled over the polished pebbles that lined its base. Evelyn watched the tiny fish swim amongst the reeds that grew in the stream, darting in tiny shoals, their silver scales glinting like knights in armour.

'Where the waters burn,' she whispered. 'Scots, wha hae wi' Wallace bled,' Evelyn said, grabbing Luke's arm, almost sending him toppling backwards off the railing.

'Burns wrote that poem over 400 years after Wishart hid the stone?' Said Luke.

'Not Robert Burns,' said Evelyn excitedly. 'The name of the poem!'

'Bannockburn,' said Luke, realising what Evelyn meant. 'It's named after the Bannock.'

'The Bannock BURN,' finished Evelyn.

'You're a genius!' Luke laughed in delight, beaming at Evelyn making her blush again. 'It's not burning water, it's a burn. A stream!'

Evelyn's face heated, blushing a deeper shade of red than before. Luke didn't notice, his eyes transfixed by the water flowing in front of him.

'Evelyn,' he said, 'do you know what the name of this stream is?'

Evelyn pulled the map she had seen earlier from Luke's bag, following his train of thought. She unfolded the massive sheet and traced her finger along the page to the town on the edge of Glasgow. A light blue line wound its way through the countryside and passed the well where they stood.

Evelyn looked up from the map.

'It's the Stand.'

'Stand where the waters burn,' said Luke, repeating the bishop's riddle. 'The Stand Burn.'

He launched himself off the railing and splashed into the ankle-deep water of the burn, sending plumes of water radiating up and out and sending a particularly disgruntled duck flapping off into the sky voicing its displeasure.

'The clue's in the burn,' said Luke, moving aside the vegetation that grew along the banks. 'Are you going to stand and watch?'

He grinned up at Evelyn from amongst the reeds. With a sigh, she slipped off her shoes and climbed under the railing to join him.

They both sifted through the frigid water, turning stones, and stirring up tiny torrents of silt that were quickly washed away by the flow of the burn.

'I've got nothing,' said Evelyn, having reached where the burn ran under the road, her black jeans now soaked to the knee.

Luke looked back at her, grim-faced and covered to the chest in mud, water, and various bits of assorted aquatic vegetation. He shifted his feet in the silt in front of the well and stumbled as something below caught his foot. He took a step back and felt along the bed of the stream with his foot. A block, too square to be natural, sat a few inches below the mud and gravel. Luke continued probing with his foot. It was neatly hewn, the edges slightly worn and rounded from centuries of erosion but undoubtably not deposited by the burn.

'There's something here,' said Luke.

Evelyn watched as he dropped onto the flat of his stomach and, with a deep breath, immersed his face in the water.

A few heartbeats passed.

'Luke?' said Evelyn, a hint of worry creeping into her voice.

'Luke?' she said again, louder this time.

Bubbles rose to the surface to the side of where Luke's head bobbed under the gentle current. A small waterfall cascaded from Luke's head as he lifted it from the burn and gasped in a deep breath.

'It's not the stone,' said Luke, shaking his head like a wet dog. 'Too big, but it has something carved on the top. Looked like a bow.'

'It must be Wishart's clue then, why else would it be there?' said Evelyn.

Luke picked a strand of river weeds from his shoulder and flicked them back into the water. 'William Wallace's seal on the Lübeck letter, it was a drawn bow and that was written only a year after Edward I took the fake stone,' he said. 'I think this could be Wishart's clue.'

Evelyn trudged through the water to where he stood next to the block. Luke squatted and put his arm into the water, feeling for the stones edges again.

'Couldn't you have done that in the first place rather than going for a swim?' asked Evelyn.

'I could have, but I wouldn't have seen the seal,' said Luke, still feeling around the block. 'And it wouldn't have been as fun.'

Evelyn shook her head at him but couldn't stop the corners of her mouth twisting into a smile.

'What did Wishart leave for us to find?'

'There's a ridge in the stone, like a handle,' said Luke, straining his shoulder to reach under it. 'It won't budge.'

Luke tugged on the stone. Nothing. He yanked again, throwing his weight backwards and nearly popping the bone out of his shoulder. The block shifted slightly but was still stuck fast in the silt.

'I think we can shift it,' he said rubbing his shoulder. 'See if you can find something to use as a lever.'

Evelyn sloshed through the water to the lighter patch of stone in the outer wall. An iron bar from an old fence sat lodged in the bank and came free from the mud with a little effort.

Luke took the bar and fitted the broken end into the ledge beneath the stone. He forced his weight down onto it, raising the edge of the stone a few millimeters.

'I think it's going to give,' said Luke, putting his entire body into pushing on the bar. The stone refused to move any further and the strain of keeping it raised the little way it had been was starting to show on Luke.

'There's another bar back over there,' said Luke in a clipped voice. 'See if you can get it out and help me shift this.'

Evelyn rushed back up stream as fast as the knee-deep water would allow and yanked the protruding bar as hard as she could. The iron bar broke free of the ground more easily than the last, making Evelyn overbalance and nearly fall into the burn completely. She steadied herself and hefted the bar ready to help Luke. She turned, just in time to see him throw the last of his strength into the lever. He tumbled backwards into the water as the lever flew from his grip and the huge stone block shifted from its seat before disappearing through the bed of the burn. She could only watch in horror as the bank of the burn crumbled, stone and soil pouring into a growing void. Luke grappled for anything he could reach to stop him sliding into the opening but his fingers found no purchase. Evelyn watched helplessly as the ground below Luke gave way and he plunged into the dark void below.

'Luke!' Evelyn screamed.

No reply came from the hole, just the sound of water trickling into oblivion.

CHAPTER 6

Approximately 20 feet below the Stand Burn, Wallace's Well, Langmuirhead Road, Robroyston, Glasgow.

Darkness. Unending, depthless. The steady dripping of water onto his head roused Luke from the grips of unconsciousness. He groaned, shifting his weight onto his arms, pushing himself up into a sitting position. Water was seeping through his clothes from the puddle he had landed in and a violent shiver had started to set in. The cold stone beneath had done little to cushion his fall. Luke tested his joints, his body ached, and he was scraped, and bruised but mercifully otherwise undamaged.

'Luke!' Evelyn's voiced echoed around his head, 'are you ok?'

Luke looked up, blinking at the light shining from the hole above his head. Water trickled over the jagged edges, the occasional pebble getting caught in the flow and clattering down the long stone shaft.

'Luke!' Came Evelyn's voice again.

'I'm ok,' groaned Luke. 'Spines are supposed to hurt when you move right?'

Evelyn's face appeared over the precipice, her red hair glowing in the halo of light.

'Can you see anything down there?' she shouted, the words bouncing off the hard surfaces and filling the void with a growing chorus.

Luke slowly got to his feet, his body still stiff from the fall. He turned his head, wincing with the movement, taking in the chamber he had fallen into.

'The bright sun was extinguished, and the stars did wander darkling in the eternal space,' said Luke, looking back up at Evelyn, 'rayless and pathless.'

Evelyn rolled her eyes. 'A simple no would have worked you know,' she said, exasperated. 'You don't have to quote Byron just because I have a degree in poetry.'

'Would you rather I quoted Howard Carter and told you I could see *"wonderful things?"*' retorted Luke.

'Only if you found Tutankhamun's tomb down there.'

Luke looked around the space again, darkness. The shaft of light coming from above cast only a faint glow over a few feet of the space Luke stood in.

'For all I know I could have,' said Luke. 'I can't see

a damn thing.'

He shuffled a few steps forward, hands outstretched, feeling for a wall.

'There's more down here,' he called to Evelyn, 'I need the torch.'

Evelyn withdrew from the edge of the hole, taking care not to join Luke at the bottom. The torch lay discarded where Luke had left it on the stone forecourt in front of the well. The water level in the burn had dropped as a result of the small waterfall now plunging into the void that swallowed Luke, making Evelyn's journey to the bank noticeably easier. She pushed herself up onto the muddy verge and to the torch lying just a few feet beyond.

'Heads up!' shouted Evelyn as she dropped the torch over the edge of the hole.

Luke looked up in time to avoid taking a torch to the temple and caught it awkwardly.

'Some more warning would have been nice,' he called to Evelyn.

'Sorry,' a disembodied voice floated back to him.

Luke flicked on the torch and shone it into the darkness in front of him. The torch beam flashed into a rough, stone tunnel. Not the smooth, polished walls formed over millennia by the flow of water, but angular and coarse, the rock torn away with blood and sweat. The cut was not fresh; a thick reddish-brown lichen spread across most of the exposed rock, grown in almost absolute darkness for centuries. The torch beam stretched a few meters down the tunnel before getting lost in the darkness beyond.

'There's a tunnel,' shouted Luke. 'I can't see where it goes.'

Evelyn tilted her head to one side, inspecting the steep edges of the shaft that led to the tunnel Luke had found.

'Wait there, I'm coming down.'

She tested the edge of the hole. Confident no more ground was going to crumble into the void she lowered herself on her hands over the empty space. Her foot found purchase on a rough jutting stone just at the limit of her reach, she stretched her other leg across to the wall to another small hold. Slowly, Evelyn made her way down the rockface, edging inch by inch down the slick stone. Her foot made contact with a stone about halfway down the wall, the surface smoother than she expected and her foot slid clean off the wall and dangled into open air. Evelyn froze gripping the stone under her hands hard enough to blanch her knuckles.

'Careful!' Luke called up.

Evelyn glared at him. 'When has telling someone to be careful ever been helpful?' Luke shrugged and held the torch steady as she searched for a firm foot hold. Evelyn shifted her weight, ready to move the last few meters to the base of the shaft. A soft crack and rattle of falling stone chips echoed into the cavern below.

'Did you hear that?'

'Hear what?'

Suddenly the stone under Evelyn's right hand gave way sending debris tumbling down the wall. Luke jumped out of the way as the rock struck the floor where he had been standing, shattering into a thousand sharp fragments. Evelyn swung wildly, her back slamming into the jagged stones, sending her toppling forwards into nothing. She fell, the floor rushing to meet her. Luke lunged, stretching out his arms under her plummeting form. Evelyn felt her body connect not with the cold stone but with Luke's arms. Her heart raced as she let out a shaky breath.

'Th..thanks.'

'Anytime,' Luke smiled.

Evelyn smiled weakly. 'You can put me down now.'

Luke let her feet drop to the floor and steadied her, still shaking slightly.

'Still more graceful than your landing.'

'Almost as dramatic though.'

Luke swung the torch back down the tunnel, the darkness seeming to stretch further than before.

'You ok to walk?'

Evelyn nodded slightly and followed the torch beam into the darkness. Water dripped from the roof of the tunnel and tiny stalactites had started to form from the minerals left behind.

'Why would anyone build a tunnel under a well?' asked Evelyn, studying the pick marks on the stones above her head.

'There's tunnels all over Glasgow,' he said pushing further down into the darkness.

'Most of them don't have secret entrances under streams though.'

'True, some have been forgotten though: the telephone exchanges under Buchanan Street, the courthouse tunnel, abandoned Victorian train lines and stations…' Luke counted them off on his hand, 'nothing I know about that's this old though.'

The tunnel continued, a line straight as an arrow through the solid stone.

'It must have taken years to build this.'

Luke stared deep into the darkness.

'It took the Romans 120 years to build the Gadhara Aqueduct. The longest stretch of tunnel was 66 miles.' He looked over his shoulder at Evelyn. 'I really hope this will be shorter.'

As if hearing Luke's wish the tunnel opened up in front of them, the torch illuminating a cavern slightly taller than Luke and about 15 feet square. The walls were straight and even, unlike the curved walls of the tunnel and entrance shaft, giving the impression of a deliberate room. It was dry in the room too, the water dripping from above stopping shortly before the arch that led into the space. Luke flashed the torch around the room.

'The stone isn't here.'

The room was all but bare with four solid stone walls and nowhere the stone could be hidden.

Evelyn stood by one of the walls, running her hand over the rough grooves left by the picks used to hew the stone and carve it to shape. Except that's not what these were. The grooves were irregular, running in different directions, cutting each other and some curving where others where straight. She dropped her arm and crossed the floor to Luke.

'No,' she said, taking his hand and guiding the torch light to the wall she had just been stood at. 'But that is.'

The light flashed across the marks of the wall. They weren't pick marks, the wall around them was smooth, near polished.

'Another clue,' said Luke. 'There's always another clue.'

He ran the torch across the lines of text on the wall.

'Can you translate?'

'I don't have anywhere to write it down.'

'I have a good memory,' said Luke.

Evelyn read the text as the torchlight illuminated it, the grooves casting shadows in the polished stone.

'Rejoice for the war is over, peace prevails and for that reason the stone must remain hidden. The deception I plotted must never be found for the sake of our great country. Wishart left the stone to me and now I near my grave he takes the secret to his.'

As Evelyn finished the final line the torch light glinted off something logged in the wall. She walked forward, hand outstretched. A small nook was carved after the final letter of the message. Evelyn plucked the tiny silver coin from where it rested.

'It's a coin,' she said, looking into the light where Luke stood. 'There's writing on it, but it doesn't make sense.'

She turned the coin over in her palm.

'ROBERTVS DEI GRA,'

She sounded the words out awkwardly. 'SCO TOR VM R EX.'

Luke walked forward slowly, each step echoing in the silence between them, and took the coin from Evelyn's hand.

'It's abbreviated Latin,' he said, standing close to Evelyn, the torch illuminating their faces. 'Robbertus Dei Gracia, Scottorum Rex.'

'Robert by the grace of God, King of Scotts.'

'Robert the Bruce.'

The pair looked at each other, grinning like children.

'Now we know who the Robert in Wishart's letter was,' said Evelyn.

'And why the real stone was kept hidden.' Luke

started looking around the room again. 'Robert the Bruce had achieved peace, Scotland was safe.'

'If he had revealed the stone the English had was fake, that they had been fooled, then it could have provoked them,' said Evelyn.

Luke moved to the far corner of the room.

'If Robert the Bruce was close to death, then the treaty of Edinburgh-Northampton hadn't long been signed,' he said, flashing the torch at the ceiling of the room. 'He couldn't risk that. He had to hide the stone again.'

'Why move it though?' said Evelyn, moving out of the darkness left in the absence of Luke.

'I don't know,' said Luke. 'But I think I've found a way out.'

He flicked the torch back up to the ceiling. The beam didn't stop at the stone but continued into a squared shaft leading vertically upwards and foot and hand holds were carved into one side at regular intervals like a ladder.

'I'll give you a leg up,' said Luke, kneeling down and cupping his hands for Evelyn's foot.

'Why do I have to go first?'

'Because if I go first there won't be anyone to heroically catch you if you fall again.'

Evelyn stuck her tongue out at him and stood in his hands crushing his fingers slightly under her heel.

'Ouch!'

'Oops,' said Evelyn innocently.

Luke stood, propelling Evelyn towards the lowest hand hold a few inches above his own reach. She grabbed the stone ledge and pulled her body up, pinning a leg against opposite walls to hold herself as she reached for the higher holds. Luke waited for her to move higher before jumping to grab the bottom hold, using the strength in his shoulders to swing himself to the next hold and the next until his toes could wedge into the small ledges below him.

They climbed a few short feet up the stone cut ladder.

'There's a flagstone,' Evelyn said to Luke below her. 'I can't shift it.'

Luke climbed higher. Evelyn shifted, holding herself with one foot and hand on the stone ladder and the others pressing against the wall as Luke climbed level with her.

'On three,' said Luke setting his shoulders against the heavy flagstone, Evelyn copying the motion. 'Three.'

They pushed against the stone, every muscle straining not only to move the stone but to keep them from plummeting back down the shaft. The stone grated against something, with a painful, gritty sound. With a final heave the stone gave way, levering backwards and dropping on to the ground with a soft thud. Luke and Evelyn blinked in the sunlight, now blazing in the morning sky. Luke pushed himself up and out of the shaft, reaching a hand back to help Evelyn.

'Where are we?' asked Luke to no one in particular.

He stood facing a line of trees and damp grass surrounding the hole they had come out of. Evelyn grabbed his shoulder, spinning him around to face the way she did.

'Ah,' Said Luke.

A short distance in front of them was a huge stone plinth topped with a Celtic cross, a sword carved into its face. Luke started to laugh.

'What's so funny?'

'He hid the stone, the symbol of them fooling the English, right under where Wallace was betrayed to them.'

Evelyn smirked. 'That's a pretty good *up yours* from someone who was talking about peace.'

'I like him even more.'

Luke walked over to the wall standing next to the monument and sat, taking the weight off his still bruised and battered body. Evelyn stood in front of him.

'I would admire Robert the Bruce more if he had told us where he hid the stone.'

'He did.'

Evelyn thought about the message on the wall.

'Now I near my grave he takes the secret to his.'

'You're getting good at this,' said Luke.

'Where is Wishart buried?'

'Where he spent most of his life.'

'In the Cathedral?' asked Evelyn.

Luke grunted and got to his feet.

'More *under* the Cathedral,' he said, 'but yes, the Cathedral.'

Evelyn moved to steady Luke on his feet, but he waved her off.

'Are you ok to walk that far?'

'I'm fine' said Luke, limping slightly towards the road.

'Really?' Evelyn said questioningly, 'because you're going the wrong way.'

Luke stopped.

'I'm going back to the well.'

'Why?'

'I left my bag there,' he said, carrying on walking. 'I think we should take the surface route back.'

Evelyn didn't move.

'Luke,' she called to him.

'What?'

'You're still going the wrong way.'

CHAPTER 7

Singl-end Cafe, Renfrew Street, Garenthill, Glasgow, Table 14

'What happened to time is of the essence?' said Evelyn, somewhat irritably.

They sat at a table by the bright cellar window that looked up onto the street above. The room was full, contented faces occupied every table and a steady stream of food was coming from the kitchens.

'Breakfast happened,' Luke said, leaning into the heavenly scents coming from the dishes being whisked past their table, the cakes and pastries in the displays more enticing and glorious than any treasure. 'And it should have happened about two hours ago. I don't like grave robbing on an empty stomach.'

Evelyn looked around carefully.

'Why don't you say that a bit louder?' she whispered to him. 'I don't think the back tables heard you!'

Luke smiled and poured himself another cup

of strong black tea from the china pot that sat between them, then offered the pot to Evelyn.

'Relax,' he said filling her cup in turn. 'I doubt anyone else in here is on a quest to find the missing coronation stone of Scotland.'

'What if whoever sent the man in the suit sent someone else?'

Luke looked around the cafe at the people happily sitting at the other tables.

'No one in here is wearing a suit,' he shrugged.

'You're not taking this seriously.'

'No,' said Luke, 'I just think if someone was going to try to kill us again, then a crowded cafe probably wouldn't be where they would choose to do it.'

'The last one tried to kill us in one of the top ten tourist attractions in Edinburgh,' Evelyn shot back at him.

'What's the chance of that happening twice?'

A waitress brought over a mountainous plate of food; Luke leant back making way for the enormous platter to be slid onto the table in front of him. Evelyn's eyes widened at the sheer volume of food, the plates piled high with doorstop sized French toast, bacon and maple syrup.

'Jesus Christ!'

'No, just a damn good chef,' said Luke, shovelling food into his mouth. 'Although I think the 5000 would have been more satisfied if they'd been served this.'

Evelyn rolled her eyes at him but looked longingly at the plate of food, wishing she had ordered something too. Luke caught her stare and pushed the plate to the middle of the table.

'There's too much for one person anyway,' he said, offering her an extra knife and fork. Evelyn took them quickly blurting a thank you before digging in herself.

'If we're going to rob a grave,' she said between mouthfuls of bread and bacon, 'shouldn't we do it sooner rather than later?'

Luke raised his eyebrow in question.

'Go to the cathedral, you know, before we get either arrested or murdered?' Evelyn continued.

Luke washed his food down with a swig of tea.

'We can't just sweep in blindly like at Wallace's well.'

'Why not?'

'For a start, Glasgow Cathedral is not only a tourist hot spot,' said Luke, taking another bite, 'it's also a cathedral.'

'Never would have guessed that from the name,' said Evelyn.

'What I mean,' said Luke, ignoring the heavy sarcasm in Evelyn's voice, 'is that even if by some miracle there's no tourists, there will still be members of the clergy wandering around.'

'And they wouldn't be too happy if they caught us rummaging around in a bishop's grave.'

'Exactly,' nodded Luke. 'Also, I'm in no rush to

fall down any more holes.'

'So how do we do it?'

Luke set aside his cutlery and cleared the table in front of him, Evelyn swiping the plate with the remnants of French toast. He reached into his bag and retrieved the map of Glasgow.

'The problem is, Wishart's grave is out in the open, in full public view,' he said. 'There's no chance we wouldn't be seen.'

'Can't we just wait until it's closed and break in tonight?' asked Evelyn.

'Do you want to add breaking and entering a church to the list of things we can be arrested for?'

'Is that worse than grave robbing?'

'Only if we get caught grave robbing.' Luke leant back in his chair. 'There's security at night—we need to go in during the day when we have an excuse to be there.'

Evelyn slumped in her chair, mirroring Luke's defeated pose.

'We need to go in during the day but have absolutely no one around,' she said, frowning at the problem.

'What if we pull a fire alarm and clear the building out? That would give us some time.'

Luke looked down at the map in front of him.

'The Cathedral is here,' he said pointing to the *Cath* etched on the page. 'There are fire stations in Calton, Springburn and Cowcaddens.' Luke pointed to the points on the map in a triangle around the cathedral.

'How long would we have?'

'Response time is under nine minutes,' he sighed. 'Probably less for a prominent place like the cathedral.'

'So not the fire alarm.'

'Let's call that plan B.'

The pair sat in silence, brains working overtime trying to solve their problem. The smiling waitress came back and cleared away the spent plates and teapot.

'We need to go to the cathedral,' said Luke finally.

'You want to just walk in and what? Ask nicely to desecrate a grave.'

'I wouldn't phrase it like that.'

'I wasn't being serious,' said Evelyn.

Luke shrugged again. 'Do you have a better idea?'

A bill appeared on the table, Luke picked up the paper and produced some crumpled notes from his pocket.

They both stood to leave. Luke headed for the wooden counter to pay the bill, Evelyn walking close behind.

'If we walk in and say, *excuse me we think the coronation stone in Edinburgh is a fake and the real one is in the tomb in your crypt, mind if we take a look..?*'

'...Then we will either be laughed out of the place, or they will call the police and we end up in prison,' finished Luke. 'And, if we try to break in or try a distraction like the fire alarm, we end up in prison.'

Luke and Evelyn walked out of the café, up the steel stairs to the level of the road and down the steep hill of Renfrew Street towards the city centre.

'Ok, so how do we not end up in prison?'

'Unless you have a way to have a building full of people and have all of them stay in one place for an extended period of time, while they, the staff and security all kindly turn a blind eye to us doing a jolly spot of grave robbing, then no.'

They turned a corner and emerged into a never-ending flow of people walking down the busy street. Men and women winding past the double row of trees running down the centre of the pavement, laden with shopping bags. A giant, cream-coloured stone building loomed at the end of the street. Evelyn's eye was caught by the banners hanging from the lampposts as they approached.

'Actually, I might have,' she said stopping next to the towering wall of the Royal Concert Hall.

'Care to share it?'

Evelyn pointed towards the lamppost and the banners hanging either side.

'Classical by Candlelight?' said Luke dubiously.

'Look at the venue.'

Luke scanned down the banner to where it read Glasgow Cathedral, 7pm.

'That just might work.' Luke considered the idea.

'We'll never get tickets,' he said checking his watch. 'Eight hours before the event.'

Evelyn chewed her lip, thinking.

'Then we don't. We get there early and hide somewhere until after the Cathedral shuts and the event starts,' she said. 'Then if anyone catches us in the crypt we have an excuse—we say we are there for the orchestra.'

Luke smiled, admiring the cunning in Evelyn's plan.

'Out of the morally questionable things we've done so far, gate-crashing an evening of orchestra is probably the most forgivable.'

Evelyn smiled back at Luke as they both weaved back through the tide of shoppers, the mammoth length of Buchannan Street stretching into the distance before them.

'Only one problem.'

'What?

'I'm going to need a dinner jacket,' said Luke walking through the glass doors of a shop.

'We're supposed to be blending into a respectable event and we look like…' he looked himself and Evelyn up and down.

'Like we've been shot at in a graveyard and driven across the country to fall down a cave that hasn't seen the light of day for 800 years,' Evelyn finished for him, 'all to find a missing stone.'

Luke tilted his head to the side. 'It sounds

ridiculous when you put it like that but pretty much.'

'I should find something too, meet back here in an hour?'

'An hour?' said Luke.

Evelyn smiled sweetly at him.

'You haven't been shopping with a woman before, have you?' she said, then walked away leaving him standing dumbstruck.

Luke checked his watch again, over an hour had passed with him sat in the high-backed chair surrounded by racks of clothing. Clicking heels snapped him to attention. He looked up to see Evelyn walking towards him. She wore an emerald-green dress straight out of the 1950's, a coal-black wool coat slung over her shoulder, held with one finger made the dark cherry of her hair stand out like a fire. Luke stood more quickly than he had meant to.

'Wow, you look…' he trailed off.

'No need to look so shocked.' Evelyn blushed slightly.

'You don't scrub up so badly yourself,' she said, her eyes took in his sleek black jacket, bright silver buttons running parallel to the lapels. She raised an eyebrow at him.

'Was the kilt really necessary?'

'Absolutely,' He said without hesitation.

Luke offered Evelyn his arm.

'Now,' he said, as she looped her arm through his, 'we have a grave to rob.'

CHAPTER 8

Glasgow Cathedral, Castle Street, Glasgow

The verdigrised roof of Glasgow Cathedral sat stark against the dark stone spires that wound towards the heavens. Flags of a hundred countries flapped gently in the breeze on the poles that lined the long precinct running towards the grand arched doors. As Luke stared up at the great window and towering spire he couldn't help but feel insignificant next to the imposing building.

The sun was dipping in the sky, casting a hazy afternoon light across the city. Luke checked his watch again.

'We have an hour until the Cathedral closes,' he said. 'Then it's three hours until the concert starts.'

Evelyn admired the giant stained-glass window that graced the front of the cathedral, held in a great stone-arched window above the door.

'It's a shame we have to miss it,' she sighed with genuine disappointment.

Luke smiled at her.

'Tell you what, if we find the stone and don't get killed or thrown in prison, I'll get tickets the next one.'

'Really?'

'Promise,' he said, making Evelyn smile back at him. 'I need an excuse to wear this again anyway.'

Luke gestured to the sharp lines of his jacket, and the green and purple tartan that he wore.

The carved oak doors, almost comically small next to the extravagance of the rest of the cathedral's face, stood open, inviting the world. A steady stream of tourists and the occasional member of the clergy filed their way in and out.

Luke and Evelyn stepped through the stone arches and into the cavernous space beyond. Light poured through the windows that surrounded the high walls, bathing every surface in a technicolour haze and making the features of the building seem overexposed and glowing. They made their way down the nave between the stone pillars that reached like tree trunks up to the higher walls and yet another set of bright, arched windows. Stacks of chairs waited in the side aisles beyond the pillars in discreet regimented lines, ready for the evening's event.

'Which tomb is Wishart's?' asked Evelyn, studying the carved stone memorials naming the great and good that occupied the resting places of honour within the cathedral.

'It's in the lower church,' said Luke. 'The stairs are just there.'

He pointed towards a stone staircase that ran underneath the north transept near where a few tourists milled, snapping pictures of the incredible architecture and colourful windows.

'We don't have long,' said Evelyn, tearing herself away from admiring the beauty of the building surrounding them. 'We should find somewhere to wait until the concert starts.'

Luke looked past her, not hearing a word she had said to him. A flick of black fabric catching his eye.

'Luke?'

Luke grabbed Evelyn's hand and pulled her behind one of the great stone pillars.

'What are you...'

'Shhh,' he cut her off.

Luke leant around the pillar to see back into the nave but snapped his head back and stood, back pressed to the cold stone. Evelyn gave him a questioning look.

'The priest stood near the door,' he half whispered.

Evelyn looked tentatively around the pillar until her eyes fell on the priest in the long black cassock, his hair even darker, almost lightless. She moved back and stood facing Luke, the pillar still obscuring the view to the priest.

'Who is he?'

'Father Keir.' Luke chanced another look around

the pillar to see Keir still loitering near the entrance. 'He is the man who rejected most of my research, including when I wanted to look for the stone.'

Evelyn looked at the priest again. His face was lined with age, his movement that of a man starting to suffer from ageing joints but in his eyes –a cold petrol blue—swam a calculation and cunning that didn't seem to befit a man of God.

'It's probably a coincidence,' she said, not mirroring Luke's concern. 'He's a priest, we're in a cathedral.'

'A catholic priest. The cathedral hasn't been catholic since the reformation.'

'So?'

'So, doesn't it seem a bit of a coincidence that a man who stopped me from looking for the stone, is here, where the stone is hidden at the same time a mysterious figure is sending killers to stop us finding the stone?'

Evelyn frowned. 'Why come himself this time and not just send another trigger-happy psychopath?'

'No idea,' said Luke.

Keir's footsteps echoed down the nave as the stiff-soled shoes clicked on the flagstones. Luke's eyes followed the priest past their hiding spot behind the pillar and towards the stairs leading to the lower church below the south transept.

'I'm going to ask him.'

'That sounds like a bad idea.'

'Probably because it is,' Luke said with a grim look. 'Go and find somewhere to hide until the concert. I'll meet you by Wishart's tomb before they close the doors.'

Luke stepped out from behind the pillar in time to see the hem of Keir's cassock disappear around a corner. He made to go after the priest but was stopped by Evelyn's voice.

'Luke,' she said, 'be careful.'

Luke gave her a reassuring smile.

'When am I not?'

Luke stepped down the curving stairs that led into the small chapel. The whitewashed walls were cast in the same rainbow of light as the cathedral above coming from the small windows set high in the walls. Father Keir was stood with his back to the stairs before a deep red-clothed alter.

He didn't turn as Luke dismounted the final step and stopped, standing not with his usual relaxed self-confidence but with a tension, rigid as the stone pillars supporting the chapel.

'Forgive me father for I have sinned.'

Keir stayed motionless, 'So I have heard, Mr Knight.' The priest made the sign of the cross and turned on Luke with a slow grace.

'You left quite the mess in Edinburgh.'

'How do you know about that?'

Keir paced towards Luke, stopping just out of arms reach.

'I have my contacts Mr Knight, as you well know.'

'Like the one you sent to kill us?'

Keir tilted his head to the side. Luke had no doubts that Keir was capable of having him killed but the priest seemed genuinely surprised at Luke's accusation.

'You think I sent that man to kill you?'

'Wouldn't be the first time,' Luke spat back at him.

Keir sighed. 'What happened in Qumran was not my doing.'

'So, it was just coincidence that it stopped me getting to the cave before you.'

'The cave was empty.'

'You didn't know that,' Luke snapped, his voice echoing off the vaulted ceiling.

The priest rubbed his forehead and walked back towards the alter.

'I am not trying to kill you Luke, or the lovely Miss Crawford,' he said. 'Even if I were I would not be so clumsy about it.'

Luke studied Keir's face, the harsh scowl he usually wore seemed softer in the glow of the chapel.

'What are you doing here Keir?'

Keir's smiled softly, only confusing Luke further. Keir had never shown him anything but thinly veiled distain and contempt. He could almost swear the priest looked, concerned?

'Give up looking for the stone, Mr Knight.'

'Why would I do that?' said Luke, hearing but not bothering to correct the childish stubbornness creeping into his tone.

'Because Luke, we may not see eye to eye, but I do not wish to see you killed.'

Luke scoffed.

'You stopped me looking for the stone once before, I'm not…'

Keir erupted in anger, cutting Luke off mid-sentence.

'Do you not think there was a reason?' The priest tempered his voice and hissed, 'The stone is powerful and people who seek power know no limits.'

'You're the one who told me not to chase fairy tales—the stone hasn't got any power,' said Luke. 'It doesn't really sing out underneath the true king like in the legends.'

Keir smirked, picking up the rosary that hung from his hip and beginning to pass the white quartz beads through his hand, a loud *click* sounding after each one fell.

'The stone is a symbol of Scotland,'

click

'a symbol of rebellion,'

click

'and if the English found out theirs wasn't real,'

click

'a symbol of treachery.'

He reached the end of the chain of beads and was left with the gothic silver crucifix in his hand.

'Symbols,' the priest said tapping the crucifix, 'have more power than any myth or fairy tale.'

Luke looked from the crucifix to the priest, locking his eyes on his deadly stare.

'I'm not letting this go,' he said defiantly.

Keir sighed and dropped the rosary back to its spot hanging at his side.

'I have to admire your tenacity,' said the priest, 'even if it is misguided.'

Luke said nothing.

'Did you know it was here that the Bishop Wishart absolved Robert the Bruce for the murder of John Comyn?' said Keir.

'At Greyfriars in Dumfries,' continued Luke. 'What's that got to do with the stone?'

Keir ignored his question and paced the length of the chapel.

'You didn't quite kill anyone in Edinburgh so I can't absolve you, but I can offer you a warning,' he said. 'The authorities have connected the man you entombed in Edinburgh to John's disappearance. They want a little chat with you.'

'Tell me something I don't know,' muttered Luke.

'They also know you're planning on attending the concert tonight.'

A lead weight dropped in Luke's stomach.

'How could they possibly know that?'

Keir flashed a wolfish smile.

'They called the university asking where you might be. Someone may have told them where to look.'

'You bastard,' spat Luke.

The priest attempted a look of pure innocence and held up his hands.

'A false witness shall not be unpunished, and he that speaketh lies shall not escape.'

'Proverbs 19:5.'

'I never took you as a religious man.'

'I'm not,' said Luke offering no further explanation. Keir didn't push the matter.

Luke thought about what the priest had just told him. Something didn't make sense.

'How did you know we would be here?' he said. 'I didn't know we would be here until a few hours ago.'

'You left quite the mess at Wallace's Well. It wasn't hard to follow,' replied Keir dryly.

Luke shook his head, unsatisfied with the answer.

'You wouldn't have gone to Wallace's Well unless…' He trailed off; Keir watched him like a viper stalking its prey.

'You called him John,' said Luke. 'How could you know about Evelyn's brother?'

Keir smiled to himself.

'You were always a perceptive one,' he said. 'Did you not stop to think where the boy got Wishart's letter from?'

'You gave it to him?'

'He came to me,' said the priest slowly, 'looking for you.'

Luke couldn't hide his surprise.

'I gave him the letter on the condition he leave you out of it.'

'Why? Because you couldn't bear me finding it instead of you?'

Keir considered his next words carefully.

'Like I said Mr Knight, the stone breeds danger and I didn't wish to see you harmed.'

Luke couldn't make sense of it. The priest's apparent concern seemed genuine but completely out of character for the man he had been at odds with for most of his adult life.

'How long have you had the letter?'

'Being both an academic and a member of the clergy has its benefits,' replied Keir, 'like access to the Scottish Catholic Archives.'

Luke's temper resurfaced.

'So, you knew the stone was a fake all along when you dismissed my research as a flight of imagination.'

'Did I really say that?'

Luke was about to spit something venomous back at the priest but Keir raised his hand and the words dissolved on his tongue.

'I knew, but I didn't know about the well until John stumbled upon the answer.'

'He's dead because of you,' said Luke coldly.

'He's dead because he ignored the warning I just gave you, just like you're going to ignore me now.'

'You're right, I am going to ignore you.' Luke smirked at him and turned to leave the chapel.

'Luke,' called Keir to Luke's back. 'One last thing.'

Luke turned back to the priest, still stood by the red-clothed alter. Keir withdrew something from within his cassock and tossed it towards the stairs. Luke caught the object. It was a book, a palm-sized bible, old and slightly battered but bound in a fine calfskin, the cover set with a silver cross and blackened in places with age. Luke looked back at Keir in question.

'In case you're in need of guidance,' said the priest.

Luke said nothing, instead slipping the bible inside the breast pocket of his jacket, before turning his back on the priest and walking away.

Evelyn looked at Luke coming up from the chapel. She could see the tension in his body, the fire that had been in his eyes had gone, replaced by something else, fear maybe? And something else that she couldn't quite place.

'I take it he isn't here to kill us?'

'No, not this time anyway,' said Luke flatly. 'We have bigger problems right now.'

'What's happened?'

'Keir tipped off the police, about the man in the

suit, about John.'

Evelyn's face fell.

'How did he know about John. The police wouldn't even believe me he was missing?'

'Long story,' said Luke.

He looked at the stone mausoleum they stood next to, the effigy worn and broken and the once crisp edges now worn and rounded.

'We still need to look in the tomb,' he said. 'You should go. If the police turn up and the stone isn't here then one of us needs to keep looking.'

'How would I do that if you were sat in a cell?'

Luke shook his head gently.

'You figured out as much as I did, I…'

'I'm not leaving. We're going to find the stone together or…'

'Die trying?'

'I'd rather not if we can help it,' said Evelyn.

Luke looked down at the watch on his wrist, the seconds ticking by too fast.

'They don't know we're here yet,' he said. 'Keir said they're going to arrest us at the concert. We have less time, but the plan still works.'

Evelyn nodded, focusing herself.

'There's a broom cupboard in the chapter house,' she said. 'It's not going to be fun, but we can wait there until the concert starts.'

'Let's go, before they check for stragglers.'

* * *

'How much longer?' said Evelyn, shifting her leg from where it was pinned between her own body and the floor, wincing at the pins and needles that bloomed in them as the blood flow returned.

'Too long.' Luke tried and failed to extract his arm from behind his back, giving up on the possibility of seeing his watch. 'When you said broom cupboard, I assumed it was designed to fit more than one broom.'

'It's not like there were a lot of options,' Evelyn shot back.

Luke decided against a sarcastic comeback given the location of Evelyn's foot in relation to himself.

'We won't have long once the concert starts,' he said after some time.

'What if it's not in the grave? It could be under it.'

'Then we're screwed,' said Luke, 'so let's hope it isn't.'

The whine of violins beginning to warm up sounded from above, muffled by the heavy floor. Breathy wind and brass notes followed as the orchestra struck up the first notes of the overture. Luke and Evelyn looked towards the low ceiling of the cupboard.

'Ready?'

'Ready.'

They both moved towards the door but became wedged between the narrow walls, pinning each other in place.

'You should probably go first,' said Luke, untangling himself and shuffling to the side to allow Evelyn past.

Music from a phantom orchestra echoed in the empty lower church: the haunting sounds of Chopin's Nocturne drifting, disembodied from above. Luke and Evelyn stood before the tomb of Robert Wishart, the headless body of his effigy lying before them, resting nestled in a high archway. The last dappled light of evening was coming through the far window casting long shadows across its surface. Luke positioned himself to slide the heavy stone lid from where it rested.

'You seem oddly relaxed about desecrating a grave,' said Evelyn, moving to help Luke.

'It's not my first time.'

Evelyn looked at him sideways.

'Don't ask.'

The pair strained against the stone slab. Nothing. The stone didn't budge but sat stubbornly in place.

Luke grunted putting every last ounce of energy into moving the slab.

Still nothing. Luke slid to the floor.

Evelyn retrieved Luke's torch from his bag and inspected the edge of the immense stone.

'It's cemented into the wall,' she said, confused.

Luke cursed under his breath.

Luke slumped against the tomb, letting his head fall back and connect painfully with the cold stone.

'It's not his grave.'

'What?'

'It's not his grave, it's just a memorial, they must have moved it,' he said, defeated.

'So, the stone isn't here?'

Luke cursed again, Evelyn joining with language that would make a sailor blush before dropping to the floor next to him. They sat, trying in vain to plan their next move.

'There's always another clue,' Luke muttered.

'Maybe it was never here,' tried Evelyn. 'We could have gotten it wrong.'

'No,' said Luke jumping back to his feet and taking the torch from Evelyn. 'Keir came to the same conclusion, and he knows more than he's letting on.'

Luke grabbed the torch, searching every inch of the tomb's effigy and the archway where it rested.

'We're missing something,' said Luke as he scanned across the finely carved effigy that filled the space. 'There…'

Luke stopped, the torch beam resting on the empty space where the effigy's head once sat.

'No…' breathed Luke. 'It can't be that simple.'

'What?'

'The effigy was defaced during the reformation,' said Luke, 'but why only remove the head?'

'You think the clue was in the head?'

Luke moved closer to the lid where the head had been. A finely carved stone pillow rested indented with where the head had sat. He reached up to his jacket and felt where the bible Keir had given him sat in his pocket.

'The stone has another name,' he said. 'A legend that a prophet named Jeremiah brought the stone to Ireland. That it was the stone that Jacob rested his head on in the book of Genesis.'

He ran his hand over the smoothed surface where the head had been.

'Jacob's Pillow,' he whispered.

'The head was removed to get to the pillow.'

Luke nodded gently, his fingers meeting a thin line just beyond the edge of the carved pillow...

The orchestra above had moved on, violins singing out the sounds of Vivaldi's Summer, the sounds piercing through the stone sharper and crisper than before.

Luke marched across the room to the prominent platform in the centre of the space, a brightly coloured cloth covering the tomb of St. Mungo.

Red velvet ropes stretched across the gaps between the towering pillars, held by brightly polished stanchions. He unhooked the rope and hefted the stanchion back to Wishart's effigy.

Evelyn's eyes widened in question as Luke fitted the round base of the stanchion between the edge of the stone pillow and the top of the slab.

'Do you think there's a Hell?'

'No?' Evelyn said, puzzled.

'That's good,' he said testing the stanchion, 'because I'm definitely going there for this.'

Luke threw his weight onto the stanchion. There was a crack and the sound of metal grating against stone. The carved pillow separated from its base with a gritty crunch. Evelyn moved to stop the top falling back into place as Luke dropped the stanchion and joined her hefting the stone sideways and resting it gently on the effigy's chest.

'It was here.' Evelyn grinned.

There was a space beneath the pillow, carved perfectly to receive a rectangular object, about two foot long and a foot wide.

'They must have known it would be found inside the tomb,' said Luke. 'So, they left Wishart to protect it again.'

'But what happened to it?'

Luke sighed and searched inside the space the stone had been.

'The cathedral was torn apart during the reformation,' he said, flashing the torch inside the small space. 'Anything seen as overtly catholic was destroyed. Either they found the stone or…'

'It was taken away before they could get to it.'

Luke clicked off the torch.

'There's nothing here.'

'Where did the stone go then?'

Luke opened his mouth to answer but was stopped by a flash of blue light from one of the small windows beyond Wishart's tomb. A siren whined; the sound almost lost in the music pouring down from above them.

'We'll have to figure that out later. We're out of time.

Evelyn looked across to the stairs leading up to the cathedral proper, waiting for the footsteps of heavy boots to come down them.

'Here, help me with this,' said Luke, with Evelyn's help hefting the heavy stone pillow back into place.

'We can still make it out. There's a door to the churchyard.'

The pair ran to the low oak door set in the north wall of the lower church. Luke shifted the heavy iron bolt and edged the door ajar. A buzz of a radio and a crackling voice made him jump back as a police officer in uniform walked along the path that led around the cathedral a few feet from the door.

'Plan B?'

'We have no plan B,' whispered Luke.

Evelyn crept to the stairs that led to the upper cathedral, edging up them slowly and crouching to peer into the nave where the orchestra played to a crowded house. The main doors to the cathedral quietly creaked open causing some patrons in the back row to turn their heads away from the musicians. Two more officers slipped through the door and stood quietly at the back of the rows of chairs, waiting. Evelyn retreated down the stairs to where Luke stood trying to see out of one of the high windows.

'Main doors are a no go too.'

Luke cursed under his breath.

'There's no way out without going past the police.'

'What do we do?' asked Evelyn.

Luke's gaze fell on the small red box sat on the wooden pillar by the stairs. He walked towards the pillar, stopping just short of the glass fronted box.

'Plan B.'

Luke slammed his elbow into the small glass panel in the front of the red box setting off the fire alarm. A piercing siren sounded almost immediately. The orchestra stopped abruptly leaving only the wailing siren sounding, followed closely by the scraping of chairs as the audience hastily made for the exits.

Luke and Evelyn made for the stairs, climbing them quickly and joining the tide of people exiting the cathedral.

'Don't run, not until we're past the police,' whispered Luke, linking his arm with Evelyn's to further pass for a couple attending an evening's entertainment. Evelyn tried not to look at the officers stood by the doors, scanning the crowd for their targets. Mercifully their eyes passed over the pair amid the chaos caused by the fire alarm.

'When we're out of sight of the cathedral we run and head for the river.'

Luke guided Evelyn out of the crowd of people as they passed through the arched doorway, heading south, not back along the flag lined precinct but instead towards the tree-lined Cathedral Square.

Luke whispered to Evelyn, 'When we get beyond that corner, get ready to...'

'Oi!' boomed a voice from behind them. 'Hold it there.'

They ignored the voice, breaking into a sprint rather than waiting to see who was coming after them.

The pair tore around the street corner dodging traffic across the busy main road, car horns blaring in their wake.

'This way!' shouted Evelyn over the clamour of the city. They ran, feet slapping the cobbled pavement, not south towards the river but deeper into the city.

'We need to split up,' Luke said between breaths. 'It'll be harder to catch us both.'

Evelyn stopped on the corner of the next road, grabbing Luke's hand, and pulling him back, painfully wrenching his shoulder, as a police car, lights and sirens blazing went screeching past them.

'Thanks.'

He checked around the corner. 'It's clear.'

Evelyn led the way onto the path that ran beside a walled public garden.

'We're not splitting up,' said Evelyn firmly. 'You wouldn't last a day on your own.'

'Is this really the time for jokes?'

'I wasn't joking,' she said flatly.

Luke couldn't argue with her.

'The stone was removed around 1560, but we don't know by who or where it went,' said Luke changing the subject.

'What about church records?'

Luke sighed. 'I was hoping it wouldn't come to that.'

'Father Keir?' asked Evelyn.

'Unfortunately,' Luke stopped and took Evelyn's hand bringing her to a halt beside him. 'If we're going to Keir for help then you should know something about him and John.'

'What does he have to do with John?'

'John went to Keir about the stone, he...'

Luke never finished his sentence; blue and red lights came blinding from the next road, tyres screeching to a stop sending foul smelling smoke into the air. An officer in uniform barrelled out of the car and ran at Luke and Evelyn.

'Run!' shouted Luke.

They tore down the road away from the pursuing police, winding through alleyways between a tangle of buildings. The path opened onto another road; Luke pushed Evelyn in front of him keeping her further away from the officer gaining on them.

Evelyn crossed the road, diving into another alley. Luke went to follow but was struck from the side, something throwing him awkwardly against the damp tarmac road. Head ringing Luke saw the car that had hit him and the uniform that was bearing down from the alleyway.

He shook off his daze and turned to Evelyn, she was turning, moving back to help him.

'No,' he shouted, thinking quickly. 'Find the Highlanders who watch the bridge.'

Evelyn stilled, unsure what to do.

'Go!'

Evelyn turned and ran, looking over her shoulder to see the police officer grab Luke as he got to his feet.

She ran into the night, not looking back again. She would follow Luke's clue. She ran knowing Luke would find a way out of this.

Luke couldn't see a way out of this. He lay face down on the cold ground, his arms being pinned behind him, cold steel handcuffs fitting tightly around his wrists. The officer said something to him before radioing the other units, telling them he had the suspect detained. Luke could do nothing but watch Evelyn disappear into the distance. He smiled to himself knowing she had gotten away; she would follow his clue and he would find her when he found a way to escape.

'On your feet,' said the officer, pulling Luke upright and guiding him towards the waiting car that had flown around the corner. 'You're a hard lad to find Mr Knight.'

'Only if you look in the wrong places.'

The officer chuckled, 'it seems like you're the one that was in the wrong place in Edinburgh.'

Luke said nothing as the officer opened the car door and guided Luke's head inside. The door slammed behind him, and the car pulled away, heading back onto the wide main road. Luke let his head fall against the window, watching the buildings move by him. Luke's eye caught a man stood on the corner, a black suit hanging awkwardly on his narrow shoulders. The man waved at Luke: a thin, wicked smile spreading across his face. Luke's heart stopped, an ice-cold dread running up his spine. The man in the suit was free, on the streets of Glasgow. Luke uttered one word:

'Evelyn.'

"Look to your consciences and remember that the theatre of the world is wider than the realm of England."

MARY I, QUEEN OF SCOTS

CHAPTER 9

*Interview Room B, Baird Street
Police Station, Baird Street,
Glasgow*

Beeeeeeeeeeeeeeeeep. Stop.

'Commencing interview of Mr Luke Alfred Knight by DI Douglas and DS Campbell.' The young detective on Luke's left spoke to the recording device sat on the edge of the table. 'For the record, Mr Knight has declined legal representation.'

Luke leant forward in his chair, resting his elbows on the edge of the light wood table that sat between him and the two detectives. He looked between them. DS Campbell, the young man who had been talking to the recording, was not much older than Luke, tidy, cropped brown hair topped a bright, friendly face, the polar opposite to the man that sat beside him, DI Douglas. Luke studied Douglas' face; deep lines grew from the corners of his eyes making the frown he was casting in

Luke's direction seem all the more threatening.

'Mr Knight, you do not have to say anything,' continued DS Campbell, 'but it may harm your defence if you do not mention when questioned something you later rely on in court.'

DI Douglas' stare seemed to be attempting to extract Luke's guilt from his soul before the questioning could start. He looked away from the man's inquisitorial gaze and back at the friendlier DS Campbell.

'Anything you do say may be used in evidence,' finished Campbell.

Luke said nothing. He locked eyes with Campbell, trying to read the younger man's feelings towards him.

'Mr Knight,' DI Douglas finally spoke, with a steely-cold voice that crept up Luke's spine to drill into the back of his skull. 'Take a look the screen.'

Douglas picked up a remote control and clicked a button at the screen on the end of the table.

'For the DIR, DI Douglas is referring to video 3, CCTV footage obtained from the National Museum of Scotland, Edinburgh,' Campbell interjected, earning a withering glance from DI Douglas.

The screen blinked to life and showed a video of Luke and Evelyn, timestamped the previous day, tearing through the corridors of the museum followed close behind by the man in the suit. The man who was not held by the police like he was, the man who Luke had seen on the streets hours earlier. His mind drifted to Evelyn. She didn't know that she was in any danger, that the man who had tried to kill them, who had killed her brother, knew where she was. The video froze on a view of the man following Luke and Evelyn into the alley that led to Greyfriars churchyard.

'Mr Knight,' said DS Campbell, 'can you tell us what happened after you entered Greyfriars with Miss Crawford and the individual pursuing you?'

Luke straightened his back, sitting upright in the chair.

'Shouldn't you be looking for the guy with gun?' he asked, avoiding the question.

'We found him,' said Douglas. 'Perhaps you would like to tell us how he ended up locked in an cage?'

'Mortsafe.'

The lines in Douglas' face deepened as his frown grew. 'What?'

'The iron cage,' replied Luke, 'it's called a mortsafe.'

Perhaps you would like to tell us how he ended up locked in a *mortsafe*?' growled Douglas.

'Perhaps you'd like to tell me how he ended up free in the city?'

'You saw him?' interrupted DS Campbell.

DI Douglas adopted his murderous glare and let out a low growl that could have been directed at Luke or DS Campbell.

'I ask the questions Mr Knight,' chewed out Douglas. 'How did he end up in the mortsafe?'

Luke slouched, letting his elbows fall back to the table. He matched Douglas' stare. Baiting him, the two men facing off like wolves over a fresh kill.

'He tripped,' said Luke flippantly. 'Very clumsy.'

Douglas looked ready to reach across the table and throttle Luke.

'Mr Knight,' DS Campbell interjected before the other two men came to blows, 'the man who pursued you through Edinburgh put an officer in the hospital when they attempted to arrest him.'

Luke failed to hide a flash of guilt, clearly leaving the man in the suit unconscious in the mortsafe hadn't been enough.

'I don't think you have anything to do with John Crawford's disappearance, but you need to tell us what you know.' DS Campbell gave Luke a pleading look, his eyes flashing sideways to DI Douglas, urging Luke not to antagonise the old detective.

Luke sighed and pulled back from the table, ending his battle of glares with DI Douglas.

'John Crawford is dead,' said Luke bluntly. 'The guy in the suit killed him and is now loose in the city with Evelyn Crawford.'

He looked from Campbell to Douglas.

'I think being a detective you can guess what he plans to do when he finds her.'

Douglas shot to his feet, sending the chair he was

sitting on skidding backwards with a screech of metal on the concrete floor.

'Mr Knight, a member of the Government is missing, an officer has been injured and now you tell me the man responsible is running around my city,' spat Douglas. 'I suggest you rethink the way you answer my questions.'

Luke bit back a retort, warned off by another sharp look from DS Campbell. Douglas turned off the screen that still showed the frozen image of Edinburgh.

'What happened in the churchyard isn't important,' he said, trying another angle. 'Why don't you tell us what you and Miss Crawford were doing at the Cathedral?'

'Taking in an evening of music?' said Luke before he could stop himself.

'While her brother is missing and the man you claim killed him was after you?' Douglas gave a forced laugh. 'Try again.'

Luke met the man's eyes. There was nothing else he could say.

'You're right,' said Luke. 'We were actually there to rob an 800 year old grave because we thought the lost coronation stone of Scotland might be in there.'

DS Campbell raised his eyebrow while DI Douglas was turning a shade of reddish purple, the hate in his eyes directed solely at Luke. He smirked.

'You know, because the one in Edinburgh Castle is a medieval fake.'

DI Douglass exploded. 'You insolent little sh...'

'Pausing interview,' said Campbell, hastily pressing a button on the recording device. 'DI Douglas, please leave the room.'

'What?'

'You heard me Douglas, out.'

DI Douglas opened his mouth to argue, but the words died in the face of Campbell's unwavering stare. He turned and stormed out of the interview room, the door slamming shut behind him.

Luke raised an eyebrow at DS Campbell.

'I thought he was your boss?'

'I looked into you Mr Knight,' said Campbell, ignoring Luke's question, 'when we connected you to John's disappearance.'

Luke watched as Campbell pulled out a chunky file and threw it down onto the table.

'Bachelor's degree in archaeology and anthropology from Bournemouth, Masters at Leicester and then five years as a research associate.' Campbell paused. 'That's when I started paying attention. In those five years you have been arrested by Bundespolezi and claimed you were recovering Michelangelo's Mask of a Faun. A year later and this time you nearly cause an international incident on the Syrian border.'

'In fairness that one wasn't my fault,' interrupted Luke. Campbell glanced up from the folder with the same cold glare that had banished Douglas and Luke sank back into the chair.

'No less than six months after and you pop up in Egypt, then Uganda, Japan, Australia, Italy and finally this year, Edinburgh, the day after John Crawford disappears and in his last known location.'

Campbell sat back in his chair, finished with his rundown of Luke's exploits.

'Who are you DS Campbell?' said Luke, curious of the man who knew so much about him.

'DS Edward Campbell, Specialist Crime Division.'

'Counter terrorism?'

Campbell opened the file he had dropped on the desk.

'Not this time; this case is politically sensitive,' said Campbell. 'Before he left for Edinburgh John reported a threat he had received. He gave no detail only that it related to something he had found.'

Luke gave Campbell a long look—his face was impassive, gone was the eager young detective that had been on display when DI Douglas had been in the room.

'Can I trust you DS Campbell?'

'That's for you to decide,' said the young detective.

Luke shrugged; Campbell knew more than he was letting on Luke was sure.

'Who exactly did John report the threat to? As

of yesterday morning, the police didn't believe he was missing.'

Campbell said nothing, fixing Luke with a level stare before sighing and leaning back, knowing Luke had gained the upper hand.

'Can I trust *you* Mr Knight?'

Luke leant forward, fixing Campbell with the same look he had received.

'That's for you to decide DS Campbell,' he said.

DS Campbell let the ghost of a smirk slip onto his face that disappeared as fast as it had shown.

'John and I are friends,' the detective paused, sadness darkening his features. 'Were friends. He called me a few days ago. He said that someone wanted something he had found.'

'The man in the suit?'

'He didn't say,' said Campbell. 'What was John looking for Mr Knight?'

'I already told you.'

'Mr Knight now is not the time to play games.'

'I am not playing games,' said Luke deliberately. 'The man in the suit is working for someone and whoever that is didn't want John to find the stone, and they don't want me to find it either.'

'The stone?'

'I told you, the Stone of Scone, the Coronation Stone of Scotland.'

Campbell rolled his eyes and got to his feet.

'Mr Knight, this is a serious matter not...'

'I'm fully aware how serious it is DS Campbell,'

snapped Luke. 'The Edinburgh stone is a fake and someone is going to great lengths to make sure that stays a secret, even as far as murder.'

'Why kill over a stone?'

'People have killed for less.' Luke rose from his chair, 'political symbols being just one of the reasons.'

The two men faced off against each other, a silent battle of wills. Finally, DS Campbell relented.

'Say I believe you and this is all about a stone,' he said. 'How do I find whoever killed John?'

'You let me go,' said Luke. 'I find the stone; I find the killer and I hand them over to you.'

Campbell sighed, running his hand through his hair.

'I can't just let you go, you're still a person of interest in John's disappearance,' said Campbell. 'Not to mention the list of petty offences DI Douglas wants to press on you.'

'Look, Evelyn is in danger, if you can't let me go then come with me.'

Luke's suggestion took Campbell by surprise, the detective taking several moments to reply.

'I can't just up and run around on a treasure hunt Mr Knight.'

'Call it following a lead if you want, either way I'm leaving.'

Luke walked towards the door but was stopped by the frame of Campbell stepping in front of him, the detective suddenly seeming far more imposing looming before him.

'Turn around Mr Knight,' the detective said using a stern voice. 'Hands behind your back.'

Luke stood stubbornly. DS Campbell grabbed Luke's arm, twisting it behind his back and slapping on a set of handcuffs. Campbell leant over to the recording device on the table, restarting the recording.

'Interview terminated.'

A long corridor led away from interview room B. DS Edward Campbell walked Luke towards the desk in the foyer of the station building.

'What are you doing Campbell?' hissed Luke.

'Shut up and walk.'

DI Douglas stood by the desk talking to the custody sergeant sat behind. Campbell spotted him and took a sharp left turn into an adjoining corridor that ended in a fire escape.

'We're going with your plan,' said Campbell quietly. 'I'm coming with you to find the stone. If that's what it takes to find whoever killed John, so be it.'

Luke smiled over his shoulder at Campbell; he'd underestimated the young detective.

They pushed through the fire door and headed around the edge of the building towards a row of cars. Campbell pulled out a set of keys and clicked the button. A dark blue BMW sat behind two police cars, its lights flashing as it unlocked. Campbell unlocked Luke's cuffs and loaded him into the back of the car before taking the driver's seat.

'When you were arrested, they said you shouted something to an accomplice,' said Campbell 'I'm assuming that was Evelyn.'

'You would assume correctly.'

'So,' said Campbell. 'Where exactly are the highlanders that watch the bridge?'

The car pulled out of the station, heading for the busy road that headed back into the city. Luke leant forward resting his arms on the two front seats and leaning into the space between.

'Only one person can tell you that,' said Luke, earning a questioning look from Campbell in the rear-view mirror. 'We need to see the Prince of Wales.'

CHAPTER 10

Prince of Wales Bridge, Kelvingrove Park, West End, Glasgow

Evelyn sat on the low wall that ran beside the bridge over the River Kelvin. A damp cold was leaching into her, right down to the bone through from the wall's capstones that were not yet warmed by the morning sun. She looked at the statue that stood a short distance from the end of the bridge, a bust of a young soldier sat atop the monument staring back at her, standing guard, watching with unseeing eyes for eternity.

Evelyn hoped she had followed Luke's clue right. Eight hours she had spent wandering the city trying to puzzle it out before she had come across the unassuming bridge in Kelvingrove Park, and to the memorial to the highland light infantry that stood before it. She had managed to snatch fleeting moments of sleep on a nearby bench while she waited for Luke but anything close to full rest remained elusive. She hadn't been able to let sleep claim her completely, all too aware that whoever wanted her dead was still out there, not to mention the danger of just being a woman alone in a city at night. Evelyn checked her phone again—nothing. Was Luke even going to be here? He could still be sat in a prison cell or worse. Evelyn shook the thoughts from her head. Luke would find a way to make it back to her, she was sure. Evelyn stopped. Why was she sure? She barely knew Luke, why did she have this absolute trust in a man she had only met a few days prior? Her thoughts were interrupted by voices coming from the river path on the far side of the bridge. She looked, hopeful that it was Luke but was disappointed by the sight of two tourists out for an early walk in the park.

Another hour Evelyn waited on the bridge, watching the people in suits heading to work with a coffee in hand, the joggers and students heading about their business, all the while hoping to see the bald head and strange different-coloured eyes of Luke Knight. She walked over to the monument by the bridge, the bronze plaque in the stone forever remembering the men of the Highland Light Infantry who never saw their home again. The figure on top of the memorial was carved in exquisite detail, the finely carved stone of his uniform seeming to flow like real fabric.

'How do you know she even figured it out?' a voice sounded faintly from the far side of the monument.

'If she's as good as I know she is, she'll be here,' another voice said, a voice Evelyn recognised.

'Luke,' she said, not quite believing what she'd heard was real.

Evelyn moved towards the bridge, slowly at first but in the sight of Luke she broke into a run. Luke stopped halfway across the bridge, Campbell standing close next to him.

'What's wrong?' asked Campbell, suddenly on alert.

Luke didn't answer him. He stared across the bridge at the woman in the emerald,-green dress running towards them, relief flooding him and dismissing the dread he hadn't noticed had built.

'She's good.' Luke flashed a smile at Campbell.

Evelyn thundered across the near span of the bridge closing the gap to Luke. She threw her arms around Luke's shoulders pulling him into a fierce hug. She stepped back, a slightly embarrassed look on her face as she noticed the other man who stood with them with a look of mischievous curiosity.

'How did you get away?'

'Technically I didn't,' said Luke, flashing a look at Campbell. Evelyn followed the look to the other man. He was tall, a clear foot above both Luke and herself, and held himself stiffly with an air of authority that seemed to outweigh his young age.

'DS Edward Campbell,' he said, introducing himself to break the awkward silence. 'I'm working John's case.'

'You went to university with him,' said Evelyn, a statement rather than a question. 'At St Andrews.'

'I did,' Campbell said stiffly. 'John always talked about you fondly.' The last words caught in Campbell's throat, a lump forming that he quietly choked back. Silent tears formed in the corners of Evelyn's eyes for her brother. They stood for a moment, wordlessly consoling each other at the loss they shared.

'What happened after I was arrested?' asked Luke, breaking the silence.

Evelyn wiped her eyes with the back of her hand.

'Nothing,' said Evelyn. 'I found the statue and the bridge and then waited for you.'

Luke breathed a sigh of relief.

'No sign of the man in the suit then.'

'The man in the suit?' said Evelyn confused. 'Shouldn't he be rotting in a prison cell?'

'He escaped.'

'He nearly killed a police officer in the process,' added Campbell.

'He's here Evelyn, in Glasgow.' Luke looked at her, concern playing across his face.

'We need to go then,' said Evelyn. 'Find the stone before he finds us.'

'Where is the stone?' asked Campbell.

'If we knew that we wouldn't still be standing here.' Luke walked across the width of the bridge and looked down the tree-lined river. 'Wishart's tomb was empty; the stone was gone and there was no clue where it went.'

'You weren't joking about grave robbing?'

'Relax,' said Luke over his shoulder to Campbell. 'It was one grave, it's not like we're the next Burke and Hare.'

Campbell shook his head and Evelyn gave him an apologetic look.

'If we can just keep the crime to a minimum while I'm around.'

'Killjoy,' Luke muttered under his breath.

Evelyn mouthed another apology to Campbell.

'Where do we go next?'

'Right,' said Luke, whirling around on one foot. 'We know the stone was taken around the time Glasgow Cathedral was looted during the Reformation.'

'So, around 1560.'

Luke couldn't help the surprised look he gave Campbell.

'John never stopped talking about Scottish history.'

'You can blame our father for that,' said Evelyn with a brittle laugh.

'What do we not know?' continued Luke.

'Who took the stone and where they took it,' said Evelyn.

Luke rubbed his temple, the strain of trying to solve an impossible problem driving a needle of pain into his head.

'We don't know who took it,' he said. 'But we know when and it's likely one of two scenarios: either the protestant forces took the stone while they *cleansed* the cathedral…'

'Cleansed?' asked Campbell.

'The cathedral was stripped of anything overtly catholic,' said Evelyn before Luke could drift into a much longer answer.

'Alters, statues, furnishings,' listed Luke, unwilling to forgo giving some elaboration to the answer. 'They even pinched the lead off of the roof.'

'What's the other option?' interrupted Evelyn before Luke could go on.

'The stone was taken by the Catholics before the cathedral was trashed.'

'How can we tell which one happened?' asked Campbell.

'We can't,' Evelyn said before putting a hand on Luke's shoulder. 'We said this last night, we need to see the records.'

'I'm not going to Keir for help,' said Luke slowly.

'He warned us about the police at the cathedral.'

'He's also the one that told the police we were there.'

Evelyn knew it was pointless to argue any more. Luke rested his head on the stone siding of the bridge, the rough stone sent tiny needle-like bolts of pain into his forehead. There had to be another way of finding what happened to the stone without going to Keir for help. A thought struck Luke and he bolted upright.

'We do know who took the stone.'

'How?' asked Evelyn.

'I'm glad you asked,' Luke smiled, 'in 1559 the predominantly protestant lords of this fine land made a move to secure Scotland as a protestant country.'

'We know, that's why the stone was taken.'

'It wasn't a smooth takeover,' continued Luke. 'The Queen Regent Mary de Guise resisted with help from the Catholic France where her daughter Mary, the future queen of Scotland was Queen Regent herself. In 1560, having lost control of Edinburgh and with de Guise's army pushing further into the country, the Scottish protestant lords turned to the English, their old enemy for help, even inviting their army into Scotland.'

Luke paused, waiting for one of them to catch his train of thought.

'The protestant Scottish were sympathetic to the English,' said Evelyn. 'If they had found the stone during the cleansing of the Cathedral it's likely it would have been revealed to the English.'

'Since the English still have a fake stone, we can assume that the one in Wishart's effigy was removed before the Reformation,' Luke finished and grinned at Evelyn and Campbell.

'Show off,' Evelyn muttered, rolling her eyes at him.

'But we still don't know where it was taken,' Campbell said from behind Luke.

'The church records would have noted what was taken from the cathedral and where it went.'

'Where can we see the records?'

Luke's shoulders fell, his face losing its triumphant look in favour of a bitter glare.

'Keir,' said Evelyn.

Luke let out a long sigh.

'Keir,' he agreed begrudgingly. 'Let me make a call.'

Luke walked away from Evelyn and Campbell, pulling a mobile phone out of his pocket and aggressively typing out a number.

'What happed between him and Keir?' asked Campbell.

'I don't know, other than he rejected Luke's work.'

Luke walked away with a phone held to his ear. He was too far away for Evelyn to hear the words but the look on his face said he had gotten through to Keir.

'Keir was looking for him at the cathedral, he knew something about John.'

'What?'

'I don't know, your lot turned up before Luke could tell me.'

Campbell's steely, professional demeanor slipped, a flash of guilt showing through the cracks.

'Why don't you ask him yourself?'

Campbell gave Evelyn a sideways glance then looked back at Luke who was sat on a bench with his head in one hand and the phone still pressed to his ear with the other.

'I don't know if you've noticed but he isn't exactly forthcoming with information about his past.'

'What are you saying?' asked Evelyn.

'I'm just saying, what do you really know about him? You should be careful who you trust.'

'He's just an archaeologist,' said Evelyn, beginning to become impatient with Campbell.

'I'm just saying you should be careful; Luke Knight is like a magnet for dangerous people.'

'I trust him,' defended Evelyn, although still not sure herself why she trusted him. 'And if you want to find out what happened to John you should start trusting him too.'

There was a cold standoff between the two, neither giving ground. Their focus was so intense that they failed to notice Luke returning from his phone call to Keir.

'Everything ok? he said looking from Evelyn to Campbell as they dropped their silent deadlock.

'Dandy,' said Evelyn. 'Can Keir help us?'

'Unfortunately, he seemed keen to be involved.'

'That's a bad thing?' asked Campbell.

'I've never known Keir to do anything out of the kindness of his heart,' said Luke sardonically.

'Mostly because I'm not entirely convinced he has one.'

'Isn't Keir a catholic priest?'

'Innocent III was a catholic and I'm pretty sure the twenty thousand Cathars he saw slaughtered at Béziers wouldn't call him kind-hearted.'

'He was the Pope not a priest,' said Campbell.

'And that makes attempted genocide, ok?' Luke fired back at him.

Evelyn stepped between the two men before their argument escalated any further.

'Enough!' she said. 'We don't have time for this. I don't think Keir is planning on committing atrocities in southern France so is taking his help really such a bad thing?'

'I wouldn't put it past him,' muttered Luke bitterly, earning a glare from Evelyn. 'We don't have much choice, but Keir will want something in return and that's never a good thing.'

Evelyn put a hand on Luke's arm. He looked at her bright blue eyes still rimmed red from tears which cooled the anger that giving Keir the upper hand had caused.

'Keir is giving a lecture at the university at two,' said Luke in a calmer tone. 'He said he would have any records in Edinburgh copied and sent to him then he would discuss it with us after.'

'The university is just around the corner,' said Campbell. 'We may as well wait there,' he finished, before turning and marching off across the bridge leaving behind Luke and Evelyn. The University of Glasgow sat on top of the hill at the edge of Kelvingrove park, the tall spire of its tower just visibly erupting above the tree line. Evelyn walked close to Luke's side, DS Campbell leading the way a few paces ahead.

'Why do you hate Keir so much?'

'I don't,' said Luke quickly. 'I just don't trust him; he's hiding something from me.'

Evelyn didn't push for more of an answer.

'You said he knew about John, last night before you were arrested.'

Luke took in a deep breath, stealing himself for what he had to tell Evelyn.

'John did come looking for my help.'

Evelyn stopped, confused by Luke's admission.

'I didn't know until yesterday,' he said quickly. 'He never asked for my help because Keir told him not to.'

'Why not?'

'I don't know, Keir said it was because he didn't want to see me hurt.'

'But he was ok with John being hurt,' Evelyn spats angrily.

Luke didn't try and quell her rage.

'That's what Keir does,' he said. 'He will play with people's lives to get what he wants.'

'But not yours.'

'Not this time?'

'Why not?'

'I don't know, that's what's concerning me.'

Evelyn clearly wasn't satisfied with the answer but Luke couldn't explain Keir's sudden worry for his safety. From experience the priest was more likely to be the one holding the gun than jumping in front of the bullet.

'How did John even know to go to Keir?' she asked finally.

'That's another answer I don't have,' said Luke. 'You can ask Keir though.' Luke nodded ahead of them.

The gothic halls and towers of the university building loomed suddenly before them. Luke and Evelyn looked in wonder at the building that could have been pulled straight from the pages of a Harry Potter novel. A castle of learning and Luke hoped the place they would learn the fate of the stone that had caused so much bloodshed.

'Are you two coming?' called Campbell from the tall gilt iron gates that cut off the mighty building from the bustle of the city.

Luke and Evelyn caught up with the detective and walked through the small entrance to the right of the ornate gateway. The grand archways leading to the university courtyards lay ahead, shadowy in the morning sunlight.

Luke stopped before the towering building, Evelyn coming to halt on his right, Campbell on his left.

Luke took a breath. 'Once more unto the breach

dear friends.'

Evelyn smirked at him. 'We're speaking to Keir not facing down a French army,' she teased.

Luke stayed stony-faced.

'Maybe not,' said Luke. 'But I know which I would rather be doing.'

CHAPTER 11

Humanity Lecture Theatre, Gilmorehill Campus, University of Glasgow, Glasgow

The last weary stragglers shuffled their way down the corridor and into their seats, far enough back in the lecture theatre that any drooping eyelids wouldn't be noticed. Some things hadn't changed since his days as an undergraduate, thought Luke, and students dragging themselves to morning lectures running on no sleep and copious amounts of caffeine was one of them. Luke, Evelyn and Campbell tagged close behind in a vain attempt to pass for students themselves and slip into the back of Keir's lecture unhampered. They had already been stopped by a bored-looking man in his mid-twenties as they approached the doorway, the man rebuffing Luke's attempts to talk his way in only for an impatient Campbell to flash his badge and warrant card, sending the no longer bored-looking man a sickly shade of white, and a look of guilt somehow being expressed by his entire body.

'I'm starting to like having you around,' said Luke quietly as they took their seats in the back row.

'I take that as high praise coming from you,' Campbell said, with only a hint of sarcasm.

Evelyn ignored the two men, instead taking in the room. It felt old, not in the way wicker furniture or textured ceilings felt outdated, but real age. The history of the place was so vivid you could taste it, smell it, breathe it in and feel the connection to long distant times. The polished wooden pews that occupied the room were the nexus of the feeling. Evelyn ran her hand along the dark wooden back of the pew as they took their seats on a back row.

'Beautiful aren't they?' Luke said softly.

Evelyn jumped, not realising anyone had noticed her admiring the pews.

'It sounds silly with everything I've seen in the last few days, but they seem almost... alive,' she said spellbound. 'Like they have this story that wants to be told.'

Luke gave her a broad, warm smile.

'Maybe they do.'

'You're making fun of me,' said Evelyn, frowning.

'No,' Luke said, a light shining in his eyes that had nothing to do with the sun pouring through the tall arched windows behind. 'These pews came from the old university, they're 17th

Century. These prosaic pieces of carved wood saw the first king of both England and Scotland, the rise of Cromwell, the return of the monarchy and the acts of union.'

Evelyn couldn't help but admire the wonder in Luke's voice as he spoke.

'They survived the Jacobite rebellion, the industrial revolution and two world wars,' he continued. 'It's sometimes the most mundane of objects that have the greatest stories to tell.'

A shiver ran through Evelyn's spine at the immensity of the history that he could see in a simple wooden pew.

'I wonder who could have sat right here,' said Evelyn wistfully.

'Some of history's greatest people studied and taught at Glasgow: philosophers, politicians, poets, writers, musicians, and more than one prime minister. Lord Kelvin, Thomas Campbell, Lord Melbourne,' said Luke, counting people off on his fingers, 'and I'm fairly sure Gerard Butler too.'

Evelyn gave him a quizzical glance and chuckled.

'You're ranking Gerard Butler alongside the man who formulated the laws of thermodynamics and Queen Victoria's closest advisor?'

'He's pretty good in *P. S. I Love You*,' shrugged Luke.

Evelyn smiled at Luke, not entirely sure what to do with the information he had just given her.

The light in the room dimmed as the thick, cream, woollen curtains were drawn across the tall windows. The steady low murmur of voices died off as a projector shone onto the white wall in front of the rows of pews, the square of light flanked by two ornate oil paintings in in dark frames, the usually vibrant pictures cast in a gloomy shadow. Father Keir strolled up onto the raised wooden platform where a long tradition of academics had delivered lectures to the room. Keir's clicking footsteps came to a stop at the centre of the stage.

'Welcome everyone,' he said softly.

Every head in the room was fixed on Keir, his congregation of adoring students hungry for the knowledge they thought he could give them. Even Luke had to admit there was something compelling about the away the man spoke. Keir clicked the button on the remote control he held and the projector flashed, changing from blank space to a photograph of a crown, lined in a fine purple velvet, trimmed in black and white fur and studded with rubies, sapphires, emeralds, and diamonds.

'Who can tell me what this is?'

A mass of hands shot into the air.

'Yes,' nodded Keir at a light-haired man in the front row.

'The crown of England.'

'Almost,' said Keir. Another set of hands raised.

'You,' he nodded to a girl sat a few seats away from Campbell.

'The Imperial State Crown,' she said confidently.

'Very good.'

The girl smiled at the priest's praise. Keir clicked the button again and the image changed. A small, gold-framed diptych occupied the space. The right half depicting what looked like Jesus and the Virgin Mary surrounded by a choir of blue clad angels. The left was simpler, four men, three of them clearly kings, crowned in gold and draped in fine furs and fabrics. The fourth man could not have been more different; his skin was painted in a darker shade than the pallid kings and he was clothed in a simple wrap of drab-brown fabric, knotted about his waist with a length of cord. The figure held a small lamb in one hand, the other resting on the shoulder of one of the kings, who knelt by his feet.

'The Wilton diptych,' Luke whispered to Evelyn.

'The Wilton diptych,' said Keir, not bothering to ask the crowd this time. 'Painted in the late 14th century by an unknown artist and for none other than this man.'

He clicked the button again, the image cropped and expanded to show the king knelt by the feet of the man holding the lamb.

'Richard II,' whispered Luke again.

'Know it all,' Evelyn teased, elbowing him in the ribs making him yelp and receive a pointed glare from a girl in the next row.

'King Richard II of England, shown here as a donor portrait in the presence of St Edmund the Martyr.' The remote clicked, refocusing the image on the first standing man with vibrant red hair and an arrow clasped in his hand. 'King of England 855-869 A.D. and ultimately martyred by Viking invaders at Thetford.'

Another click. The image changed to the man in the simple clothes holding the lamb.

'John the Baptist,' continued Keir. 'Prophet and the baptizer of Jesus.'

Another click. The projector slowly changed to the final man, standing between Edmund the Martyr and John the Baptist. It could have been the stark white hair or the air of wisdom that the artist had captured but he seemed older, important, and noble.

'And finally, St Edward the Confessor, King of England until his death shortly before the Norman invasion in 1066. Who can tell me what he is holding?'

No hands raised; a nervous silence fell across the room as Keir's interrogative look drifted across the crowd.

'No one?'

Luke studied the king's hand. He held a ring, simple and golden and set with a single large sapphire.

'What is it?' whispered Evelyn.

Luke gave her a slight shrug and noticed the surprise on her face, not sure whether it was from him not knowing what the object was or rather admitting to the fact.

'Can't know everything.'

'Pity,' said Keir. 'St Edward has one miracle attributed to him, the miracle of the ring. Edward was a deeply religious man, when he was approached by a beggar and having no money at the time, the king gave the beggar his own ring.'

Keir paused, observing the reaction to his lecturesome story.

'Many years later two English pilgrims became lost in The Holy Land and were saved by none other than John the Evangelist, one of Jesus' twelve disciples. John gave them the ring to return to England with a message for the king, that in six months he would be dead.'

'Interesting definition of a miracle,' muttered Campbell. Luke stifled a laugh and nodded to him in agreement.

Keir shot a scolding look in their direction.

'After Edward's death,' he continued in a sterner tone, 'the ring and other relics accompanied his body to Westminster Abbey, that is until the mid-16th century when it disappeared from Westminster during the dissolution of the monasteries.'

Keir clicked the remote again and the projector screen went blank.

'Now, not one of you knew about the ring and not one of you could tell me what happened to it after the dissolution,' Keir clicked the remote one last time. The screen returned to the image of the Imperial state crown. 'Except I would wager most everyone in this room has seen at least a part of this holy relic.'

A low murmur erupted across the room, discussion rampant after Keir's revelation.

'The sapphire in the cross that tops the most famous crown in the world, is, as tradition tells, none other than the sapphire from the ring of St Edward.'

'But if it was lost during the reformation, how did it end up in the crown?' asked a dark-haired girl in the second row.

Keir smiled. 'An excellent question. You see the ring wasn't lost, it was taken,' he explained. 'It could have been that only one person knew where it was and to all others it was lost. But eventually it made its way into the imperial state crown and almost everyone in Britain knew where it was even if they didn't know what it was, hidden in plain sight.'

Keir turned off the projector and leant on the wooden railing that cut off the stage from the pews.

'The problem with locating a lost relic as a historian, archaeologist or even a theologian, is that most of the time someone actually knows where it is; they may be alive or long dead but if you are not careful you can spend a lifetime looking for something only to find it was never really lost, only hidden.'

'If you don't know where it is, how is hidden any different to lost?' called out a tall, young man from somewhere to Luke's left.

'If something is lost, there is usually very little to go on, something that is hidden however, someone knows where it was put and therein is the problem. If something was hidden, it's usually because whoever hid it didn't want it to be found by the wrong people. To prevent something hidden from becoming lost, clues are often left, whether you're the right or wrong person to find it, you simply have look for the clues hidden in plain sight, like with the ring's sapphire in the Crown,' said Keir with a knowing grin. 'All deciphering history is, is asking the right questions and looking for the things that others have missed.'

A wave of applause passed through the room. Keir nodded graciously and made eye contact with Luke, sitting motionless at the back.

'I have some time to take questions before we take a short break.'

Every hand in the room went up, every hand, except those belonging to Luke, Evelyn, and DS Campbell.

The last of the students filed through the door and into the corridor beyond, leaving only Luke, Evelyn, and DS Campbell still sat in their places at the back wall of the room and Keir, who collected together his materials ready for when the students returned.

'You had more to learn from that than most Mr Knight,' said Keir, looking up from his notes. 'There are enough lost things in the world to bury you.'

Luke got to his feet and walked slowly down the shallow stairs towards Keir.

'And there are enough pieces of the true cross out there to build a hundred of them,' he said, stopping short of the stage and leaning against the fine wainscoting that clad the walls. 'What's your point?'

'No point,' sighed Keir. 'I've already given up on telling you to give up your search. I see you've acquired another follower,' he nodded at Campbell.

'A condition of my freedom. Although he's useful to have around, I might keep him.'

'I am sat right here you know,' said Campbell trying to sound offended.

Luke ignored him.

'What did you find out about the stone?'

'Straight to the point as usual,' said Keir giving Luke a long-suffering look. He pulled a sheet from the stack of notes. 'Much like Edward's ring, the stone wasn't lost, just taken, and luckily for you it was taken from a Catholic church around the same time, so I already had access to the records.' He handed Luke the sheet.

'What's this? asked Luke.

Evelyn had walked down the stairs while they spoke and now stood reading over Luke's shoulder.

'It's a letter sent from The Scots College in Paris dated December 1566,' said Keir. 'It's not addressed to anyone nor is it signed but you may find the contents interesting.'

Evelyn took the page from Luke and began to read.

The Bruce was responsible for this college's existence from his alliance with France and it is only right that it has been able to protect Scotland's greatest treasure from the English these last few years, as he once did. I understand that although France has been its home it must return to Scotland as you did. Your husband's land hid it well and I would maintain it is best protected beneath his seat.

Your most faithful friend and advisor.

'You never told me you spoke French,' said Luke with mild surprise.

'You never asked.'

'So, the stone was taken to France?' asked

Campbell.

'And then brought back.'

'But we still don't know by who or where it went.'

'Not true, the letter tells us everything,' said Evelyn. 'We know it was given to someone who was Scottish but spent time living in France, who had a husband who owned the land where the stone was first hidden.'

'Glasgow,' added Luke for Campbell's benefit.

'And we also know their *most faithful friend and advisor* left Scotland for the Scots College in Paris.'

'And you know who had the stone just from that?' scoffed Campbell.

'The person who would have need of the coronation stone of Scotland,' said Evelyn, smug. 'Mary Queen of Scots, who was married to Lord Darnley, Earl of Lennox, which included Glasgow.'

'Now who's the show off?' mocked Luke.

Evelyn stuck her tongue out at him childishly and said, 'I did a project on Mary and Elizabeth in school, although I never thought it would be any use until now.'

'Who sent her the letter though?' asked Campbell, ignoring Luke and Evelyn's digression.

'I believe I can answer that,' said Keir. 'James Beaton was the Bishop of Glasgow during the reformation. He fled to Paris with many of the relics that were rescued from the reformation and was Mary's ambassador, advisor and confidant.'

'The stone was sent back to Mary and Beaton

told her to hide it somewhere in Lennox,' said Luke chewing his lip. 'Brilliant, so we've narrowed down the search from somewhere in the world to somewhere is western Scotland.'

'Should find it in no time,' said Campbell sarcastically.

The three of them stood there wondering at the impossibility of finding the stone in such a massive area to search. Keir watched them curiously from the stage.

'If you had ever paid attention in my lectures Luke you might have learnt something, particularly in this case,' he said after several minutes. All three heads turned his way, waiting for him to continue. 'The stone isn't lost, it was hidden.'

Luke, Evelyn, and DS Campbell all looked at him blankly.

'Someone knew where it was, maybe a clue was hidden in plain sight, and no one knew what they were looking at.'

'Like the sapphire from the ring being front and centre in the crown,' said Campbell.

'Nice to know at least one of you was paying attention.'

The gears in Luke's brain whirred as he processed what Keir had said.

'Evelyn, can you read the last line again.'

She scanned down the page Keir had given them.

'Your husband's land hid it well and I would

maintain it is best protected beneath his seat,' she said. 'Why is that important? We said its hidden somewhere in Lennox.'

Luke smiled, his idea playing out.

'Beaton told us exactly where he wanted Mary to hide the stone, we need to take it literally.'

'Ok...?' said Evelyn.

'Lennox's seat, their principal residence.'

'Where was that?' asked Evelyn.

Luke turned to Keir, opening his mouth to ask the same question.

'Balloch Castle,' came Campbell's voice.

Luke turned back slowly, a look of surprise and mild confusion on his face.

'Did you do a school project too?'

Campbell shrugged. 'We used to go to Loch Lomond all the time in the summer when I was a kid. We visited the castle a few times.'

'Lucky for us you both remember useless information from your childhoods,' said Luke turning back to Keir. 'I never thought I would say this Keir but thank you, sincerely.'

Keir inclined his head, once again adopting the humble modesty that is expected of a priest.

'Luke,' called Keir as the three started to leave, 'remember, you aren't the first to look for the stone and you won't be the last, don't get buried by it.'

Luke said nothing in return, simply inclining his head as the priest had done before continuing on his way out of the room, leaving Keir to his lecture with the students that were beginning to filter back into the room.

'So, we're just going to run blindly into a castle and look for some clue to where the stone is?' said Campbell.

Evelyn half smiled at him.

'That's about how it's worked so far, occasionally while watching over our shoulder for someone trying to kill us.'

'Not this time,' said Luke without looking at them. 'We have a stop to make first.'

CHAPTER 12

Royal Exchange Square, Queen Street, Glasgow.

'But why a traffic cone?' said Evelyn in a state of utter confusion. Luke looked up at the mounted statue of the Duke of Wellington that stood before the towering Corinthian columns that formed the portico of Glasgow's Gallery of Modern Art.

'The statue was supposed to mend social and political division, to be a symbol of British character,' he said, 'but it really just exemplified the disconnection between the rich and the poor. Why build a statue and not a school?'

'That still doesn't explain the traffic cone.'

They continued walking down the road and towards the road that led to the wide-open expanse of George Square.

'It might have been 140 years later, but the statue is still a symbol of authority, sticking a cone on its head is a subtle rebellion. It's an example of Scottish spirit and humour, refusing to take imposed authority seriously.'

Evelyn looked back over her shoulder at the jaunty, orange cone that perched on the bronze duke's head.

'But why a traffic cone?'

'It was done by a drunk student,' said Campbell before Luke could launch into another rhapsodic speech about the symbolism of a traffic cone. 'Students seem to find traffic cones hilarious.'

'So, a traffic cone… because it was funny?'

'Essentially,' said Luke.

A sparse crowd loitered around the bright George Square that sat before the impressive city chambers building, some taking photographs of the statues on their plinths and columns while others simply enjoyed the warm sunshine. Luke led Evelyn and Campbell through the square to the foot of a towering statue that stood at the square's centre, between the four green lawns that flanked both its sides.

The top of the plinth was over double the height of even Campbell and topped with a column that reached towards the sky, where it ended with a statue of a man draped in a fine cloak and holding a book in his left hand. The monument towered over the eleven others in the square, standing high above those of Queen Victoria and Prince Albert, taller than even that of Robert Burns and Thomas Campbell. Luke made a short, fast bound across the last few feet between where he stood with Evelyn and Ds Campbell at the base of the monument. A wooden bench sat in front of the flowerbed that surrounded the plinth. Luke leapt onto the bench, elevating himself above the people who stood in the square.

'Where's the coward that would not dare fight for such a land?' called Luke theatrically as he paced up and down the short wooden bench.

'What's he on about?' asked Campbell.

'It's *Marmion* by Walter Scott,' she said pointing to the top of the column, Campbell craning his neck to see the statue of the poet that stood there.

'Canto the fourth, stanza thirty to be exact,' said Luke still standing on the bench. 'And it's true, who would not fight for somewhere like Scotland?'

'Listen Knight we don't have time for this.'

Luke stopped pacing and spun on his heel to face Campbell and Evelyn.

'You're right,' he said, 'but something Keir said made me think, whoever has the stone has Scotland and who wouldn't fight for that? We aren't the first to look for the stone.'

Evelyn and Campbell stood patiently, looking up at Luke as he continued pacing the bench.

'The stone was hidden, and someone knew where—how else would Beaton have known to take the stone from Wishart's tomb to Paris? All of the clues we followed to get there were untouched since Robert the Bruce re-sealed the well tunnel and carved the message on the wall.'

'Ok, Beaton found the stone another way,' said Evelyn. 'The secret was probably passed down through the bishops. I doubt the stone got hidden in Wishart's effigy without his successor knowing about it.'

Campbell looked impatient.

'How is this helpful?' he said.

'If Mary took the stone and hid it at Balloch then it isn't likely that Lord Darnley knew nothing about it.'

'Darnley wouldn't need the stone though; he was already married to the most powerful woman in the country,' said Evelyn as Luke jumped down from the bench to stand back with his companions.

'You're right, he wouldn't but he isn't the man who made a move for the throne.'

Campbell put a hand to his forehead trying to stave off the stabbing pain of the headache he knew was coming.

'Is this going to be another history lesson?'

Luke smiled wickedly.

'Well since you asked,' he said. 'In 1567 Henry Stuart, Lord Darnley and heir to the Earl of Lennox was murdered.'

Evelyn gasped with all the overacted theatricality of a classic Agatha Christie movie. Luke shot her a withering look.

'Sorry,' she said without a hint of sincerity whilst

stifling a giggle.

'The would-be killer first, quite dramatically, tried to blow up Darnley and having failed that instead strangled him. And where had the queen and her husband just returned from?' Luke gestured around them with his arms outstretched towards the great city.

'Glasgow,' he said simply.

'You think someone murdered Darnley to get to the stone?' asked Campbell with a renewed interest.

'You're the detective, you tell me,' said Luke. 'It's not like it would be the first time.'

Luke winced, immediately regretting his flippancy, Evelyn's brother being one of those murdered for the stone. He flashed her an apologetic look. She waved him off, knowing he hadn't meant to provoke the still raw wound.

Campbell thought through the report of the crime Luke had given him.

'If whoever did it wanted information about the stone, they wouldn't have tried to blow Darnley up first,' he said. 'You can't get anything from a dead man.'

'Why murder him then if it was about the stone?' asked Evelyn, who had perched herself on the edge of the bench where Luke had stood.

'Unless they already knew about the stone and just needed Darnley out of the way,' said Luke. 'DS Campbell.'

Campbell snapped his head back to Luke from where he had been observing the crowd forming near the cenotaph at the far end of the square.

'Yes?'

'A man is murdered and shortly after a prominent gentleman kidnaps the man's wife with the aid of 800 heavily armed soldiers,' said Luke. 'Who's murder suspect number one?'

'The prominent gentleman; it doesn't take a detective to work that one out,' Campbell replied with a snort of derision.

'I'm assuming you're referring to Lord Bothwell,' said Evelyn. 'It's not exactly a revelation that he murdered Darnley so he could force Mary into marriage.'

'No, it's not, but it does present us with a problem.' Luke sat on the bench next to Evelyn and pulled the map out of his satchel.

'Balloch is an hour away, not ideal but not too far,' he said pointing to the area near the bottom of Loch Lomond. 'However, if Bothwell did murder Darnley and kidnap Mary to get the stone, it won't be at Balloch.'

'Where would he have taken the stone?' asked Evelyn, leaning over the map.

'Bothwell's marriage to Mary sparked a civil war less than a month after he kidnapped her,' said Luke. He flipped the map over, found a black marker pen in his satchel and drew a crude outline of Scotland on the blank back. 'Bothwell had a castle at Dunbar where he took Mary after supposedly murdering Darnley.'

Luke drew a small mark on the coast just east of Edinburgh.

'But after being defeated at the battle of Carberry Hill, leaving Mary behind to be imprisoned, he fled,' Luke continued. 'First to Huntly Castle...'

He drew another mark somewhere north of Aberdeen.

'...Then to Spynie Palace,' another mark on the northeast coast. 'And finally, he sailed from Aberdeen to Shetland where his treasure ship fought a battle against Sir William Kirkcaldy in Scalloway,' he said, drawing a line from Aberdeen to where the Shetland islands sat in the far north.

'Bothwell had the stone on the treasure ship he took to Scalloway?' asked Campbell.

Luke scowled.

'I really hope not,' Luke replied. 'After being battered by cannon and by storm Bothwell and his ship ended up in Denmark where he was imprisoned and died.'

Evelyn took the pen from Luke and put a dot on the map some distance east of the outline of Scotland.

'The question is, did Bothwell find the stone, and if he did, where did he take it?' said Luke with a strange lack of confidence. He thought for a moment, his frustration clear to see.

'I have a different question,' said Evelyn. 'Why

did you bring us here to figure this out?'

Campbell levelled a suspicious frown. 'That's a point, what's George Square got to do with Mary Queen of Scots?'

Luke avoided eye contact with both of them, instead suddenly taking a great interest in a discoloured patch of stone by his foot.

'This is the only statue of Walter Scott I knew of in Glasgow.'

Evelyn stared at him quizzically.

'You mean we walked halfway across the city when there is a lunatic with a gun hunting us,' she said, 'just so you could quote Scott with a better backdrop?'

Luke smiled at her sheepishly.

'I thought it would be better to show Keir's point,' he offered in weak explanation.

Evelyn smiled and shook her head. Somehow, she wasn't even surprised he felt the need to take the time to walk to the Scott statue just to make a show of his thinking.

She tried not to laugh at the absurdity of everything and caught Luke trying not to fall into hysterics himself. The pair locked eyes, completely missing Campbell once again staring off at something happening on by the cenotaph at the end of the square.

'Keir made another good point,' said Campbell, reaching inside his jacket for the Glock 17 pistol that sat snug in a shoulder holster. 'We aren't the last to look for the stone either.'

Luke and Evelyn broke their eye contact and looked at Campbell. They leant in opposite directions around the plinth of Scott's statue following Campbell's eyeline to the point that had him was transfixed. The man in the suit stood by one of the white marble lions that flanked the cenotaph at the top of the square, his razor-thin lips twisted into a smile as he spotted the heads of Luke and Evelyn poking out from either side of Scott's plinth. The man's hand slid inside his jacket and withdrew the stout 1911 Luke had taken from him in Greyfriars.

'How did he know we were here?' said Campbell.

'No idea,' said Luke, grabbing Evelyn's hand, 'and I'm not sticking around to ask.'

He pulled Evelyn to her feet and took off towards the south entrance of the square, Campbell following close on their heels. They had just made it past the statues that stood sentry where the square gave way to the road and city beyond when the first shot rang out, breaking the peace of the square with its sharp crack and sending screams of terror ringing across the space. Bodies scattered for the nearest cover. Razor-sharp chunks of stone sprayed across Luke as the bullet clipped the base of the statue by his head. He threw himself down beside the heavy stone plinth, Campbell and Evelyn sheltering behind the one on the opposing side of the path.

Silence fell; all Luke could hear was his own heart beating in his ears. But then the heavily accented voice called out from the square.

'Enough, Mr Knight.'

Luke risked a look around the plinth. The man in the suit stood next to the bench in front of the Scott statue. Luke's heart thrummed harder as he saw the man holding a young woman at gunpoint, her whole body paralysed with fear.

'Out you come Mr Knight,' the man in the suit said with a twisted glee, 'or she dies.'

CHAPTER 13

Statue of Field Marshall Lord Clyde, South Entrance to George Square, Glasgow.

Luke felt a chill permeate into every muscle in his body, petrifying flesh and fixing him in place, another statue in the square's collection. Only his eyes could move, the terrified woman sobbing silently, the barrel of the gun levelled at her head and the long arm that held it running to the man in the suit.

'Did you hear me Knight?' the man's voice took on a harsh snarl. 'Time's running out.'

Luke stayed frozen for too many excruciatingly long heartbeats. The world seemed to slow down and distort, sounds and shapes stretching and blurring before snapping back to reality with a jarring speed, cold sweat prickling over his body, he moved to step out from behind the plinth.

'Luke, what the hell are you doing?' hissed Campbell.

Luke looked at him where he sheltered behind

the opposing plinth.

'Just keep him talking,' Campbell said, fixing Luke with a hard stare. 'Don't do anything stupid.'

'You have met me, right?' said Luke flashing a smile to hide the pit of crippling fear that had formed inside him.

'Knight, half the city would have heard that gunshot,' Campbell said, half reprimand and half desperate plea. 'Armed response will be here in minutes; this is Glasgow not downtown Baghdad.'

Luke ignored him. Evelyn was huddled behind the statue, body frozen somewhere between fear and rage. The unmistakable slick click of a gun's slide being drawn back made Luke's muscles tense.

'Time's up,' said the man in the suit with a deranged relish.

'Wait!' Luke threw himself out from behind the plinth, the gun whipped towards him and levelled over his heart.

The man in the suit sneered at him, his finger hovering over the cold steel trigger.

'Stupid boy, so ready to die and for what?' the man gestured with the gun to where the woman he had held at gunpoint still sat, petrified, then to the statue where Evelyn and Campbell sheltered. 'A stranger, a stray and the man who arrested you?'

Luke studied the man's face, his eyes were as

cold and dead as before, the knife blade smile that didn't just threaten but outright promised violence, but something was wrong, something Luke couldn't quite place.

'A deal's a deal, let her go,' said Luke nodding to the woman.

The man in the suit sneered and gave a quick flick of the gun barrel, dismissing his hostage who hesitated before scrambling across the pavement to shelter.

'I'm in no rush for anything,' said Luke, forcing his voice to stay steady. 'But pulling a gun in the middle of the city, I'm guessing you are.'

The man bristled visibly and tightened his grip on the gun.

'You should have listened to the priest, Knight,' the man spat. 'You should have kept your nose out of things that don't concern you.'

Luke tilted his head; how did the man know that Keir had warned him? The man was growing more agitated with every passing second, all too aware of the impending arrival of police with a lot more firepower than his.

'If you wanted me dead you would have killed me already, what do you want?'

'Where is the stone?' the man asked with an icy menace.

Something clicked in Luke's mind.

'You're not trying to stop me finding the stone,' he said slowly. 'You want it for yourself.'

'My employer is most insistent on possessing the stone,' spat the man.

'And you have no idea where it is,' laughed Luke mockingly. 'You really are an idiot aren't you.'

The man bristled and lurched forward, the barrel of the gun now only an arm's length from Luke's head.

'An idiot insults the man pointing a gun at them.'

'You aren't going to shoot me,' said Luke with a sudden cockiness that defied the situation, walking forward so the cold metal of the gun pressed against his forehead.

'Are you willing to bet your life on that?' sneered the man.

Luke locked eyes with him.

'Yes actually, I am,' Luke gave him a victorious smile. 'If you kill me, you lose the stone. You're lucky I didn't keep my nose out of it.'

'You will tell me where the stone is,' ground out the man, struggling to keep his temper in check.

'Why would I tell you the only thing keeping me alive? Any minute this square is going to be flooded with lights and sirens and you'll be face down in cuffs before you can say excessive force. Your employer will never get the stone.' Luke put as much spite into those final words as he could, delighted to see the man's steely-cold demeanour falter and the shining cracks of panic show. He was surprised when this didn't happen, the man instead looking past Luke, his knife edge lips curling into a twisted smile.

'I wouldn't be so sure Mr Knight.'

Luke turned slowly, not trusting the man in the suit. Behind him Campbell and Evelyn no longer sheltered behind the back statue's plinth. Instead, Campbell lay sprawled face down on the pavement, unconscious but breathing softly. Luke's eyes trailed to Evelyn, stood to the left of Campbell's unconscious body. She wasn't alone, a man stood next to her holding another identical 1911 pistol to her head, a man in an identical poorly fitting suit.

'Oh, that's just cheating!'

Luke turned back to his own suited gunman; his face identical to the other except... Luke could have kicked himself; his face was undamaged, unbruised. Evelyn's gunman on the other hand had an angry purple bruise around his right eye from where Luke had slammed it into a wall at Greyfriars, his nose even more crooked than before and his weight not being fully supported by his injured leg.

'Twin criminals? That's original,' said Luke sarcastically.

The unscathed twin scowled at him.

'Let's try this again, tell me where the stone is, or she dies.'

A gun cocked behind Luke, he didn't turn, didn't dare take his eyes off of the gun aimed at him.

'Even if I wanted to tell you where the stone was

I couldn't, I don't know!'

The gun steadied over Luke's heart.

'I find that hard to believe Mr Knight,' said the man calmly.

'Do you really care less about her life than a bit of old rock?' shouted the twin behind him.

A siren blared in the distance, the man in the suit facing Luke tensed, his time was up.

'Last chance Mr Knight, where is the stone?' He said the last words slowly, deliberately, biting out every syllable.

'I don't know!' Luke spat back.

The man in the suit nodded at his twin over Luke's shoulder. The hammer of a gun clicked backwards as it was cocked, the sound followed by a high yelp from Evelyn.

'Wait!' Shouted Luke, the man in the suit held up his hand. 'Scalloway.'

Luke hung his head, defeated.

'The stone is in Scalloway.'

The man in the suit tilted his head to the side, studying Luke.

'I thought you didn't know where the stone was, how do I know you aren't lying?'

'I don't, but Scalloway is the last place Bothwell went before his defeat.'

'Bothwell?'

'James Hepburn, the Lord of Bothwell,' said Luke, pinching the bridge of his nose. 'He probably stole the stone from Mary Queen of Scots and took it to Scalloway after... It's a whole thing please don't ask me to go over it again.'

The man in the suit considered this new information for a moment.

'Scalloway is in Shetland,' he said menacingly. 'You better not be trying to send us on a wild chase Mr Knight.

'If the stone is anywhere, it's in Scalloway,' Luke said forcefully, locking his stare with the man's.

'Sill, I think we need some insurance,' the man looked past Luke again. 'Corban, take the girl.'

'No.'

Luke spun around in time to see the twin he guessed was Corban go to grab Evelyn. Quicker than Luke's eyes could follow, Evelyn lashed out a savage blow that landed on Corban's already battered and broken face. He howled like a wounded dog and dropped to his knees. Evelyn sprang to her feet and took off down the road opposite the southern entrance to the square. Luke turned back to the twin facing him, he threw himself forward and wrapped his arms around the man's legs causing him to fall and hit the pavement with a heavy, dull thud. Luke got up and ran after Evelyn, Corban only a few paces in front of him, his twin slowly getting to his feet behind. A fleet of police cars and riot vans screamed into the square as Luke gained on Corban.

A taxi pulled out of a side street into Luke's path

cutting him off from his pursuit. He jumped and slid across the bonnet, narrowly avoiding being sent tumbling by the careless driver.

'Not this time,' Luke whispered to himself as he landed on the far side of the bonnet and continued to gain ground on Corban.

The colossal glass roof of the St Enoch shopping centre loomed on the horizon as Evelyn sprinted past a group of workmen repairing pipes that ran underneath the road. Corban reached an arm into his jacket to retrieve the gun that he had put back in its holster. Luke pushed with the last of his energy and caught up with him just as the barrel of the 1911 pistol cleared the edge of the holster. Luke needed to do something before Evelyn found herself with a bullet chasing her down the street. He threw himself sideways, blindsiding Corban and sending him tumbling over the low fence that surrounded the men at work and into the deep trench where they were mending the pipe. Luke fought to steady himself and stop his body following Corban into the trench. He carried on running, looking back only to see the confused faces of the workmen who had suddenly discovered that it was raining men from above them.

Evelyn turned left and disappeared around the corner of a building. Luke was only seconds behind her, he turned the corner and with a flash of pain to his cheek found himself staring up at the sky from the cold road.

'Luke!' squeaked Evelyn. 'I'm so sorry, I thought you were the man in the suit.'

Luke shook off the daze that surrounded him and let Evelyn help him to his feet.

'It's fine,' he said quickly, 'Corban is busy inspecting the roadworks, but his brother can't be far behind.'

Evelyn stole a look back around the corner and saw a seething and slightly dishevelled Corban being helped out of the trench by his brother.

'Are you ok to run?'

Luke felt where the bruise on his cheek was now forming and nodded.

'You have one hell of a right hook,' he said, wincing slightly.

'Thanks, but we can discuss that later.'

She grabbed Luke's hand and pulled him down the road after her. The pair ran away from the city centre and towards the busy junction of roads ahead. The stunt with the roadworks had bought them some time but the suited men were gaining on them again.

'We can't keep this up,' said Evelyn, between gasping breaths.

Luke just nodded, unable to speak between deep breaths. He looked towards the stone tower that rose from the middle of the junction, a protruding monolith so out of place on the busy metropolitan road. Luke turned back to see their pursuers less than a hundred meters behind.

'This way,' he called to Evelyn, dragging her suddenly to their left and just out of sight of the two suited men. The pair ran full speed at the strange tower, Luke piled into a small door at its base, throwing his full weight into it with his shoulder and causing the door to fly open with a clang of reverberating steel. Evelyn collapsed against the far wall of the cramped room inside the tower as Luke slammed the door behind them, praying Corbin and his twin were too far back to have seen their intrusion.

'Where now?' asked Evelyn. 'We're trapped in here.'

Luke ignored her and started moving around the room stamping on different areas of the floor with one foot.

Evelyn looked at him quizzically.

'Have you gone mad?'

Luke kept stamping, the echo of his foot slapping against the floor bouncing off the old stone walls.

'We could never outrun them on the streets,' said Luke still stamping. 'We needed to put some distance between us and them without them knowing where we are.'

'So, your solution is to trap us in a tower in the middle of the road.'

Luke stamped again, but the slap of his foot striking the solid surface didn't come, instead a dull thud echoed around them. Luke smiled like a child that had been handed a chocolate bar. He dropped to his knees and pulled a small metal pointing trowel from his bag and fitted it into the gap between two of the floors paving slabs.

'Do you remember when I told you there were tunnels all over the city?' he said leaning his weight on to the trowels handle. Evelyn nodded, watching Luke curiously.

'If I'm right then we aren't trapped in here.'

'And if you're wrong?' Said Evelyn.

Luke leant harder in the trowel. With a screech of metal on stone, the slab in front of Luke lifted enough for him to slide his fingers underneath and pry it up further. Luke carefully lifted the stone and laid it flat on the ground beside where it had once sat. A black hole occupied the space where the slab had been, Luke pulled out his torch and flashed the light into the hole. He looked back at Evelyn with a smirk.

'I'll let you know if it ever happens.'

CHAPTER 14

Tolbooth Steeple, Glasgow Cross,
High Street, Glasgow

Luke landed with flat-footed thud. The drop from the floor of the Tolbooth Steeple was further than he had judged, and the hard landing jarred his back. The air in the space below the eminent tower was thick with long accumulated dust that had been disturbed by Luke's entrance, over a century of dirt and grime now cascading through the air in tiny nebulas picked out by the light effusing from the hole above. Luke pulled the torch out of his jacket pocket and clicked it on. He flashed the beam around the dark space illuminating more miniature dust storms, the worst of them now settling back to the ground, and more spider webs than a bad haunted house. A solid red-brick wall faced Luke, the bricks rough and handmade, the coarse mortar that held them together beginning to crumble from years of neglect. He turned, the torch light flashing across the brickwork before flooding into a long, dome-roofed tunnel that stretched beyond the torch's limit.

'Heads up,' called Evelyn from above.

Luke looked up in time to see his leather satchel plummeting towards him at an alarming pace. He moved just in time to catch the falling bag and avoid taking its considerable weight straight to his head.

'Some warning would have been nice.' Luke slung the bag over his shoulder, Evelyn muttering an apology from the roof of the tunnel.

'Watch your step when you land,' Luke called up blindly, his eyes fixed, studying the uneven cobbled floor of the tunnel. 'It's a longer drop than it looks.'

Luke had barely finished his warning when Evelyn dropped down beside him. Her foot slid on the uneven stones sending her flailing into Luke. The pair tumbled to the cold cobbles causing Luke to let out an 'ooofff' as the air was knocked from his lungs.

'If this was a movie, you would have caught me,' Evelyn said stiffly, propping herself up on an elbow.

'Then next time call Harrison Ford,' Luke groaned and awkwardly got to his feet. 'Anyway, I caught you last time.'

'Does that make you half as good as Indiana Jones?'

Luke rolled his eyes at her, getting up off of the dusty floor and cracking his back, a loud popping click like bubble wrap running up his spine.

'We should move, someone will find that hole sooner or later,' said Luke, nodding towards the square of light above.

Evelyn picked up the still shining torch from where Luke had dropped it when they had fallen. She flashed the beam of light into the tunnel, the light tapering into the distance before being swallowed entirely by the oppressive darkness.

'Are you sure this is a good idea?'

'Honestly?' said Luke, joining Evelyn's side, 'until today there were only rumours it even existed.'

Luke gave a reassuring smile that failed to convince Evelyn that following Luke as he started into the tunnel was a better option than taking their chances with Corban and his brother.

The air in the tunnel grew damp and stale as they ventured further down its length. It was, for the most part, in good repair, the careful brickwork keeping out the worst of the damp that seeped through the ground from the nearby river. The low rumble of traffic echoed from the curved ceiling of the tunnel, the occasional passing of a heavier vehicle causing small showers of dirt and dust to clatter gently on the worn cobbles.

'Where exactly does this go?' said Evelyn nervously.

'No idea,' said Luke, turning to see the look of panic beginning to set in on Evelyn's features. 'Like I said, there was only rumour it existed so there's only rumour of where it goes.'

'Then where does rumour say it goes?' Evelyn said through gritted teeth as the rumble of traffic above caused another miniature avalanche of dust.

'The tolbooth used to be the site of executions, hangings.'

Evelyn grimaced, rubbing her neck involuntarily.

'But in 1814 a new courthouse was opened next to Glasgow Green, which was arguably a much nicer setting for a family-fun event like a public execution.' Luke stepped around a shallow pool of water that had come to occupy nearly the entire with of the tunnel, he offered Evelyn a hand to step across behind him. 'A tunnel was built between the new courthouse and the gallows to move the condemned.'

'Nothing like a cheery story for a stroll through a pitch-black tunnel.'

Luke shrugged.

'History isn't exactly all sunshine and daisies, anyway, the tunnel was used until the last public executions in 1865 and the tunnel remained until the 1980's when it was filled in. But there was rumour of a second tunnel that ran from the courthouse to the old tolbooth to move prisoners who hadn't been granted a public hanging.'

'So, this is the second tunnel?'

'Only one way to find out,' said Luke pointing further down the tunnel with the torchlight.

'There were no records of a second tunnel but there's no reason this couldn't be it.'

They walked on wordlessly, the oppressive silence and darkness doing nothing to the grim legacy of the cold tunnel.

'Why was the first tunnel filled in?' asked Evelyn.

'Yet another piece of history destroyed by modern living,' said Luke theatrically. 'The weight of traffic was causing it to collapse.'

Another lorry rumbled overhead, shaking a thick haze of dust into the air.

The pair froze in their tracks. Luke moved the torch beam slowly towards the ceiling, both his and Evelyn's eyes following its lead to the thin layer of bricks that held back the earth.

'Maybe we should pick up the pace.'

'Mmm hmmm,' murmured Evelyn, not taking her eyes off the arched brickwork.

Luke and Evelyn's footsteps echoed off the cobbles as they took the tunnel at a brisk walk, motivated by the ever-present rumble of traffic not so far above. The tunnel began to veer to the right, the long sweeping profile cutting the torch beam shorter and doubling the claustrophobic darkness that seemed to creep from the walls themselves.

'What do we do when we get to the end?' asked Evelyn, more in an attempt to ignore the sense of dread biting at her heels than anything else.

Luke didn't answer immediately, considering

their options.

'Like I said there are two options, either Bothwell took the stone from Darnley's estate or...'

'He didn't.'

Luke made a grim face, 'Not a lot to go on.'

The curve of the tunnel grew sharper, the torch light now only illuminating a few paces in front of Luke and Evelyn.

'But you think Bothwell took the stone.'

'What makes you think that?' asked Luke, curiously.

Evelyn gave him a confused look. 'You told the other man in the suit that the stone was in Scalloway, that Bothwell took it there?'

She stopped, letting the dark engulf her back as Luke carried on several steps before stopping. Realising Evelyn was no longer by his side he spun round, half blinding Evelyn with light.

'What's wrong?' he said, genuine concern colouring his tone.

'You were lying to him,' Evelyn said slowly, 'you don't think Bothwell took the stone.'

'I wasn't lying, not entirely, I didn't know for sure.'

'His brother had a gun to my head,' snapped Evelyn.

'And he had one to mine,' shot back Luke. 'Anyway, he didn't know I was lying.' Luke let the silence fall back upon the tunnel, the echoes of their shouts fading into the distance.

'Hell, I wasn't even sure I was lying.'

Evelyn felt the flare of anger die inside her, cooled by the guilt that Luke had unwittingly let bleed onto his face.

'Why don't you think Bothwell took the stone now? You dragged us all the way to George square just so you could tell us you think he took it.'

Luke snapped back into himself.

'You can thank Corban and his brother for that actually.'

Evelyn gave him a dubious look.

'Two things,' said Luke holding up the first two fingers on his right hand. 'One, the twin whose face we haven't broken had no idea who Bothwell was. If he had found the stone, he would have used it to gain power, reputation but instead he died in exile.'

'He could have lost the stone during the fight in Scalloway.'

Luke smiled. 'Which brings me onto two,' he said counting off his points on his fingers. 'The men who attacked Bothwell were loyal to Mary's son, James VI of Scotland.'

'And the First of England,' said Evelyn, Luke's realisation dawning on her too. 'If they had gotten the stone then it would have been in the hands of the future king of England.'

'And we wouldn't be looking for it now,' finished Luke. 'Nor would the twin's employer, or your brother.'

Evelyn still flinched on hearing her brother being mentioned, the barely staunched wound being torn back open each time. Luke moved on quickly, sensing her discomfort.

'I don't think the stone ever left Balloch,' he said. 'When Mary escaped Loch Leven castle she didn't run, she raised an army, she wanted Scotland.'

'The Stone was the symbol of her right to rule.'

'The symbol of her defiance, her rebellion, as it was to Robert the Bruce before her,' nodded Luke.

'How do you know *she* didn't take the stone from Balloch?'

'The Battle of Langside, Mary's last stand, fought about two miles that way,' Luke pointed down the tunnel in the direction they were heading. 'Scholars say she was headed for Dumbarton Castle, but I'll give you two guesses what is just a hop, skip and a jump beyond.'

Evelyn didn't need to say it out loud, the last hope for a queen, for a country and it remained lost, buried by time. Except nothing is truly lost.

'Mary was trying to reach the stone,' the sounds from above had died completely, the silence in the tunnel so complete even Evelyn's softly spoken words echoed around them. 'Not lost, hidden, and someone knew where.'

'Mmm,' murmured Luke in agreement. 'The idea was right, but we were following the wrong person.'

Luke spun on his heel before another silence fell.

'To answer your question, that's what we do when we get out of here, we go to Balloch.'

Evelyn followed Luke further along the tunnel, the tight curve beginning to straighten again.

'We need to find Campbell first,' said Evelyn, 'before we go to Balloch.'

'I got the impression the two of you didn't like each other.'

Evelyn shrugged. 'He knows Balloch and besides it's my fault he got knocked out, Corban was after me not him.'

'Half the police in Glasgow were headed for that square, Campbell will be fine, we'll find him.'

'Still, I feel bad for leaving him in the square.'

Evelyn folded her arms in front of her, looking down at her feet she nearly ploughed into Luke who had stopped dead in front of her.

'I think we have bigger problems than Campbell.'

Evelyn's eyes followed Luke's torch to the wall of the tunnel, or rather, where the wall had once stood. The entire Left side of the tunnel, from the floor to the centre of the ceiling, had collapsed. What had to be tens of tonnes of soil and rubble that formed the city's foundations had spilled into the tunnel, blocking all but a small gap where the ceiling curved back down toward the right wall, just out of Luke's reach.

'Here, hold this,' said Luke, handing the torch to Evelyn and dropping his satchel to the cobbles. He planted one foot on the loose mountain of rubble, nimble as a cat he scaled the short distance to the space between the rubble and the ceiling.

'Can we get through?'

Luke looked through gap, the light from the torch catching glimpses of the tunnel beyond.

'The rest of the tunnel looks clear, no way we can fit through though.'

Luke slid back down the slope on his side, digging his foot into the soil to slow his descent, coming back to the floor accompanied by a tiny avalanche of stone and soil.

'Why don't we just turn back, see if we can reach the hole into the tollbooth?'

Luke squatted and started to rummage in his satchel.

'Why would we do that?' he said pulling out his trowel from the bag. 'Just need to make the hole bigger.'

Luke hopped back up and walked back over to the blockage. He put the trowel between his teeth and climbed back up to the hole.

'Are you sure that's a good idea?' asked Evelyn dubiously as Luke wedged himself between the wall and one of the more stable sections of the rubble.

'It's fine,' he said, chipping away at the blockage, sending a steady stream of stone, broken brick, and soil down onto the floor. 'Victorian engineering is solid stuff, this tunnel has been here over 100 years, it's not going anywhere now.'

'He says clearing away where it's collapsed,' said Evelyn under her breath.

'What was that?'

'Nothing.'

After several minutes of shifting rubble the hole had widened enough for a person to squeeze through. The air was thick with dust, dampening the light of the torch and somehow making the tunnel seem gloomier than before.

'Ready?' asked Luke.

'Would it make a difference if I said no?'

Luke shrugged as much as his precarious position would allow him. Evelyn sighed and crossed the tunnel to pick up Luke's bag, tossing it up to him. Luke caught the bag, slipping slightly and causing another stream of rubble to fall.

'Need a hand?' asked Luke, reaching as far has he could behind him and offering Evelyn his hand.

'I'm fine,' she said tersely.

'Sure?'

Evelyn nodded silently, staring at the tiny space between the between the brick and the base of the gap.

'You're not claustrophobic, are you?' asked Luke, noticing the tension in Evelyn's body.

'No,' she replied quickly. 'But I'm not overly fond of a tonne of rubble falling on top of me.'

Luke pushed his satchel through the hole, hearing it tumble to the cobbled floor on the far side.

'I promise you the bricks aren't going anywhere,' he said manoeuvering himself into the hole feet first. 'And right now, this is your only way out.'

Evelyn nodded again, watching Luke squeeze through the hole in the rubble and disappear onto the far side.

'You can do this,' called Luke's disembodied voice. 'Just keep moving forward and don't stop.'

Evelyn looked at the hole again, steeling herself. She threw the torch, landing it on the edge of the hole and leaving her in darkness. The lack of light seemed to amplify the sounds of traffic above. Evelyn hesitated, one hand on the wall of rubble.

'Just ignore it,' said Luke. 'Focus on my voice.'

Evelyn shook her head, clearing the thoughts intruding her mind. She climbed the short distance to the hole and picked up the torch, shining its light into the space.

'You're almost there,' said Luke seeing the light flickering through the hole. 'It's not as far as it looks.'

It looked like a grave, thought Evelyn. The hole beneath the brick ceiling no more than two feet wide and a fraction longer than Evelyn was tall. She took a deep breath and hauled herself into the hole, holding the torch in front of her she inched slowly towards the open end, towards escape. Evelyn's arms broke free of the hole, her head following close behind. She dropped the torch, letting it roll down the slope to Luke waiting below.

'See, you made it.' Said Luke.

Evelyn opened her mouth to reply but was cut off by a chilling groan followed by the cracking of mortar splitting from bricks. Evelyn froze. The wall on the right of the tunnel bowed, the bricks held together by nothing other than friction.

'Evelyn,' said Luke, his voice shaking slightly as he fixed his stare at the bowing wall. 'Jump.'

'What?'

'Jump now!' he shouted.

Evelyn threw herself the last few inches though the hole, pushing off the pile of rubble she flew through the air and collided with Luke who wrapped his arms around her and propelled them both as far away from the blockage as he could. The bowed wall gave way, spilling another mountain of soil, brick, and rubble into the tunnel, flooding the space where Luke and Evelyn had been moments before.

The dust settled slowly to the cobbled floor, Luke and Evelyn lay inches from the edge of the rubble, breathing heavily and staring at the pile that could have been their tomb.

'Well,' said Luke between breaths. 'At least I caught you this time.'

Evelyn stared at him, unsure whether to laugh or slap him, so settled for both.

The tunnel came to an end not far beyond the

collapse. A short cast iron spiral staircase wound its way to the roof of the tunnel and to a small wooden hatch. The damp at this end of the tunnel had eaten away at the metal, leaving a rusted, reddish ghost of the once fine stairs. Luke and Evelyn climbed the first few steps tentatively, testing the strength of the corroded metal but finding it was more stable than its condition made it look.

'Did you say this tunnel comes out in the courthouse?' asked Evelyn.

'If the stories are true, why?'

'Well, we are technically still fugitives.'

Luke stopped below the hatch and chewed his lip in thought.

'I guess no one is going to come looking for us here then,' he said, pushing the hatch open and climbing the last of the stairs.

Evelyn followed close behind him.

'I'm not sure I trust your judgement anymore.'

CHAPTER 15

Basement Storage Cupboard, Southwest Corner of the Glasgow High Court of Justice, Saltmarket, Glasgow

The stone slab that had sat on top of the old wooden hatch to the tolbooth tunnel, concealing its existence for the last century, crashed onto the floor as Luke threw his shoulder into the underside. The sound, like a canon being fired, exploded into the small room that the tunnel came up into.

Evelyn cringed at the racket.

'Do you think there's any way no one heard that?' asked Luke, peering tentatively into the room beyond the hatch. Banker's boxes lined the walls, stacked on heavy, almost industrial looking wood and metal shelves. They were caked in a thick coat of dust but otherwise were crisp and well maintained. The shelves ran from floor to ceiling on every wall, the boxes stacked high enough to hide any trace of the brickwork behind and creating a fortress of cardboard and forgotten paperwork.

Luke pushed the hatch fully open, letting the heavy boards clatter on top of the fallen stone that had covered them.

'Are you trying to let everyone know that we're here?' said Evelyn in a pointed whisper as she climbed the last few stairs to join Luke in the room full of boxes.

Luke shrugged slightly, walking around the room and reading the box labels that were still intact.

'In for a penny,' he said, picking the lid off of one of the boxes and peering inside.

Evelyn stepped carefully around the hole in the floor and tried to look over Luke's shoulder.

'What is it?'

'Just old court records,' said Luke, pulling out a stiff sheet of parchment. 'Very old court records. I guess this is some sort of archive.' He put the page back in the box with great care before dropping the lid back into place. Evelyn moved past him to another shelf of boxes, the labels had faded, the lettering faint and ghostly. The third box along the shelf had a label that was in a marginally better condition than its fellows, the black block type was still patchy in places. The lack of light didn't help. Evelyn squinted at the label.

M scell eous Lett rs

Cl rks of Sessions Offi e

Edinburgh

Evelyn put her hands to the corners of the box's lid, her fingers leaving imprints in the layer of dust that had settled over the box, untouched for who knew how long. The lid slid cleanly off, Evelyn breathed in the smell of old paper that emanated from the box.

A sudden crash of stone against stone exploded behind her. Evelyn jumped at the noise, dropping the lid and spinning around to see Luke standing where that entrance to the tunnel had been, the heavy stone slab sitting crooked, one edge overlapping the adjacent stone.

'Sorry,' said Luke, noticing Evelyn's shocked expression. 'My fingers slipped.'

He kicked the edge of the slab, knocking it back seamlessly into place.

'What were you looking at?'

Evelyn took a deep breath, feeling her heartbeat return to its normal rhythmic thump. Luke moved over to the box that Evelyn had started to open.

'What are letters from the Clerk of Sessions Office in Edinburgh doing here?' he said to the air, whipping off the lid of the box. The musty, old paper smell drifted back into the room, Luke let it draw him in, the smell of knowledge, discoveries waiting to be found. Luke reached into the box; his fingers had barely grazed the first of the thick, heavy pages when he froze. He tilted his head to the side, his hand still resting on the stack of papers.

'Did you hear that?'

Evelyn listened for a moment before replying, 'What?'

The faint clicks of a door's latch popping open and muffled voices drifted from not so far beyond the room where Luke and Evelyn stood.

'Time to go,' said Luke, his voice hushed but with an edge of panic.

He slid the box's lid back into place and grabbed Evelyn's hand. Luke pushed the door open just enough that there was a hair's breadth of a view into the corridor beyond.

'It's clear,' he said pushing the door fully open and moving quickly away from the voices that grew louder and clearer with each passing moment. The pair started down the corridor but quickly came up against a dead end, the corridor ending only a short distance beyond the room they had left behind, in a featureless brick wall.

The voices grew closer, clear enough now to pick up the full measure of conversation.

'Is there another way out?'

'You know as much as I do,' said Luke, looking around them frantically for another chance at remaining undiscovered. 'Back to the tunnel,' he said, failing to see any other option.

The shadows of two figures appeared at the junction of the corridor just beyond the room of boxes, the shapes strange and elongated by the artificial lights.

'No time,' said Evelyn, she looked Luke in the eyes, the fluorescent light deepening the contrast of the greens and browns, making the hazel colour even more striking. Luke caught her look.

'What is it?'

Evelyn flashed a glance back at the growing shadows.

'Trust me.'

Before Luke could question any further Evelyn had grabbed the lapels of his jacket and pulled him towards her, pressing her lips firmly against his. Luke's hand slid instinctively around her waist, pulling her closer. The footsteps rounded the corner and stopped, the two voices breaking their conversation at the same time. Evelyn broke away from Luke, ready to do her best act of embarrassment at being caught stealing a romantic moment, leaving Luke in a stunned, silence. Evelyn turned to face the pair of arrivals when one of them called out.

'Evelyn?'

'Daniel!'

'Daniel?' said Luke, his usually sharp brain struggling to process the last thirty seconds of his life.

Daniel strode towards them, his mirror-shined leather shoes squeaking on the polished concrete floor.

'Evelyn Crawford, well I never,' he said pulling her into a tight embrace. 'I thought it was you, what are you doing down here of all places?'

Daniel spoke with the schooled refinement of someone born into the highest of society, each word careful and clear in a way that made the thick accent he piled onto the words painfully spurious.

'Daniel I...' spluttered Evelyn, lost for words, '... could ask you the same thing?'

She looked sideways at Luke and caught him raise an eyebrow at her.

'Luke this is...'

Before Evelyn could finish her sentence Daniel turned to Luke and extended a hand towards him.

'Daniel Montrose,' he said looking Luke up and down as if he were sizing up his opponent. 'Evelyn and I were... friends growing up.'

Subtle, thought Luke.

He was older than both Luke and Evelyn, only by a handful of years but enough that the fine lines in his face were beginning to deepen. His platinum blonde hair was slicked back and shone in the dim lights, not a strand out of place. Just like his suit and his shoes, not one aspect of his appearance wasn't carefully manufactured and styled. Luke had never met anyone so disingenuous.

'Luke Knight,' said Luke, taking the hand Daniel held out with a near painfully tight grip and shaking it once.

'A pleasure,' said Daniel with a thin-lipped plastic smile. Luke met his icy-blue stare, Daniels's grip on his hand tightening enough for the bones to grind against each other. Luke forced himself not to wince despite the pain that lanced through his hand.

'I imagine it is,' said Luke, not bothering to reign in his hubris. If Daniel wanted a contest, he wasn't going to deny him the pleasure.

The smile slipped from Daniel's face, he dropped Luke's hand and turned back to Evelyn.

Luke 1 - 0 Daniel, thought Luke to himself making an involuntary grin crack across his face. He caught Evelyn rolling her eyes at the testosterone-fuelled battle of wits that she had just witnessed.

'I'm so sorry to hear about John going missing,' said Daniel. 'We were always close those years back home.'

Evelyn forced herself to keep her expression blank: she would not let her tears betray her, not now.

'That's actually why we're here,' she said, moving on from any emotion. 'We think John might have been in Glasgow before he…' she choked on her words, the image of Corban's cruel grin filling her mind.

'Disappeared,' she finished. 'Luke is helping me.'

Daniel shot Luke a cold look.

'Is that what you were doing down here?' he said. 'It certainly looked like you were firmly... involved with the case.'

Evelyn flushed slightly at Daniel's thinly veiled jab.

Luke 1 - 1 Daniel.

The man who had accompanied Daniel cleared his throat. He could have been a carbon copy of Daniel, the same mirror-polished shoes, expensive suit, and glossy slicked-back hair. Luke looked between the man and Daniel. Even the same look of smug self-importance, Luke smiled to himself.

'My apologies, Evelyn, Mr Knight, let me introduce my associate, David Paterson.'

Paterson said nothing, merely inclining his head slightly before returning to his statuesque watch from the edge of the corridor.

'David is assisting me with some business I have while I'm in the city.'

'Business that brings you to a courthouse basement?' asked Luke, curious despite his growing desire to be anywhere else but in the same room as Daniel.

'I'm looking for some information on a piece of contested family property, rightfully it's mine but unfortunately the proof I need has been… missing for a long time,' he said, stepping slowly towards Luke. 'I thought it might have been in Edinburgh, but it looks like it has been moved here.' Daniel lifted his arm, gesturing around him at the dim basement.

'Not the clerks records?' asked Evelyn quickly, seeing Luke bristle at Daniel's swaggering.

'You've found them?' said Paterson making everyone jump by breaking his silence.

Evelyn nodded, 'They're in the room just back down the hall,' she said pointing at the door to the room that she and Luke had found their way through after escaping the tunnel. 'Boxes of them.'

A broad, full-toothed smile spread across Daniel's face, revealing lines of brilliant white teeth. The smile was the first genuine thing Luke had seen in Daniel.

'You may have just made my day.'

Evelyn smiled back at him, the two holding each other's gaze for several seconds.

It was Luke's turn to clear his throat, making a point of looking down at the watch on his wrist. Evelyn broke off from Daniel and turned to Luke.

'We would love to stay and help but we have to find Campbell and get ourselves to Balloch.'

'Balloch?' asked Daniel curiously, 'what was John doing there?'

'That's what we're hoping to find out,' Luke

replied.

An awkward silence fell over the corridor. Daniel had his eyes fixed on Evelyn, clearly the feelings he had for her had not changed in the intervening years. Evelyn hadn't noticed, or at least had pretended not to.

'Well,' exclaimed Daniel theatrically, 'I won't hold you up any longer, let me walk you out.'

'There's really no need,' Evelyn started, trying to make an excuse to leave unescorted.

'I insist,' said Daniel, putting an end to the discussion. He offered an arm to Evelyn which she took politely, before striding off down the corridor back the way they had come, leaving Luke to trail in their wake. Paterson didn't follow, instead crossing the hallway and disappearing through the door into the room with the boxes of papers. The corridor led a short distance through the basement, a heavy door stood before them, Daniel keyed in a code on the handle and pushed it open with a click to reveal the foot of a polished marble staircase. Evelyn and Daniel were busily engaged in small talk, leaving Luke to admire the courthouse. The area beyond the threshold to the stairs was a stark contrast to the dreary basement. Compared to the open brickwork and polished concrete floors, the stairway was a picture of opulence: creamy, dark-veined marble lined the floor, reaching out to finely plastered and painted walls. It was more than Luke had expected from a government building.

'What is it you do Mr Knight?' asked Daniel, remembering Luke walking behind them.

'Luke's an archaeologist,' Evelyn answered for him.

'An archaeologist?' said Daniel, genuinely surprised. 'I was expecting police and private detectives to be hunting for John, not historians.'

'Archaeologist,' said Luke reflexively, then giving a small shrug. 'My job is to look for lost things with scraps of clues from the depths of history,' he said. 'Looking for a lost person isn't so different.'

'A person and some bits of old pot seem pretty different to me,' scoffed Daniel.

Luke clenched his fist digging his nails into his palm before letting his hand fall back open, dismissing his irritation. A courthouse probably wasn't the wisest place to start a brawl and besides, he'd promised Campbell he'd try not to break the law, although Daniel was definitely testing the limits of that promise.

'And what do you do Montrose?' asked Luke, deciding to change the subject was the safer option.

'Daniel's a lawyer,' Evelyn smiled up at Daniel. 'He was always the dull one,' she said giving him a friendly shove.

The stairs ended in another corridor, the décor the dry utilitarian style Luke had expected to find in a government building. Plain pine doors led off from the corridor to offices and meeting rooms, the whole place felt as staged as Daniel himself.

'Careful who you call dull,' he shot lightheartedly back at her. 'Your precious Walter Scott was a lawyer you know, I'm surprised your historian didn't know, I thought all they did was collect facts?'

Evelyn gave Luke an apologetic look, but he couldn't let it go this time. 'Appointed Sheriff depute of Selkirk in 1799 and Principal Clerk of Sessions in 1806,' said Luke. He turned his head to look Daniel in the eye. 'I'm surprised a lawyer knew that.'

It was a weak shot, but he would take it.

Luke 2 – 1 Daniel.

Daniel didn't offer a retort, instead turning back to strike up conversation with Evelyn. Luke couldn't help but smirk, and that's the match.

'Also,' said Luke, interrupting Daniel. Luke continued walking, catching up to the lawyer, 'I'm an archaeologist not a historian, I thought details were important for lawyers?'

Luke brushed past him and headed for the door at the end of the corridor, pushing them open to reveal the bright, open foyer of the new court building.

Daniel and Evelyn's conversation caught up with Luke as they stepped through the door, joining him in the imposing space.

'I hope you find what you're looking for in Balloch,' he said, surprisingly sincerely. 'Anything you need here's my number.'

He handed her a small white card, simple black lettering showing what Luke assumed was Daniels's name, phone number and probably some suitably important sounding job title.

Luke started to walk towards the door as Daniel and Evelyn said their goodbyes, Evelyn's footsteps clicking across the polished floors to catch him up.

'Mr Knight,' Daniel called across the echoing foyer.

Luke stopped and rolled his eyes.

'I'll catch you up,' he said to Evelyn, leaving her by the large open door, before turning back to Daniel, striding across the floor towards him.

'Thank you for helping Evelyn, we all want to find John,' said Daniel extending a hand towards Luke who took it hesitantly, surprised by Daniel's sudden affability. Daniel didn't release Luke's hand, instead pulling Luke towards him, speaking in a low voice, not wanting his parting words to be overheard.

'Leave this for the police. I don't want Evelyn in the same trouble as her brother—leave her out of it!' he hissed.

Luke pulled his hand out of Daniel's vice like grip.

'Evelyn can make her own choice,' Luke shot

back at him. 'And I think you'll find she's far more capable than you're giving her credit for.'

He didn't bother waiting for a reply, Luke spun on his heel and strode towards the wide glass doors of the courthouse to join Evelyn.

* * *

The grey light of the late afternoon cast long, dark shadows across the riverside path, the blue-grey expanse of the Clyde calm and flat reflecting the city back at Luke and Evelyn as they walked back towards the city.

'What did Daniel say to you?'

Luke huffed a laugh. 'He thought this was all too dangerous for you.'

'He's just being a good friend.'

'Sounds like he was more than a friend,' said Luke derisively.

'Are you jealous of him?' asked Evelyn, a wicked smile spreading across her face.

'Why would I be jealous?'

Luke winced as Evelyn's smile faded; he hadn't meant his words to come out as sharp as they had.

'About what happened...'

'It's fine,' interrupted Luke. 'It was good thinking.'

The pair walked on in silence, passing the

concrete steps of the Clydeside Amphitheatre.

'Where are we going?' asked Evelyn.

'We need to find Campbell before we go to Balloch,' said Luke.

They stopped in the shade of one of the tall oak trees that lined the grassy riverbank. The last gleams of the failing light setting the river afire with shades of red and orange.

'He could be anywhere,' said Evelyn. 'Have you tried calling?'

Luke held up his phone, a long spidering crack running though the dark screen. 'The cobbles in the tunnel aren't the softest of landings.'

Evelyn chewed her lip, watching a boat glide down the river, it's rippling wake scattering the glowing light on the water.

'What about the hospital?' she said, 'He took a bad blow to the head.'

Footsteps crunched on the grass behind them.

'Takes more than that to keep me down.'

Luke and Evelyn turned to see DS Campbell walking toward them, his unmarked car flashing blue and red lights parked on the road at the top of the bank.

'You two have half the city out looking for you,' he said, 'I thought it was better if I found you first.'

'Only half?' said Luke feigning offence.

'The other half are still looking for the man in the suit.'

'Men, plural,' said Luke. 'The one we met in Edinburgh is called Corban.'

Campbell rubbed his forehead. 'This day just keeps getting better.'

The last of the afternoon sun dipped behind the horizon leaving the riverbank in the rapidly descending darkness.

'What now then?' asked Campbell.

'Balloch,' said Luke simply.

'Balloch? Didn't you drag us all the way to George square just to explain why the stone wasn't there?'

Luke gave his best look of innocence.

'You missed a few things while you were unconscious.'

'Clearly,' said Campbell. 'Want to fill me in?'

'Long story,' Luke said walking towards Campbell's car, 'I'll explain on the way.'

Campbell gave Evelyn a questioning look. She shrugged in reply before following Luke.

Campbell let out a long breath before joining them and muttered, 'here we go again.'

CHAPTER 16

Great Western Road, somewhere between Clydebank and Dumbarton, West Dunbartonshire

Night had fallen fully by the time Luke, Evelyn and Campbell had made it through Glasgow's evening traffic, the roads practically gridlocked with people impatiently travelling home. Luke had tried for the better part of the trip out of the centre of the city to goad Campbell into putting on the lights and sirens to get through the traffic despite Campbell's insistence that he couldn't just use them whenever he wanted and that they were only for emergency use, and before Luke asked, no this did not constitute and emergency, meaning what should only be a half-hour drive was already nearly at the hour mark.

The lights and sounds of the city were behind them now, replaced by unlit countryside, made darker by the tall trees lining the road. Luke watched out the window for the gaps in between the shadowy trunks to see the silvery moonlight dancing across the mirrored water of the river.

'Do you really think the stone is still going to be there?' asked Campbell from the driver's seat.

Luke continued looking out of the window, 'all the evidence says it is.'

'All the evidence said it was in Wishart's grave and Wallace's Well.' Campbell rested his hand on the top of the steering wheel, rubbing the still sore spot on his temple with the other. 'And until a few hours ago, bloody Shetland.'

Luke turned to Campbell and offered him a weak smile.

'Basil Brown spent a year excavating three mounds in a field near Ipswich, all three of those mounds gave up nothing but scraps, a handful of clues to what was once there.'

Campbell let his head fall back against the seat with a soft thump and let out a groan that made Evelyn stir from where she slept on the back seat.

'Don't act like you don't love history lessons,' said Luke with a smile.

Campbell couldn't stop the huffed laugh. 'Are you sure you don't need to go and find a mound in a field, so you have a suitable backdrop for your point?'

Luke shot him a mock frown. 'No need for the sarcasm, point taken.'

Luke ignored Campbell's laugh and continued. 'At first Basil had dismissed the biggest mound. Looters had gotten there first sometime in the last thousand years and sunk a trench straight into the middle. As it turns out part of the mound had been destroyed by an early medieval ditch so what looked like the middle of the mound wasn't.'

'Has this actually got anything to do with finding the stone?' interrupted Campbell.

'If you let me finish,' said Luke. 'The point is Basil Brown went by the best evidence he had and came up empty three times, but he didn't give up. New evidence made him go back to the mound he had dismissed, the mound that contained one of the greatest treasures in British history.'

'Sutton Hoo.'

'Very Good,' smirked Luke. 'I'll make a history student out of you yet.'

The pair laughed, hushing themselves again when their outburst caused Evelyn to mumble her fatigued disapproval.

'Only one problem,' said Campbell after they were sure Evelyn was asleep again. 'Basil Brown dug three empty mounds, right?'

Luke nodded.

'You've only come up empty twice.'

'That's not really…'

'And when he found the ship and all the treasure didn't a load of stuffy academics swoop in and take over?'

'When did you become such an expert?' Luke cried, his voice rising to an unusually high pitch. 'And anyway, it's just an analogy.'

Campbell grinned, enjoying how easy it was to

wind Luke up and not letting on that all he knew about Sutton Hoo came as a result of watching Ralph Fiennes in *The Dig*.

The road curved gently north, taking them out of the tree-lined countryside and into the outer reaches of suburbia. The fiery sunset glow on the river that had been extinguished, rekindled by the faint orange warmth of a thousand lights in a thousand windows and Dumbarton castle, sitting on the bank, becoming like the sun, disappearing over the horizon in a flare of floodlights.

Campbell's eyes flicked up to the rear-view mirror, catching a glimpse of Evelyn, still sound asleep.

'What happened to you two after the square?'

'What do you mean?' said Luke quickly, a little too quickly. 'Nothing.'

Campbell gave him a slow sideways look.

'I mean, how did you shake off the man... men in suits?' Campbell corrected himself. 'But now I'm wondering what else happened?'

Luke glowered at him. 'Nothing happened,' he said firmly.

Campbell just gave him a look that made it clear he didn't believe Luke for a second.

The two locked stares in a silent battle, Campbell's eyes only flicking away for a split second to stop himself letting the car drift off the road.

'Fine!' exclaimed Luke. 'Jesus Christ, DI Douglas

should have let you take the lead on my interrogation.'

'Unfortunately, rank beats talent,' said Campbell with a grin. 'Now spill it Knight, what happened?'

Luke drew in a deep, steady breath before letting it out with a sigh.

'We slipped Corban and his brother at the tollbooth. There's a tunnel that goes from there to the courthouse at Jocelyn Square,' added Luke at Campbell's puzzled look.

'The tunnel came up in the basement of the courthouse. We were trapped, and someone was coming so Evelyn kissed me,' said Luke frankly.

The car veered suddenly to the side, tyres screeching as Campbell fought to get them back on a straight course.

'It's not that bloody surprising!' said Luke indignantly.

'Pothole.' Offered Campbell, trying to suppress a childish grin. Evelyn murmured softly from behind them, sleeping soundly though the car's erratic movement.

'Anyway,' Luke said through gritted teeth. 'She only did it as a distraction, which I guess worked since the man who walked round the corner was her ex.'

Campbell choked on a laugh, earning another exasperated glare from Luke.

'I expect that was pretty distracting for him.'

'I don't know about distracted but he definitely

wasn't happy about it,' said Luke. 'Not as unhappy as he was about me helping Evelyn find out what happened to her brother.'

'Is that what you two were arguing about just before I turned up?'

Luke turned his head slowly towards Campbell who was focusing intently on the road.

'How did you know we had been arguing?'

Campbell lifted a hand off of the wheel, not looking away from the road, and pointed at himself.

'Detective.'

Luke rolled his eyes.

'Apparently he thinks I'm putting her in danger,' he said, ignoring Campbell's question.

'He has a point.'

'How am I putting her in danger when she came to me?'

Campbell thought hard about how to phrase his next words. He gripped the wheel tighter causing the leather to creak under his hands.

'You forget I did my homework on you when you got tangled up in this... mess.' Campbell looked at Luke. 'I can see why someone would think you're a dangerous person to be around.'

'I'm just an archaeologist,' Luke protested.

'How many archaeologists have been responsible for sparking an international incident?'

'Probably quite a few actually.'

'Ok,' said Campbell. 'How many archaeologists

under the age of 30 have caused one international incident, let alone four!'

Luke brows lowered in a perplexed frown.

'Four?' questioned Luke. 'The disagreement in the Judaean desert, the miscommunication in Qala-e-Bost with the Afghan police,' he counted each of them off on his fingers, he paused thinking for a moment. 'Oh, and there was that little misunderstanding at the Lebanese border.'

Campbell huffed a laugh at Luke's understatement.

'Little misunderstanding?' he said. 'Is that what you call fleeing Syria on a camel with a pickup truck full of heavily armed terrorists on your arse?'

Luke smiled at the memory of racing across the burning sands, the sun blistering down and the ring of gunshots echoing behind him. He had to admit it was one of the tighter spots he had ever gotten into and indeed, out of. There was a legend that The Holy Lance, the spear that pierced Jesus' side on the cross, was smuggled into Palmyra when the city of Antioch fell during the first crusades. Luke had followed the trail to the Valley of Tombs and the Tower of Elhabel. Unfortunately, as he soon found out, the militant group that had captured the city were embarking on a jolly day of cultural destruction, destroying the temples at Bel and Baalshamin before moving on to the necropolis and its towers. Luke had been too late to stop the tower's destruction but not too late to see one of the men holding a carved wooden box that contained the clue to the lance's location. In hindsight stealing from terrorists probably wasn't the smartest idea, the group had caught up with him Northwest of Damascus resulting in Luke riding towards the Lebanese border like a bat out of hell. He had lost the box but thanks to the Huey that flew in, and the tan-skinned soldier hanging out of the helicopter's side door, he had kept hold of his life, just.

'Ok, I will give you that one,' said Luke, not bothering to suppress his ridiculous grin.

Campbell just shook his head.

'That's still only three?'

'Tibet,' said Campbell flatly.

Luke chewed his lip in thought, trying to recall what had happened in the east.

'You don't mean that argument with Zhao?' asked Luke. 'I would hardly call that an international incident.'

Campbell exploded, his voice raising an entire octave.

'You stole a car belonging to General Zhao of the People's Liberation Army, abandoning him and their entire exploration party in the middle of the Himalayas while shouting, *"Even Li Shang couldn't make a man out of you"!*'

'Was that bit really in the report?'

Campbell shot him a pained, exasperated glare.

Luke shrugged, putting on his best look of innocence.

'He shouldn't have stolen my scroll.'

Campbell couldn't contain it anymore, he broke out into a laugh, setting Luke off and causing them both to fall into a fit of hysterics.

Campbell wiped a tear from his eye, regaining control of himself, his ribs aching at the effort.

'You see my point though.'

'In my defence,' said Luke, struggling to keep a lid on his laughter, 'it's not me that's dangerous.'

Campbell sighed. 'You might not be, but you have a talent for attracting danger. You're like sugar to wasps. I can see why he was worried.'

Luke looked back at Evelyn, her face soft and sound deep in rest. Was he putting her in too much danger?

'If I'm such a risk to be near,' said Luke, turning back to Campbell. 'Why are you still sticking around?'

Campbell smirked. 'Even special branch isn't all gun fights and car chases, some of us like a bit of danger.'

Luke raised an eyebrow at him, but Campbell ignored it.

'Besides, John is… was my friend, I want to know what happened to him.'

Luke let his head fall back against the soft car seat.

'We find the stone; we find who was responsible.'

He let out a mirthless laugh. 'At least before I knew who was trying to kill me.'

The road veered hard to the right, Campbell followed the bend before turning down a small side road and slowing to a stop at the side of the inky dark road. The engine whirred down to a stop plunging the car's occupants into a haunting silence.

'Why are we stopping?'

'It's late, there won't be anyone at the castle until morning, and we ARE NOT breaking in,' said Campbell in a forceful voice that Luke wondered if they were taught in police training.

Luke opened his mouth to argue but was cut off by Campbell. 'Sleep. The stone's been lost for 400 years, it can wait another few hours.'

Campbell stretched his legs as much as the restrictive space of the car's footwell would allow and leant back in his seat.

'Anyway, if you're right, you might soon find out who's trying to kill us,' he said, closing his eyes.

Luke didn't protest again but he couldn't rest, not for a minute. Somewhere out there was a story waiting to be finished, a lost history to be uncovered and a killer to be unmasked. He stayed upright in his own seat, staring out at the dark wilderness and the distant glint of the waters of Loch Lomond far beyond.

'Maybe,' he said softly. 'But I'm not sure that's a good thing anymore.'

CHAPTER 17

Balloch Castle Country Park, Balloch, West Dunbartonshire, 16 miles Northwest of Glasgow

'I thought you knew where this place was?' Luke disentangled the sharp tendril of bramble from his jacket, unhooking the vicious thorns from the fine fabric. They had been walking for half an hour and didn't seem to be any closer to the castle on the banks of Loch Lomond. Instead, the trio found themselves ensnared by another thick hedge of briar that divided the countryside into neat parcels of land. Campbell cursed loudly as his leg caught on more of the hooked thorns.

'Yes, I do know where it is, if we were going by road, like normal people,' he said bitingly. 'Not like I'm trying to storm the freaking Bastille!' Campbell ripped himself free of the hedge, staggering forward, only avoiding an unwelcome meeting with the ground by the grace of Evelyn's hands steadying him.

'I don't remember the Bastille being surrounded

by fields and hedgerows when I was in Paris,' said Luke flippantly.

Campbell steadied his footing and opened his mouth to throw something acidic back at Luke but was interrupted by Evelyn.

'Why couldn't we just take the road?' she said. 'It's a public park, isn't it?'

'Somehow those two suited lunatics have tracked us down twice, using the roads. Being seen by people would make it easier for them to do it a third time.' Luke picked a twig off his jacket and flicked it back into the hedge. 'I'd like to see them find us when even we don't know where we are.'

Campbell looked at Luke with his head tilted to one side. 'I'm sure there's some logic in there somewhere.'

Evelyn shrugged and started towards the woods on the opposite side of the field.

Their feet crunched through the untamed, crisp grass that bordered the woods. The day was still young enough that the dew which clung to the long blades sprayed into the air and soaked their shoes as they walked.

'What are we going to do if they do track us down though?' asked Evelyn as they passed the tall trunks of the trees that stood sentry at the woods edge.

'Run?' said Campbell hopefully. 'And let the proper authorities deal with them.'

Luke ducked under a low branch.

'As far as they know we are still chasing after the stone in Scalloway. With any luck they're on their merry way to kill us there.'

Campbell batted away a thin whiplike branch that sprung back at him as Evelyn brushed past.

'Since when have we had any luck?' asked Evelyn.

'Excellent point,' said Luke. 'Good thing we have the proper authorities with us.'

He smiled at Campbell who gave an exasperated glare back. Evelyn stifled a giggle, covering her mouth with her hand. Campbell followed her eyes, putting a hand to his head to find a tangle of leaves and twigs tangling his usually well-groomed hair. He made a low growl, brushing at his head and sending a small tree worth of bits of leaf and twig to join the litter already on the ground.

'What's the castle like?' asked Evelyn. The forest's densely packed trees had thinned out, a clear path now winding towards the far side of the woods.

'I always thought it looked more like a house from the outside than a castle,' Campbell replied. 'I've never seen the rest of it.'

'You came here all the time as a kid, and you never went inside?' Evelyn asked, somewhere between suspicion and curiosity.

'You can't,' said Campbell simply.

Luke stopped dead.

'What exactly do you mean by, *"you can't"?*'

He turned slowly to look Campbell in the eye.

'It's closed to the public; it was used by the park rangers, but it's been derelict for years now.'

'And you didn't think to mention this before?'

'You never asked,' said Campbell, mimicking Luke's usual flippant attitude.

Luke chewed on his lip, frustration taking up residence on his face.

'Why did we wait until the morning if we're going to have to break in anyway?'

'Because we aren't going to break in,' said Campbell firmly.

'Do you have a key to the place you haven't told us about too?'

'No,' said Campbell, ignoring Luke's sarcasm. 'We're going to do this properly and find someone in charge and ask for their help.'

Luke rolled his eyes.

'That means no breaking in, no criminal damage and no stealing anything,' Campbell looked between Luke and Evelyn. 'Agreed?'

Evelyn looked at Luke and shrugged. Luke forced out a begrudging reply. 'Agreed.'

'Excellent,' said Campbell, starting again towards the far side of the woods.

Evelyn smiled at Luke, a broad, full-toothed grin.

'What?' said Luke.

'It's good to see there's at least one person who can tell you what to do.'

Luke gave her a half-hearted glare that achieved nothing but making her laugh and causing Luke's own mouth to twist into a smile.

'Are you two coming?' called Campbell.

Luke rolled his eyes making Evelyn laugh at him once more. She brushed past him catching up with Campbell a little way down the path.

Luke looked up at the sky and exasperated, sighed.

'This is why I work alone,' he muttered before following on behind Evelyn.

The woods petered out into open parkland. The grey-blue water of the Loch was just visible on the horizon, picturesque against the backdrop of lush, rolling hills. Luke, Evelyn, and Campbell strode along the path that cut through the long untamed grass of the park, the blades and colourful wildflowers moving gently in the breeze coming off the Loch. They followed the path as it curved gently to the east, the crenelations of the castle's tall stone tower began to appear over the tops of the trees as they drew ever closer. Luke admired the grand building as it came fully into view. The dark stone walls seemed to loom above the tranquil park that it sat in, making the place seem more impressive than its small size should allow. As impressive as it was, Campbell was right, it did look more like a house than the castle of a ruling family, and a distinctly

19th century house at that thought Luke. The bricked up arrow slits and crenelated battlement that edged the roof were likely more for show than serving any functional purpose.

'I was expecting it to look more...'

'Castle-like?' finished Luke.

'Yeah, that,' Evelyn said with no small amount of disappointment.

'I said it looked more like a fancy house than a castle,' said Campbell.

The three of them continued walking around the perimeter of the castle. Cold, grey Harris fencing cut off three sides of the structure, the latticework of stiff steel wire somehow more forbidding than the high stone walls behind. A modern defence, lesser in stature and substance but with an authority undiminished by time. Plastic board signs had been cable tied to sections of the fence, repeating every few metres along each section. Luke stopped in front of one of the groups of signs. The first plastic board was just a brightly coloured array of company logos, an advertisement of all the groups involved in the ongoing restorations—nothing useful. It was the second of the signs that had caught Luke's attention: a short history of the park and its eponymous castle.

'800 years of history in two paragraphs,' he said quietly to himself. 'That's depressing.'

'Anything useful?' asked Evelyn, appearing at

Luke's shoulder to read the sign.

'Only that we're in the wrong place.'

Campbell's face fell.

'How are we in the wrong place?' he said. 'Is there some other Balloch castle that I don't know about?'

Luke turned on his heel to face Campbell and the shimmering loch.

'Yes actually,' he said, suddenly chipper. 'Right there.'

Campbell frowned at him and turned his head slowly to look where Luke was staring. Campbell scanned the view: nothing but open grass leading to the loch. He rounded back on Luke with a quizzical look on his face.

'Have you been smoking something Knight?'

'Look harder.'

Campbell turned fully around to face the direction of the loch, studying the area carefully. The lush green trees of the park casting a gentle shade against the emerging sun for the few early visitors to enjoy. The path that ran from the castle, starting out as gravel but morphed into a neatly trimmed tramline that continued to the water's edge that bordered the park. Definitely no castle. Nothing that so much as broke the gentle slope of the land beyond a slight rise in the earth near just before the water's edge.

'You know I could arrest you for wasting police time, right?'

Evelyn finished reading the sign on the fence and walked the few short steps to join Luke and Campbell.

'It's not there anymore,' she said. 'The ruins of the first castle were broken apart to use to build that one.' Evelyn pointed at the new castle behind them.

'It looks like a Victorian folly because it is one,' said Luke flatly. 'But on the upside, you can still see the original.'

Luke inclined his head towards the low mound that stood barely above the ground level on the slope before the Loch. 'Granted it's not as grand anymore.'

Silence fell between them as they looked between the old castle come earthen mound and the new castle built from its carcass, the high battlement wall and castle dressings taking on an almost gaudy aspect in light of its newly learnt heritage.

'What now then?' asked Evelyn. 'If they salvaged the old castle for the new one surely they would have found the stone.'

'Maybe, but who's to say they knew what it was if they did?'

'What's one block of grey stone amongst a thousand others?' said Campbell.

'Exactly,' Luke replied.

'You think they might have built it into the castle then?' said Evelyn with just a hint of horror in her voice.

Luke took a deep breath and studied the high walls of the new castle, trailing his eyes down the lichen mottled stone.

'No idea,' he said after letting out his breath. 'Still, it's worth a look.'

He strode off towards the steel fence that surrounded the castle. Planting one foot on the bottom of the thick frame Luke reached for the top of the fence, grabbing the high bar, and pushing himself up so the top of the fence sat level with his waist.

'Umm Knight, what do you think you're doing?' came Campbell's strong, for police use only, voice.

'Going to take a look around?'

'I said we are not breaking in, get down.'

Luke dropped down from the fence, landing with a flat-footed *SLAP* on the tarmac path.

'Technically I wasn't breaking in, so it's only trespassing,' he said, 'which isn't even a crime!'

'I don't care, we agreed no breaking in.'

'But.'

'No!'

Campbell's last word came with the full force of the law and was enough to make even Luke know there was no point arguing.

'Do you have a different plan?'

'Yes, actually I do,' said Campbell smugly. 'We passed a site office for the renovations, someone there must have some information that could tell us what happened to the stone.'

Luke frowned.

'As an academic I can't argue that proper research might be a good idea,' he said. 'But I'm still saying my way would have been more fun.'

Campbell smiled victoriously, finally managing to keep Luke under some sort of control.

'Good, after you then.'

Campbell stood aside, opening the path back around the house to Luke, who took a last longing look at the castle and the unbroken fence line. He tore his eyes away and made to start down the path.

'Actually,' said Evelyn suddenly, stopping the two men. 'I'm going to look at where the old castle was.'

Campbell looked at her sceptically.

'There might be something left there,' she finished, sounding less than convincing.

'Perhaps I should go too?' chimed in Luke. 'You know, expert eye and all.'

Campbell frowned at the pair, his illusion of taking charge disappearing like the walls of the old castle.

'I can't think of a reason why not.' Not through a lack in effort of trying to think of one on his part.

'Excellent,' said Luke. 'We'll go look at the old castle, you go to the site office and meet back here in an hour.'

The glare had not left Campbell's face.

'Fine,' he said shortly, 'just promise me you won't break into the castle.'

'You have my word,' said Luke.

Campbell gave them one final look of warning, promising trouble if they broke Luke's word before striding away from them.

Luke and Evelyn watched Campbell as he walked away, leaning in unison to see him disappear around the far side of the castle.

'Just to be clear,' said Luke, 'you were planning on breaking into the castle too, right?'

Evelyn flashed him a mischievous grin.

'Of course.'

'How are we going to get in?' asked Evelyn. Luke dropped down from the fence landing to her left.

'I was thinking the front door,' he replied earnestly.

Evelyn stared after him as he started towards the turreted entrance.

'Are you serious?'

Luke grabbed two hanging hi-vis vests that were hanging off a hook on the inside of a transit van's open back door. Stooping mid-stride, he snagged the two battered, white hard hats that lay at the foot of the door.

'Put these on,' he said handing one set of vest and helmet to Evelyn. He slid his own vest over the battered dress jacket he still wore, the helmet topping off the ensemble. Complete with the kilt it did make him look like a reject from some strange avant-garde fashion show, but he carried on walking unphased.

A flurry of workmen shuffled in and out of the large front door to the castle, clothes already speckled with paint and plaster before the day had even begun. The door itself was set back into a porchway, the outside of which had been styled to resemble the barbican of a real medieval castle, rectangular with turrets flanking a stone archway.

'Just keep walking and act like you're supposed to be here,' Luke whispered to Evelyn as they approached the door. He walked with a calm confidence that Evelyn struggled to mimic, surely they wouldn't get away with walking in the front door, not dressed the way they were, they would stick out like a sore thumb on a building site. Evelyn's heartbeat soared as they arrived at the castle door, Luke muttered hellos, tipping his hardhat to a group of stone masons loitering outside, sneaking in a morning cigarette.

To Evelyn's amazement the three men nodded back to Luke and continued on with their conversation. No interrogation, no suspicion, not as much as a second look.

Beyond the door the entrance hall had lost some of the grandeur it had been built with. The walls and floor had been stripped back to bare stone and wood; plastic covers coated the floorboards protecting them from the heavy footfall of steel-toed boots. Luke grabbed Evelyn's hand and pulled her after him through a cracked oak door, away from the main area of renovation work.

'That had absolutely no right to work,' said Evelyn, stepping around something covered in a billowing white dust sheet.

Luke crossed the short space to another door on the opposite wall, kicking up billows of dust into the thin streaks of light that streamed through the boarded up window.

'If there's one thing I've learned sneaking into places I shouldn't be,' he said easing open the door and peering into the space beyond, 'a hi-vis and confidence can get you in anywhere.'

'Seriously?'

'No one looks past the high vis, works every time,' Luke looked back at Evelyn with a smirk. 'Well almost but if I'm honest Balmoral was probably pushing my luck.'

Evelyn crossed the room, joining him by the door.

'One day I have a lot of questions for you.'

'Just ask Campbell for the files,' Luke replied, 'this way.'

The next room was as bare as the hallway they had come in through, barer even. No warm wooden boards covered the floor. The grey stone walls ran straight into the heavy flagstones. It was near pitch black as the door swung closed behind Evelyn, the two small windows set into the front wall tightly boarded over. Evelyn tried the light switch to the right of the door frame, nothing: the tiny golden switch failing to do anything more than make a *click* that echoed in the darkness. Luke pulled the torch out of his bag and flicked the bright beam on, casting it around the room.

'What are you going to do with the stone if it's here?' asked Evelyn.

Luke continued scanning the walls.

'It's not my decision, the stone belongs to Scotland.'

'Hasn't history proven that the stone causes nothing but death and violence?' asked Evelyn.

Luke walked to the far corner of the room and squatted next to one of the large stones, brushing his hand over the surface.

'The stone doesn't cause anything, it's just a stone. The men and women who seek power are the ones who cause the violence. The stone is just a symbol, an excuse.'

Evelyn chewed her lip and walked across the stone floor to Luke, heels clicking as she did.

'Is it a good idea to give back that excuse?'

Luke looked up at her and shrugged.

'A symbol's meaning can change. What was the focus of rebellion in the right hands can become a symbol of pride, of hope, of being better than we are now.'

'And you think it will change?' Evelyn asked sceptically.

'Your brother seemed to think so.'

Evelyn bowed her head, a sad smile forming on her face.

'Speaking of symbols,' said Luke brushing dust and debris away from a stone, three courses up from the floor. The shallow grooves now cleared he flashed the torch onto the stone.

'What is it?' asked Evelyn?

A cross was incised into the stone, a saltire, the arms crossing in the shape of an X. In each vertex of the cross a small rose had been carved.

'The arms of Lennox,' said Luke.

'Part of the old castle,' whispered Evelyn. 'Do you think it has anything to do with the stone?'

'Maybe,' said Luke.

He scratched at the mortar around the stone, it was crumbling, weathered and friable from years of wear.

'Here hold this.'

He handed the torch to Evelyn and fumbled in his bag, after a few seconds pulling out a small chisel and a wooden mallet.

'Where did you get those from?' asked Evelyn confused.

'The van outside belonged to the stone masons,' Luke replied. 'I saw these when I grabbed the vest, thought they might be useful.'

Luke fitted the end of the chisel against the

mortar line. Evelyn kept the torch steady on the wall. Neither of them heard the door quietly creep open behind them and a dark figure step through. Luke lifted his arm slightly, wooden mallet tight in his grip, ready to strike the first blow to dislodge the stone.

'You won't find anything,' boomed a voice from the shadows by the door.

Luke and Evelyn both jumped, Luke dropping the mallet and chisel to the floor with a clatter.

Campbell stepped into the beam of Evelyn's torch.

'I said no breaking in.'

'We didn't,' protested Luke, 'the front door was open.'

Campbell's glare silently told Luke not to push it. He opened the door, letting a hazy light back into the room and waited for Evelyn and Luke to pass through before following.

'How do you know the stone in the wall wasn't important?' asked Luke as they moved back through the room with furniture covered in dust sheets and into the stripped hallway.

'I spoke to the castle's steward,' said Campbell. 'They haven't found anything in the renovations that references the old castle, apart from the stone with the carving.'

Luke frowned.

'Then it was worth taking the stone out, it might have had something on another side,' he said.

'Even if there was it doesn't change the fact that the stone isn't here.'

'Why so sure?' asked Evelyn.

'The steward was very keen to tell me the history of the two castles,' said Campbell. 'And it turns out there's a third castle in the story.'

'It's weird hearing you give the history lesson,' said Luke.

Campbell ignored him and continued.

'Balloch was the seat of the Earls of Lennox but in 1390 they decided it wasn't secure and took up residence in another castle.'

'So, when the stone was hidden at the Lennox's seat….' said Evelyn.

'It could have been at the other castle,' said Luke, dejected.

The trio walked across the open area in front of the castle towards the gate through the fence. The sun had risen high in the sky while they had been inside. The Loch in the background shining like a mirror, dazzling.

'Exactly, but luckily they didn't go far.' Campbell looked past Luke and Evelyn to the shining loch.

'And this castle is still there… mostly.'

Luke looked over his shoulder.

'Well, an island is definitely more secure.' He turned back to Campbell and smiled. 'I guess we just need to steal a boat.'

Campbell did not return his smile.

CHAPTER 18

The Inchmurrin Ferry, Loch Lomond, Argyll, and Bute, 1.5 miles from the shore of Inchmurrin.

Cold freshwater misted Luke as the small wooden boat motored across the blue-grey loch towards the island of Inchmurrin that sat like a jewel on the water's surface. Despite Luke's best attempts, the boat that was ferrying them from the mainland was decidedly not stolen, or as Luke had tried to argue, borrowed with every intention of returning. After a short argument that ended with Campbell informing Luke that, yes even if he put it back, stealing a boat was still illegal, they had instead trekked back across the mosaic of fields to Campbell's car, and driven the short distance along the bank of Loch Lomond to the small village of Arden to board the ferry that ran to the island. Luke had perched in the bow of the sleek wooden boat watching the thin strip of golden sand draw closer. Campbell and Evelyn had taken up one of the wooden benches at the boat's stern, both looking less than thrilled with the method of transport.

'Not a fan of boats?' Luke had asked Evelyn as they had left the dock at Arden. She had simply shaken her head and walked unsteadily to the spot she still occupied. He hadn't bothered asking Campbell the same question, the shade of sickly green he had turned as soon as the boats engine had stuttered to life was all the answer Luke needed. The short stretch of water between the mainland and the island only took fifteen minutes to cross but Luke had made the most of the journey so far, getting as much information as he could about the island from the ferry's small but surprisingly knowledgeable crew. The young man at the helm had furnished Luke with all the tales of the island that had been passed down to him from his father who had run the ferry, and his father before him. A tiny island with a long history, from the monastery where the island got its name and cattle raids by the legendary Rob Roy to the castle being the refuge of a defeated Robert the Bruce, and the hunting lodge of kings thereafter all the way to James VI and I, son of Mary Queen of Scots.

'Hunting for what though?' Luke had said softly. Had the first Scottish King of England known where his mother had hidden the coronation stone, the symbol of his power? Had he even known the one he had been crowned on was a fake, thought Luke.

'Mostly deer, there's still a good few of them

about,' the man had said, oblivious to the truth of Luke's question. The remainder of the journey had passed with nothing other than the gentle splash of water against the wooden boat and the gentle hum of the engine to break the stillness of the loch. The island had grown to fill most of the horizon, with a short, pebbly beach taking place at its southernmost end. A wooden jetty reached out from the track at the top of the shoreline into the water like someone building the road hadn't noticed the land had ended. The boat's engine chugged as the skipper bumped the throttle, controlling their speed and guiding the boat towards the middle of the long jetty. With a final shudder as the engine was thrown into reverse, the boat glided beside the jetty and came to a stop against the wooden platform with a gentle bump. The deck hand who Luke had been talking to jumped from the gunwale to the jetty with a thick rope, pulling the boat securely against the jetty and tying it off to one of the large iron rings bolted to the wooden boards. Evelyn and Campbell made a beeline for the jetty no sooner than the boat had been tied off. Two of the crew were helping the passengers off the boat, a short queue forming across the width of ferry.

Luke idled at the back of the queue gazing up at the hill that overlooked the beach and the jetty.

'At least the castle won't be hard to find,' Luke said to himself as he admired the cold grey arch that stood resolute atop the knoll and from what Luke could see above the trees that lined the shore, was the only part of the castle that still remained as such. Luke hopped off the boat nodding his thanks to the young deck hand helping him. Evelyn and Campbell were perched on a boulder at the end of the jetty waiting for Luke. The colour had returned to Campbell's face, and both now wore a weak smile instead of the sickly grimace that had been set during the journey. He strode down the jetty towards them, the wooden boards creaking underneath each step.

'There, down the ruffles wall did glow. The zun upon the grassy vloor, An' weakly-wandren winds did blow, Unhinder'd by a door.'

Campbell looked at Luke quizzically.

'Did you hit your head coming off the boat?'

'It's a poem by William Barnes,' chimed in Evelyn. 'The Castle Ruins.'

Campbell turned to her. 'And was he drunk when he wrote it?'

'It was written in an old Dorset dialect; Barnes was a bit of a linguistic purist and thought his native dialect was the closest to pure Saxon English.'

'I'm still lost,' said Campbell. 'Why is this relevant. Dorset is about as far as you can get away from here.'

'The Castle in the poem is a ruin, so is that one,'

Luke pointed towards the stone arch on the hill. 'I was just pointing it out.'

Campbell rubbed his temple, trying to suppress the urge to argue more. 'Couldn't you have just said that?'

Luke cocked his head and gave a half-mouthed smirk.

'That wouldn't be as much fun,' he said and turned to start down the track that led from the jetty to the castle. 'Shall we?'

Campbell frowned at him as he shifted himself off the rock and onto the jetty, Evelyn following close behind. Luke caught his frown and slapped a hand onto Campbell's shoulder.

'Cheer up, at least this won't take long,' he said straight-faced. 'There's not much to look around, the place is a bit of a ruin.'

Evelyn tried and failed to cover up her laugh as she hopped off the rock next to Campbell as Luke strolled down the wooden jetty. Campbell's look could have burned holes through the back of Luke's, already dishevelled, jacket.

'I could shoot him, no one would ever know,' muttered Campbell to himself. 'No Chief Inspector, last I saw him a man in a dodgy suit was running after him with a gun.'

Evelyn coughed a spluttering laugh and gave him an apologetic smile before catching up with Luke. Campbell let out a long breath and looked up at the cloudless sky. 'I bet you think this is hilarious too.'

He looked back to Luke and Evelyn as they reached the track at the end of the jetty. As Much as he hated to admit it, if anyone could find a lost national treasure and find who killed John, it was Luke bloody Knight.

'There's not exactly a lot to go on,' said Evelyn looking up at the castle.

Luke shrugged.

'Still more than there was at Balloch.'

'That's not exactly difficult,' said Campbell.

The trio stood at the bottom of the castle hill. Up close there was more still standing than they could see from the jetty. Sort of. The natural steep sides of the outcrop that the castle sat on had been exaggerated by wide, deep ditches on two sides that made the ruined structure seem somehow still daunting. A few loose courses of wall remained sporadically across the hilltop. It was hard to make out any sort of plan from their position at the foot of the steep slope but to Luke it looked like there had once been a central building with some sort of enclosing wall isolating the castle even more than the hill and the island.

'Well, we're not going to find anything down here,' said Luke, making his way towards the footworn track that led up the shallower side of the hill. 'Onward and upward.'

Evelyn watched Luke bound up the track, barely stopping at the summit before trekking off towards the main body of ruins.

'He doesn't stop does he?'

Campbell didn't take his eyes off the castle.

'From what I've read and seen the last couple of days,' he added 'once Luke Knight has his mind set on something, there's not a lot that could stop him, and not a lot he would stop for.'

He turned towards Evelyn, his eyes levelling at the petite, cherry-haired woman, but he wasn't looking at her, more like through her at something else entirely, concern or something akin to sadness marring his face.

Evelyn shivered, quickly following Luke's path up the hill, joining him at the ruins.

Campbell took a deep breath, steadying himself before taking the track up the hill himself.

Luke and Evelyn stood in the centre of what had once been the castle. From within the ruined walls the layout of the medieval castle became clear. The main building had three rooms. The first, closest to the track that led up the hill, had little remaining beyond the ghost of a window that once looked out west across the loch. The second room was a similar story, the skeleton of the room sticking out of the net of grass and ivy. The final room had the most story to tell, not that it was a long one. The walls held the traces of a handful of windows and thin arches' slits, some of which had been blocked by now crumbling stones at some point in their life. An opening in the far wall led to the hint of a tower adjoining the outer enclosing wall. Luke thought, a gatehouse maybe.

'Three rooms, three of us,' said Evelyn, breaking Luke from his trancelike observation. 'Divide and conquer?'

Luke said in agreement, 'worked for Julius Caesar.' He walked straight for the far room and leaving Campbell and Evelyn to search the two smaller rooms. Luke paced the perimeter of the room; the walls were rough he noticed, the occasional dressed stone but the majority resembling rubble held together with a rough mortar filled with tiny fragments of broken seashells. He crouched next to part of the crumbling ivy-covered wall and peeled off part of the sprawling green tendrils that covered the masonry. The wall underneath stood to the height of Luke's waist, just barely showing the remnants of a windowsill. Luke ran his hand across the surface of the stone, the tips of his fingers finding the rough mortared grooves between the stones.

'Huh,' said Luke to himself, the mortar under his hand suddenly becoming smooth, finer than before.

'Well, that's not medieval.'

Luke jumped to his feet and continued his circuit

of the room, noting other spots where the wall had been repaired sometime in the recent past. He reached the gap in the wall that led to the remnants of the gatehouse tower—what was left of it anyway—not enough to spend much time looking at, thought Luke. He looked around at the exterior walls, they stood high on this side of the castle, a tangle of brambles like leafy barbed wire stopped him getting close but they were easily twice his height at the tallest point.

'Anything over there?' called Evelyn.

Campbell's reply followed shortly. 'Nothing.'

'Same story here,' said Luke dejected, walking back across the centre of the far room to where Evelyn had joined Campbell in the middle of the castle. He hopped down from the floor of the far room, landing with a soft thud on the grass-covered ground.

'There's some fairly modern repairs but...'

Evelyn looked at him, concern on her face. 'Luke? What's wrong?'

Luke had stopped dead, his eyes widening slowly. He turned and jumped back into the far room then, almost immediately, turned and jumped back down again. Evelyn and Campbell watched in a bewildered silence as Luke repeated the jump back and forth twice more.

'The floor!' exclaimed Luke, jumping back up to the far room and casting his gaze across the skeletal walls. 'Oh, that is clever.'

Campbell leant close to Evelyn.

'I think we broke him.'

Luke flew across the room to the wall that dropped down to the tangle of brambles.

'Luke, what is it?' shouted Evelyn.

Luke turned back towards her, the spring back in his step.

'Floor, wall, window,' he said, dropping back into the room with them. 'What do you see?'

'Three of the five basic architectural elements of a building?' said Campbell dryly. 'Maybe you should just tell us, save some time because of the whole hired killers with a shady puppet master hot on our backs.'

'Where would be the fun in that?' smiled Luke.

'Not getting murdered sounds pretty fun.'

Evelyn had circled the far room while the two boys had argued, she leant her hand on the frame of an arched window, looking at the narrowing stonework that formed an arrow slit that ran lower than the sill of the arch.

'The room's been rebuilt,' she said.

Luke's heads spun to look over his shoulder at her.

'And?'

Evelyn looked at him, the room he stood in was lower than hers, the floor of the far room cutting her view of him off just below the knee.

'This room is higher than the rest of the castle.' Evelyn walked back across the room. 'Do castles have cellars?'

Luke's mouth turned up at the corner. 'Not bad for a poet, Crawford.'

He didn't notice Evelyn's cheeks flushing a pale red as he took up position in the centre of the far room and spun on his heel to take in the tumbled piles of masonry that had once been a seat of power but reduced to ruins by nothing but time. Well, time and people thieving stone for houses.

'Time,' said Luke facing his companions again. 'Time changes everything right?'

'Right,' said Campbell.

'Wrong, time is an abstract concept, it can't directly affect anything. Time didn't reduce this castle to ruins, the elements and people did.'

'What's your point?' said Campbell, his patience wearing noticeably thin.

'Years of harsh weather might have crumbled the walls but it sure as hell didn't repoint the masonry a hundred years ago.'

'Or remodel those windows,' chimed in Evelyn.

'Exactly,' continued Luke. 'Like Evelyn said, everything about the architecture of this room says it should have a space below it.'

'But there's no entrance to it,' said Campbell.

'Not anymore.'

'Someone covered it up, like how the window was blocked.'

Luke smiled. 'Now he's getting it. At some point in its history this room was rebuilt in part: the arrow slits became arched windows, a window was bricked up and most importantly, the entrance to the room below was concealed.

'Why?'

'To keep the stone hidden,' said Evelyn.

Luke flashed her a wide smile that she returned.

'Isn't that a bit of a leap?' Campbell said sceptically. 'I mean, some medieval Earl did some home improvements and that means there's the lost coronation stone of Scotland under the floor? It's just guesswork.'

Luke said defensively, 'precision guesswork.'

Campbell raised an eyebrow at him.

'Anyway, I don't think the search is going to take long.'

Campbell rubbed his head and snapped. 'I would ask why but I'm sure you're going to tell us anyway.'

Luke recoiled physically from Campbell's outburst, levelling his eyes at him. Luke had only known the man for barely more than a day but still concern coloured his face at the detective's sudden irritation.

'If you insist,' said Luke, unsettlement replaced, albeit weakly, with his usual flippant attitude.

'You see,' he continued, walking towards the tumbled window on the northwest wall, 'when you're sad like me sometimes you know things like how to tell how old mortar in a wall is.'

He stopped by the repair he had noticed earlier

and nodded towards the branch like seams of new mortar.

'For instance, that doesn't look very medieval.'

Campbell scoffed. 'Is "not very medieval" some of your precision guesswork?'

'19th Century if you want to be pedantic,' Luke shot back. 'My point is, someone has been patching up the castle in the last hundred or so years.'

'Why?' asked Evelyn, brushing past Campbell to join Luke in the far room.

'Maybe they wanted to stop the ruins being more ruined,' said Campbell sarcastically.

Luke shot him a deliberately antagonistic smile. 'Yes actually.'

'Seriously?'

'Same thing has happened at hundreds of castles, tombs and other assorted ruins, hell even half of Stonehenge has been propped back up and cemented into the ground,' said Luke.

Evelyn frowned. 'Even Stonehenge?'

'All in the name of preservation.'

Campbell asked, 'so that's what happened here?'

'No,' replied Luke. 'Well yes, well… sort of.'

He started towards Evelyn.

'The repairs to the wall, the windows, sure, we'll call them slightly overzealous restoration,' he stopped a pace before Evelyn, face to face with her delicate features. He looked down at her feet, Evelyn's eyes following his.

He said, 'But why repoint the floor?'

They all stared at the place where Evelyn stood. The spot beneath her feet where Luke had stood minutes before, at the patch of ground where he had scuffed away the carpet of grass and moss to reveal the extent of the carefully re-laid floor. The finer, brighter mortar outlined a near perfect square in the old stones, just large enough in width to fit the shoulders of a grown man.

'Because they didn't want anyone to know they found something,' said Evelyn, breaking their trance.

'And why not patch up some walls while you're at it,' continued Campbell. 'Hide what you did to the floor in plain sight.'

The smile on Luke's face was genuine. 'Do you two need me or are you going to solve this one on your own?'

Evelyn looked up at him, her blue eyes glowing in the sun.

'Right now, we need you to figure out a way in, we can't just dig up a castle in broad daylight.'

'I think you mean we shouldn't dig up a castle in broad daylight,' quipped Luke, casting a wary glance at Campbell. 'We could easily do it but some people get a bit grumpy about that sort of thing.'

Campbell let out a long breath, trying to send his irritation with it.

Luke hid his smirk from the detective, there was

the disapproval he was waiting for.

'Unfortunately, I don't see another option,' said Luke. Evelyn stepped quickly off of the patch of bare floor as Luke drew a well-worn brick hammer from his bag and knelt by the re-laid floor.

Campbell frowned at the hammer and then at the man on the end of the arm holding it.

'Did you steal that from the masons at Balloch?'

Luke turned his head to look at Campbell.

'One thing I've learnt in life detective, don't ask questions you won't like the answer to,' said Luke and swung the hammer towards the outer line of mortar.

CHAPTER 19

Inchmurrin Castle, Inchmurrin, Loch Lomond, Argyll, and Bute

Pale dust blew across the hilltop that supported Inchmurrin Castle, billowing into the air like a sandstorm across a desert before collecting against the crumbled walls in tiny dunes. Luke let the hammer slide from his hand, landing with a clang on the small collection of stone he had amassed next to him. He stood back, wiping the dust and sweat off the smooth curve of his head and admiring the small hole that had been opened in the floor of the far room. The afternoon sun had risen high in the sky in the time it had taken to chip away the Victorian mortar and reveal the narrow portal to the celler and the temperature had moved from pleasant to sweaty and uncomfortable with it, making everyone involved in the excavation thankful for the occasional cool breeze blowing in from the Loch.

'Who's going down there then?' asked Campbell peering dubiously into the dark space.

'Well volunteered,' Luke returned Campbell's

glare with an evil grin which only made the detectives face harden further. Luke cut off his smile; it probably wasn't the best idea to test the patience of a man with a gun and handcuffs.

Evelyn coughed, hacking out the lungful of dust she inhaled as Luke shrugged off his jacket, knocking the caked-on grime that had collected on the fabric into the air in a hazy cloud, like an old rug being beaten in clean—a very old rug.

'Here, hold this,' he said tossing the jacket to Campbell and taking up position at the edge of the hole. He leaned over the precipice, the burning sun barely penetrated an inch beyond the limit of the hole, and beyond that? Nothing but darkness extending into an infinite unknown as far as Luke could see.

'How far to the floor is it?' asked Evelyn, joining Luke by the hole.

'Your guess is as good as mine,' said Luke grimly, tearing himself away from staring into cellar and turning to face Evelyn and Campbell. 'Only one way to find out.'

He didn't give them time to ask how, taking a step backwards, a step closer to the edge. Evelyn's eyes widened as Luke lifted his foot for another step. As fast as she could force her body to move, she closed the short distance between them, lunging for him and grabbing a fist full of his crumpled shirt. Evelyn threw her weight backwards, stopping Luke mid-step. His eyes met

Evelyn's, their usual fiery blue just as vibrant but cold with anger and what Luke thought looked like... fear.

'There are other ways of finding out than throwing yourself in half-cocked and blind,' Evelyn bit out.

Luke looked down at his foot, teetering on the rough lip of the hole, the other a few inches behind it, dangling over empty space. He shifted his weight, dislodging a lump of mortar, sending it tumbling into the darkness to clatter against the floor moments later.

'Careful Crawford, if you're going to react like this every time I do something reckless and irresponsible it's going to make the day dreadfully long.' He looked back up at her and winked. 'Plus, people might start thinking you care about me.'

Evelyn rolled her eyes, the coldness replaced by exasperation. She relaxed her arm enough to let Luke fall back an inch before catching him again. She didn't let him fall far but it was enough to wipe the smirk of his face and scramble to get both his feet firmly back on solid ground. It was Evelyn's turn to wear a wicked grin.

'You're right, there are other ways of telling,' he said resigned, disentangling his shirt from Evelyn's grip. 'But none quite as fun.'

Evelyn's brows furrowed, her attention lapsing for a second, long enough for Luke to take his final step backwards, backwards out of Evelyn's reach, backwards into the empty space where the castle floor had been but now only empty space remained. Luke disappeared into the darkness, his shoulders scraping past the edges of the narrow hole.

Evelyn and Campbell looked at each other then back at where Luke had disappeared beneath them. They both rushed forward, dropping to their knees and trying in vain to see into the impenetrable darkness.

Evelyn yelled into the dark, her voice echoing off unseen walls. 'Luke!'

She let a heartbeat pass, and another.

'Luke!' Campbell shouted beside her.

'I'm ok.' Luke's disembodied voice echoed from below.

Evelyn slumped back in relief.

'I'm going to kill him.'

Campbell let out a held breath and chuckled, it sounded half-hearted even to him.

'Probably not the best thing to say in front of a police officer,' he said looking back into the hole. 'Although I can't say I would stop you.'

Luke was plunged into darkness, rapidly closing a gap between his feet and a floor he couldn't see. The floor in question was a little further than he had thought, causing him to land awkwardly and tuck into a roll to avoid an injury. The darkness was as absolute within the cellar as it was looking in from above, the small square of sky provided only a thin column of light, barely more than a dusky haze surrounded by the sea of black. Luke propped himself up from the floor. The stone was smooth under his hands, cold and damp from the years of isolation but not overgrown with moss and weeds like the castle above, the darkness saving it from being retaken by nature. Luke shifted his hand, his fingers meeting something small and rough. He held the broken chunk of mortar up to the faint light beneath the hole before sending it clattering into the far reaches of the cellar.

He heard Evelyn's voice call out from above, the sound echoing and amplifying off the walls. He got to his feet stiffly. Maybe there were better ways to find out how deep a hole goes.

He heard his name called out again, Campbell's thick accent replacing Evelyn's bright voice.

'I'm ok.'

Luke slid his hand into his satchel, fumbling blindly for the cold metal of his torch. His hand closed around the handle, pulling the torch out into the air and Luke gave a small prayer to whoever would listen that it hadn't broken when he rolled out of the jump. Someone must have listened; Luke slid the small plastic switch forward and a beam of light shot from the torch onto the far wall of the cellar.

'Sit tight, I'm going to have a look around.'

There wasn't much to speak of in the cellar. Four simple stone walls with a flagstone floor and as far as Luke could see from the torchlight, no side rooms, or corridors. Bare, empty, a room made of stone, but no sign of the one he was there to find. Luke's eyes caught a shadow at the far end of the cellar, two flat shapes lying on the floor, set in contrast by the torchlight. Seeing nothing else of interest he crossed the room towards the shapes to find a flagstone that had been lifted from the floor and broken in two. The jagged pieces then laid crudely atop the space they had covered.

'What can you see?' called Campbell.

The sudden break in silence caused Luke to jump, dropping the torch to the stone floor with a worrying crack and plunging him back into darkness.

'Bugger all now,' snapped Luke.

He knelt, searching for the torch in the vain hope it still worked. Mercifully the bulb in the torch blinked into life, emitting its warm light, a shadow sat across the beam from a long crack across the glass. The broken flagstone lay just a few feet from Luke, he knelt next to the pieces. The stone had been broken recently, as recently as the repairs had been made to the floor above anyway, tiny chippings of stone dug into Luke's knees as he knelt. He cursed, if the stone was here, it's unlikely it was anymore. A glint of gold underneath the broken flagstone caught his eye.

He put the torch on the floor, casting distorted shadows on the wall behind. The pieces of the broken slab slid away with little effort leaving behind a shallow rectangular depression in the floor. No more than a few feet deep and sat right at the centre, placed carefully, was the source of the glint.

'Well, you don't belong there,' said Luke curiously. He picked up the object and paused, looking around hesitantly, half expecting its removal to trigger some cartoonish booby trap, before slipping it into his pocket. He stood, frustration furrowing his brows. Why was there always someone a step ahead? With one last scan of the cellar, Luke walked back to the column of light coming from the castle above.

'Any chance of a hand out of here?'

No sooner than Luke had finished his sentence, a rope dropped from above. Luke quickly sidestepped to avoid the heavy coil hitting him, letting it instead land in a heap on the floor.

'That was quick.'

Campbell's head appeared in the square of sky, 'I guessed you probably wouldn't have thought as far ahead as how to get back out.'

He couldn't argue with that.

With a grunt of effort, Luke hauled himself over the edge of the hole, finding Campbell's hand waiting to help him to his feet.

'Where did you get the rope from?'

'It's an island with a bunch of boats, I figured there would be some rope somewhere.'

Luke frowned, 'And none of us thought of that before I jumped?'

'You didn't exactly wait around for suggestions,' said Campbell. 'What did you find down there anyway?'

Luke looked at him grimly. 'An empty Stone of Destiny shaped hole with no trace of a stone. Someone beat us to it by at least a hundred years.'

A boat motor chugging across the loch was the only sound in response.

'So, there was nothing?'

Luke smiled reaching into his pocket, 'I didn't say nothing.'

He withdrew a large, gold pocket watch, leaving it dangling from a chain a few inches in front of his face. Evelyn took the watch from him. A simple clock face sat behind the murky glass, once an ivory white it had yellowed with age. Two delicate metal hands pointed towards sharply printed roman numerals. The back of the case was rough on her hand. She turned it over. The bright gold back had been engraved with a fine scrolling script but below, three sets of initials had been crudely scratched in.

If The Spider Shall Fail

W.S. T.T. A.F.

'What the hell does that mean?' blurted Campbell.

'I think Miss Crawford will be the expert here.'

Evelyn took the watch from Luke; she ran her finger delicately across the fine grooves of the engraving.

'But if the spider shall fail, I will go to the wars in Palestine, and never return to my native country more,' she said in an awed hush. 'The Spider and The King.'

Luke stepped slowly towards her and looked down at the watch in her hands.

'That explains who W. S is.'

Campbell cleared his throat. 'Umm, can someone explain this for those of us who aren't historians or poetry experts?'

Evelyn shook herself out of her fixation on the watch. 'The Spider and The King, it's a story from Walter Scott's *Tales of a Grandfather*, it's stories of Scottish history,' she said, quickly, nearly tripping over her words in excitement. 'After being crowned king in Scone in 1305 Robert was on the run from the English, he took refuge in a cave where he watched a spider try and fail to build a web, the spider failed six times as Robert had, watching the spider he vowed if it succeeded to build the web on the seventh try, he himself would try a seventh time to reclaim Scotland.'

Evelyn and Luke couldn't contain their glee.

'So, you're saying that's Walter Scott's watch.'

'Possibly,' said Luke with a shrug.

'And he left it here in place of the stone, and the story about the spider is what? A clue to where he moved it?'

Luke took the watch gently from Evelyn's hands and held it up to his eyes. He twisted the crown hearing the mechanism winding, clicking back into life followed by a faint *tick tick tick* as life flowed back into the hands on the watch face. The trail wasn't dead, just dormant, waiting for the next person to take up the trail.

'It would seem that way, wouldn't it?' Luke flipped the watch over. 'But not just Scott.'

Campbell looked over Luke's shoulder at the gold circle glinting in the sun.

'Who are T.T. and A.F.?'

Luke turned his head to Campbell, grinning an inch from his face.

Campbell's face fell. 'History lesson?'

'You kind of asked for this one,' said Evelyn.

Campbell nodded, accepting his fate as Luke grinned, full-toothed.

'Oh yes you did,' he said enthused. 'The year is 1817, the Prince Regent, soon to be known as George IV, issues a royal warrant to Mr Walter Scott to recover the "*lost*" Honours of Scotland, the crown jewels not seen in over a hundred years.'

'Why do you say "*lost*" like that?' asked Campbell, mimicking the air quotes Luke had used.

'Because they were never lost,' said Luke derisively. 'Sometime around the Act of Union in 1707 they were shut in a box in Edinburgh Castle and not looked at again. The warrant was less to recover the Honours than to check they were still where the monarchy thought they had left them.'

'It's not lost if someone knows where it is,' Evelyn added.

'Exactly, now, the recovery of the Honours wasn't the idea of the young Prince George but was the result of not insignificant prompting by Scott and his good friend, one Adam Ferguson.'

'A.F.,' finished Campbell.

Luke dropped the watch into Campbell's outstretched hand.

'Sure, Scott got a Baronetcy and Fergusson was appointed deputy keeper of the crown jewels of Scotland for their recovery, pretty good motivation, but, I wonder if it was all just an excuse to look for one of Scotland's other lost royal treasures, one that Prince George didn't even know was missing, one that, as far as he was aware, he'd been crowned sat atop.'

The high sun dipped behind a cloud, stealing the warm breeze, and leaving behind a frigid wind blowing off the loch.

'Ok,' said Campbell processing, 'but who is T.T.?'

Luke opened his mouth, barely getting halfway through the sentence. *'Now that one I admit, I don't know,'* when Evelyn said slowly:

'Thomas Thompson.'

Campbell and Luke turned to her in unison.

'Thomas Thompson,' she said again, more confidently.

Luke and Campbell looked at her blankly.

'When I was studying Scott, I read a book of his letters, one was about the appointment of a new deputy Clerk, Thomas Thompson. Scott raved about his excitement for what Thompson would discover, that he was a font of knowledge on Scottish history.'

Evelyn Smiled at Luke and Campbell's expressions.

'Giving history lessons is fun,' she winked at Luke. 'I see why you do it.'

It was Luke's turn to roll his eyes at her. Campbell was still processing the storm of information.

'If this story about Robert the Bruce and the spider is a clue, then we just need to go wherever it happened,' he said, reinvigorated that they had finally got a heading. 'Where is the cave?'

'Kings cave, Machrie, on the Isle of Arran,' said Luke, strangely monotone and cold.

'Ok then that's worth a try!' Campbell started towards the track off the castle mount.

'Or was it King's cave in Drumadoon, or Blackwaterfoot?' continued Luke walking towards Campbell. 'Kirkpatrick-Fleming, Dailly, Campbelltown maybe?'

Campbell frowned at him.

'Everywhere wants to claim a piece of the Bruce legend.'

'Ok you've made your point,' growled Campbell.

'What about Daniel?'

'What about him?' said Luke spinning on Evelyn.

'There were the records from the Clerk of Sessions office in the courthouse in Glasgow, maybe there are letters between Scott and Thompson that might have a clue to which cave it is.'

'Still failing to see what Daniel has to do with this,' said Luke irreverently, furrowing his brows in mock confusion.

Evelyn ignored Luke's childishness. 'He has access to the records; he could help us.'

'I think we're doing fine without Mr Perfect's help.' Luke winced, his words coming out with an overtone of jealousy that he hadn't intended.

Evelyn narrowed her eyes.

'Are you jealous of him?'

'Jealous?' Luke snorted. 'I just don't trust him.'

Evelyn threw her hands up. 'He's a good man.'

'He's a lawyer.'

'He's trying to do good, he's standing in the next election, trying to make a change.'

Luke's laugh was vicious. 'A politician, that's your argument to make me trust him?'

'Will you two cut it out!' Campbell yelled, the force in his voice making Luke and Evelyn stop dead.

'Have you forgotten why we're looking for the stone or do you just not care?' Luke was in Campbell's crosshairs.

'We find the stone, we find who killed John and you're throwing away help just because of some petty rivalry?'

For once, Luke kept his mouth shut. Campbell forced down his emotion, not letting his walls break.

'Exactly, I'll call...'

'And you,' Campbell turned on Evelyn. 'Your brother is dead, or have you forgotten that? You seem more interested in running around with Knight than you do in finding the stone.'

Campbell knew he'd gone too far but he didn't care, enough was enough.

'How dare you,' Evelyn spat, her eyes raging with anger. 'How dare you. John was my family, not yours.' Evelyn cursed the tears blurring her vision.

Campbell walked up to Evelyn, stopping by her side. 'Then start acting like it!'

He brushed past her, heading out of the ruined castle to the track beyond.

'You weren't the only one who loved him.'

'He was my brother,' shouted Evelyn after him, the tears she had been keeping in for days, now flooding down her face. 'Who was he even to you?'

'He was...' Campbell stopped, the words he wanted to say failing in his throat. He looked back over his shoulder one last time and bit out, 'my friend,' before walking away. Disappearing from sight.

Evelyn stood, not feeling the bite of the cold breeze, not feeling anything. A shadow loomed over her as Luke quietly stood by her side.

'Give me your phone, I'll call Daniel.'

She reached into her pocket and pulled out her phone, handing it to Luke without looking.

Luke took it and left Evelyn staring across the island.

He crossed the ruined threshold of the castle and stood with his back to the land, looking across the grey water. He let out a breath and dialled the number in Evelyn's phone. He had some serious damage control to do.

A sound from behind him made Luke's head snap around, a chiming, like a ringtone.

'There's really no need to call, Luke.'

'Daniel?'

Something hard hit the back of Luke's head. A dull, sickening pain bloomed, bringing with it a foggy darkness into the edges of his vision, his ears ringing. Luke felt his body fail him, sliding to the ground. Luke heard a scream behind him. He couldn't force his body to move, his muscles shutting down completely. A face loomed over him, sneering, bruised.

Corban laughed but the sound didn't reach Luke's ears, the ringing growing too loud. The haze in his vision spread closing across the light until all was black.

CHAPTER 20

Darkness there and nothing more

Luke was vaguely aware that he was moving. Consciousness drifted back slowly, a nauseous ebb and flow like the tide, waves of darkness drowning him, dragging him back to nothingness. The periods of lucidity grew longer, hazy flashes of light and stabs of sound, like a radio being tuned in and out, reached him in bursts. Thoughts flew through Luke's head, too fast, too many. Focus Luke, said a voice from somewhere in the dark of his mind. His thoughts stilled. Answer the questions that will keep you alive.

'Am I alive?' Luke questioned himself.

Something jolted his body making pain explode from the back of his head and lighting the dark with a blinding starburst.

'Ok definitely alive.' Luke focused on his thoughts, trying to fight through the pain and keep his grip on the last thin strands of consciousness.

What would keep him alive?

Someone had attacked him. The twisted smile on Corban's battered face formed in Luke's mind. The twins; he should have been more careful. Another face replaced Corban's the soft brown hair and narrow eyes, the phoney accent. Daniel. It was Daniel. It had always been Daniel.

Not important right now, focus.

Where was he?

Moving, definitely moving, but where?

He was sat upright, that much he could tell, against something hard, but warm, not stone or concrete, wood maybe? The floor beneath him was moving, seeming to rise and fall, smoothly, rhythmically, like…

A boat!

Why the hell was he on a boat?

Luke forced his eyes to open, his body protested, still recovering from the blow to his head. Luke pushed on, peeling his eyelids apart just enough to see through. The light was blinding after the absolute darkness. The long rays of the low afternoon sun whited out Luke's vision, like a photograph that had been overexposed. Luke screwed his eyes back shut, the pain in his head nearly as blinding as the light.

'Come on Luke,' he whispered.

He blinked, forcing his eyes to stay open long enough to focus on the surroundings.

He was definitely on a boat, that much he could see. An expensive boat at that. As his vision cleared a polished, exotic wood deck came into view, dotted with chromed cleats and railings, shining like jewellery around the neck of an aristocrat. Something shifted at the edge of his vision, a person, their body elongated and distorted to Luke's eyes in the flare of the light. The figure moved towards Luke; it spoke but the words evaporated into the fog lingering in Luke's head.

The figure moved closer again, crouching to look Luke in the face. Daniel.

The fog in his head vanished, replaced by a fire. Luke snapped fully awake and lunged for Daniel. Adrenaline overcoming the weakness in his muscles. It wasn't enough, he was too slow.

Daniel took a casual step back, moving out of Luke's reach and instead sending him sprawling to the polished deck and causing another wave of sickening pain to lance through his head.

Daniel leant over Luke's body.

'Excellent, you're awake,' Daniel drawled dryly. 'I was beginning to think Corban had hit you too hard, he does get a little overzealous sometimes.'

Luke winced hard, fighting against the heavy blanket of pain that was threatening to take him over again.

'Get him up,' snapped Daniel, a disgusted sneer twisting his features. 'I was really expecting more from a man of your reputation, Mr Knight.'

Solid arms hoisted Luke roughly off of the deck,

one of the twins he assumed, and dumped him back into the hard wooden chair he had woken up in.

Luke bit down on a cry of pain. 'Give me a minute to stop seeing stars and I'll make you regret underestimating me,' he ground out.

Daniel seemed genuinely amused by Luke's threat.

'It's good to see Corban didn't damage your ego.' He leaned toward Luke, hovering next to his ear, and whispered viciously, 'if I, were you, I wouldn't go trying anything stupid.'

Daniel shifted to his right, giving Luke an unobstructed view across the deck to where Evelyn sat in an identical chair. Her expression filled with a barely contained rage, like a wolf locked in the cage of her mind. Someone stood next to her, Corban's twin, his arms crossed casually across his body, pointing the cold steel barrel of the 1911 pistol at Evelyn. Luke shot to his feet trying to cross the short space to her but was stopped by a vice like grip on his shoulder that forced him awkwardly back into his seat.

'Don't worry she's quite safe.'

Luke snarled like an animal, baring his teeth. 'You dare.'

'Dougal is under strict instructions not to lay a finger on her,' Daniel paused, focusing intently on Luke, 'provided you do as you're told.'

Luke opened his mouth to threaten him again

but stopped, he looked back at the man stood next to Evelyn, his anger replaced momentarily by amusement.

'Dougal?' Luke said with a smirk.

Daniel frowned. 'Yes?'

'Corban and Dougal?'

Corban's rough accent growled behind Luke's head.

'You have some sort of problem with our names?'

Luke turned to look at Corban's bruised face.

'Not at all,' he said. 'Just, Corban and Dougal the twin criminals, really? What was the problem, Ronnie and Reggie already taken?'

Luke's head snapped around and before he knew what had hit him, pain shot through his jaw as well as his head. Corban raised his hand to punch Luke again but was halted by a waved hand from Daniel.

Luke spat a mouthful of blood onto the deck, feeling the split in his lip sting as he did.

'Ouch,' said Luke sarcastically.

Daniel sighed theatrically. 'For future reference, that's an example of something stupid.'

'Noted,' spat Luke.

'The same goes for you Evelyn, make good decisions and I won't hurt Luke,' Daniel's smile was that of a jackal. 'Much.'

Dougal chuckled mirthlessly, moving to stand before Evelyn. He leant down to her height.

'I would listen to him,' he said running a finger

across her cheek. 'It would be a shame to ruin such a pretty face.'

Evelyn smiled sarcastically, he frowned, confused as Evelyn threw her head forward catching him with her forehead across the front of his face, breaking his nose with a sickening crack.

'Bugger,' said Dougal. He stumbled back, pinching the bridge of his mangled nose, his face distorted with rage at the sight of the blood that came away on his fingers.

'Oh look, you're identical again,' Evelyn smiled.

Dougal snapped, raising his arm and struck Evelyn across the face with the back of his hand. Evelyn righted herself in the chair, her cheek shining, already beginning to bruise. Tears stung her eyes, but she refused to let them fall, she wouldn't give him the satisfaction. Luke made to lunge for Dougal but was halted by the pressure of the gun barrel held to his head.

'That's enough,' snapped Daniel. 'All of you.' He aimed the last pointedly at Dougal who shrunk back into himself like a scolded child.

'Mr Knight, if you could keep a cage on your insolence for five minutes, I think it would benefit everyone.' Daniel's exasperation was audible.

Luke looked past him to Evelyn, sat slumped in her chair. Her hands were bound behind her with a length of mooring line. She hadn't stood a chance at defending herself, taking the full force of Dougal's blow. Luke could see the bruise on her cheek growing darker already as she raised her head. Luke met her eyes and projected a silent, '*Are you ok?*'

Evelyn nodded, just a slight inclining of her head, too subtle for Daniel or the twins to notice but enough to tell Luke, '*I'm fine.*' The corner of her mouth twisted into the ghost of a wicked grin. '*I gave worse than I got.*'

Luke smiled weakly before turning back to Daniel, his features hardening.

'What do you want Montrose?'

Daniel chewed his lip, bemused.

'Come now Luke, they told me you were intelligent.' He laid a hand on Luke's shoulder and hissed. 'We both know what I want.'

Luke shook him off and swallowed, the salty, metallic tang of blood pooling from his lip slid into his throat.

'I don't know where the stone is.'

'I find that hard to believe,' said Daniel dryly.

Luke locked Daniel's stare and doubled down, stubbornly.

'I don't know, the castle was a dead end, someone beat us there by a hundred years. Give or take a few decades,' he added flippantly.

Daniel sighed and reached inside his jacket, retrieving something that he kept out of Luke's sight.

'Well, that's unfortunate, I go to all this effort

to track you across the country.' Daniel held up a sheet of paper, unfolding it slowly. 'You know after John betrayed me, I thought I would never find the stone. Imagine my joy when I found none other than his own sister on the trail, it really was a stroke of luck. How disappointing that you're telling me the stone is... lost in time.'

Luke's head snapped up; his eyes focused on the sheet of paper.

'That's how Scott describes it anyway,' Daniel smiled at Luke's stunned confusion 'That is who got to Inchmurrin before you isn't it?'

He handed Luke the sheet of paper. It was old, a heavy, expensive, cotton fibre sheet written on in a fine cursive script only achieved by a fountain pen in an expert hand.

Dear Thomas,

Firstly, I must thank you for your assistance. Your knowledge of our great country's past is truly without parallel, I fear without it we would have been buried by our task as you yourself are by the books that proved our salvation. It is a cause for joy that the Honours are restored to their rightful place. I fear I must report that the search for certain other objects of significance to our nation have not been as fruitful and that we have been left in the dark.

It would appear those secrets are lost in time.

Yours,

Walter Scott.

Luke raised his head from the page only to see Daniel's smug face. He sauntered towards Luke and plucked the page out of his hands, folding it neatly in half before tucking it back in his breast pocket.

'What do you suppose that means Luke, "lost in time"?'

'I don't....' Luke started.

Daniel held out a large gold pocket watch, dangling from its chain, *the* pocket watch. Luke reached instinctively for his own pocket where that watch had been. Gone.

'A word of advice,' said Daniel exasperated, reaching back inside his jacket, 'don't lie to me again.'

Daniel held out a long, elegant, blackened steel revolver. The brass trigger guard and backstrap glinted in the sun like the pocket watch, nearly as stunning thought Luke, if it weren't for the fact it was pointing at him.

'1851 Colt Navy,' said Daniel twisting the barrel

of the revolver, aligning a chamber with the cocked hammer. 'Not my usual style but I couldn't help but admire the poetry of killing an archaeologist with an antique.'

Luke didn't breathe, didn't flinch. He stared down the cold octagonal barrel. Daniel's eye squinted, looking along the iron sights at Luke's heart.

'If it should come to that.' He let his arm fall, taking the gun off of Luke with it. Luke let out a slow breath, unable to hide that the gun had rattled him.

'Now, let's try this again, where did Scott take the stone?'

Daniel swung the watch back and forth in front of Luke's face, like he was trying to hypnotise the answers out of him.

'I'm assuming you figured out the Scott's clue, lost in time, very clever,' he said sarcastically. 'But *if the spider should fail,* what does that mean?'

'I…' Luke began.

'Don't lie to me!' Daniel exploded. Regaining his composure he hissed, 'poor John lied to me and what a waste that was.'

Evelyn spat from behind him. 'He was your friend you bastard, he trusted you and you killed him.'

Daniel sauntered over to where Evelyn sat tied to the chair. 'John was an unfortunate loss, collateral damage in the pursuit of a greater end.

He tried to take the stone from me, to deny me, it's rightful heir.'

'Rightful heir?' snorted Luke. 'You?'

Daniel's head snapped back to Luke.

'Yes, Mr Knight, the stone and its promise of power are mine, it belongs to me.'

'It belongs to Scotland, to the people!' Argued Evelyn to Daniel's back. He ignored her.

Luke fixed Daniel's glare. 'It belongs in a museum.'

Daniel frowned, confused at Luke's sudden smile. Luke looked past him, catching Evelyn's eye.

'I've always wanted to say that.'

Evelyn rolled her eyes. 'Is this really the time?'

Luke wiped the smile off his face and focused back on Daniel.

'Regardless of where it belongs, it's not worth killing for!'

Daniel let out a slow breath through his nose and rocked on his heels.

'But that's where you're wrong, it's not the stone itself that's worth killing for, it's the power, the power over a country.'

Luke gave him a sceptical look.

'You know just having the stone doesn't make you king, right?'

Daniel wiped a hand down his face, his growing frustration becoming difficult to tame.

'You're missing the point Mr Knight, this

country is ready for a revolution, a rebellion. All it needs is a spark, a symbol and a man with the vision to use it.'

'And that would, be you?'

'Who better?'

'I can think of one or two,' Luke said under his breath.

Corban's hand cracked Luke across the back of his head. The sickening ache in his head bloomed anew making him sway in his chair, fighting the urge to vomit.

'Thank you Corban. I did warn you Mr Knight.'

Luke pushed past the pain, regaining his focus on the egotistical maniac in front of him.

'Why? Why would you go to all this trouble just to start a political crisis, what's in it for you?'

'What else?' said Daniel, as if the answer were painfully obvious. 'Power and money, quite a bit of money in fact.'

'Let me guess,' spat Luke, disgusted. 'You're going to set yourself up as the hero, the new William Wallace smiting the English in politics and become the obvious choice for a leader, a king in an independent land.'

A broad, full-toothed grin spread across Daniel's face.

'That's a very entertaining story Mr Knight, you should write fiction. It might sell better than your last book.'

Luke bit back a retort to Daniel's stab, the

inevitable blow from Corban wasn't worth calling him an asshole.

'My plans aren't nearly so dreadfully convoluted.' Daniel strutted back and forth across the deck, grandstanding and preening like a peacock. 'Yes, setting myself up in power is a part of it, only a small part mind, a mere drop in the ocean, and it's the ocean I really want.'

Luke frowned.

'Or rather what's under the ocean.' Added Daniel.

Understanding dawned on Luke's face.

'North sea oil,' he said in disbelief. 'All of this has been about oil.'

'Of course, the oil that lies under the North Sea will be the black gold in my crown,' said Daniel triumphantly. 'You see, I learnt something interesting about international law, once I have made this country free of England, natural resources that were shared will have to be divided. It just so happens that a lovely little agreement in Geneva means that Scotland will have rights to over 91% of the oil in the North Sea that is currently shared amongst this *"United"* Kingdom.'

He said the last with the disgust of a person who had trodden in something unpleasant.

'But the oil won't be yours, it'll belong to Scotland!' said Evelyn with expert condescension.

Daniel turned slowly on his heel, and moved,

stalking towards her.

'You see Evelyn that's where you're wrong, like Luke said, I have the stone, I spark a rebellion and make myself the hero who regained our freedom, the obvious leader. Yes, Scotland will control the oil, but I will control Scotland and there has never been a better time than now, which is why I need you to stop lying to me Mr Knight.'

Luke frowned, why now? What was the rush? Something flapping in the wind on the distant banks of the loch caught Luke's eye, tiny flags forming strings of red, white and blue bunting lined the road that ran along the shore. 'The coronation; you need to do this before the King's coronation.'

Daniel sighed, 'as I said, I am under some time pressure, being crowned on the Stone of Destiny is the monarch's symbol of rule over Scotland. If I can show the stone is fake then the power it commands is just as fraudulent, and the people have the push they need to rebel.'

'Murder, kidnapping, treason... anything else you want to add to the list?' spat Luke.

Daniel raised the barrel of the gun.

'You still can't profit from it, not unless you steal from the country,' said Evelyn quickly, 'that can only go on so long before you get caught and exposed for the bastard you are.'

Luke chewed on his lip, he was missing something, focus.

'Exploration licences,' he said suddenly.

Clearly his brain had been running slowly because of the blows from Corban and what he suspected was a fairly strong concussion. Evelyn and Daniel both looked at him with surprise.

'He won't control the oil, but he will control the exploration licenses.'

Daniel began to clap slowly, a surprised admiration curling the corners of his mouth into an involuntary smile.

'Maybe I did underestimate you, Mr Knight.'

Luke stared daggers back at him.

'You see Evelyn, I will have control over who gets to explore and extract oil that will belong to Scotland,' continued Daniel. 'And it just so happens that I, or rather a shell company that can't be linked back to me, own large shares of several oil companies that I have a sneaking suspicion will be the ones winning bids for exploration licences under my rule.'

'And all hidden behind a mask of patriotism,' Luke mocked.

A deathly silence fell across the boat, the only sounds the gentle waves splashing against the hull and the seagulls flying overhead.

'You're mad,' said Evelyn viciously, splitting the silence.

Daniel sneered at her, moving closer, like a predator stalking its kill.

'You know that's exactly what your saintly

brother said when he found out why I wanted the stone.'

Evelyn recoiled at Daniel's mention of John, her emotions threatening to spill over.

Daniel continued, 'he refused to tell me what he had found too, let's not let history repeat itself.'

Evelyn spat on Daniel's dark, polished shoes. 'Murderer.'

Daniel looked disappointedly at her; he didn't bother wiping his shoe clean.

'I told you, John sealed his own fate.'

'You pulled the trigger,' she hissed, all the venom of a viper behind her words.

'Actually, I had Corban do that,' he said flippantly.

Something in Evelyn snapped, she threw her body forward, fighting against the ropes binding her to the chair, the rough cord cutting into her bare wrists. She didn't care, she fought, trying to tear Daniel apart but not reaching him. Daniel stood a mere step out of her reach with a bored expression.

'If everyone is quite finished,' he said, turning his back on Evelyn, leaving her shaking with rage, and addressing Luke.

'I am going to ask you One. Last. Time.' He paused after each word, every rest a threat. 'The clue on the watch, what does '*if the spider should fail mean*'? Where is the stone?'

'Screw you,' Luke spat.

It was worth the blow to the jaw from Corban.

Daniel raised the barrel of the revolver to Luke's chest.

'Try again.'

'Up yours?'

The grin fell from Daniel's face.

'I can see we are going to have to try a change of tack,' he sighed. Daniel clicked his fingers and from behind him Evelyn yelped. Daniel stood aside letting Luke see Dougal pressing the cold steel muzzle of his 1911 pistol against Evelyn's temple.

'I would really hate to do this,' said Daniel.

Luke's mind went into overdrive, the bath of adrenaline washing away the lingering fog. He couldn't take his eyes off the silver barrel. Off of Evelyn's panicked face.

'Stop this Daniel, I don't know where the stone is.'

'I think you're lying,' said Daniel turning the pocket watch over in his hand to look at the face, '30 seconds, then shoot her.'

Dougal nodded at Daniel's back, his attention hadn't shifted from Luke.

Luke shot to his feet, knocking the chair back painfully into Corban's shins, stopping him from pinning Luke to the seat with his talon like fingers.

'Call off your dog Montrose, I don't…'

Daniel ignored him. 'Time's ticking Luke.'

He tossed Luke the watch, the golden circle falling into Luke's hand. He could feel the gears of the movement counting away the seconds against his palm.

'Ten.' Daniel started counting.

Tick.

'Nine.'

Tick.

Luke made towards Daniel but was halted by Corban, having shoved aside the chair, grabbing the back of his jacket.

'Daniel stop!' he shouted.

'Eight.'

Tick.

'King's Cave,' Luke blurted.

Daniel held up a hand, staying Dougal, he examined Luke with an equal measure of suspicion and triumph.

'So, you were lying to me,' said Daniel. 'Tut tut, very naughty.'

Luke seethed. 'I didn't lie to you, it's a line from *The King and the Spider*, the clue is the cave Robert the Bruce took refuge from the English in.'

'King's Cave,' finished Daniel.

'Yes,' spat Luke, 'but there are more of them than there have been Kings of Scotland, it could be any of them.'

Daniel walked slowly towards Luke, positioning his face a hair's breadth from Luke's.

'Then figure it out,' hissed Daniel. 'If anyone can

then it's the brilliant Luke Knight.'

Luke rubbed his forehead and snapped.

'Fine, just give me some time.'

Daniel's face softened, becoming almost friendly.

'Of course, I'm not an unreasonable man Luke,' said Daniel. 'You still have seven seconds.'

Luke started.

'Daniel…'

'Seven.'

'There's no way…'

'You're wasting time Knight,' said Daniel mockingly. 'Six.'

Luke's mind raced, too many, there were too many choices.

'Five.'

And that wasn't helping, the watch ticking echoed in Luke's ears drowning out all other sound. He could just tell Daniel any place, send him on a wild goose chase. And when he finds nothing then he kills us, death now or death later, not much of a choice.

'Four.'

Think, think, thought Luke, his mind rattled through the possibilities, the impossible task of deciding on just one.

'Three.'

Where? He needed more time, more information.

'Two.'

'It's on the Isle of Arran.' Shouted Evelyn.

Daniel spun around to her.

'Say again?'

Evelyn took a deep breath, steadying her nerves.

'In the stories The Bruce retreats to an island after his defeat by the English. The only King's caves on islands are the two on the Isle of Arran and one on Ratlin Island,' she said slowly, aware of the gun still to her head and the finger of the man whose nose she'd just broken curled around the trigger. 'Ratlin belongs to Northern Ireland. Scott wouldn't risk taking the stone out of Scotland, that leaves Arran.'

Daniel strode over to her, chewing his lip in thought.

'You said there are two king's caves on Arran, which one is it?'

'I don't...'

'Do not tell me you don't know!' exploded Daniel.

Evelyn, to her credit, didn't back down, didn't even flinch at his outburst. Luke couldn't help but admire her strength.

Evelyn fixed Daniel's glare, biting back.

'I don't, but two caves are a lot less to search than you had before.'

Daniel laughed, mirthless and fake, just like everything else about the man.

'Well, well, it looks like Evelyn has learnt a thing or two from you Luke.'

Luke didn't return his amusement.

'She was brilliant long before she met me.'

Luke caught Evelyn's blush over Daniel's shoulder. Daniel turned to follow Luke's eye. He stopped smiling when he saw Evelyn's face.

'You're right Mr Knight.' Daniel paced the deck, waving a hand at Dougal to drop the gun. 'Lucky me having two brilliant experts to find me the stone.'

He stopped pacing in front of Luke, once again smiling cruelly.

'Shame I only need one.'

Daniel raised his arm, the Colt Navy revolver still clasped in his grip. Luke was helpless as Daniel's finger squeezed, the hammer dropped striking the cap on the chamber and igniting the powder inside.

Evelyn cried out, but the sound was extinguished by the crack of the lead ball leaving the barrel, travelling on its inexorable path.

Luke felt the impact like being kicked in the chest, unimaginable pressure, but no pain. He looked down at the hole in his jacket, the edges of the fabric singed, black. Black at the edge of his vision. He looked back up at Daniel's face, sneering, triumphant and Evelyn distraught, fighting against the ropes, against Dougal.

The darkness spread. Luke stumbled back, collapsing into the low railing that curled around the gunwale.

He was falling, then his head hit water, the cold

engulfing his body, then nothing. Darkness there, and nothing more.

Daniel blew the smoke away from the barrel of the revolver before handing it to Corban who waited with a cloth to wipe down the handle.

Evelyn was spitting venom at him, but he didn't care, the stone was within his grasp.

'Dougal.'

'Yes sir?'

Daniel smiled. 'Set a course for Arran.'

Dougal turned and started towards the helm.

'Oh, and Dougal.'

The suited killer stopped and faced Daniel.

Daniel nodded towards Evelyn, still hurling abuse at him. 'Shut her up will you.'

"A ruin should always be protected but never repaired – thus may we witness full the lingering legacies of the past."

SIR WALTER SCOTT

CHAPTER 21

200 Meters North East of Inchmurrin Castle, Inchmurrin, Loch Lomond

Campbell stormed down the hillside crowned by the tumbled ruins of Inchmurrin Castle. The look on Evelyn's face as he had left the summit was playing on his mind. Had he been too harsh? No. She needed to know how he felt as much as he needed to say it out loud. He took the path through the castle ditch at a quick pace, turning left away from the jetty, towards the west coast of the island and the sparse copse that edged the rocky shoreline. He trudged down the shallow embankment towards the water's edge. The grass gave way to a treacherous mosaic of moss-covered stones that Campbell's smart, rubber-soled shoes, while being great for city policing, were very much not suited for crossing. His foot skidded across the top of a flat stone, painfully twisting his knee in the process, Campbell swore lashing out and kicking a small stone that went skittering across the ground before splashing into the loch with feeble plop. He let out a frustrated growl cursing the pain in his knee and beginning to regret kicking the stone as his toes protested at the impact. He risked a few more steps before dropping wearily onto one of the larger boulders. His limbs felt heavy, the adrenaline leaving his body and taking the last of his temper with it. The silence in the copse was welcomely serene after the chaos of the last day, the narrow band of trees cutting off the shore from the rest of the island, a rare slither of peace in the world. Campbell sighed, guilt over his outburst creeping up on him nauseatingly quickly. He should apologise, not for what he said, he stood by that but his delivery left a lot to be desired. He turned his head, looking across the gentle grey of the loch, the perfect mirrored surface had been broken by the radiating wake of boats passing the island.

Campbell gazed at the broken reflection on the water's surface, the trees and the castle mount distorted by the low waves twisting the features into a surrealist portrait of the landscape. He could just make out the commanding figure of Luke atop the knoll, framed by the ruined castle walls. He'd been unfair to Luke, he was trying to help them, hell he had no reason to even care about John. To Luke he was no different to any other missing person and now he's been put through more than any sane person would put up with. Although, if he was honest, he wasn't sure Luke was entirely in his right mind. Campbell blew out a long breath, steadying the nerves that were feeling the effects of the adrenaline leaving his system. He made to push off from the boulder and head back towards the castle ruins to make his amends when a woman's shout broke the stillness of the island. Evelyn? Campbell risked his ankles and sprinted across the jagged rocks. He stopped short of the edge of the copse and shielded himself behind one of the more heavily vegetated trees. Luke was no longer standing on the hill, instead his wiry frame was slumped in a ragged pile over the low broken wall with the sneering face of one of the twins looming above, too far away for Campbell to make out which one. The suited hitman spun at a shout from someone walking out from the ruined castle, the other twin dragging a struggling Evelyn in tow. Campbell strained his vision at the man giving orders to the twins.

'You bastard,' hissed Campbell under his breath.

He'd only met Daniel Montrose a handful of times before, but he couldn't mistake the smug, self-righteous face that made him want to reconsider his stance on police brutality. Daniel. John's own friend had ordered his murder. Campbell had to check his anger before he ran back up the knoll and killed Daniel with his bare hands. Luckily Campbell's voice of reason shouted louder than hate, even with his police issue Glock 17 pistol the odds of him overpowering three armed men on his own were slim. He was no use to Luke and Evelyn dead and he doubted Daniel would have any qualms about having him killed. Campbell backed further into the cover of the copse, positioning himself so he still had a view of the ruined castle. Bitter helplessness, not a feeling Campbell was used to, but he could feel nothing else as he watched Luke being dragged unconscious down the slope of the knoll, Evelyn still struggling against one of the twins close behind. There was nothing he could do. He should never have left them at the castle. Another body and they might have stood a chance against Daniel and the twins, another set of eyes and they might not have been taken by surprise. It was his fault.

'Focus!'

The voice in Campbell's head cut through the noise of him spiralling towards the black.

It was right, self-pity was getting him nowhere. he could think of a way out of this, he *had* to think of a way out. Campbell shifted to his left, his foot catching on a rock mostly hidden by moss and dead leaves, making him flail for a grip to stop his stumble. His hand caught on the spindly lower branches of the tree he had sheltered behind, his weight suddenly thrown against the slender trunk shook the tree alarmingly and disturbed a crow roosting high in the branches, sending it flapping into the sky with a disgruntled *caw.* His grip slipped on the loose bark sending him falling painfully onto the rocky ground.

Campbell winced, cursing under his breath he froze, glued to the spot.

He risked a look towards the castle and immediately wished he hadn't.

The gaunt faces of the twins were trained on the thin tree line hiding Campbell. Daniel, only a few steps behind them had lost his smug grin, replaced by a thin-lipped, predatory glare.

'Just turn around, keep walking,' muttered Campbell in a half prayer to whatever god was listening.

Apparently none of them.

One of the twins, the one with the bruised face, Corban—that's what Luke had said the other twin had called him while Campbell had been unconscious—reached into his jacket.

Campbell cursed again as Corban withdrew the sleek 1911 pistol, holding it with his arm crooked, the barrel pointing towards the sky.

There was nothing he could do now, Campbell held his breath and reached slowly for his own gun.

'Corban,' Daniel's voice echoed across the island. 'go and see what that was, we can't afford any more delays.'

Corban didn't move, his head shifted back and forth, eyes scanning the trees.

'It was just an animal, let's go,' growled Dougal.

'What if it's the detective?'

'Then he's going to be stuck on the island and won't be our problem anymore,' said Dougal condescendingly.

'I don't think...'

'I don't pay you to think Dougal,' snapped Daniel. 'I pay you to do what I goddamn tell you, got it?'

Dougal ground his teeth, straining against the urge to argue.

Corban padded towards the tree line.

Think. Campbell reached slowly for the holster at his hip, maybe he wouldn't have a choice about taking on three armed men.

Closer, Corban was almost at the copse's edge, there was no way of hiding from him once he broke the line tangled brambles that shielded Campbell.

There was nothing for it, Campbell took a deep breath and pulled his pistol free. If he was going down he wasn't going to make it easy for them.

A twig snapped somewhere in front of him, followed by a yelp from Corban as a huge ginger tomcat jumped out of the briar clutching a very dead bird in its jaws.

Corban cursed. 'It's just a bloody cat.'

Campbell let out a slow unsteady breath, relief flooding his body.

He watched as Corban re-joined Daniel and his brother, grabbing the still motionless Luke before continuing their path away from the castle.

Campbell didn't move until they were out of

sight. He watched them take the track, not towards the jetty he, Luke and Evelyn had arrived on but instead along the western coast towards a whitewashed farmhouse.

He got to his feet and picked his way towards where the cat sat with its quarry licking its paws. He leant down and scratched the cat between its ears.

'You might be my new best friend.'

Campbell looked back towards the farmhouse and stepped back into the copse. Carefully picking his way across the uneven ground he followed Daniel and the twins from the cover of the woods that lined to the coast.

The trees grew denser and the untamed briar and bramble snagged on Campbell's clothes as he passed the farmhouse, still trailing Daniel and the twins as they cut off the track and made towards a narrow strip of beach that led to a rickety private dock. The needle-like thorns of wild rose embedded themselves into the fragile skin on the back of Campbell's hand has he crouched behind a tangle of bushes at the edge of the strip of beach, forcing him to bite back a yelp.

A small rowing boat was moored to the dock, bobbing gently on the calm loch water. The twins heaved Luke into the tiny boat, leaving him slumped against the bow, before forcing Evelyn onto one of the hard wooden seats. The rowing boat was barely big enough to fit all five of them and sat low in the water from the extra weight. Corban cast off the mooring rope and pushed off of the wooden dock, starting them gently out into the open loch before picking up a pair of oars and slotting them into the brass row locks.

Campbell let out the mass of curses he had held in until he was sure the rowboat was far enough out they wouldn't hear him and picked the rose thorns out of his hand.

The rowboat was headed towards a sleek, modest-sized, wooden yacht anchored just north of the island.

'Of course you have a yacht,' muttered Campbell.

The rowboat bumped against the dark wooden hull of the yacht, bobbing on the placid water as Corban dropped the oars and threw a mooring rope over one of the chromed cleats set into the deck and pulled the rowboat tight alongside the yacht.

Campbell's anger, mixed with frustration threatened to overwhelm him. He could do nothing but watch as Luke and Evelyn were unceremoniously bundled into chairs that had been arranged facing each other on opposite sides of the narrow deck. Evelyn struggled as one of the twins roughly bound her hands behind the chair.

Luke's limp form was left unrestrained, slumped awkwardly and still out cold. At least he was only unconscious. It had been more than a few minutes since he had been knocked out and

Campbell knew how dangerous that could be, much longer and...

Campbell stopped his thoughts before they went there. He needed to keep the dark away.

'Focus. Think,' said the voice in his head.

He couldn't do this on his own, he needed to call in help. He was going to be in a whole heap of trouble for the mess he had caused, not to mention aiding persons of interest in evading the police, but he was out of options.

He reached into his pocket for his phone, his fingers brushed against something sharp and he snatched them away.

'You have got to be kidding me,' he muttered gingerly, trying for his phone again only to find the screen shattered, the glass spiderwebbed in a thousand tiny shards from where it had struck the rocks after he had fallen.

He swore and shoved the broken phone back into his pocket.

He was on his own. No backup and up the creek without a...

Campbell's eye caught something sticking out of the sand at the other side of the narrow beach.

Another rowing boat sat upside down, long abandoned, against the grassy bank that formed the edge of the beach. It was half-buried by sand and fine gravel that had been blown over its form by months, if not years of Scottish wind.

Campbell glanced back at the yacht, still

anchored, still gently rolling side to side on the shimmering loch.

Daniel stood with his back to the shore, leaning in close to a groggy, but mercifully conscious Luke.

Campbell let out a long held breath. Luke was alive, but that was a small victory.

The barrel of a long silver revolver glinted from Daniel's hand, the weapon extended towards Luke and joined shortly by one of the twin's 1911 pistols trained on Evelyn.

Campbell swallowed, his mouth was as dry as sand. He couldn't wait any longer.

'For the love of God just don't provoke him,' said Campbell in vain hope that Luke would know when to keep his mouth shut.

He broke the cover of the tree line and walked briskly across the sand towards the buried boat.

The elements had really done a number on the little wooden rowboat.

The once crisp, white paint on the hull was peeled and flaking, exposing the wood underneath.

As Campbell drew closer he could see the picture wasn't much better. The springy cedar wood had been bleached by the sun to a skeletal white. Dry and brittle, the planks were riddled with alarming cracks. He doubted the wreck of a boat was even watertight but there weren't exactly a lot of other options.

He dropped to his knees as he reached the boat. The sharp points of the fine gravel within the sand digging into the skin on his shins.

There was nearly a foot of sand covering the stern of the rowboat where it sat with the bow sticking up in the air, making it look like an attempt at a scale model of the titanic sinking into a sea of sand.

An oar was discarded in the tangle of grass on the bank behind the rowboat, the wood was just as bleached of colour and cracked as the boat was. Campbell snatched it from the bank, tearing out clumps of grass and weeds that had grown around it.

He dug the blade into the sand, shifting it in swathes and slowly revealing the boat's form.

The sand must have built up quickly, thought Campbell as he revealed the buried hull. The paint was discoloured but still intact. The bare wood of the gunwale too had escaped the sun's bleaching.

Campbell checked back over his shoulder at the yacht, hoping its occupants were still too preoccupied to look back at the beach.

Luke was on his feet now, gesturing angrily at Daniel.

Campbell smirked, he'd like to see what it would take to keep that man down.

With the boat free of its tomb, Campbell righted it on the sand, letting the wreck sit on its keel.

Wreck was the word for it. The interior of the

row boat was in a better condition but then again, that wasn't much of a competition. Thankfully most of the splits in the wood didn't seem to reach all the way through the planks, only a handful allowing daylight through the hull.

'Still beats swimming,' muttered Campbell, although he wasn't sure he wouldn't end up in the water at some point given the thing keeping him dry.

Despite its relatively small size, it took an effort to drag the rowboat through the sand to the water's edge.

'Here goes nothing.'

Campbell heaved the boat the final feet so that it sat fully in the loch. By some small miracle the splits in the hull all sat above the waterline, that was until Campbell boarded the rowboat, his weight causing it to sink slightly and allow a thin, steady stream of water through the cracks.

'Give me a break.' Campbell dug the oar into the water with as much effort as he could muster, the need to get to the yacht now even greater.

The single oar didn't provide much propulsion and soon Campbell was hot, sweaty with the effort of keeping the rowboat moving. He strained against the weight of the water, stroke by stroke closing the gap between him and the yacht.

He could hear their voices, Luke and Evelyn... and Daniel, their vicious argument drifting to him on the breeze.

He was only a few hundred feet from the yacht now, he dug the oar back into the water, over and over, willing the little boat to move faster.

Something was wrong.

Campbell raised his head, the voices had stopped. He looked towards the yacht just as a single gunshot cracked the stillness of the isolated patch of loch.

The world froze. Time returned in slow motion, all sound absent except Campbell's own heartbeat.

He could do nothing but watch Luke stumble back, a thin wisp of smoke still lingering on the barrel of Daniel's revolver. Luke collapsed, tumbling over the gunwale of the yacht and hitting the water like a dead weight.

The world returned to normal all at once, catching Campbell off guard.

He abandoned the oar and dove overboard without a second thought.

The water of the Loch was frigid, the air from Campbell's lungs ripped away by the cold the second he was submerged and making him want to gasp in mouthfuls of the air he had left behind.

'Focus.'

He hung suspended in the stillness of the loch, willing his heart to calm, fighting the urge to breathe.

Campbell opened his eyes, the cold, fresh water was crystal clear below the surface, clear enough that he could see the crumpled form of Luke sinking into the murky depths. The cold was like a belt tightening around Campbell's chest. He kicked for the surface, gulping in air as his face broke the water. There was no time to fight the shock.

He dove again, kicking hard after Luke's body as it drifted further and further from reach. Campbell's lungs burned with the need for air, the basic instinct to breathe threatening to overpower reason. Luke was almost within his reach now, Campbell threw out his arm desperately towards Luke's body.

His fingers closed around Luke's billowing jacket, clamping tightly onto the sodden fabric. He pulled Luke towards him, arresting their descent and wrapping an arm tight around Luke's waist.

Luke was almost weightless in the water, making it easy work to half float and half swim back towards the surface.

Campbell's lungs were on fire, every inch they crept back up the louder his mind screamed at him to breathe. Breathe. Breathe!

The frigid water had eaten away at every last ounce of strength. Campbell's grip failed. Luke slipped from his grip and plummeted faster than Campbell could react. He ignored the part of his brain creaming for air and dived after Luke. Campbell could barely feel his arm make contact with Luke but he forced muscles to hold on. He hadn't realised how far they had sunk. The dappled surface of the water was impossibly far. Every fibre of his body was crying out for him to stop, to just take a breath. He ignored them and swam. With the last of his energy Campbell kicked towards the light, breaking the surface with an explosion of water and dragging Luke up beside him.

The sudden brightness was blinding, the sun reflected off of every facet of the rippling loch creating a disorientating silvery kaleidoscope.

Campbell looked around desperately for the row boat, trying to see through the glare but there was nothing but empty water.

It must have drifted while he was retrieving Luke.

There was no sign of Daniel's yacht either… no sign of anything he recognised.

He turned in the water, looking for anything at all.

There was land not far behind them. He started towards it, not caring what it was as long as it was dry.

His limbs ached, the adrenaline leaving his body and taking his strength with it. He struggled to keep a hold of Luke and keep moving.

How far had they drifted under the surface?

The island they were heading for wasn't Inchmurrin. It was smaller, much smaller, barely a hundred meters across.

A thick cloud drifted in front of the sun, cutting out the glare on the water.

Definitely not Inchmurrin.

Without the blinding light he could make out the ragged tumble of rock that made up the island. It was smaller than he had thought, but beggars can't be choosers. Land was land and it couldn't come soon enough. Even in the water Luke's weight was a strain on Campbell's sapped muscles. He pushed harder wincing against the pain in his limbs.

There was no gentle sandy coast on the tiny patch of land, instead the rocky shore seemed to erupt from the loch like it had been picked up and dumped there by some giant long in the past, out of place and in a stark contrast to the other islands in the loch.

Campbell struggled onto the boulders closest to the waterline. The rough stone cut into his palms as he braced himself against them and heaved Luke out of the loch.

Rivulets of water ran from Luke's clothes across the stone as Campbell pulled him clear onto the shore.

Luke's body sat limp, sprawled like a ragdoll across the rocks.

Campbell stared at the small ragged hole that was torn through the breast of Luke's jacket... straight over his heart.

He pulled the damp fabric away from Luke's chest, muttering prayers and begging that if they were ever going to be answered it was now.

Luke's shirt was peppered with tiny burn marks, the gun had been so close the black powder was still burning when the shot found its mark.

Campbell stopped.

Had it found it's mark?

Luke's shirt was far from the brilliant white it had been but there was a colour missing.

There was no blood, not so much as a drop staining the front of Luke's shirt.

Campbell stared in confusion at the hole in Luke's jacket.

How was there no blood?

Luke's chest rose so softly Campbell wasn't sure if he had imagined the movement.

He leant forward, reaching out to test the pulse in Luke's neck.

Campbell's fingers barely brushed the edge of Luke's throat when he sat bolt upright, sucking in air with a violent gasp.

Campbell jumped back with a start.

'He shot me,' said Luke in surprise.

Campbell stared back at him, open-mouthed, dumbstruck.

Luke's tone shifted from surprised to indignant.

'That utter bastard shot me.'

CHAPTER 22

Inchgalbraith, Loch Lomond, Luss, Argyll and Bute

'I really liked this jacket,' said Luke a little dismayed. He had propped himself up against the trunk of a tree that grew dangerously close to the edge of the island whilst holding his jacket out in front of him and wiggling his finger through the ragged hole in the breast.

Campbell still stared at him, mouth agape, like the Luke sat before him was a ghost that had risen from the depths and left behind Luke's actual body.

'You're not dead.'

Luke didn't look up from his jacket.

'Good spot,' he said dryly.

Campbell blinked, trying and failing to process the impossibility of Luke's survival.

'How are you not dead?'

Luke stopped probing his jacket and slipped something out of the inner pocket, before tossing it through the air to Campbell.

'Do you have a moment to talk about our lord and saviour Jesus Christ?' he said with a smirk.

Campbell opened his hand to see a small leather-bound bible with a silver crucifix set into the cover. Except where the effigy of Jesus should have been nailed to the cross he had instead been nailed by a .36 calibre lead ball that had bent the entire cross in on itself before coming to rest Leviticus deep in the thin bible pages. He turned the desecrated book back over and ran his fingers across the cracked leather. The tiny book might have stopped the shot but it had struck with enough force to bulge out the back of the book where it had hit. Campbell looked back up at Luke to see him experimentally prodding at a deep blackish-purple bruise over his chest.

'Someone up there must be looking out for you,' mused Campbell.

Luke winced as his fingers grazed the centre of the radiating bruise.

'Trust me,' he said through gritted teeth, 'if there is a God I'm going to be firmly on their naughty list.'

'God isn't Santa Claus,' laughed Campbell. 'You being alive is part of the plan. The world's not done with you yet.'

'Big white beard, always watching you, rewards the good, punishes the bad...' Luke counted off on his fingers grinning. 'You believe in God?' he asked curiously.

'Yes and no,' shrugged Campbell. 'My family are catholic but…'

Luke didn't wait for the rest of the sentence, he knew it wasn't going to come and he wasn't going to push for it either. Instead he got stiffly to his feet and wrung out his jacket before tying the damp fabric around his waist.

Campbell stayed transfixed by the few thin pages that stopped the force of a bullet.

'Why were you carrying a bible if you don't believe in God?'

Luke took a few shaky steps towards Campbell.

'I never said I don't believe in a God,' he said, grimacing at the pain in his chest. 'I just have issues with people telling me all the reasons why I'm going to hell.'

He took the bible from Campbell, holding it in the air between them before putting it back in the pocket of the jacket round his waist.

'That still doesn't explain why you have a bible in your pocket,' pushed Campbell, following after Luke as he began to pick his way around the narrow coast of the island.

Luke picked his way across the rocks. The ground quickly became loose underfoot, the consolidated rocks covered in a tumble of what looked like blocks of dressed stone.

'It was gift from Keir,' said Luke. 'I thought it was just a bit of good old catholic guilt in an attempt to stop me from robbing a bishop's grave but nothing with that priest is ever it's face value.'

Campbell nodded along to Luke's explanation.

'Hang on,' he stopped in his tracks, 'you robbed a bishop's grave?'

'You sound like you're surprised,' said Luke, smiling back over his shoulder.

'I thought there might have been a line somewhere.'

Luke shrugged, feigning a look of innocence. He continued to walk around the island, Campbell following behind. They rounded another overhanging tree, nearly walking straight into the corner of a crumbled square tower.

'Where are you going?'

'To the boat,' said Luke over his shoulder.

'What boat?'

Luke stopped and scanned the curving shoreline.

'The boat you got us here on,' he said as if it were obvious. 'We're not on Inchmurrin anymore and I'm assuming you didn't swim the entire way here.'

Luke frowned and turned back to Campbell.

'Where did you leave it anyway?'

Campbell walked to Luke's side and cleared his throat, raising his arm to point away from the island's shore and into the open water.

Without the dazzling glare of the sun it was easy to spot the ragged rowing boat.

'Ah,' said Luke flatly.

The boat was drifting, stranded in the middle of the Loch halfway between them and what Luke assumed was the northern shore of Inchmurrin. Not that it would be much use to them even if it were only a few feet away. The cracks in the hull had let in enough water to cause the boat to list alarmingly to starboard and even as they watched, it dipped lower and lower into the water.

'Well…,' said Luke, 'that's going to be a problem.'

The wind picked up across the loch, rustling the leaves on the island's trees and pushing the rowing boat steadily further away from Campbell and Luke.

'Maybe there's another boat on the island somewhere,' said Campbell hopefully, scanning the curving coastline.

'There won't be,' said Luke. 'No one lives here, not anymore anyway.'

Campbell rounded back on him.

'And how do you know that?' he scoffed. 'We don't even know where we are!'

Luke scuffed his shoe against the stones that made up the shore of the island.

'You see how the island looks like someone dumped a huge pile of rocks into the loch?'

Campbell nodded, still looking at Luke sceptically.

'That's because they did.'

'Who's they?'

'The people who lived here a hair under 3000 years ago,' said Luke.

Campbell waited for more from Luke.

'And they were...?'

Luke frowned at him suspiciously, not used to being asked to elaborate on a history lesson.

'Well, if you believe the Romans, and more specifically the geographer Ptolemy then they were a tribe called Damnonii.'

'Is that what they were called?'

'It's what Ptolemy called them and unless you happen to have a time machine in your pocket there's no way to prove otherwise.'

Luke stooped down and picked up one of the smaller loose stones that laid over the island's foundations.

'Anyway,' he continued, 'these Scottish Iron age people were pretty accomplished engineers and for one reason or another decided to put their skills to practise by building crannogs, these little artificial islands to live on.'

'And that's what that stone is?' said Campbell nodding at the stone in Luke's hand.

'No,' said Luke. 'This is from the castle behind you.'

Campbell turned to see that the crumbled wall they had almost piled into was actually a somewhat still intact, mostly, tower built across what must have been nearly the entire width of the island.

'Now I'm no expert,' said Luke vain attempt at modesty, 'in Scottish geography that is — medieval castles and Iron age feets of engineering I'm pretty damn good — but a crannog with a castle slapped on top of it? There's only one of those I know about which makes me pretty sure that were stood on Inchgalbraith, ancestral home of Clan Galbraith and Ptolemy's Damnonii.'

'Brilliant,' said Campbell, smiling broadly. 'Now how do we get off of the ancestral home of the Damnonii and the Galbraith's?'

'Haven't the foggiest,' said Luke, forcing his voice to stay bright. 'We need to find a way to get off this island and go after Daniel before Evelyn…,' Luke's throat caught as he remembered Evelyn, still at Daniel's mercy. 'My point is we can't do anything stuck here, we need to find a way off.'

'And how are we going to do that?' said Campbell frustratedly. 'The boat has all but sunk, we have no way to contact anyone and I don't know about you but I'm in no rush to try and swim back to civilisation.'

Something in the sky above Campbell's head caught Luke's attention, his eyes moved tracking it across the horizon and towards the loch.

Campbell carried on talking. 'So unless these brilliant Iron age people also built a lovely bridge to the mainland we are up the creek literally without a paddle.' Campbell let out a hysterical chuckle, 'hell, for all its worth we may as well try and magically sprout wings and fly out of here.'

Luke was still watching the sky behind Campbell.

'Are you even listening to me?'

Luke levelled his stare back at Campbell, his eyes wide.

'Yeah,' he said, 'we're going to fly out of here.'

Campbell looked at him blankly.

'You know I was joking about that right?'

* * *

'No! Absolutely not. Not going to happen.' Said Campbell forcefully.

He was stood by the ruined tower, shielding his eyes as he looked up at Luke who stood, clinging to the rugged masonry, his feet level with Campbell's shoulders.

'If you have any better ideas,' said Luke, shifting his weight to see further over the low trees to what he had watched cross the sky, 'then I'm all ears.'

He looked back down at his feet to see Campbell still staring up at him.

'Well?'

'Give me a minute.'

Luke pushed off of the wall dropping back to the ground with a soft thud.

'Look, Daniel has a head start on us, he has Evelyn, he knows where the stone is and every minute we're stuck here he's just getting further ahead of us.'

Campbell wiped a hand down his face in frustration.

'Yes, but I'm pretty sure in the police operational handbook it says "*When on duty, don't steal planes, it's a crime*".'

'That's an oddly specific code of practice,' said Luke flippantly. 'I wouldn't have thought it would come up enough to have its own entry.'

Campbell gritted his teeth and let out a small growl in frustration.

'Anyway,' Luke continued quickly, 'I thought you lot were allowed to commandeer cars in an emergency?'

Campbell sighed. 'I don't think that rule applies to this situation.'

'Why not?'

'Two reasons: first,' Campbell held up one of his fingers, 'that rule applies to cars. *That* is a plane.' He pointed in the direction the plane had landed then held up a second finger.

'Second, and most importantly, we are not in some Hollywood action movie where the police are allowed to do that!'

Luke towed the ground with the point of his shoe.

'So you're not allowed to commandeer cars…. or

planes?'

'No.'

'Then I would like to circle back to my earlier question.'

Campbell scrunched his eyes shut and rubbed at the headache blooming in his temple.

'And that was?' he asked exasperatedly.

Luke attempted an innocent smile.

'Do you have any better ideas?'

Campbell started noncommittally, 'well...'

'Then that settles it, your moral objections have been noted, now let's go liberate that plane, rescue Evelyn, find the stone and stop that egotistical son of a bitch that shot me,' Luke interrupted before Campbell could continue, his face wearing a slightly unhinged smile.

'Sounds easy when you say it like that,' said Campbell sarcastically.

He sighed then followed Luke as he started across the island towards the waiting plane.

'When this is all over, I'm blaming everything on you.'

The pair skirted the edge of the crumbling wall, navigating through the thick undergrowth.

'Just tell them I took you hostage,' said Luke over his shoulder. 'What's one more charge for the record.'

The island was even smaller than it had looked. The widest point barely reaching the same length as a football pitch. It didn't help that the stone tower took up nearly all of the available space on the island and the tangle of trees took care of what little was left. This left little space for navigation and forced Luke and Campbell to pick their way along the uneven, rocky coast to the northern shore.

Luke climbed over a particularly large fallen lump of castle wall and leant against the trunk of a tree that grew at a precarious angle over the loch.

The Cessna seaplane sat on two long pontoons on the surface of the loch, moored at the end on a long jetty that jutted out from a large island to the north. An outboard motor chugged away on the back of a boat heading away from the island towards a larger quay on the west coast of the loch.

'How long before they come back?' asked Campbell, coming to stand beside Luke.

'No idea,' replied Luke, still watching the boat get closer to the mainland and, more importantly, further away from them and the plane. 'So, we better get a move on.'

Luke started towards the loch, the cold water chilling his legs as it soaked back through the still damp fabric of his trousers.

'Wait,' Campbell grabbed Luke's shoulder, stopping him before he dived headfirst into the frigid water. 'Your plan is to just swim over there and then fly away?'

'Pretty much, yeah,' nodded Luke.

'What about the keys?'

'What keys?'

'The keys to start the plane?' asked Campbell as if it were obvious.

'Planes don't have keys,' replied Luke, taking a step back out of the water. 'There's probably a lock over the throttle but the ignition is just a switch.'

Campbell narrowed his eyes, skeptical of Luke's claim.

'That really doesn't seem very secure.'

'Makes our life easier,' Luke shrugged.

Campbell shook his head at the thought of the clear potential of a sudden rise in the number of plane thefts should that particular morsel of information become more widely known, as he followed Luke into the loch and towards the seaplane.

Despite Campbell's fatigue from stopping Luke from almost drowning and Luke's from being the one doing the drowning, not to mention recovering from a gunshot to the chest, it didn't take them long to cross the stretch of loch between Inchgalbraith and the waiting Cessna seaplane.

Luke hauled himself up onto the slatted jetty, his clothes once again drenched and pouring water like rain onto the wooden boards.

Campbell was close behind, heaving his exhausted body out of the Loch and flopping heavily onto his back, panting.

'Not tired are you?' Luke jested, offering a hand to help him up.

'I know you don't remember but while you were busy drowning,' said Campbell between deep breaths, taking Luke's hand and pulling himself to his feet, 'I almost killed myself trying to save your arse.'

'And my arse is very appreciative, now hurry up.'

Campbell bent double and rested his hands on his knees, still dragging in air.

Luke cast an eye at the chiselled muscles that Campbell's sodden shirt clung to.

'I knew all those muscles were just for vanity.'

Campbell's head snapped towards Luke, a glare creasing his brow. He stood upright, the exhaustion and deep breathing masked by stubborn pride, and walked past Luke towards the plane, not dignifying the comment with a response.

Luke ran his hand down the cool, smooth metal wing of the plane as he walked towards the cockpit door.

He reached out towards the handle and stopped, instead resting his hand against the flat of the door.

'What's wrong?'

'It's just,' said Luke, a hint of despondency in his voice, 'I'm an archaeologist about to get on a seaplane and I haven't had to run away from a giant boulder or outraged indigenous people. It's just a little disappointing.'

Campbell shook his head. 'You watch too many movies.'

Luke shrugged as Campbell spotted something coming towards them from the far shore of the Loch.

'Anyway, I wouldn't write off the outraged indigenous people just yet.'

Luke spun around to see the motorboat heading back towards them at a rate of knots. Two men were stood pointing towards Luke and Campbell and making hand gestures that, despite the distance, looked less than friendly.

'Ok, time to go.'

Luke yanked open the cockpit door and put a foot onto the step to climb in.

'Wait, don't you need to do pre-flight checks or something?' asked Campbell with a tinge of panic.

Luke stepped back onto the wooden jetty and looked quickly across the plane from tail to nose.

'Wings, propeller, engine, looks good to me, now move!'

Luke threw himself up the steps into the cockpit of the Cessna, sliding over to the left seat leaving Campbell to take the right hand side.

Campbell slammed the door shut behind him and snapped the handle locked. He turned to see Luke reaching out towards different switches only to pull his hand back and leave it hanging in the air before reaching for another switch, all the time muttering under his breath.

'You know how to fly this thing right?'

'Sort of,' said Luke hesitantly.

Campbell blinked slowly.

'What do you mean sort of?' he ground out. 'You can't sort of fly a plane, you either can or you can't!'

Luke turned to him, momentarily pausing his study of the switches.

'I've flown planes, just never seaplanes.'

'Isn't it the same?'

Luke shrugged. 'Sort of.'

Campbell craned his neck, looking out the side of the plane to see the motorboat coming towards them. It was gaining ground quickly, already having halved the distance to the plane since Campbell had spotted them coming.

'Any time you want to start moving would be great.'

He looked back in time to see Luke use a pair of spanners to snap the padlock off of what he assumed was the throttle cover. Luke dropped the spanners back into a small tool bag behind the pilot's seat and reached forward to turn a large switch to the right.

'When I say so, I need you to make sure all of the circuit breakers are pushed in.'

Luke pushed another lever all the way into the panel of instruments then did the opposite to the lever next to the throttle.

'And those are?'

Luke pushed the throttle in a quarter of an inch. 'Those buttons behind your wheel,' he said, pointing with his other hand at the bank of buttons in front of Campbell.

'Lights,' muttered Luke waving his hand across the multitude of toggles and switches before finding the ones he was looking for.

'Circuit breakers?'

Campbell ran his finger across each row of buttons on the panel in front of him.

'All good.'

'Cool, cool.' Luke nodded taking a deep breath. He flicked a row of switches sparking to life the panels of instruments.

'What does that oil temperature gauge say?'

'Uhhh,' hesitated Campbell, taking a second to locate the oil temperature gauge amongst the dizzying array of dials. '95.'

'Celsius or Fahrenheit?'

'Fahrenheit,' said Campbell more confidently.

Luke nodded, pushing the throttle forward halfway.

'Cold start it is then.'

He flicked a switch, starting the fuel pump and pushed the lever next to the throttle in for only a few seconds before pulling it back.

'Luke, sure you're up for this one?' asked Campbell, nervously watching, gripping the edge of his seat.

Luke finished the checks then leant back in the seat, all too calm for Campbell's nerves, and smiled. 'Just a walk in the park, Kazansky.'

Campbell frowned, 'What?'

'Top Gun.'

'Never seen it.'

Luke shook his head. 'Philistine. Anyway, ready?'

'Ready?' said Campbell, sounding anything but ready.

Luke pushed the ignition bringing the engine roaring to life, the propeller spun faster and faster as he pushed the throttle forward.

The plane began to move forward, gliding across the surface of the loch. Luke adjusted the wheel taxiing the seaplane to an open stretch of water.

The motorboat carrying the plane's irate owners was rounding the coast of the island, speeding after the seaplane. Campbell cursed under his breath as their shouts carried over the sound of the engine.

'Any time you want to get us airborne would be good.'

Luke leant into the throttle, pushing the engine slowly to full power. The plane picked up speed, racing across the loch, beginning to lift from the surface as Luke pulled the wheel towards him. The motorboat was seconds too late, the group on board being showered with the water pouring off the seaplane's floats as it climbed towards the sky.

Campbell couldn't suppress a smile as he watched the scene below out of the cockpit's side window.

'That was close.'

Campbell looked to Luke when he didn't answer. Luke had put a set of large headphones over his ears and was pointing towards them.

Campbell found the matching set in front of him and slipped them over his own head.

'I said that was close.'

'Just a bit,' came Luke's crackling reply in Campbell's ears.

Luke manoeuvred the plane, heading west and quickly clearing the edge of the loch.

'Where are we going?'

Luke levelled the controls, setting the plane's course.

'They're heading for Arran, the only way there from the loch by boat is down the river Leven to the Clyde and then into the Firth.'

'Is that even possible?' asked Campbell.

'It's how they used to get the steamers into the loch,' replied Luke. 'The river's changed a lot since but a small boat should be able to make it, especially this time of year when the water's higher.'

He looked across to Campbell who was waiting for him to continue.

'We could try and follow the river and catch up with them, but they had a good enough head start that they could have reached the Clyde by now.'

Campbell cut in, catching where Luke was going.

'So we get ahead of them; cut them off.'

'Exactly,' said Luke. 'That's why I'm taking a shortcut…'

A crackle of static buzzed in both their headsets, interrupting Luke.

'What was that?'

'Probably just interference,' replied Luke, checking the radio settings. 'I wouldn't worry about…'

The static interrupted him again, this time followed by an authoritative woman's voice.

"…Unidentified aircraft this is His Majesty's Naval Base Clyde, please acknowledge and identify yourself…"

Campbell turned slowly towards Luke, a look somewhere between panic and abject horror on his face.

'Please for the love of God tell me the end of that sentence isn't "over Faslane"?'

Luke shrunk back in his seat.

'Ok, I won't tell you that.'

'Jesus Christ man,' Campbell shouted. 'It's a nuclear submarine base, I know nothing about flying and even I know that's restricted airspace.'

'Must have slipped my mind,' muttered Luke.

"…Unidentified aircraft this is His Majesty's

Naval Base Clyde, please acknowledge and identify yourself..."

Came the crackling voice again. 'Say something,' said Campbell.

'...This is chshhh-rcraft G-LSIS Chshhh,' Luke said, faking the sounds of a faulty radio. *'Radio chshh-lty...'*

He clicked the radio off.
'That should buy us a second.'
'Really?' asked Campbell incredulously.
'Probably not.'
The voice crackled again.

"...aircraft G-LSIS you are approaching restricted airspace, please adjust your course south immediately..."

'What happens if we keep going?' asked Campbell.
'If we keep ignoring their requests?' said Luke, strained. 'Eventually they'll scramble a jet to intercept us.'
Campbell turned a shade whiter.
'I think it might be a good idea to adjust our course then.'
Luke held the controls steady, he needed to get ahead of Daniel, he wouldn't let that bastard get the drop on him again.

"...aircraft G-SISJ you are approaching restricted

airspace, please adjust your course south immediately, acknowledge …"

Campbell stared at Luke, half questioning if he could grab the controls and fly them out himself.

'Luke, why aren't you adjusting our course?' asked Campbell as calmly as he could. 'The lady asked very nicely.'

Luke chewed his lip. 'What if we miss Daniels's yacht? What about Evelyn?'

Campbell pinched the bridge of his nose.

'Remind me what happens if you keep ignoring them?'

Luke gritted his teeth, his cool slipping as he said.

'An RAF Typhoon comes and blows us out of the sky…'

He looked sideways at Campbell. Campbell didn't need to tell Luke that they were less help to Evelyn if they were dead.

'Point taken.'

'So we take the long way round yeah?'

In the end logic won. Luke eased the plane south, away from the threat of hostilities and back towards the distant Clyde and let out a long breath.

'Long way round works too.'

CHAPTER 23

400 meters South of the Wreck of the Merchant Vessel Captayannis, The Firth of Clyde, approximately 2 Kilometres North of Greenock, Renfrewshire

'Then try harder!' hissed Daniel.

The yacht coursed swiftly across the calm waters where the River Clyde morphed from an already mighty river into the widening expanse of the Firth. Progress had been slow navigating the serpentine course of the Leven, pushing Daniel's limited patience, not to mention temper, to a breaking point.

'I told you, I don't know,' spat Evelyn, 'and you shot the only person who could have figured it out.'

If looks could kill the one Evelyn gave Daniel would have been a dagger pushed slowly with spite right into his heart. She wouldn't give him the satisfaction of seeing her break, although each word threatened to catch in her throat and betray her. She couldn't ignore the grief, so she focused on the anger instead, letting the raging inferno of hate for the man stood in front of her, the man who killed her brother and Luke, burn any tears before they came.

Daniel's frustration wasn't masked so easily. The refined, collected man who had presented himself to the world as strong, a leader, level-headed and quick-thinking, was now pacing back and forth across the short stretch of deck, gesturing with the revolver in his hand and muttering curses.

He stopped, an idea striking him mid-pace. He rounded on Evelyn.

'Then how about we play a little game, to help you think?'

Evelyn stared back at him, not breaking eye contact, still refusing to answer.

Daniel reached into his pocket and pulled out a small flask. The body of the flask was a dull copper, the shiny metal browned like an old penny. Evelyn could just make out faded etchings in the metal, tangled stems of roses wreathing a rampant lion, proud and roaring.

Evelyn couldn't help but smirk.

'What?' snapped Daniel, his hand pausing halfway back to his pocket.

'Nothing,' smiled Evelyn sweetly — clearly the irony of the union of the two symbols on the flask was lost on him.

He shook his head, then continued to reach back into his pocket, pulling out two small lead balls and two squares of cloth.

'You told me there are two caves where the stone could be hidden on Arran, correct?' said Daniel, carefully pouring a measure of black powder from the flask into one chamber of the revolver, dropping in the wad of cloth after before turning the cylinder.

Evelyn watched his hands move, loading the black powder, the wadded cloth and then turning the cylinder again and repeating the process a third time, then a fourth, a fifth and a sixth until the cylinder had turned a full revolution around its axis.

Daniel rolled the lead balls around in his hand, the dull clinking lost in the wind before it reached Evelyn.

'Two Caves,' he said placing one of the balls over the opening of a cylinder before turning it in line with the ramrod under the barrel. Daniel unclipped the rod, leavening it down and pressing the ball deep into the cylinder.

'Two balls.' He spun the cylinder, letting it click around before loading another ball.

'Two chances.' Another clicking spin and the lead balls were lost, seated snugly inside the chamber. Evelyn's gorge rose at the sight of the hammer on the pistol being cocked back. Her belligerent defiance wavered for a moment, the smile slipping from her face as the barrel of the gun waved towards her.

'I'm going to ask you again where the stone is. Don't!' snapped Daniel, fighting to keep a reign on his temper as Evelyn opened her mouth to answer, 'don't say you don't know, you can work it out.'

Evelyn closed her mouth, letting her scowl settle back over her brows, steadfast against the gaping barrel of the gun pointed at her.

Daniel continued. 'You're going to figure out which cave Walter bloody Scott put the stone in.'

'And why would I do that?' said Evelyn caustically.

Daniel held the Colt revolver up to his face, admiring the sleek, cold blue steel.

'Like I said, two chances. There are two loaded chambers, four empty.' Daniel levelled the barrel back towards Evelyn. 'Two chances, you tell me you don't know, or I think you're lying I pull the trigger. You more than anyone should appreciate the poetry of it, each shot is like the stone, we know the bullets are in the gun, but not where, missing but not truly lost.'

'I prefer Tennyson,' Evelyn quipped.

Daniel frowned.

'Which cave did Scott write about in the Bruce story?'

'Shouldn't you be having one of your lackeys do your dirty work like they did with John,' shot back

Evelyn, ignoring the question entirely.

'I'm impressed,' she laughed sarcastically. 'I didn't think you would have the ball...'

A flash exploded from the barrel of the gun, smoke pluming into the air as the lead ball whistled past Evelyn and gouged a splintered groove into the gunwale behind her.

Evelyn couldn't stop her body from making itself as small a target as being bound to the chair would allow. Slowly she calmed her racing heart and peered back up at Daniel. The smoke cleared to show his disappointed expression as he spun the revolver's cylinder, letting it come to a rest over another chamber.

'A word of advice,' he said slowly, cocking the hammer back, ready to fall again. 'When I make a promise, I keep it.'

'That's a first for a politician,' said Evelyn, failing to hide the wobble in her voice as she tried to steady her nerves.

Daniel ignored her and began pacing, two steps forward, turning, two steps back.

'Blackwaterfoot, Uamh an Rìgh,' drawled Daniel. 'The king's cave, that one I've heard of, it was used as a church as I remember it.'

He stopped pacing and rounded on Evelyn.

'It wouldn't be the first time the stone was hidden in a church now would it?'

Evelyn swallowed, fighting the anxiety forming like a lump in her throat.

'What if I told you it was? How would you know I wasn't just saying anything to stay alive?'

CLICK

The hammer on the revolver fell, striking bare metal. Evelyn flinched but no shot rang out.

Daniel strode towards her, spinning the cylinder again.

He bent down and hissed in her ear. 'You had better be very convincing then.'

He sprung back upright.

'So,' he said voice suddenly bright, 'Blackwaterfoot?'

'I doubt it,' Evelyn said through gritted teeth, relenting. She tried not to keep glancing at the gun, two shots still waiting in the chambers, 'even in Scott's time the cave was a tourist attraction, he wouldn't have risked the stone being found that easily.'

Daniel chewed his lip, thinking for a moment, pointing the gun slowly at Evelyn.

'You better not be lying to throw me off, Crawford.'

Evelyn choked out a humourless laugh.

'It could be any of them!' Evelyn snapped. 'The King and the Spider is just a story, Bruce never even went to the caves, Scott could have picked any of them to write about.'

'That's not good enough,' shouted Daniel, his voice growing louder with each word.

'What do you want me to say? The stone's in the

king's cave near Machrie, because Scott thought the rich history nearby made a beautiful poetic landscape to end the stone's story!' She snapped back.

CLICK

Evelyn was too riled to flinch as the hammer fell.

'Do not mock me Evelyn.' Daniel's words had a vicious, ragged edge, the polished accent slipping to it's true rough timbre. 'If the stone isn't in Blackwaterfoot, then it's in one of the others. Which one?'

'I don't know!'

'Then you're no use to me!' bellowed Daniel, spinning the cylinder violently and yanking back the hammer.

'Fine,' she yelled back. 'Then I guess you're just going to have to kill me.'

Daniel's anger broke its dam, he lashed out with his foot, kicking the chair that had held Luke, breaking its leg and sending it skittering across the deck.

He swore and rounded on Evelyn.

'In 36 hours, I will start a revolution, right at the place where this all began. I can't do that without the stone,' he hissed, his voice taking on a threatening placidity. 'I don't have time to search an entire island. You may not be a history scholar but you know Scott better than most, so where did he put it?'

Evelyn smirked at him, only flaring his temper

more, just as she'd hoped.

'First mistake Daniel, never tell the person you're threatening that you're desperate,' she laughed in his face. 'Now I know even if you kill me, I still win, Luke still wins and John still wins.'

Daniel reigned in his anger, instead he actually laughed. A cruel biting laugh.

'Can a dead man really win?'

The words hit Evelyn like a punch to the gut.

'Maybe my plan will be delayed, but I will take what's mine, one way or another,' sneered Daniel. 'And you, your traitorous brother and that bloody Luke Knight will still be dead.'

A clamour from the bow of the yacht interrupted Daniel before he could continue.

They both snapped their heads towards the noise to see Corban lying face down on the deck and a figure standing on the curving prow, silhouetted by the low afternoon sun, dripping water from his clothes.

'I think you'll find rumours of my death have been greatly exaggerated.'

CHAPTER 24

25 minutes Earlier

2000 feet above the Wreck of the Merchant Vessel Captayannis, The Firth of Clyde, Approximately 2 Kilometers North of Greenock, Renfrewshire

'See anything?'

Campbell shielded his eyes from the flare of the sun. His hand was pressed between his forehead and the Cessna's window, acting like the brim of a cap as he searched the dazzling water far below for any sign of Daniel's yacht.

'Honestly,' he said looking away from the window and blinking hard through the sunspots that danced in front of his eyes, 'if I look out there much longer I might never see anything again.'

The low afternoon sun had been a constant and unwelcome companion since they had reached the Clyde and started their search west towards the Firth. It wasn't just the search that had been hampered, the glare through the windscreen of the Cessna had all but blinded Luke, forcing him to fly more by the plane's instruments than anything he could actually see.

'I'm going to turn us around,' said Luke. 'We must have passed them by now.'

He dipped the wing to the left, dropping in altitude and sending the plane in a gentle curve back up the river.

With the sun behind them the view of shimmering river became clear enough to make out the tiny shapes of boats and ships passing up and down the wide expanse, leaving v-shaped wakes criss-crossing the gentle waves.

Campbell resumed his scanning of the river, head moving back and forth in perfect, regimented sweeps.

He growled in frustration. 'There must be thirty boats down there that could be the yacht. We need to get lower.'

Luke chewed the inside of his cheek, flexing his hands on the yoke in front of him.

'I can only take us down a little further,' he said warily. 'If we start cruising below 1000ft our friends in the navy might start sending love letters again.'

'As close as you can get us,' replied Campbell, 'otherwise, we have no chance.'

Luke pitched the nose of the Cessna down,

dropping the plane towards the water.

'Ok, keep your eyes peeled. I'll make another pass and...'

A sound like a suppressed explosion joined by the screech of steel going through a shredder made Luke snap his head to the plane's wing in time to see a cloud of feathers surrounding a red mist streaking along the bottom of it.

Luke didn't have time to take in the sight, the yoke in his hands yanked itself sideways, throwing the plane violently and sending Campbell careering into Luke's side.

Luke fought the tumble, bringing the plane back to level.

'What the hell was that?' gasped Campbell, sucking in lungfuls of air as his heart raced.

'Bird strike,' said Luke tightly. 'We took it on the wing so there shouldn't be a problem.' He let out a slow breath.

'Providing we don't get any more and we don't take it to anything vital we shouldn't have a problem.'

Campbell settled back into his seat. 'And if we do?'

'Then we have a problem.'

'Maybe steer clear of the sugar boat then,' said Campbell, his nerves restored to intact.

'The what?'

'Sugar boat,' Campbell said again. He leaned across Luke and pointed out of the window.

A silvery knife cut through the river below, the half-submerged form of a ship well over 100 metres long stuck out of the river like a rusting steel island.

Flocks of seabirds circled above the hulking wreck, occasionally dropping down to the ship's carcass only to be replaced by another lifting into the air in an unending battery creating some sort of whirling Hitchcockian nightmare.

'What the hell is that?' asked Luke.

'Merchant ship that was carrying sugar back in the 70s,' said Campbell, subconsciously taking on the same inflection as Luke's history lessons. 'It got holed by the anchor chain of another ship and was sinking so the captain ran her aground on a sandbank.'

'And in 40 years no one, ever thought to move it?'

Campbell shrugged. 'Tale as old as time, no one owned up to it being their responsibility, so there it stayed,' his face darkened. 'And now it belongs to the birds.'

Luke gave him a slow side-eyed look, only mildly concerned that the pair of them had probably been awake far too long now.

'I'll take us out wider,' he said, easing the Cessna gently towards the northern shore. 'I'd rather not have survived getting shot only for my obituary to read death by poultry.'

The plane began its circle of the merchant ship, gliding in a gentle arc away from the storm of wings.

'Wait!' yelled Campbell, throwing his arm in front of Luke and pointing out of the pilot side window. Luke jumped back in his seat causing him to jerk the yoke and rock the wings violently.

'Maybe we don't jog the person keeping the two-tonne hunk of metal in the air.'

Campbell muttered a swift apology but kept pointing towards the wreck of the sugar boat.

'Look.'

Luke checked the controls and glanced out of the window at the water below. At first he saw nothing but the expanse of blueish grey and the swarm of flapping wings above the wreck. But then, there it was, in amongst the weave of wave and wake Luke saw the sleek, albeit minute from their altitude, wooden yacht cutting its way across the Firth just south of the bird-infested wreck.

'Got you!' whispered Luke viciously.

Campbell fell back into his seat as Luke banked the plane away from Daniel's yacht, heading north of the wreck.

'Umm Luke mate, you're going the wrong way?'

'We can't exactly land the plane on top of them, can we?' said Luke.

'What's your plan then?'

Luke shrugged. 'I was thinking violence and a healthy serving of sarcasm.'

'Ok, but seriously, you do have a plan?'

Luke turned his head slowly towards Campbell, a sharp, lupine smile revealing two rows of white teeth.

Campbell's skin turned a similar shade as the blood drained from his face.

'I don't like that look.'

※ ※ ※

'Next time, I'm making the plan,' said Campbell irritably, batting at a beady-eyed herring gull that was pecking at his leg.

'Quiet.'

Luke didn't look up from his vantage, lying prone on the cold metal of the Cessna's high single wing. Campbell lay beside him, still trying to fend off the persistent gull that was still pecking at the hem of his trouser leg. With a final kick he finally dislodged the bird sending it back to circle the sky with near a hundred squawking seabirds above the colossal wreck Luke had used to shield the plane from Daniel's yacht.

'Anything?' asked Campbell, turning his attention back to Luke.

Luke lowered the binoculars he had found tucked behind the pilot's seat and handed them to Campbell.

'It's them,' said Luke tersely. 'I can only see one of the twins.'

Campbell watched the yacht through the

binoculars. Evelyn was still tied to the chair as she had been in the Loch. He couldn't help but smile at the defiant look on her face as Daniel grew redder with anger at what he was sure was the same stubborn, rebellious attitude that John had always had.

'Corban's on the bow, Dougal must be at the helm.'

Campbell's view of the world through the binoculars flashed past as he aimed them at the bow of the yacht and the perpetually sneering face of Corban.

Luke pushed himself up from the Cessna's wing and shucked off his still damp jacket.

'Do you want to go over the plan again?'

Campbell lowered the binoculars and squinted through the setting sun at Luke.

'No, you've been shot, drowned and concussed,' he said grimly. 'I still think I should go instead.'

Luke feigned offence, 'And deny me the look on Daniel's face when he sees me alive?'

Campbell rolled his eyes.

'Just make sure the plane is ready to fly.'

'Just try not to get yourself shot again,' retorted Campbell.

Luke grinned, 'no promises.'

He stood on the wing and jumped feet first into the water below, plunging through the gentle waves and surfacing a moment later to start towards the yacht.

'If we survive this,' muttered Campbell to himself, 'I'm going to kill him myself.'

❖ ❖ ❖

Luke cursed the heavy sodden wool of his clothes as he hauled himself out of the water. He gritted his teeth trying not to give himself away by grunting at the strain of lifting himself onto the bow of the yacht on burning muscles.

The distance between the wreck of the sugar boat and Daniel's yacht hadn't been far but the current had been relentless, fighting Luke at every stroke.

By some miracle no one on board had spotted Luke in the water: Daniel too busy interrogating Evelyn and, as Luke peeked over the edge of the gunwale, Corban was still holding vigil over the south side of the Firth.

As quietly as he could Luke manoeuvred himself over the chromed railing that topped the gunwale and onto the deck. His clothes poured water onto the polished deck, the drops hitting the wood with a gentle *tap, tap, tap.* Corban's head twitched, his ears picking up on the noise. Just as he turned Luke rushed forward but too slowly. Corban caught his attack and the pair scuffled, forcing Luke back against the side of the yacht.

Daniel's voice exploded from the stern of the

yacht, furious.

'...and that bloody Luke Knight will still be dead.'

Luke struggled against Corban's surprising strength.

'You!' hissed Corban.

'Me,' Luke smiled back before throwing his head forward, catching Corban across his still bruised brow. The connection made a dull echoing thud and Corban's grip on Luke slackened as his body slumped to the deck.

Luke shook his head, clearing away the stars pushing into the edges of his vision, head-butting Corban probably wasn't good for the concussion.

He turned towards Daniel and Evelyn to see them both staring at him open-mouthed. So much for taking the boat by surprise, thought Luke.

'I think you'll find rumours of my death have been greatly exaggerated,' said Luke, patting at his torso as if testing his own corporality.

Daniel's face was stuck somewhere between outrage and sheer astonishment.

'How?' he said, letting the words slip out unintentionally.

Luke swaggered towards them.

'Let's call it divine intervention.'

He flashed a look towards Evelyn, her wrists were red raw, burned by the rope that lashed her to the chair. His eyes moved up to her face, a broad smile shone back at him, accompanied by a dark bruise across her cheek were Dougal had hit her. He would make sure to pay him back for that. He turned his attention back to Daniel.

'You owe me a new jacket.'

Daniel shook off his shock and raised the revolver in his hand at Luke.

'Sorry, where are my manners?' said Daniel calmly. 'I'll have my man get one for you.'

He didn't take his eyes off of Luke.

'Dougal!'

Luke took a step towards Evelyn but stopped as Daniel tightened his grip on the gun.

'Just let us go and you can have the stone,' said Luke, 'we won't follow you, we won't try and stop you, just let us walk away.'

'I don't think so Knight,' said Daniel. 'Not to say I don't trust you but, well... can you blame me?'

Luke edged his feet further towards Evelyn.

'The stone isn't worth more lives Daniel.'

'The stone is worth a hundred lives,' Daniel spat, seething. 'The stone is Scotland and people have killed far more to take it in the past than I have.'

Heavy footsteps clunked across the deck. Luke watched from the edge of his vision Dougal walk slowly towards them, his own 1911 pistol extended. He stopped by the crumpled form of his brother long enough to prod him with the toe of his shoe eliciting a pained groan. Satisfied, Dougal continued forward looking to Daniel for instruction.

'If you know the past,' said Luke before Daniel could give commands to Dougal, 'then you know it's never gone well for the men who have tried to take it by force, no matter how much death they leave in their wake! Edward the First might have thought he had the stone but Robert the Bruce still kept Scotland.'

Daniel's demeanour turned deathly calm, his cold eyes focusing on Luke alone.

'Then I'll make sure history doesn't repeat itself.'

He lifted the revolver moving beyond Luke's chest to his head, and closed his finger around the trigger.

There was no way to stop the shot but Luke threw his body to the side just as Evelyn kicked out at Daniel, her foot connecting with his knee, forcing the bone painfully sideways with a grim, popping snap.

Daniel roared, his finger tightening fully on the trigger and firing the revolver as his leg collapsed under him.

The shot went wide, sailing past Luke and grazing Dougal's shoulder.

Luke saw his only chance; he rushed across the deck and delivered a swift knee to Daniel's head knocking him back to the deck, before continuing forward.

He skidded to a hault beside Evelyn and stopped to untie the ropes binding her wrists.

'Luke!'

'Yes I know you thought I was dead, I'm your hero, you can sing my praises once we're out of here,' Luke smiled up at her.

Evelyn frowned back at him and said again, rather more urgently.

'No, Luke,' she said again nodding towards he bow.

Luke twisted to see Dougal, red-faced with murder in his eyes getting to his feet and raising his gun with his uninjured arm.

Luke turned back and dropped the ropes in his hand. 'Ok, Plan B.'

He grabbed hold of the chair and, before Evelyn could object, threw himself over the gunwale into the Firth taking the chair and Evelyn with him.

The pair crashed through the water in a swirl of foam and bubbles. Luke kicked hard towards Evelyn and grabbed a small black-handled knife from his ankle. He gripped the ropes and deftly cut through the fibre, freeing Evelyn from the chair.

Moments later they both broke the surface, Evelyn coughed, gasping lungfuls of air.

'You bastard!' she stuttered, shivering in the frigid water.

'Most people say thank you.'

'Most people haven't been thrown overboard.'

Luke's retort was cut off by a splash behind them.

They turned in time to see Dougal emerge from

the water, impervious to the cold and wasting no time to begin his pursuit.

'Can you swim?'

Evelyn flexed her shoulders, still stiff from being restrained and nodded.

'Head for the wreck,' called Luke as they started away from Daniel's yacht.

He needn't have worried about Evelyn falling behind, within a minute she had pulled far ahead, leaving Luke's aching body to struggle on behind her.

Dougal was closing the distance between them with an alarming pace, even with his injured arm doing little to propel him forwards.

Luke pushed on, ignoring the pain in his shoulders. The sun was getting low in the sky, once again casting a fire across the Firth.

He strained his ears over the sound of the water washing over his head for the sound of the Cessna's engine

'Come on Campbell.'

'Come on Campbell,' Campbell growled at himself. He had tried and failed twice to get the plane's engine to start the way Luke had shown him.

The gleaming propeller on the nose of the plane juddered a few rotations, catching the glowing amber sunlight before petering out yet again.

He glanced out of the window for any view of

Luke and Evelyn. The Yacht drifted gently in the distance but the sun glinting off the water made it impossible to make out anything smaller than a boat.

He turned back to the swamp of controls before him. Luke had told him to get the plane ready at any sign of trouble and the gunshots that had rung out minutes before was definitely trouble.

Campbell went through the engine startup one more time. Taking a deep breath he pushed the ignition. The engine stuttered again, the propeller juddering.

'Oh come on you piece of...' Campbell shouted, slamming his fist down on the console.

The engine stuttered before exploding into life, the propeller spinning in a silver blur in front of the windscreen.

Campbell yelled in triumph and started taxiing the Cessna across the water, breaking the cover of the sugar boat and heading for Daniel's yacht.

A tiny figure in the water waved their arms in the air. Campbell slowed the engine coming to a stop just short of them. He left the pilot's seat and threw open the side door.

Evelyn swam hard for the plane, struggling to climb onto the floats that supported the seaplane. Campbell's hand appeared in front of her face, she took it and was hauled into the cabin.

'Where's Luke?' asked Campbell.

Evelyn coughed, clearing the water that had

found its way into her throat. 'He was right behind me.'

Campbell leant out of the door.

Luke was grappling with Dougal a few meters beyond where Evelyn had been, kicking up a torrent of white water, the suited man trying to force his head underneath the surface. Luke broke free with a desperate gasp and swung his elbow back catching Dougal in the temple. Luke slipped away and swam for the waiting Cessna. He felt something wrap around his ankle as Dougal dragged him back. Luke yelled at a sharp pain that burned across his leg, he rolled onto his back and kicked Dougal in the jaw with his other foot.

Dougal crashed back into the water leaving Luke free to swim the short distance to the plane.

Campbell was waiting by the door to drag Luke aboard, he fell to the floor of the cabin panting as Campbell slammed the door shut behind him.

'Luke, your leg,' said Evelyn, concerned by the small pool of blood that had formed beneath Luke's leg.

He lifted the hem of the damp woollen kilt revealing a long, thin gash that extended several inches from just below his knee.

'Dougal must have gotten hold of my knife,' hissed Luke as he prodded at the cut.

Campbell rubbed a hand across his forehead. 'When I told you not to get shot, that didn't mean get stabbed instead.'

Luke flexed his ankle, testing the muscles running down his calf. 'It's only a scratch,' he said with a wince. 'No time to worry about it now, Daniel and the discount Krays won't be down for long.'

'Can you still fly?'

Luke let Evelyn help him to his feet and half walked, half hopped towards the cockpit.

'If Douglas Bader could fly with no legs I can deal with a light stabbing.'

He slumped into the pilot's chair and gestured to Campbell to take up the co-pilot position.

Luke manoeuvred the plane in a wide circle, lining up a clear path for takeoff.

'Now it's a race for Arran,' said Campbell as Luke pushed the throttle forward, bringing the Cessna up to takeoff speed before pulling back on the yoke, guiding the Seaplane in a gentle climb.

'We're not going to Arran,' said Luke.

'What?' echoed Campbell and Evelyn in unison.

Evelyn rushed to the side of Luke's seat. 'You can't let Daniel get the stone! This is about more than John now.'

'She's right,' continued Campbell, 'if Daniel gets the stone this whole country is screwed.'

'That's why we aren't going to Arran,' Luke said calmly. 'The stone isn't there.'

Campbell narrowed his eyes at Luke. 'You're going to have to explain that one.'

'I thought the inscription of the watch left too

many options,' said Luke. 'And when Daniel read the letter...'

A loud metallic clang cut Luke off.

'Another bird strike?'

Luke looked out of the pilot's window, his face turning grim at the view.

'Not this time.' Luke yanked off his headset and strode purposefully towards the cabin door, Leaving Campbell to grab the controls.

'Keep it steady.' Luke pulled open the door and stepped out onto the pontoon.

The rush of air was like standing behind a jet engine making Luke grab hold of the ladder that led to the cabin to keep his balance.

'Knight!' Dougal's rough voice roared from the other end of the pontoon. He stood clinging to the beam that supported the wing with one hand and a small black handled knife with the other.

'That doesn't belong to you,' Luke shouted back, nodding at the sgian dubh Dougal had taken from him.

Dougal smiled viciously.

'Then let me return it.'

He launched himself at Luke, ignorant or unafraid of the vast empty space beneath him.

Luke caught him, still holding onto the ladder with all his strength to stop Dougal taking them both off the pontoon. The tip of the knife caught him in the shoulder, tearing cleanly through the cotton shirt but only grazing skin.

Luke tried to throw the suited killer off him but was only rewarded with a fist to his jaw for the effort. The blow loosened Luke's grip on the ladder and both men fell to the pontoon, sliding dangerously towards the abyss.

Luke threw out an arm catching one of the struts and moved to get to his feet. Dougal was faster, already standing he kicked at Luke's hand, trying to dislodge his grip.

Luke shifted his hand quickly leaving Dougal's foot to strike the bare metal. Before he could recover the attack Luke grabbed the foot and twisted, forcing Dougal to turn and drop to his knee. Luke scrambled to his feet and moved to attack. At the last moment Dougal rolled onto his back, kicking out and catching Luke square in the chest, knocking him backwards.

Luke landed hard on the flat on his back. The air rushed out of his lungs at the impact, winding him and leaving him stranded, vulnerable.

Dougal struggled slowly to stand over Luke, he smiled the cruel, malevolent smile again, adjusting and readjusting his grip on the knife.

Luke coughed, forcing the air back into his lungs but it was too late, Dougal raised the knife.

'Come back from this one Knight.'

Luke looked around desperately his eye catching a movement in the sky behind the gleaming knife.

'Hey Dougal!' Dougal looked blankly at Luke, the

knife stopping, hanging in the air.

Luke smirked. 'Duck.'

The look of confusion on Dougal's face didn't have a chance to form fully. An explosion of feathers replaced the space that Dougal's head had occupied.

Luke rolled onto his stomach to look over the edge of the pontoon.

Dougal was already a speck in the distance only disappearing moments later in a splash of white foam.

Luke winced, 'come back from that one.'

He got steadily to his feet, gripping onto the ladder behind him. He stood on the first rung and pulled the cabin door open and stepped stiffly inside, pulling the door shut behind him.

Evelyn and Campbell stared at Luke open mouthed as he turned towards the cockpit.

'You saw that then?' said Luke, noticing their faces.

Evelyn got out of the pilot's chair making room for Luke. 'Is he...?'

'Put it this way,' Luke said, collapsing into the chair and putting on a headset, 'four more and I'm technically an ace.'

Campbell shook his head. 'Well *Ace*,' he said sarcastically, 'do you want to tell us where we're going?'

Luke tilted the controls, turning the plane

smoothly back inland up the Clyde.
 'Only if you have the time.'

CHAPTER 25

Somewhere over Renton, West Dumbartonshire. Approximately 14 miles Northwest of Glasgow.

Scott's pocket watch swung in the air between Evelyn and Campbell. Luke kept one hand on the plane's yoke, flicking the watch back and forth with the other like a hypnotist.

'I thought you said the watch was a red herring?' Evelyn grabbed the watch mid-swing and pulled it from Luke's grip.

'I said the inscription was,' Luke returned his hand to the controls, 'not the watch.'

'Could we maybe skip the cryptic statements and history lessons this time?'

Luke looked across to Campbell, theatrically affronted.

'Luckily for you it's not a history lesson that's needed,' Luke said, then turned to Evelyn, 'it's a matter of poetics.'

Evelyn studied the pocket watch in her hands, the hands on the face had long since ceased their orbit of the watch-face but that was hardly surprising, even most modern watches will only last a few days without winding let alone over a century. Given the time it had spent sat beneath the castle on Inchmurrin the watch was in a surprisingly healthy state. The silvery metal was almost unblemished save for a thin scratch disappearing off the edge of the case.

'Those secrets are lost in time.'

Evelyn hadn't seen Luke and Campbell watching her from the cockpit and jumped as she turned back to them.

'Lost *in* time, not to time,' Evelyn repeated the words. 'The phrase is lost to time.'

'Scott's letter,' said Luke smiling.

Evelyn disappeared behind the pilot's seat, fumbling through the tool bag Luke had returned to its place.

'Does someone want to fill me in?'

Luke turned to Campbell.

'Daniel had a letter written by Walter Scott to Thomas Thompson, telling him the secrets to the stone were lost in time.'

Campbell frowned.

'But we know Scott found the stone and Thompson helped him.'

'Exactly!' Evelyn said excitedly, popping back up from behind the chair. 'Scott was a writer and a poet, every word he wrote was considered and chosen carefully. So why would he get the phrase he finished the letter with wrong?'

She lifted a narrow flat headed screwdriver and slotted it into the seam between the watches bezel and case beneath the scratch.

'Because it was a clue,' Campbell said quietly before turning to Luke. 'Is she right?'

Luke shrugged.

'I hope so, or she's about to ruin a rather nice watch.'

The thin edge of the screwdriver found the hairline seam, sliding into the groove and lifting the case barely a millimetre away from the watch.

Evelyn's eyes stayed focused, she twisted the screwdriver, leavening the case until it popped away from the watch with a metallic pop.

She tipped the separated case into her hand and looked into the exposed innards of the watch.

It was no surprise that it had stopped working. Jammed within the fine gears and springs was a folded square of fine paper.

Evelyn eased it free. The paper was thin like the pages of a bible allowing it to be folded thin enough to be hidden within the watch. She opened the thin sheet gently to its full size. The watch slipped from her fingers and was only saved from hitting the floor by Luke's reflexes.

'What is it?' asked Campbell, watching the awed expression that had emerged on Evelyn's face.

She didn't answer, instead letting her arm fall between Luke and Campbell.

Luke switched the plane to autopilot with the digital screen that sat in the centre of the instrument panel. He took his hands gingerly from the yoke then, once he was confident in the capability of the flight control system, turned and took the paper from Evelyn's hand.

He studied the paper, his brows furrowing as he focused.

'Well?'

'It's a poem,' said Luke, handing the page to Campbell.

> *Talorcan the king there died*
> *by Britons fury fell.*
>
> *Nested and wreathed, by the holiest yew.*
>
> *Auld long since have the trees*
> *downed carousel,*
>
> *ever graced the sight but of blind eyes few.*
>
> *Fairies light on faces dawn,*
>
> *From crooked hill sunlight adorn.*
>
> *Weary hunter follow sweet Charlotte's stare.*
>
> *Glory or death brought to men,*
>
> *Who hunt across highland glenn,*

For their destiny beneath Carrick's Chair.

'Just once,' Campbell said exasperated as he finished reading the page, 'it would be brilliant if one of these clues could be a bloody set of directions. You know, how hard would it be?'

He threw the page back to Evelyn, then, in an almost impeccable imitation of a P.G. Wodehouse character, said, 'What ho old boy! Sorry for all the fiddle-faddle, never can be too careful! I left the stone next to the old dovecote, just take ten paces from the castle, turn left at the big tree and X marks the spot! Jolly good hunting.'

Luke stared quizzically at him for a moment before Evelyn spoke.

'But he has, Scott wrote a lot about Scottish history, poems and novels. 'This,' she said waving the page at Campbell, 'is like a map drawn with words.'

'Where are we heading then?'

Evelyn's answer was usurped by a loud beep and a orange light blinking to life on the instrument panel.

Luke swore under his breath and tapped the fuel indicator dial beneath the light.

'If we don't decide and land soon,' he said tightly, 'then the answer is down and with haste. Right tank is empty and left is on its way out.'

Evelyn read the first line of the poem over.

'Talorcan's fall, that has to be the first clue.'

'Ok, who was Talorcan?'

'King of the Picts,' said Luke,' but there were two of them: Talorcan Mac Enfret and Talorcan II.'

Evelyn looked at the page.

'Slain by Britons.'

'Talorcan II was killed at the battle of Mugdock by the Britons of Alt Clut.'

Evelyn chewed the edge of her lip.

'There's a Mugdock just outside Glasgow, near Milngavie. Is it the same one?'

'No one's ever pinned down an exact site for the battle,' said Luke glancing at the fuel gauge 'but given the circumstances it gets my vote.'

'What about the rest of the poem?' asked Evelyn.

'We'll figure it out after we land. How far outside Glasgow is Mugdock?'

Campbell answered. 'Maybe 10 or 11 miles.'

Luke flashed a look at the fuel gauge just as the warning light for the left tank flashed its fiery orange. 'This could be interesting.'

* * *

The sun had dipped low behind the horizon as the Cessna drifted lower over Milngavie. Tiny twinkling lights were beginning to spark to life with the coming night. Luke strained his eyes, at the hazy open countryside that spread out before the hills. Another flash of orange flooded the cockpit, the fuel warning lights shining in tandem and both indicator needles sitting firmly on empty.

The seaplane dipped lower still, houses growing larger in the view below. Lower still and as Evelyn watched from one of the thick square windows in the cabin, cars and even people, small as ants, became visible despite the lack of light.

'Err Luke,' she said leaning over the shoulder of the pilot's seat, 'I can't help but notice we're getting quite close to the ground.'

Luke stayed focused on the open countryside beyond the town.

'Kind of need to be close to the ground to land.'

Evelyn frowned. 'But this is a seaplane.'

'I know,' he replied shortly.

'Don't seaplanes, you know, by definition, need to land on water?' she asked, mild panic starting to set into her voice.

'Yep,' he looked over his shoulder at her. 'Might want to buckle up.'

Evelyn half-jumped back into the cabin and scrambled to fasten the lap belt across her waist.

Campbell re-fastened his own belt.

'You know what you're doing right?'

'Word of advice my friend,' Luke gave him a tight-lipped smile, 'don't ask questions you won't like the answer to.'

Campbell muttered a prayer and gripped the side of his seat hard enough that his knuckles turned bone white.

The plane dropped lower, Luke's eyes scanned back and forth across the horizon until they caught the flat inky-black void in the ground that he had been searching for.

Luke swore softly so the others wouldn't hear, they were too close and too high, the plane needed to circle around and come in lower but he couldn't risk it, not with the Cessna already running on vapour.

'Hold on!' he shouted, loud enough that Evelyn and Campbell could have heard without the headsets.

He sent the plane into a steep dive towards the dark path of land, the engine whining and airframe creaking at the sudden strain.

The ground that rushed towards them was as dark as the night sky, exactly as dark. Not ground at all, the surface of water reflected the sky above.

Luke levelled the plane, fighting the yoke as it tried to rip itself free of his grip. The plane lowered again, touching the mirrored surface of the water and sending huge ripples radiating towards the shores. Too fast, too fast, TOO FAST thought Luke.

He controlled the plane onto the water, the drag of the water around the floats was immediate, forcing the occupants of the plane forward in their seats.

The far shore was rapidly growing closer. *Still too fast.* Luke cut the engine, letting it fall idle and forced the elevators up, slowing the plane more.

The sudden drop in speed made the Cessna's nose pitch down, lifting the tail high into the air, still careening towards the shore.

A chorus of shouts erupted from Luke, Campbell and Evelyn. The plane slowed further as the rocky bank at the water's edge came ever closer.

* * *

'Well, that could have been worse.'

Luke stood on the edge of the reservoir, hands on hips, admiring the seaplane which had come to rest wedged nose-down and tail in the air at a near perfect forty five degree angle against an outcropping of stone.

Campbell was crouched, hands on his knees hyperventilating while Evelyn rested a comforting hand on his back.

'I'm... going... to kill him,' Campbell forced out between gasps.

'Hey, I landed the plane, we're all alive. What more do you want?'

Campbell shot upright and half pulled the pistol

from the holster on his hip. Evelyn grabbed his wrist, unsure whether he would actually shoot Luke this time.

She stalked forward. 'That was the most half-arsed, irresponsible… reckless!' She stopped trying to grasp the right words. 'I don't know why I'm surprised, it seems like you put about as much thought into it as you did your attempt at a rescue.'

'I tried to tell him,' snipped Campbell from the background.

Luke turned to both of them. 'It worked didn't it, both times.'

'More by luck than judgement,' said Campbell under his breath.

Evelyn glared at Luke, folded her arms and breathed out heavily through her nose.

'Ok, I'm sorry,' Luke sighed.

Evelyn's mouth twitched into the ghost of a smile at the rare victory.

Luke smirked. 'Next time I'll use my whole arse when coming up with a plan.'

Evelyn's vision turned red as Luke turned and strolled away from the reservoir and the wrecked plane. 'Campbell.'

'Yeah?'

She chewed her lip. 'You can shoot him now.'

CHAPTER 26

Craigmaddie Reservoir, Mugdock, Stirlingshire. 8 miles north of Glasgow.

Darkness had fallen fully by the time Luke, Campbell and Evelyn had recovered as much as they could from the newly monolithic Cessna, not that there was a lot left to salvage. Much to Luke's surprise and relief, tucked neatly behind the last row of seats in the cabin was a pair of sturdy leather boots which Luke eagerly swapped for his own water logged brogues.

Luke hopped across the rocks that lined the northern bank of the reservoir, joining Evelyn and Campbell on the gravel pathway that led off into the darkness. Few lights lit the space immediately surrounding the water's edge leaving only the warm light of the full moon and the twinkling of hundreds of stars to cast their light on the landscape, the reservoir just far enough from civilisation for the sky to be untouched by the murky orange glow of modernity.

'I don't suppose either of you found a torch?'

Evelyn turned to face Luke at the sound of his voice as Campbell fumbled inside his jacket and brought out a slim black torch that he clicked on with a button on the back, like one an FBI agent in some American crime show might use.

Luke shielded his eyes from the sudden flare of light and held out his other hand into which Campbell dropped the torch.

'Where is Talorcan's grave then?' Campbell asked, looking around into the darkness.

Luke nervously cleared his throat. 'Eh… no one knows.'

Campbell rounded on him. 'Ok,' he said with a careful calmness. 'What about where he died? The battlefield.'

'No one knows that either,' Luke gestured around him to the empty countryside. 'Generally in the vicinity of Mugdock is about as close to where Scott hid the stone as Talorcan is going to get us.'

Luke opened his mouth to continue, noticing the frown Campbell was giving him through the darkness.

'I have an idea on that actually,' interrupted Evelyn.

She sauntered over to Luke and plucked the torch out of his hand.

'Like you said before, Scott wouldn't waste words, everything is deliberate.'

She held out the page and cast the torch across the swirling writing. Luke and Campbell shuffled closer, taking advantage of the small light.

'I'm not sure about most of it but these two lines stood out,' said Evelyn, pointing to the two short lines in the middle of the poem. 'Faeries light from the crooked hills, it means nothing in English but Crooked fairy in Gaelic is…'

'*Cam Sìth,*' said Campbell. 'The Campsies.'

'It seemed obvious, they're kind of hard to miss from here, even in the dark.'

Luke looked up at the imposing dark shadows of the Campsies in the distance. They were striking, a part of the landscape but somehow more, separate, important. Even when he had first seen them, the first time he had come to Glasgow, he couldn't help but stop and stare. In the sunlight they were magnificent, so perfectly representing the beauty of Scotland that he couldn't help but imagine that they had been sketched into existence by some great landscape painter, as if McCulloch had awoken one day and found the scenery lacking.

The fall of night didn't detract from their brilliance, but instead cast them in mystery, like the magic of the creatures that gave the mountains their name emerged under cover of darkness.

'Great, so we've narrowed it down to about 20 square miles.' Campbell's words snapped Luke's attention back to the poem.

'Charlotte.'

'I prefer Edward but close enough.'

Luke took the page from Evelyn and read the lines again.

'No, the next line in the poem, follow Charlotte's stare. Who's Charlotte?'

'It could be his wife, Charlotte Carpenter?'

Something sparked in Luke's mind, connections forming. He read the poem over and over, muttering a seemingly random assortment of words.

'*Auld,*' said Luke clearly, putting a stop to his musings. 'It's the only word in the poem in Scots and not English.'

Evelyn and Campbell looked at him blankly, clearly waiting for the rest of the explanation.

Luke held up his hand in a silent request for the torch which Evelyn tossed through the air into his open palm.

'It's all in lines 2-4, the yew trees isn't talking about Talorcan's grave, he just gets us here. The yew trees surround the second clue, except they aren't there, a "Downed Carousel" of yew trees.'

Campbell frowned. 'That possibly makes less sense than the poem.'

'It does unless you take the next clue, "blind eyes",' said Luke poking his finger at the page. 'A circle of yew trees that has only been seen by eyes that can't see.'

'Like eyes in a painting?' Evelyn offered.

Luke nodded. 'Or sculpture, carved into stone.'

'And for those of us who don't know poetry or sculpture?'

Luke turned to Campbell and grinned.

'Auld wives,' said Luke putting the torch under his chin and casting his features in an eerie, over-exposed glow. 'On Craigmaddie Muir stands three stones, one perched atop the other two. Carved into the stone are faces, sightless and speechless staring out.'

'Is there a point to this?'

Luke dropped the torch and gave Campbell a nettled look.

'I'm getting to it, can you just…' Luke held up his hands in the universal sign for wait, 'ok?'

Campbell rolled his eyes and Luke put the torch back under his chin, relaunching into his story.

'Legend says these stones were the site of strange rituals, human sacrifice and magic, the secrets of what went on shielded by a circle of yew trees. And the name of these stones: Auld Wives' Lifts.'

Luke took the torch away and said brightly.

'Of course, most of the legends are probably a load of rubbish but the point is, Scott often wrote about folklore and the yew trees were long gone by the late 1800's so the stones would have had a clear view of the mountains.'

'So there's something on the stones that will show us where in the mountains the stone is hidden?'

'Like a map or something?' asked Evelyn.

'As much as I would love to finally have a nice detailed map to where we need to go,' said Campbell dryly, 'I think if Scott had chipped that into the stones someone would have noticed it in the last hundred years.'

'Only one way to find out,' Luke shrugged. 'Speaking of a map, I don't know where the stones are in the day let alone at night.'

Evelyn pulled a tatty, folded Ordnance Survey map from the top of her boot.

Luke raised an eyebrow. 'Unusual place to keep a map.'

She slapped the map onto Luke's chest and said tartly, 'When was the last time you saw a dress with pockets?'

Luke took the map without further comment.

The map was worn and well-used; deep creases cut through the colour leaving lines like great rifts criss-crossing the landscape. By some luck the area of the reservoir and the stones was relatively unscathed and helpfully a simple plastic compass had been attached to the cardboard cover. Hardly a replacement for the golden, brass compass that Luke expected was still on Inchmurrin with the rest of the contents of his satchel but beggars can't be choosers.

'Right,' said Luke turning his back on the reservoir after tracing the route with his finger across the tattered drawn landscape. 'Onwards.'

* * *

'Next time,' grunted Campbell as he freed his foot from a thick, boggy puddle, 'I'm setting the route.'

The path had been, if a little muddy, relatively solid under foot for the first mile between the reservoir and Auld Wives' Lifts. The easy going had quickly turned when Luke had suggested, instead of following the path to the north, cutting across the moorland directly to the stones.

Luke stepped onto one of the few patches of solid ground and turned the torch on Campbell.

'How was I supposed to know there was a bog here?' said Luke defensively. 'It's not like it says on the map, *Watch out, there be water here!*'

Thick fog had rolled across the muir as night had fallen fully and the temperature in the air plummeted. Luke's torch beam flared across the blanket of water vapour forcing Campbell to shield his eyes, smearing mud across his brow.

'Yes it does!' shouted Campbell, his voice raising an octave. 'That's what all the blue patches are.'

'What blue patches?'

Luke flashed the torch down at the crumpled map illuminating the area of the muir and the smattering of small blue circles that indicated the small ponds formed by the runoff from the surrounding sodden ground.

Luke looked up sheepishly form the map. 'Ok, that one's on me.'

Evelyn stepped daintily onto the higher ground next to Luke and plucked the map from his hands.

'*I* will take it from here. I've seen what happens when you two are left to make the plans.'

Campbell stumbled to join them.

'Hey, I'm not the one who crashed the plane.'

'Ditched, not crashed. There's a difference,' said Luke defensively, 'and are you ever going to let that go?'

'It was an hour ago!'

'Not the point.' Luke turned back to Evelyn only to be met with empty air.

'You're still not getting the map back,' called Evelyn from the mist up ahead.

Despite their size, the thick fog and the opposing darkness made the stones near impossible to find even with the aid of a map and compass. No landmarks could be picked out in the distance, in fact there was no distance. The flare of the torch across the blankets of white fog made it impossible to see anything until you practically walked into it.

Coincidentally, this is exactly how Luke finally, quite literally, stumbled across the stones. The jagged corner of the stone connected with the shallow bone of Luke's shin. He grabbed his leg and hopped on one foot, biting back a less than manly yelp at the sudden eruption of pain that was completely disproportionate to the injury.

Evelyn emerged from this mist shortly after. Luke straightened quickly and tried to ignore the throbbing in his shin.

She walked past him, up to the face of the large boulder resting on the two others and ran a hand across the rough surface. Hidden amongst the natural valleys and troughs of the stones surface were deeper carvings, neat lines etched into the stone that, when cast in shadow as the torch beam passed across them, joined together.

'Names?' said Evelyn. Luke limped closer to her.

'Victorian Graffiti,' said Luke. 'Funny how a hundred years is all it takes for graffiti to go from ASBO to history.'

Campbell appeared from the mist like a ghost summoned by the mere mention of crime.

'I don't care if it's history in a hundred years, I'd still give Banksy an ASBO if I caught him.'

'Or her.'

Luke and Campbell turned to Evelyn.

'What?' she said provocatively. 'Are you saying only men are allowed to be artistic vandals?'

Both men knew better than to try and dig their way out of the inevitable hole they would end up in and remained silent.

Evelyn smirked, her carmine lips twitching to

the side as a thick blanket of fog drifted between her and the two men, muting the colour. She turned back to the stone and let out a strangled gasp as a face appeared behind the shifting fog. No, not a face, another carving. Crude features scratched into the stone forming a lurid visage frozen in an unblinking glare.

'Green men,' said Luke behind Evelyn's shoulder making her jump again. 'Some say they date back to the medieval, some even older.'

'And are they?' asked Evelyn unable to break the stare of the empty carved eyes. She felt the skin on her neck prickle as the hair stood on end. Like the eyes of the people who carved the faces deep in history were still out there, watching from the fog.

'Possibly, some of them look pretty Pictish but it's hard to date stone carvings,' Luke said brightly dispelling the tension that had built. 'But I'm pretty sure they're Scott's "Blind Eyes" '.

Luke circled the stones, the fog relented as a light breeze blew gently across the muir, curling into tiny whirls as the air was channelled and manipulated by the natural amphitheatre that surrounded the stones.

More faces were carved into the rough stone; some were simple, round, flat, almost featureless with eyes and mouth only picked out by shallow, straight lines, while others, while not necessarily finer carved, showed depth, fully formed features frozen in time.

Eight faces in total he counted, returning finally to the first where Evelyn still stood, now accompanied by Campbell.

'Look at this,' Campbell pointed at one of the names carved into the stone.

The carving didn't much stand out from the rest, perhaps it was slightly finer carved than many of the rest, the strokes deliberate and neat. But none of that would have caught the eye immediately, only closer study would reveal the differences. The name seemed familiar to Luke but he couldn't place it.

Lucy Ashton

Luke looked back at Campbell and Evelyn, a question asked with his expression rather than words.

'The Bride of Lammermoor, Lucy Ashton was the bride in Scott's *The Bride of Lammermoor*,' Evelyn said excitedly.

'Another wife,' Luke huffed a laugh, 'and maybe another.'

He moved his gaze up from the carved name to the face that sat above it.

'Hello Charlotte,' he said softly.

'I can't imagine Scott's wife was all too happy with that portrait,' Campbell said dryly.

Luke couldn't argue with him. Joke or not, the face couldn't be called feminine, nor attractive in any way. The shape of the face and the majority of the features were almost nonexistent, only superficially etched in to give the impression of a head. But the eyes, someone, presumably Scott, had taken care to carve the eyes in a finer detail, clear enough that there could be no doubt in the direction they were staring, unblinking, for eternity.

'Weary hunter follow sweet Charlotte's stare.' Luke turned to Evelyn and Campbell, 'I don't know about you two but I'm pretty bloody weary.'

Two heads bobbed in silent agreement.

'Not to put a damper on this, but where are we following her stare to?' said Campbell. 'In case you haven't noticed I can't see the feet at the end of my legs in this fog let alone wherever along an indefinite line Scott hid the stone!'

Luke looked down at his feet then back to Campbell and opened his mouth.

'It was a figure of speech,' interrupted Campbell with a long suffering groan.

'We don't need to see where we're going.' Luke and Campbell turned to Evelyn's voice.

She waited, expecting one or the other to catch onto her idea. Neither man spoke.

'Really?' she said and held up the map.

They looked at her blankly.

'Jesus Christ, it's a miracle you two got off that island on your own,' she huffed and pushed past them to the face on the stone.

Evelyn shone the torch on the ground, searching for a moment until she found what she was looking for; a small stick about as wide as a thumb and near perfectly straight. The stick fit snugly into the carved face's eye socket. Evelyn took the compass from the map and measured a bearing from the stick. She translated this to the map and, using the straight edge of the ruler drew a straight line, projecting out from the tiny mark denoting the stones, across the paper landscape in the exact direction the face of Charlotte stared.

'The stone is somewhere along that line,' said Evelyn triumphantly.

Luke and Campbell leant over the map.

'Where did you learn that?' asked Luke.

'Be prepared,' said Evelyn and flashed a Scouts three fingered salute.

Luke chuckled at the childish grin that had broken out on her face.

'Great, so all we need to do is walk along that line until we trip over the stone,' said Campbell sarcastically. 'Or failing that, into the Atlantic.'

Luke stared into the fog as Evelyn glared daggers at Campbell.

'We know it's in the Campsies,' snapped Evelyn, 'although I admit that's still a lot of land.'

Luke snapped his head back to the map.

'Evelyn, where does that line pass through?'

Evelyn cocked her head to the side, tracing the line across the map.

'A lot of empty land and a few houses,' she said disappointedly. 'Why?'

Luke chewed the edge of his lip thinking. 'Specifics, place names,' he said, leaning over Evelyn's shoulder. 'There's still a line of the poem left.'

Evelyn traced back along the line.

'Dunglass Hill, Strathblane railway, ehhh,' she tilted her head again to read the small black text 'Ballagan Glenn, Earl's Seat, Dichtey Burn.'

'Wait,' exclaimed Luke. 'What was that last one?'

'Dichtey Burn?'

'No, the one before that.'

Evelyn moved her finger back up the north face of the mountains to a point at their heart.

'Earl's Seat.'

Luke stepped back, grinning like a Cheshire cat. 'Quiz time.'

He ignored Campbell's groan.

'Robert the Bruce was King of Scotland and the man who we can blame for us ending up in this situation, But what was his title before king?'

'Earl of Carrick,' said Campbell quickly.

Luke looked momentarily taken aback.

'Not just a pretty face Knight,' grinned Campbell, pointing at his chiselled jaw.

Luke smirked at Evelyn's rolling eyes.

'Ok, question two. The last line of the poem said, *"For their destiny beneath Carrick's Chair"*. We can assume that "destiny" is the coronation stone or

Stone of Destiny, but what is a chair?'

'Something you sit on?' said Campbell slowly.

'A seat,' Evelyn corrected him. 'That's one-all pretty boy.'

'Tie breaker, Carrick's chair could then also be read as?'

'Earl's Seat,' they said in unison.

'Precisely,' said Luke, then frowned. 'How far is Earl's Seat?'

The map rustled as Evelyn roughly measured the distance between the stones and the highest point of the Campsies.

'About five miles.'

'Perfect.'

Luke spun on his heel and started into the fog.

'Shouldn't we wait for the fog to clear?' asked Evelyn.

'Sure,' said Luke stopping in his tracks. 'We can make camp here next to an ancient battlefield, beside the creepy face stone that might have been used for dark rituals and human sacrifice.'

Campbell and Evelyn looked at each other then back at the stone.

The fog rolled across the staring faces, unmoving in the rock.

'No, you're right we should get ahead while we can,' said Evelyn quickly, half running to catch up with Luke.

Campbell took one last look at the unnerving effigies before walking as calmly as he could after

Luke and Evelyn only for his nerve to give out. He broke into a jog to catch up to the pair that were disappearing into the mist.

'Hey, wait for me!'

CHAPTER 27

Earls Seat, Campsie's Fells, 578m elevation, 10 miles north of Glasgow on the boarder between Stirlingshire and East Dunbartonshire

A lack of light never helped a search, but the true darkness on the mountains had all but buried any hope of finding the stone. Luke turned on the spot, a full axis as if the earth turned around the point at his feet. There was nothing out there, or rather nothing out of the ordinary. Grass, stone, exposed earth, and a surprisingly well-maintained fence for the top of a mountain. But nowhere obvious for a centuries old ceremonial stone to be hidden, although, as Luke thought about it, what would an obvious place for a centuries old ceremonial stone even look like? And anyway, why would it be hidden in an obvious place, surely, they should be looking for inconspicuous place. But what would that look like? Not that he would admit it but Campbell's X marks the spot was sounding good right about now.

'Are you going to help look or are you happy doing a piss poor lighthouse impression.'

Luke looked down at Campbell's bemused face and clicked off the torch.

He hopped down from the concrete plinth that he had stood on, onto the soft almost springy ground and winced. The cushioned surface wasn't enough to stop a lance of pain from the impact tearing through his leg where Dougal had stabbed him.

'Just trying to shed a little light on the problem.'

He toed the ground, seeing the earth depress under the weight of his foot and then, slowly, spring back, like it was being inflated from beneath.

'Unfortunately, I don't think this will help here.' said Luke as he slipped the doused torch into a pocket.

Evelyn trudged along the line of the wire fence to where Luke and Campbell stood beside the plinth.

'This is hopeless.' she said dropping the fold of her dress that she had held to keep the hem from snagging on the jagged rocks of stone that sat beside the fence.

'I'm not sure I'd see the stone even if I tripped over it!'

'She's right,' said Campbell, 'I could barely see the path up here let alone tell the stone apart from any of these.' He planted his foot on the closest rock. It wobbled, only seated an inch into the ground.

Luke looked at the dark horizon, the only hint of orange glow in the west coming from the distant glimmer of fluorescent bulbs in, Stirling maybe or Falkirk? He wasn't even sure what he was looking at, there was a reason Archaeology was on his office door instead of Geography, aside from the fact he had put it there. Although in all likelihood he wouldn't have an office to go back to after everything that had happened in the last few days.

'From crooked hill sunlight adorn,' said Luke tearing his eyes from the horizon. 'Scott really had thought of everything.'

Campbell stopped pacing along the fence line.

'Hang on, you want to just wait for sunrise and then keep wandering around until we find something?'

There was a dull thud as Luke slumped against the concrete plinth and slid to the ground.

'Pretty much.' he raised his arm and looked at Campbell. 'Best come get comfortable.'

Campbell's eye roll was practically audible, he stomped off following the same search pattern he had been following muttering under his breath.

Evelyn stifled a snigger and settled herself on the ground next to Luke.

'Not going to keep exploring with Dora.' Said Luke nodding backwards at the silhouetted figure of Campbell marching regimented grids in a futile search.

Evelyn laughed. 'No, as much as I love roaming wild mountainsides, I think they're far more beautiful when I can see the scenery.'

Luke shrugged, staring off into the distance once more.

'I don't know, the dark has its charms, the world becomes a different place, this endless eternal space that you could wonder pathless the problems of the day extinguished.'

'That was almost poetic.'

Luke turned to her. 'I should hope so, it was Byron.'

Evelyn's head snapped to him. 'That wasn't Byron.'

Luke smiled. 'Well… I was paraphrasing.'

They both laughed. The threat of the day still hanging over them momentarily forgotten.

Luke studied her face as she turned back to the horizon. Her usual bright colours had been muted to a rainbow of monochrome in the absence of light, even as he watched new shades were painted onto her features as his eyes adjusted to the dark.

'I guess you're right, but my favourite things about the dark are still the lights, the stars, the moon,' she said staring into the distance, 'even the streetlights in Cumbernauld look pretty from here.'

'I would argue stars and moonlight have a tad

more appeal than fluorescent bulbs.'

Evelyn tilted her head back, so her face was basking in the pale grey moonlight.

'I always found stars sad, they're lonely, so many in the sky and still so far apart,' her voice had turned wistful. 'And most of them are ghosts of burntout suns that are so far away that for us light hasn't gone out yet.'

'A sky full of ghosts,' nodded Luke, 'it's a lot like people really.'

Evelyn raised an eyebrow at him. 'The fact that there are 7 billion people on the planet but we're all still isolated and alone?'

'No, that even when our light goes out, others can still see us. No one's ever really gone as long as someone remembers them.'

Luke met Evelyn's eyes; he could see the tears she was holding back shimmering across their surface even in the dark.

'Who said that?'

'I did.' Smiled Luke.

Evelyn gave a short laugh, and a weak smile tweaked the corners of her lips.

'You know that was really was almost poetic.'

'Better than Byron?' He smirked.

'Don't push it.'

❋ ❋ ❋

Sometime in the early hours Campbell had

finally given up his search and perched himself between the rocks next to the plinth.

The thick cloud that had rolled in turned out to be a blessing, keeping the night warmer than clear skies would have allowed and making the wait on the mountain marginally more comfortable.

Luke watched the first strokes of dawn paint the horizon, burning off the feathery cloud and leaving in place wild blush streaks that darkened with every passing minute.

He nudged Evelyn awake; she stirred stretching the stiffness from her neck as her face contorted.

'Remind me not to buy a concrete mattress.'

'I would but I'd be too impressed you found a concrete mattress to buy,' said Luke thoughtfull, 'anyway wake Campbell, sun's coming up.'

Luke hopped to his feet leaving Evelyn to shake Campbell awake, causing him to jump and topple backwards over the stone he had been resting.

By the time he had righted himself Luke was already back atop the concrete plinth, turning a slow circle and surveying the mountain.

'Exactly below my feet is the highest point in East Dumbartonshire, Earl's Seat, and Scott's poem said the stone is hidden beneath,' said Luke to the empty air, 'but it can't be on this spot.'

'Why not?' asked Campbell as he hefted himself from the ground.

Luke tapped his foot on the plinth, 'The

Ordnance Survey didn't place the first trig point until 1936. If the stone was hidden at exactly the highest point they would have found it.'

'Would Scott have even known where the highest point was? The whole summit is Earls Seat, the stone could be anywhere!' argued Evelyn.

'You're right but he must have marked it somehow,' said Luke, he thought out loud. 'There must be something a marker that's gotten overgrown or a…'

'An X?' said Campbell.

'Yes, except not that because we're not following a pirate map,' Luke replied irritably. 'There must be something were missing from the poem, like…'

'An X carved into a stone?'

Luke snapped his head to Campbell, his expression noticeably frustrated. He opened his mouth to snap something back at Campbell, but the words died in his throat.

'Oh, you have got to be joking.'

Campbell's face was the picture of smug triumph. At his feet, cast in a dark shadow by the now streaming rays of the sun against the lighter stone was an incised X about four inches square, carved with stark, deliberate, lines.

'Ehhh, what was that about pirate maps?' Asked Campbell.

Luke stomped over to the stone and dropped to

the dewey grass, his face mere inches from the carved X.

It had been there some time, the interior of the craving having the same weathered patina as the rest of the stone, so close you would never notice if it weren't for the shadow from the rising sun making the lines darker, even then you could walk past it.

Campbell looked down at Luke, lying prostrate at his feet.

'So, what say ye Cap'n Blackbeard?' He said in an over the top impression of a pirate. 'Is this where the treasure be buried?'

Luke got slowly to his feet and sighed.

'This one time, once, I will admit X marks the spot,' Luke recoiled physically at the words. 'But it's nothing to do with treasure maps or pirates.'

He shook his finger at Campbell and turned to walk away but stopped, rounding back on him.

'And another thing Blackbeard was a violent, murderous criminal from Bristol,' said Luke, his voice sounding almost hurt. 'Don't ever accuse me of being from Bristol.'

Campbell had no words as Luke once again turned and walked purposefully towards the fence.

'What's wrong with Bristol?'

Evelyn shrugged and followed Luke, leaving Campbell frowning in confusion.

'I don't understand, why an X?' She asked to

Luke's back. 'It isn't part of the poem.

Luke walked along the fence line, stopping at each wooden upright and giving it a hard shove, testing its seating in the ground.

'Do you know where the phrase x marks the spot comes from?'

'You know you have a habit of answering questions with a question.' Replied Evelyn with a humph.

Luke didn't offer a reply, simply looking over his shoulder with a blank expression waiting for her answer.

Evelyn growled under her breath, 'I don't know, pirate maps?'

Luke turned back to the fence and continued down the line, testing the posts.

'Actually no, not into common usage anyway,' said Luke grimly, 'when military executions by firing squad took place, a target would be put over the heart to focus fire, sometimes a just a plain white circle but often with an X.'

'X marks the spot,' she said softly. 'Why would Scott mark the stone with that?'

The post under Lukes's hand shifted as he put his weight on it. He gave it a soft kick where it met the ground causing the wood to flake away. Spongy, rotten, perfect.

He threw his weight against it, pulling it away from the tacked-on wire and splitting it from the end still stuck in the ground with a wet crunch.

He hefted the post, testing its weight before carrying it back to the death marked stone.

'Scott was a military man, part of the Edinburgh volunteers, Sir Fergusson even more so, he had been serving for twenty years by the time he and Scott recovered the lost honours, and he was appointed Keeper of the Regalia.'

Luke heaved the fence post into the air and dropped the flat end onto the ground, letting it strike the earth with a dull thud.

'You see, Scott was a friend to the prince, the future king, so why would he not declare he found the stone?'

'The same reason we're trying to stop Daniel getting it,' said Campbell, 'it would drive a wedge between Scotland and England.'

'It was a rhetorical question but yes,' said Luke, moving a few inches and thumping the post onto the ground again. 'But that leaves a problem, by protecting the symbol of country they love, keeping part of the honours, one of the most important aspects of every coronation, of every King and Queen, from the future King, it was treason, and what was the sentence for treason?'

'Death.' Evelyn said bluntly.

Luke hit the ground again, the sound of the blow dying softly.

'I have another question,' said Evelyn, watching Luke's strange ritual of hitting the ground, listening, moving a foot or so and repeating the process 'What the hell are you doing?'

Another muted thud as the post connected with the ground.

'Improvising,' said Luke, followed by another thud, 'usually if I wanted to find where someone dug a pit a few centuries ago I would break out some lovely shiny survey kit that beeps and shows me nice clear pictures of whats beneath my feet.'

Thud

'But since we're lacking in time, wanted by the police and a murderous politician.'

'Not to mention 50% of Bonnie and Clyde since you sent his brother for a high dive.'

Luke glared at Campell.

'Yes, thanks for reminding me I have a target on my back.'

'Or an X on your chest.'

Luke's frown deepened; he regretted that particular history lesson.

'Anyway, given that and I'm assuming neither of you have twenty or so grand lying around I'm going retro.'

'Ugg hit ground with stick.' Mocked Evelyn in an impression of a caveman.

Thud

'Not that retro,' said Luke with a suffering sigh. 'It's called bowsing, early archaeologists developed the technique, it's crude but fairly genius. It's essentially very early reflection seismology, you see when I hit the ground it sends sound waves that we can hear. Ground with different compaction has different acoustic resonance...'

Evelyn interrupted, 'Luke while fascinating: police, murderers, time.'

'Good point.'

Thud

'Basically, disturbed ground echoes.'

Luke brought down the wooden post again, as if to illustrate his point the dull thud changed to a slight echo.

Luke looked up at Campbell and Evelyn and smiled. He turned over the post, so the splintered end touched the ground and dragged two long ragged lines over the hollow sounding earth.

'X marks the spot.'

CHAPTER 28

Earl's Seat, Campsies Fells, 578m elevation, 10 miles north of Glasgow on the Border between Stirlingshire and East Dunbartonshire

'I think you're making it up.'

Luke scraped the ground with the corroded bracket he had stripped from the fencepost and fashioned into a makeshift trowel.

'Look, there's a different colour here,' he said prodding at the patch of bare earth, 'and the soil is looser, crumbly, friable.'

Campbell stared at the turfless ground where Luke had peeled away the surface of the earth to show a patch of bare soil about a metre across.

'Of course, how could I not see the clear difference between the muddy brown soil and the other muddy brown soil.'

'Look, someone has dug a hole here, I don't argue with you about laws so trust me.'

Campbell snapped incredulously. 'You do

nothing but argue about the law!'

Luke stopped scraping the ground. 'And so far you've done nothing but question my archeological insight,' he said calmly, before returning to scraping the earth. 'At least when I question laws it's in the interest of expediting the situation.'

Campbell knew it was pointless to try and argue, instead throwing his arms up in exaggerated despair and stomping off to do another circuit of the mountainside.

'He's going to throw you in a cell when this is all over if you aren't careful,' said Evelyn with a short chuckle.

Once this was all over—her words made it sound like they had started looking for the stone months, even years beforehand, she'd almost forgotten only days ago her life had been normal: no murderers, lost treasures or plane crashes. And John had been alive. Even when he was missing there had been hope until it had been ripped from her by Corban's cruel twisted grin, his glee at telling her John was dead. Once this was over that was all she had to go back to. Books full of dead poets and memories of happier times. Before this stupid rock had ever come into her life.

Evelyn knelt on the soft ground beside Luke and peered into the hole.

A rectangular hole. about two foot square and getting on for a foot deep had been dug away under Luke's hand.

Evelyn had to agree with Campbell, the ground did all look the same. How Luke knew where a hole had been dug over a century ago she had no idea.

'I doubt it,' said Luke, not looking up from his work.

'Why's that?'

'He's the one who let me out in the first place.'

And also how Campbell had ended up entangled in this mess. 'They didn't hang around before burying this,' said Luke, snapping Evelyn out of her bitter spiral. 'Clearly Scott and Ferguson wanted the stone out of their hands as soon as they could.'

Can't blame them, thought Evelyn sourly, but asked out of curiosity, 'how do you know?'

Luke pointed his makeshift trowel at the wall of the hole.

'The edges of the cut they made, they're ragged, hurried and uneven,' he scraped some more at the soil inside the hole, 'and this infill, it's almost indistinguishable from the natural ground, it hasn't been washed-in slowly and it's loose, it hasn't been packed in, just dumped back in and covered with the turf.'

'I can't see the difference even after you've pointed it out,' said Evelyn. She watched Luke break away the crumbling soil from a firmer, consolidated edge. Yes, she could see the way the loose fill flaked easily away from the undisturbed ground, but only as it did so, there was no way she could see where that solid edge might go, what shape it would make or where it would stop. It was almost like a poem, the story is revealed line by line, you don't know what's coming next and it only makes sense once the last words are revealed.

'You feel the difference more than see it,' said Luke, still focused on his work. 'It just takes practice, and a bit of precision guesswork.'

Evelyn smiled at that.

The sound of the makeshift trowel cutting through the soil changed suddenly. No longer a soft, dull, low pitched brushing of soil, instead a harsher, sharp sound of the metal blade against something hard.

Luke and Evelyn both stopped dead at the sound and looked at each other.

'It could just be a stone,' offered Luke.

Evelyn frowned at him, 'we're looking for a stone…'

'Really?' said Luke sarcastically, 'and this whole time I thought it was the Holy Grail we were after.'

He turned quickly away from Evelyn's scowl and continued moving the earth carefully away from whatever had caused the sound beneath.

'What I meant was, we're on a mountain covered in stone. This could be nothing.'

A murky shape slowly took form in the soil,

rectangular, like the hole that contained it and only barely smaller. The hole cut no more than was needed to closely house it.

'Granted if this is nothing it would be the most conveniently-shaped nothing I've ever seen.' Luke scraped across the top of the rectangle, revealing, inch by inch, the smooth carved surface. The improvised trowel caught on something protruding above the stone surface with a metallic clunk, metal striking metal.

Luke stopped dead, his hand not moving beyond what the makeshift trowel had struck.

'Evelyn, describe the Stone of Scone to me,' he said shakily, 'just to make sure I'm not jumping to conclusions.'

Luke turned to her when no answer came. An awed stare met his broad grin as Evelyn knelt slowly to the edge of the hole and reached a hand out, brushing her fingers across the rough, soil-stained surface.

'Beauty is truth, truth beauty, —that is all ye know on earth, and all ye need to know...' said Evelyn.

Luke looked sidelong at her and raised an eyebrow.

'I don't know what it looks like Luke, I'm a poet not a historian,' she said, meeting his eyes. 'But I don't need to know anything other than it's beautiful.'

'It almost seems a shame to describe it after

that,' said Luke carefully probing under the metal object protruding from the stone, 'but none the less, a block of sandstone, weighing over 150 kilos, a cross carved into the surface.'

He gently eased up the rusted metal that was fused to the end of the stone.

'And an iron ring at each end so you could actually lift the thing.'

He grinned at Evelyn who had allowed a broad smile to bloom at the sight of what had to be the stone. The stone that was not lost but hidden, its glory obscured but still so bright.

Luke's fingers found the second cold iron ring. He lifted it gently from the soil and gave a gentle tug, testing its strength.

Luke swallowed the lump that had formed in his throat.

'Here goes...'

'Nice to see those survived the century underground,' Daniel's venomous voice echoed across the mountainside. 'It'll be easier for you to get it out for me.'

The iron rings clinked onto the stone, slipping from Luke's hands as he rounded on Daniel's voice.

Morning sun cast his form in shadow. Two more figures stood beside him. Luke couldn't make out their features in the glare, he guessed the shorter figure was Corban but the third...

Luke cursed to himself as a cloud drifted

across the sun revealing Campbell's face, teeth gritted and body tense but not struggling, no, the glinting silver barrel of Corban's 1911 pistol pressed hard into Campbell's ribs put a stop to any resistance before it began.

Corban dug the pistol in harder, as if to emphasise the threat, making Campbell wince but stand firm.

'I really have to thank you Mr Knight, without you I might never have found the stone out here.'

Daniel sauntered across the grass towards Luke and Evelyn.

'Now why don't you bring it to me?'

Luke shot to his feet and stormed towards Daniel, stopping inches from his face. He stood shaking with rage.

'How?'

How had Daniel found them so quickly? Their arrival at the reservoir might have been less than subtle but they could have gone anywhere from there.

Daniel leant in close to Luke's ear and hissed, only loud enough for Luke to hear.

'Don't make this difficult Knight.'

He stepped back, resuming the carefully scripted bravado.

'Come on Mr Knight, you've done the hard work for me this far,' he sneered, 'why ruin a good thing?'

'How are you always only one step away?'

Luke regained his composure, ignoring Daniel's demands, he stared the grinning man in the eye, unflinching.

Daniel's grin faltered, he took a step back, out of the range of Luke's intense stare.

'One thing you should know Mr Knight, money opens a lot of doors: museum archives, government records, police tracking systems.'

Daniel's smile returned at the last. He ignored Luke's frown and strode slowly to where Campbell was still held at gunpoint.

'Surely you know every police vehicle is fitted with a tracker DS Campbell? It makes it very useful to find someone who's on the run in an unmarked car.'

Daniel clapped his hand to Campbell's cheek once, then again.

Campbell lunged forward baring his teeth, poised to rip Daniel apart.

'Ah, ah, ahh,' Daniel taunted as the barrel of Corban's pistol was forced so deeply into Campbell's ribs that he buckled, dropping to one knee with a shout of pain.

'No one likes a hero, Detective. Perhaps I should take this, just in case you have any ideas.'

Daniel pulled Campbell's own pistol from its holster on his hip and weighed it in his hands before turning back to Luke, holding the gun carelessly in the air.

'Money opens other, more fun doors too, parties,

palaces,' Daniel paused and grinned again, 'private helicopters.'

As if on command the sleek pointed nose of a Bell 222 helicopter rose above the crest of the mountain behind Daniel.

Luke and Evelyn shrunk back from the onslaught of wind from the helicopter's downdraft as it hovered low over the open mountaintop, the relentless thudding of the rotor wings cutting through the air almost deafening.

'After that mess you left at the reservoir, it wasn't hard to find you. Now Mr Knight, the stone if you will,' Daniel shouted over the noise. 'You know how this goes.'

He nodded to Corban who moved his pistol to rest on Campbell's temple as Daniel levelled Campbell's own Glock at Evelyn.

'What's more important to you Knight?'

Luke turned and marched towards the hole and the stone still lying within. Daniel had won, there was nothing he could do.

Evelyn caught his shoulder as he passed her and shouted.

'What are you doing? You can't give him the stone.'

Luke shrugged. 'Nothing's worth more than you. Either of you.'

He carried on walking before she could argue further. The helicopter's downdraft had blown soil back across the stone. Luke brushed his fingers across its surface, cleaning the debris. A country for a detective and a poet, a country for his friends. It seemed like an obvious choice. He dropped to his knees and dug his hands down one side of the stone, levering it onto its end before, heaving it from the hole. Moving the stone took all of Luke's strength. The solid block of sandstone weighed more than a grown man, not to mention the weight of what it represented and the weight of what it meant to hand it to Daniel.

'Into the helicopter if you don't mind, Mr Knight.'

Luke glared death at Daniel but didn't protest. He hefted the stone, the muscles in his back screaming at the strain.

Step by slow step he half-stumbled towards the waiting helicopter. He couldn't bear to look back and see Daniel's smug expression at watching him struggle with the stone. So close, they were so close and fell at the final hurdle. No, not fell, they were cheated and who says this has to be the end.

Finally, Luke reached where the helicopter had perched on the mountain, no longer hovering but neither fully landed, still poised to lift off at a moment's notice.

The faceless visored helmet of the pilot tracked Luke the last few steps to the side door. He kept his head low as he reached the door, dropping the stone onto the soft grass and sagging at the relief from the weight.

'Do hurry up Knight, some of us have appointments to keep.'

The helicopter's rotors whipped above him carrying Daniel's words away with their relentless onslaught. Luke ignored him and stared up at the spinning blades, they were too fast to pick out an individual, a blur against the bright sky, both present and invisible at the same time, moving through space practically unseen.

Luke refocused on the door, popping the handle and letting it fall open on its hinges. It was an effort to heft the stone back off the ground, let alone get it to the height of the door. He gritted his teeth and hauled the stone onto the bed of the cabin, pushing it safely inside and wincing at the shriek it made sliding over the metal surface.

Only Daniel's smug face met him as Luke turned his back on the stone.

'You've won,' bit out Luke, 'now leave.'

A faint smirk tweaked the corner of Daniel's mouth.

'Come on Knight, you didn't think it would be that easy did you?'

He stalked towards Luke, chuckling faintly to himself, like a hyena cornering its prey.

'I'm disappointed,' he said stopping short of Luke. 'I expected some more fight from you.'

Daniel's final words were followed with a sharp exhale and a dull thud as Luke's fist connected with his stomach, fast as the blades above their heads, in a swift hook. Daniel doubled over, wheezing, gasping to regain the breath that had been knocked out of him.

'Is that enough fight for you?' hissed Luke in Daniel's ear. 'I hate to disappoint.'

Luke shoved Daniel's folded form away from him, twisting Campbell's pistol out of Daniel's grip before turning the sleek black gun on him.

'Call off your dog Montrose,' said Luke, nodding in the direction of Corban whose head was darting between Daniel, Luke and his own gun, still pointed at Campbell.

Daniel raised his hands calmly in a mock surrender.

'If you're going to point a gun at me Mr Knight,' he said, not breaking Luke's gaze, 'you had better be willing to pull the trigger.'

A soft click echoed above the whir of the helicopter's rotors as Luke pulled back the Glock's slide, chambering a shining brass case, in response.

Daniel held his stare for a few more moments before calling to Corban.

'Do as he says.'

Corban hesitated, looking to Daniel before finally dropping his gun. Campbell shook off his grip and picked up the shining Colt, training the barrel on Corban before slowly walking backwards and joining Luke.

'What now Mr Knight? Do you expect me to beg? Give you the stone and wait for the police?'

Luke looked down the barrel of the pistol at Daniel, his hands still lazily raised, then flashed a glance at the waiting helicopter with the stone nestled inside, at Campbell with the 1911 pistol in his white-knuckled grip pointed unwavering at Corban, and Evelyn. Her shock of auburn hair like fire in the sunlight, burning like her glare at Daniel. People have killed for less, thought Luke as he turned his focus back to Daniel. His hand tightened around the pistol's hard plastic grip; the cold metal of the trigger pressed into his finger.

Luke let out a slow breath and relaxed his hand, dropping the gun slightly. 'Leave.'

Daniel's eyebrow raised in genuine surprise.

'Get in your helicopter and leave.'

'Luke,' started Evelyn, her voice a mix of hurt and fury, she rushed forward only to be stopped by Campbell's outstretched arm, 'you can't.'

Luke turned to her and offered a slight shake of his head, a silent apology.

Daniel levelled his gaze at Luke, suspicious of the seemingly easy surrender.

'I guess you'll be taking the stone first?'

Luke dropped the gun to his side and shrugged defeated.

'What's the point? You said it yourself, you have the resources, the connections, even if we took the stone you would just find us again and take it back.'

'You know Knight, I admire that you had the courage to try and stop me,' Daniel took a step towards Luke, the vicious, predatory grin cutting across his face, 'and the brains to know when you'd lost,' he chuckled to himself.

Luke bared his teeth and pointed the pistol at Daniel once again hissing, 'leave.'

Daniel backed down a step at the hate gleaming in Luke's eyes, he nodded to Corban and started towards the helicopter.

Luke, Evelyn and Campbell watched on as the two men climbed into the helicopter cabin, the stone still resting on the floor. Daniel gave them a mock salute before slamming the door shut and signaling the pilot to take off.

Evelyn shook off Campbell's arm and rounded on Luke.

Pain erupted across his cheek as her hand connected hard enough to make his eyes tear up.

'How could you just let them go?' she shouted, the hate in her eyes now turned on Luke. 'After everything you just give them the stone and let them win?'

Luke flexed his jaw and said calmly, 'is that really how little you think of me?' Evelyn stopped her rage and frowned at him in confusion.

'We had to let them go, if we had taken the stone and run Daniel would have just hunted us down and we would be back where we are now, same story different setting.'

Luke handed Campbell back his Glock 17 pistol and brushed invisible dirt from his hands.

'Now Daniel thinks he's won and for the first time we're the ones hunting him.'

'It was all a trick?' smiled Evelyn.

'Why didn't you tell us?' asked Campbell tucking the Glock back into its holster and Corban's Colt into the waistband of his trousers.

'I had to make it believable,' shrugged Luke.

'Great,' Campbell continued, 'just two small problems, we have no idea where Daniel's taking the stone and since my car is still in Balloch and you crashed the plane...'

'Ditched,' protested Luke, 'it was a ditch landing.'

'Crashed,' repeated Campbell. 'We are in the middle of nowhere without any transport.'

Evelyn Cleared her throat.

'Actually, I think I can help with that. When I was on his yacht Daniel said he had to get the stone *"back to where this all started"*.'

Luke rolled his eyes. 'That vain, pretentious bastard.' Luke turned to Evelyn and Campbell. 'He's setting himself up as the saviour, the new heroic leader and a new King of Scotland. Where else would an ego like that go but where the Kings of Scotland were crowned, the home of the coronation stone, where it all began.'

'He's taking it to Scone,' said Evelyn, shaking her head. 'We can still stop him.'

'That's all well and good,' said Campbell. 'Now how do we get there?'

'Oh ye of little faith,' smiled Luke, patting Campbell on the shoulder. He reached into his shirt pocket and pulled out a sleek, black phone, waving it in front of Campbell.

'I'm sure Daniel won't mind me using up some minutes,' said Luke with a grin, admiring his hand. 'He really should keep a closer eye on his pockets.' Campbell shook his head, disapproving on principal. Luke flicked the phone on and dialed a number.

'Who are you calling?' asked Evelyn. Luke's face turned hard and somber.

'You know the saying, if you can't beat them,' he said grimly, 'find someone worse.'

CHAPTER 29

Killearn, Stirlingshire, 17 Miles North of Glasgow

'The answer is no Luke.' Luke could hear the click of Keir's heels across the wooden floor of his office down the phone line.

For half the journey off the Campsies Luke had failed to convince Keir to get off his bony, pious arse and help them. Although in fairness, using those exact words probably hadn't helped matters.

A creak echoed in Luke's ear as Keir sank into his desk chair. 'I warned you once to let this go,' he said, weariness softening his tone. 'I'm not going to help you put yourselves back in front of a gun.'

'If you don't help us you're letting him change the face of Britain, you're putting an entire country at the mercy of a sociopath,' snapped Luke.

'As opposed to politicians who are usually so empathetic?' Keir sighed, leaning back in his chair with another creak of strained wood and leather. 'I already have Mr Crawford's murder on my conscience, I'm not about to add the three of you to it.'

Campbell and Evelyn walked a short distance ahead, picking their way along the gentle track that led to the edge of the town. Luke turned his attention back to the phone and the priest.

'You didn't seem to have any reservations putting me in danger in Qumran.'

'Are you ever going to let that go?' snapped Keir.

When no answer came from Luke he continued. 'That was different, there was more at stake and for the record, I didn't tip off the Israeli's, I just happened to be in the right place to finish what you started after they caught you.'

Luke bit back a retort, arguing with Keir would get him nowhere.

'All I need is for you to delay Daniel long enough for us to get to Scone.'

'What makes you think I could do that, even if I wanted to?'

Luke screwed up his eyes, pinching the bridge of his nose, frustration threatening to turn into anger.

'You know as well as I do that the church has a stake in the Stone, they protected it for half a century, kept their deception of Edward I a secret, are you really telling me an organisation worth more than the GDP of Iceland can't even make a bloody phone call?'

'I'm sorry Luke, I'm not going to be the one to lead you to your own execution,' said Keir softly but firmly.

'So you'd rather let us face the sword alone, unaided?'

He was silent for a moment before finally replying, 'better than swinging it myself.'

The line went dead with a decisive click, leaving Luke without a retort.

'Sanctimonious prick,' he shouted, launching the phone across the field.

Campbell's head tracked the arc of the phone through the sky and to its final rest in a small stream. 'I take it that went well?'

Luke glared at him and rubbed his temple. 'We're on our own.'

He carried on towards the end of the track and to the road beyond.

'What's the next bright idea?' shouted Campbell, hurrying to catch up.

Luke stopped at the edge of the road as the blurred shape of a car whistled past into the town.

'Well?'

He turned away from the road to where Evelyn had stood at his side.

'Plan's still the same,' he said after a moment. 'We get to Scone, stop Daniel and get the stone back. We just have less time to do it in.'

Evelyn chewed on the corner of her lip. 'What about Balloch? Go back and get the car. I doubt

Daniel will be tracking it anymore.'

'That's a three hour walk. Without Keir slowing them down we would never make it to Scone in time to stop Daniel,' said Luke.

Another car whipped past them on the road, a glare from the high sun flashing off the glass and into Luke's eyes making him turn his head away. 'What about trains?'

'Not round here,' laughed Evelyn, 'closest one would be back in Glasgow.'

'Well, what….' Luke started when Campbell brushed past him and strode purposefully into the road and raised his hand at the car speeding towards him. The squealing breaks made Luke and Evelyn spin towards the road. The car had barely come to a stop and already Campbell prowled towards the driver's side window, his warrant card on full display.

The man in the driver's seat wound down the thin window letting out a stream of surprisingly inventive curses. 'What are you playing at ya daft twa…'

'Sir, please step out of the car.' Campbell spoke in the way only a seasoned police officer could, a voice that could command attention in any situation. Except it seemed, from the man in the car.

'Are you aff yer heid, a could a hit ya,' the man shook his head, 'jumping in front o cars like that.'

'Sir!' Campbell said more forcefully, finally

making the man's attention snap to him.

'I need you to step out of the vehicle, I am commandeering this car under section 42 of the Police Special Powers Act 1979.'

'Are ye now?' The man stared at Campbell for a long moment, judging the young detective, scanning for any sign of his conviction slipping. Finding nothing the man clicked off his seatbelt and opened the door.

'What do you need it for anyway?'

'I'm sorry but I can't discuss any aspect of an ongoing investigation,' the words came out of Campbell like a well-rehearsed line. He extended his hand for the keys that the driver still gripped tightly.

'I'll have your car back to you by tomorrow,' said Campbell by way of assurance.

The man seemed reluctant to hand over.

'No a scratch on it,' he added.

The man grudgingly handed him the keys. Campbell took them and waved over to Luke and Evelyn who were still stood on the track watching, amused at the exchange.

'Hang on, who are they?' the man said indignantly seeing Luke and Evelyn reach the car.

Campbell's eyes widened slightly as his brain grasped for an answer.

'Ehh, my partners,' he said slowly, then with confidence regained, 'DC McGregor and DC Renton.'

Luke raised an eyebrow at him and muttered under his breath,

'And you say I watch too many movies.'

Campbell glared at him as the man looked Luke and Evelyn up and down, his brows furrowed in a dubious frown.

Luke followed the man's eyes down to his clothes, the tattered and blood stained shirt and frayed kilt. He looked across to Evelyn whose once fine dress wasn't faring much better.

'We're under cover,' said Evelyn quickly, noticing the man's growing suspicion.

'Aye, are ye now?' he said with a huffed laugh.

Thankfully the man didn't question further, instead standing aside to let Campbell past and into the driver's seat.

Luke moved towards the passenger door, brushing past Campbell.

'Police special powers act?' he whispered, flashing him a wry smile.

'Shut up and get in the car,' Campbell hissed back, pushing past Luke and dropping into the driver's seat. He went to shut the door but found it stopped by the man's hand on the frame.

'Back here, tomorrow, no a scratch.' It wasn't a question.

Campbell said nothing and nodded once. Apparently satisfied the man removed his hand and Campbell shut the door and fired up the engine. He pulled away slowly down the road that wound through the town.

Evelyn watched out of the back window until the man was far out of sight of the car, disappearing behind the bend of hedges that lined the road.

'I didn't know the police could actually commandeer cars?' she said curiously, leaning between the two front seats.

'They can't,' said Luke, far too amused by the situation.

Evelyn turned to Campbell for more explanation.

'We needed a car,' he continued, shrugging, 'I figured if even Knight believed police could borrow a car whenever they wanted, there was a good chance a random member of the public would too.'

'Not sure if I should be flattered or offended by that,' said Luke.

'Mark the day! The irreprehensible DS Edward Campbell breaking the law?' teased Evelyn, making both her and Luke burst out laughing.

'What happened to, "I'm a police officer I can't break the law"?' asked Luke.

Campbell frowned at him and bristled.

'Given the list of crimes I've already committed helping you two?' he searched for the right words, then shrugged, his face and tone softening. 'Fuck it.'

Luke and Evelyn's mouths both dropped open.

'Who are you and what have you done with Campbell?' said Luke.

Campbell grinned at them both then turned back to the long, empty road and planted his foot on the accelerator, sending them careening towards Scone, towards the Stone and to Daniel.

"You doubt? I Mak Siccar"

RODGER DE KIRKPATRICK TO ROBERT THE BRUCE ON THE KILLING OF JOHN COMYN 10 FEBRUARY 1306

CHAPTER 30

Scone Palace, Scone, Perthshire, 35 Miles North of Edinburgh

Luke couldn't help but bathe in the wonder of the objects that lined the walls of Scone Palace. No, not just what lined the walls, the walls themselves, the fine wallpaper, vaulted ceilings that stretched down halls and the intricate plaster moulding that decorated the space. Even the plainest of furniture that stood around the fringes of rooms seemed to draw the eye.

A hiss from Campbell pulled Luke away from his fascination with the furnishings.

'If you're done bothering the bookshelves.'

'Honestly,' said Luke wistfully as his eyes danced across the warm leather spines and the delicate gilt of the books that surrounded them, 'I might need a few minutes.'

Campbell rolled his eyes and shoved Luke through the door into a bright room lined with cabinets full of fine porcelain.

'He's not here,' said Evelyn from behind them.

'We've been into every room in this place and there hasn't been a hint of Daniel or the bloody stone.'

It was true, thought Luke, it had been late in the day by the time they had finally driven down the long road into Scone Palace but even then they had not been greeted by the media circus they had expected Daniel to have amassed to broadcast his monumental declaration that he, and he alone, was responsible for the return home of the Stone of Destiny; the symbol of Scottish kings and queens and a reminder of a nation defiant to oppression. Luke could practically see the smug look on Daniel's face as his plan fell into place and they were too late to stop him. A pointless conflict ignited not for the love of a nation—that he could have at least understood, if not condoned. No, Daniel only did anything for the love of power, money and fame: greed hidden behind the attractive cloak of patriotism.

But there had been no media circus and as yet not so much as a glimpse of Daniel's face, smug or otherwise.

They had spent the better part of an hour searching the palace as much as the red nylon rope, as impenetrable to the public as any locked door would allow and when that failed the private rooms beyond. Nothing. No Daniel. No Stone. No options.

'He's here somewhere, we just need to keep

looking.'

'Where?' snapped Evelyn. 'We've been through this house twice and nothing, what good is looking again going to do?'

'Well unless you can think of some poem about Scone that says where narcissistic psychopaths might be we haven't got any better idea.'

Campbell pushed past her and made for a door in the opposite wall.

'The surrounding woodland scenery is very grand,
It cannot be surpassed in fair Scotland,
Especially the elegant Palace of Scone, in history renowned,
Where some of Scotland's kings were crowned.'

Campbell stopped on the threshold, his shoulders rose and sunk slowly as he took and let out a long breath.

'The City of Perth by William McGonagall.'

Luke smirked at Campbell, amused at not being the target of the detective's exasperation for a change.

'Unless the next line is about a wonderful room in the palace that's perfect for political plots then, my point still stands.'

Evelyn stuck her tongue out at him, choosing not to dignify Campbell's snipe with a response.

'Mature,' said Campbell dryly. 'My apologies to Mr McGonagall for calling his poem useless.'

'In fairness you wouldn't be the first,' said Evelyn. 'His work isn't exactly famous for being good.'

'It's also factually wrong,' interrupted Luke, his brows furrowing as he crossed the room to the bright, leaded window. 'The kings weren't crowned at the Palace, the Palace wasn't even built until the 1800's.'

Campbell rubbed his forehead. 'There's a time for being a pedant, Knight.'

'There's always time to be a pedant, Detective, details are the difference between truth and fiction.' Luke clamped a hand on Campbell and Evelyn's shoulders and guided them towards the window. 'Even if you can forgive the frankly tortured rhyme, McGonagall has got the basic facts wrong, kings were crowned on Moot Hill just over there.'

Luke pointed to a wide green strip of land before the woods, just north of the palace. A single building stood in the clearing: a small chapel built from blocks of pinkish stone, lighter than the deep red of the palace stonework and topped with a dark pitched roof cornered with four matching spires. The hill was unusually quiet, lacking the mass of tourists that roamed the palace and grounds.

'Why there?' asked Evelyn. 'If Daniel wants a show why a drab chapel over a palace?'

'I'm glad you asked,' said Luke with a toothy grin.

Campbell rolled his eyes and hissed under his breath, 'For Christ's sake.'

'Could be a lot of reasons. Moot Hill was the site of first parliament under Constantine II, the site of proclamations and laws. Obviously, it was the sight of coronations and where Kenneth MacAlpin first brought the stone of destiny.' Luke ignored Campbell who was making a show of checking the time on an invisible watch.

'But as much as it pains me to say, I think Daniel knows his history, of the Stone anyway.' Luke continued, 'do you know where the name Moot Hill comes from?'

'Do enlighten us,' said Campbell sarcastically, earning a warning slap from Evelyn.

'As you wish, in the early coronations noblemen would bring soil from their land in their boot to the hill so they could pledge their allegiance and the king wouldn't have to risk travelling across the kingdom.'

'Daniel wants to make his claim of power over all Scottish soil at once,' finished Evelyn. 'That's a wee bit histrionic.'

Luke gave a non-committal shrug. 'Everything Daniel's done has been about the symbolism, why break the habit? The nation is in a liminal space, the passing of crowns, a time when the depth of tradition comes to the front of the public consciousness. Symbols have a greater power now than they have in the last seven decades and as much as I hate to give him credit, Daniel knows that and will take advantage. '

'The road has been closed off and the tracks up to the chapel too,' Campbell said, peering out of the rippled glass towards the road they had arrived on.

He was right, in the time they had been in the Palace, steel crowd control barriers had been erected across the road that ran between the palace and the chapel, cutting off access to traffic and pedestrians.

'No security through,' mused Luke.

'About time we caught a break.'

Campbell moved the heavy linen curtain out from the edge of Evelyn's view.

'Luck isn't something we get Crawford.'

Evelyn's shoulders tensed as she watched a man in a suit disappear around the side of the chapel. It was too far to make out his face but she knew.

'Corban.' The name left a bitter taste in her mouth.

Campbell let the curtain fall, cutting through Evelyn's bitter trance.

'A dog never strays far from his master.'

Campbell turned away from the window and strode for the hallway that ran from the room.

'What are you doing.'

He stopped and shrugged at Luke. 'I assumed we were going with the usual plan?'

'And that would be?'

'Stumble blindly into danger with no plan, no backup and, let's be honest, no chance of it going well, then hoping for the best.'

Luke frowned at Campbell as the detective wavered in the doorway, watching him expectantly.

A hand fell on Luke's shoulder. 'He has a point.'

Luke didn't look at Evelyn. 'I know, but I don't like him being the one suggesting the reckless plan,' he said uneasily, turning to her slowly, 'it means I have to be the voice of reason.'

She patted him on the shoulder with a weak smile then made for the doorway where Campbell waited. Luke followed, stopping where the Detective leant against the frame.

'You've changed.'

'I've just spent too much time with you Knight,' he smirked then started down the hallway.

The sun was dipping low across the horizon, casting a red glow into the long hallway and throwing long shadows against the walls. They climbed a short set of stairs through the exit and into the obligatory gift shop. Luke stopped near on the threshold of the exit and called ahead. 'I'll catch you up.'

Evelyn and Campbell looked back at him. 'What are you doing?'

'Find somewhere to watch the chapel, I'll be there in a second.'

Luke disappeared back inside without another word.

Evelyn shrugged to Campbell before continuing

to the edge of the building. They moved to the corner of the crenelated tower, hidden from the chapel by the airy hedges.

'Any sign of Corban?'

Evelyn strained her eyes at the side of the chapel Corban had slipped around.

'Nothing,' she said flatly. 'Promise me something Campbell.'

Campbell looked at the back of her dark, burning hair, concern toning his face. 'What?'

'When we find him,' Evelyn's voice was cold, 'Daniel's mine.'

She turned to look at the detective when no answer came.

Campbell swallowed the lump in his throat. 'If by yours you mean yours to turn over to the police...'

The look of pain in her eyes told him that not what she meant.

He let out a measured breath, 'I'll never forget he was the one that took John away from you.' He paused. 'And from me, but we have to be better than Daniel.'

Evelyn held his gaze, her silence saying more than words could, the almost hidden emptiness behind Campbell's eyes, the masked pain. She hadn't seen it before but in that moment she knew she wasn't the only one who had lost a part of her heart. She reached out and gripped his hand.

'Any movement?' The pair jumped apart at Luke

appearing along the wall beside them holding a long leather-wrapped object in his hand. If he noticed the tears staining both their eyes he made no comment.

'What the hell is that?' hissed Campbell, his usual brusque manor back in place.

Luke looked to the sword he carried then back to Campbell.

'A sword…' he said slowly.

'I think he means, why the hell do you have a highland broadsword?' added Evelyn.

'They had them in the gift shop and I didn't want to go in unarmed,' said Luke as if it were obvious while shedding the sheath from the cold steel.

'But it's blunt and this isn't 1746,' said Campbell sufferingly. 'Besides, Daniel and Corban aren't going to be using swords.'

He pulled the gun from the holster on his hip.

'Ouch!' exclaimed Campbell, rubbing the spot on his arm where Luke had just slapped him with the flat of the blade.

'It might be blunt but it's still heavy enough to hurt,' said Luke. 'Besides, I've told you, I don't do guns.'

'Could have done without the demonstration,' Campbell grumbled.

Luke ignored him, instead hefting the sword and breaking the cover of the bushes.

'What's the plan, just walk in the front door?' asked Evelyn incredulously.

'Why not? Like Campbell said, stumble blindly into danger with no plan, no backup and hope for the best.' Luke smiled at her.

'Front door seems like the most reckless way in.'

CHAPTER 31

Mortuary Chapel, Moot Hill, Scone, Perthshire, Approximately the former site of the Parish Church of Scone and the Abbey of Scone.

The small gothic chapel that sat nestled in the grove of trees on Moot Hill may not have been a great fortified structure like the Bastille or Kenilworth; the gently sloping manicured grass certainly wasn't an obstacle that warranted a feet of military engineering to traverse like Alexander the Great's causeway to besiege Tyre. But, the chapel had one strategic advantage that none of those great structures had: one single door, one way in and one way out. Luke studied the arched portal from where they now stood, hidden from the structure by the thin tree line.

'We're seriously going to just walk in?' asked Evelyn, leaning over Luke's shoulder to get a clearer view of the chapel.

The first signs of Daniel's press conference had begun to appear along the road beyond the palace, the vanguard of unwitting soldiers that would spark Daniel's political war.

Luke slid back behind the tree's dense trunk.

'Unless you've been holding out on us and you can actually walk through walls, I don't see another option.'

Evelyn gave him a sharp side-eyed glance, not bothering to dignify his sarcasm with a response.

'I know it's the only way in, what I meant was what are we going to do? Just rush in and tackle him to the ground.'

Luke looked pointedly between Evelyn and Campbell.

'*We*, aren't doing anything, I lost the stone to Daniel so it's me who has to get it back.'

Not waiting for their inevitable protest Luke turned and started out from the tree line towards the chapel only to be stopped by a vice-like grip on his shoulder, yanking him backwards.

Luke protested but to no avail, Campbell had him pinned against the wide tree trunk, the detective's full weight holding Luke's shoulder against the rough bark.

'Listen Knight,' he hissed, 'I did not get shot at, drag your dead weight out of a loch, nearly get blown out of the sky by the RAF and then get held at gunpoint again just for you to swan back into the firing line. We all lost the stone to Daniel and two of us have much more reason to stop him than you do.'

'He's right, John tried to stop Daniel on his own

and look what happened,' the words caught in her throat. 'No one else is going alone.'

Luke didn't respond. He saw the look in Evelyn's eyes, the one that Campbell shared in his, this wasn't his fight, not entirely. Sure, Daniel had tried to kill him, repeatedly, but Luke's wounds would heal, they might leave a mark but what Daniel had done to Evelyn and Campbell cut far deeper, leaving scars that might never fade.

'So, if we could give it a rest with the heroic, self-sacrificing bullshit,' continued Campbell, 'we can finish this together.'

Luke nodded once, firmly and felt the pressure on his shoulder ease as Campbell stepped back. Luke straightened and moved to adjust the collar of his shirt that had been pushed out of place but his hands stopped, frozen at the voice that growled from behind Evelyn and Campbell.

'How touching.' Corban leered out of the shadows into the dying light. He wore a thin-lipped grin, like that of a hunter that had cornered his prey.

He reached inside his jacket and drew a wicked, long, curving knife.

'You killed my brother,' he said, pointing the tip of the knife at Luke.

'Eye for an eye,' Evelyn spat.

Luke took a step past her, closing the space between him and Corban's knife.

'Also, technically it was a seagull.'

Corban's grin fell, twisting into a vile hate-filled sneer.

'Mr Montrose said he didn't want guns here, didn't want to risk making a scene.' Corban twisted the knife in the air, the silvery blade glinting in the last of the evening sun. 'Unlucky for you really, because I'm going to enjoy this.'

He levelled the blade again slowly, then, swift as an arrow, he lunged towards Luke, slashing the knife upwards in a great arc.

The blade sailed through the air, inches from Luke in a blur of silver and Luke felt himself falling as Evelyn tackled him out of the blade's path.

Luke recovered in time to see Campbell's foot connect with Corban's chest, sending him hurtling backwards into the trunk of another tree.

'You two go,' Campbell shouted over his shoulder, a lethal calm coming over his body. 'Stop Daniel, I've got this prick.'

Luke helped Evelyn to her feet. 'What happened to not going it alone?'

'A lunatic with a knife.'

Luke nodded. 'Excellent point.'

Corban groaned, pushing himself up from the tree.

'Go!' said Campbell more forcefully.

Luke held Campbell's stare and bowed his head before making for the chapel, Evelyn in tow.

Campbell turned his attention back on the suited killer.

'No back up detective?' Corban mocked. 'Pity.'

Campbell caught Corban's arm as he thrust the knife again, locking his own arm over it and turning his body away from the blade so his back was to Corban.

'Your brother was taken out by a seabird,' he forced Corban's arm against his leg, bending the joint at an unnatural angle and forcing him to let go of the knife, 'I think I'm good.'

Corban broke out of Campbell's grip and lashed out with a fist before he could recover his footing.

The blow exploded on Campbell's temple and sent him staggering against the tree, the world continuing to move after he stopped.

He had barely stopped the ground spinning when Corban was on him again. Campbell blocked the first blow, barely, and returned a solid fist cracking into Corban's ribs.

He stumbled back and Campbell took the opening. Air rushed out of Corban's lungs as Campbell slammed his fist into the man's stomach then, as he doubled over, a swift uppercut that sent the killer on a short trip to the ground.

Campbell walked slowly over to Corban's prone form. The killer was trying to lift his weight from the earth on shaking arms. Campbell stopped by his side and put a foot on the man's back, forcing him back to the ground.

'I should kill you where you lie.'

He pushed his heel harder into the back of Corban's ribs, feeling the bones under his foot begin to bend. 'But lucky for you, I'd rather see you rot in a cell for the rest of your miserable little life.'

He lifted his foot from Corban's back and made to restrain the killer's arms.

Corban rolled suddenly and grabbed Campbell's foot, pulling the detective's legs from under him and toppling him.

As the suited killer knelt on Campbell's chest, it became all too clear what he had been crawling for the knife was back in his hand and hanging in the air, poised to plunge towards Campbell's heart.

'You should have killed me, detective,' spat Corban.

Campbell struggled to free himself but Corban's knee dug deeper into his sternum. The knife rose higher.

Campbell, unable to draw his eyes away from the hanging knife, searched blindly for anything that could stop the blade piercing his chest.

Corban smiled and plunged the knife just as Campbell's hand closed around a smooth chunk of stone sitting half-buried in the turf. He closed his eyes and swung his arm, tearing the stone from the ground in a desperate riposte to Corban's attack. The stone connected with Corban's head with a bone-splitting crack.

A dead weight collapsed onto Campbell, the knife, carried by the momentum of Corban's falling body, sunk into the ground over Campbell's shoulder, cutting a thin line through his shirt and the skin beneath as it did.

Campbell lay there for several seconds, breathing heavily. It took some significant effort to shift Corban's lifeless body off him, the small man being surprisingly heavy for his stature. A thin trickle of blood oozed from the wound on his temple, Campbell reached for the pulse in Corban's neck. He was alive and breathing shallowly. Shame, thought the dark part of Campbell's brain. He removed his belt and tied Corban's hands to the slender trunk of a young tree then stepped back. His foot knocked into something hard and he looked down to see the a reddish pink stone, the stone he had used to brain the man who had tried to stab him. Blood had already dried on the edge of what wasn't a piece of random geology, but instead a broken part of a neatly carved block, part of some long forgotten wall.

Campbell stooped to pick up the stone, throwing it in the air and catching it in his hand.

'I guess Luke was right, history is useful.'

✸ ✸ ✸

What little light was left by the setting sun barely penetrated through the heavy leaded windows of the chapel. It was smaller on the inside than it appeared, the space within only further constrained by the towering alabaster carving that adorned the western wall. Three men in Stuart dress were surrounded by ornate, flowing lines and watched over by two silent angels, reclining on a platform above. It was beautiful, the detail giving the figures motion, bringing them to life. Almost. Beautiful but cold, the bone white of the alabaster touched the figures with a sense of death that seeped out into the room beyond, the illusion of life with all of the vibrancy leeched out.

Luke stepped silently through the iron gate that sat within the doorway. His feet moved carefully across the flagstones, a cat stalking a bird as it preened its feathers, ignorant of shadows licking at its heels.

Deep red cloth laid draped over the alter that sat before the carved figures. Daniel moved his hands away from one of the candles that lined the alter, shaking the match he held and extinguishing the flame.

Flickering light danced across the pale stone faces, at times reflecting the alter cloth, spattering ghostly crimson stains over the stone. Luke felt Evelyn's presence by his side but kept his eyes on Daniel's back.

'Well Mr Knight, I am…. disappointed.'

Daniel was bathed in the warm glow of the candles as he pulled a cloth over the stone that sat atop the alter, the light sapped the colour from the bare skin that Luke could see, diluting Daniel's already muted tone to the waxy pallor of the statues.

'Did you really think I wouldn't come for it?'

He turned from the alter, the shining golden hilt and fittings of an aged cavalry sabre flashed as he moved and clattered against his side.

'No,' the familiar sneer spread across Daniel's face, 'I thought you'd be here sooner.'

He stepped slowly across the stone floor, circling. Luke mirrored his steps, following the slow dance across the chapel.

'And Evelyn, now you I thought had more sense than to come here, after all, the last Crawford who tried to stop me here ended up, to paraphrase Dickinson…' Daniel stopped and locked eyes with her, "sharing a carriage."'

Evelyn felt the sharp pain of her nails cutting into her palm, her hands were curled so tight it felt as though the bones were going to tear through the thin skin of her knuckles.

Luke put a hand on her shoulder but she shrugged it off and stalked towards Daniel. Step by slow, measured step she crossed the short distance to stand inches from him. 'He knew! He knew what you were doing, that no matter what pretty mask you wore, deep down, you're nothing but hate and rot and vile. You don't love this country, I'm not even sure you're capable of love.'

Daniel bristled and hissed back at her, 'John was weak, he wanted the stone to be given back to the people. So what if it served my own ends to find the stone? He still got what he wanted, the people have the true stone!'

'And you have the people?' spat Evelyn.

'Precisely,' Daniel took a step closer to her, 'and you would still have your brother.'

Evelyn threw her fist at Daniel's face, connecting her white knuckles with the fragile bone of his nose.

Daniel recoiled, burning pain searing beneath his eyes. 'You bitch.'

Blood flowed down Daniel's chin, dripping like grim rain, patters echoing across the chapel even over his garbled curses.

Metal shrieked as Daniel ripped the sabre at his side free of its scabbard and whipped the blade blindly towards Evelyn, his eyes still blurred from the tears streaming after the blow to his nose. Luke pulled Evelyn back, putting his own body between her and the shining sword.

'You'll be begging me to let you join your brother when I'm done with you,' Daniel seethed, flicking blood from his hand across the floor.

'One more move and she'll be talking to a corpse.'

A click echoed from the door, Campbell stepped through the opening, pulling back the slide of his Glock and chambering a round.

Daniel's face was impassive but the tip of the sword dipped, hesitant.

'Detective, always a pleasure,' he said without hint of warmth in his voice. 'Corban?'

Campbell smirked. 'Taking a nap, unfortunate side effect to getting brained with some masonry.'

Daniel's face hardened. 'Pity.'

'Stoned on the job,' Luke sighed and shook his head. 'Just can't get the henchmen these days.'

Campbell kept the gun's barrel steady, stepping sideways across the chapel floor to stand beside Luke and Evelyn.

'Give it up Montrose, you're not walking out of here with the stone.'

'Then we have reached an impasse,' said Daniel. He wiped the blood drying on his hand away on his fine jacket, no longer caring for the image. 'You say I won't walk out with the stone but you know I can't let you leave with it either.'

Luke hefted the sword at his side. 'Then I guess one of us isn't leaving.'

Silence fell across the room. Luke could hear his own heartbeat drumming in his ears, could almost hear those of the people beside him. The world outside the chapel ceased to exist, there was only the moment here, a deadlock. Luke saw Daniel breathe out slowly, the muscles in his shoulder almost imperceptibly tightened, coiling like the body of a viper.

Daniel struck out with the sabre, stepping out of the line of the gun and thrusting the blade at Campbell's chest like a bolt of cold lightning.

Luke was faster. He brought the broadsword up in an arc, catching Daniels blade and sending the tip of the sabre away from landing its fatal strike but not far enough to clear the detective completely. The flat of the sabre clattered into Campbell's hand, knocking the gun from his grip to clatter across the flagstones.

Daniel shoved off Luke's blade, stepping back and rounding the sword on Luke.

'You know Knight, before your constant meddling was just tiresome, but now I'm really pissed off.'

Daniel's face was flushed, contorted with an unrestrained rage. 'I'm going to make sure you can't come back this time.'

Luke shrugged and raised his sword. 'As you wish.'

The strike came faster than Luke had expected, Daniel struck from the right giving Luke only seconds to bring his sword up to parry. Steel rang against steel, echoing around the chapel. Luke wound his blade higher and thrust towards Daniel, striking him square on the shoulder. Daniel recoiled, pressing his hand against the spot the sword struck.

He took his hand away, confused at the absence of pain and lack of blood.

'You came for me with a blunt sword,' Daniel said, amused. 'I'm not sure if I should be offended or admire your bravery.'

'Offended,' said Luke as he struck at Daniel who easily parried the blow, 'admiring my bravery would mean I thought you could beat me.'

The swords came apart with a ring of hardened metal.

Luke and Daniel exchanged strike after strike filling the chapel with a deafening hum of clashing steel like a hundred out of tune church bells. Neither man gained the upper hand as they danced across the small space.

'You say I'm the evil one Knight, but it's you who are denying the people their history, denying their choice to be free.' Daniel's attacks were getting more frantic, wilder and looser. 'I'm a patriot, a hero.'

Luke parried another strike, Daniel's blade resting in place a moment too long. Luke exploited the mistake. He grabbed Daniel's arm with his free hand and forced it down until the tip of the sabre clashed with the ground.

'Please, Mel Gibson made a more convincing Scottish hero!'

Luke punched out with his sword hand, slamming the heavy basket hilt into Daniel's face with a sickening crack.

Daniel collapsed back, catching himself on the wall.

'And I'm not taking away their choice,' continued Luke stepping forward and pressing the blunted tip of the sword into Daniel's chest. 'I'm just stopping you from making it for them.'

Daniel spat a mouth full of blood onto the flagstones and roared, he pushed off the wall slapping Luke's sword away with the flat of his own.

Luke parried the first strike but the second found it's mark. Daniel feinted right drawing Luke's guard then cut left, too fast. Luke could only move his body to avoid taking the blade in full. The sabre's tip sailed through Luke's shirt as if it weren't there leaving a burning line across his chest. He looked down, a scarlet stain was blooming across the fabric, wicking through the fabric along the weave.

Luke dropped to one knee, putting the sword's point into the ground and leaning heavily to stop his body giving way completely.

'Goodbye Mr Knight.' Daniel raised his sabre and drew back the blade, leaving it hanging in the air, ready to deliver its final, fatal cut.

Time slowed as Luke watched the razor-sharp steel fall towards him. Somewhere in the distance he heard his name, Evelyn? Campbell? He couldn't tell who. There was nothing but him and the sword coming towards him, closer and closer.

Even Daniel's sneering face disappeared, only the blade remained. Mere inches from his head now, Luke closed his eyes and let out a slow breath and dropped to the ground throwing his hand out to brace against the floor as he ducked below Daniel's cut. He felt the air, heard the swoosh of the sword passing over his head. He didn't get the chance to relish in the confusion on Daniel's face, instead thrusting the blunted tip of his sword upwards and into Daniel's ribs as his momentum carried him onto the blade. Luke sprung to his feet and swung the dull broadsword, not at Daniel's body but at his arm. He felt the bones break under the blade as it connected. Daniel let out a blood-curdling scream and dropped the sabre, his hand no longer able to support the weight with the bones in his arm splintered and useless.

Luke caught the falling sabre by the hilt in his left hand and turned its momentum back on Daniel, drawing the edge across his thigh.

Daniel collapsed to his knees, blood from his wounds leaking onto the stone floor in a slowly growing pool. Luke almost pitied the figure cowering at his feet. Daniel cradled his ruined arm, the arrogance stripped from him. Luke put the sabre against Daniel's chin, forcing his head up, forcing Daniel to look at him.

'Come on Knight,' Daniel laughed weakly. 'If you're going to kill me get on with it.'

Luke's face remained unchanged, hard and impassive. He left the tip of the sword pressing into the delicate skin on Daniel's neck. 'I'm not going to kill you,' he said, letting the sword fall away.

Daniel let out a breath as Luke walked away and began to laugh slowly.

'I always knew you were weak.'

'I'm not going to kill you,' Luke continued as he reached Evelyn and Campbell, 'because you're not mine to kill.'

Daniel stopped laughing.

Evelyn took the hilt of the sabre that Luke offered her. She weighed it in her hands, turning the blade over so it trailed along the stones, screeching behind her as she stalked towards Daniel. She raised the sword and laid the point against his ruined shirt.

The tip of the sabre cut into Daniel's chest, splitting the skin over his heart and sinking slowly deeper. Evelyn stilled her hand, letting the blade sit only a centimeter into his flesh.

'I should kill you for what you did to John,' she leant on the sword, making it sink just a fraction deeper, 'what you've done to me, to Luke and to Campbell.'

The sword inched forwards a shade with every name.

'And what you tried to do to this country, my country.'

She twisted the sword, opening the wound and letting blood flow freely down Daniel's chest, finally eliciting the cry of pain she had been yearning for.

Campbell made towards her, to stop her from piercing the heart that had torn hers out, but was stopped by Luke's hand on his arm.

Evelyn was numb, the cold hilt of the sword bit into her hand as she gripped it hard but she felt nothing. A dissonant serenity not unlike that of the alabaster statues set over her. Stone-faced and impassive she pulled the sword back, leaving Daniel to slump to the floor, panting.

Shivers racked his body, adrenaline coursing through his veins and flowing down his body with the blood from the wound that was already beginning to clot.

Evelyn crouched low, leaning close to Daniel's ear and whispered.

'You're not worth it.'

Her whisper echoed around the chapel, the silence within so absolute. She rose and threw the sabre aside. The blood-stained blade clattered discordantly across the stones and came to rest in a forgotten corner of the room.

Evelyn found Luke's arm around her shoulder and let it guide her into a tight embrace. Her trance broken, silent tears fell down her cheeks in tiny rivulets. She felt Campbell's hand squeeze her shoulder and his usually hard voice softly say, 'it's done.'

It was done. Daniel lay on the cold stones by the alter sobbing quietly.

No, not sobbing. Luke's head snapped up. Laughing. Daniel was on his feet, Campbell's lost Glock in his hand, the yawning barrel like the maw of a terrible beast, pointing at Evelyn's back.

'If you're going to kill me,' Daniel smirked, 'make sure you finish the job.'

His finger tightened on the trigger.

Luke spun with Evelyn in his arms, his body replacing hers. Black flickered at the edge of his vision as his eyes met the deep fear in hers. Not fear for herself but for him, Luke realized as the gunshot cracked the air.

He screwed his eyes shut and… nothing.

Absolutely nothing. Luke peeled his eyes open and the dim candle-light flooded in. He wasn't dead. Had the bullet missed or was he in shock? Was adrenaline masking the pain from the searing lead tearing through him. No. He would have felt the impact at least. Luke spun to Daniel, the gun was still extended but the barrel was cold, no faint trail of smoke from burning gasses.

Daniel's smile faltered as his eyes trailed down to his chest. The blood-stained shirt he wore almost hid the neat hole the bullet had torn. He staggered the gun clattering to the ground as his legs gave way and his body folded awkwardly onto the floor.

Blood splattered the carvings behind the alter, strangely bringing life and colour to the quiescent figures as it drained from Daniel.

A footstep on the stone floor broke the silence left in the wake of the gunshot. Three heads spun towards the door. Black robes fluttered through the air as Father Keir stepped fully into the room and strode past Luke, Evelyn and Campbell without acknowledgment. He made towards Daniel's bleeding and broken form lying slumped like a discarded toy against the alter. Keir knelt in front of him, his pale white rosary beads clicking against the stones as he sank, and reached a hand for Daniel's head. He took Daniel's hair in his hand and forced his head up, made him look into Keir's cold eyes. 'I make sure.'

CHAPTER 32

Mortuary Chapel, Moot Hill, Scone, Perthshire, Approximately the former site of the Parish Church of Scone and the Abbey of Scone.

Luke didn't have much experience with death. Actually, that wasn't entirely accurate, death had been a constant companion for much of his recent life. Both those who had been buried in the earth for such a time that anything other than skeletons had long since been eaten away by time and decay, and the more recent. Unexpected war graves, if they could even be called such a thing, soldiers resting where they fell amongst barbed wire and shell holes, vestiges of clothing still clinging to the bones and names stamped on the metal around their necks. Even above the ground Luke wasn't unaccustomed to the violence in the world. War zones and cut throats were an unfortunate accompaniment to the world he lived in. But the difference was he had never been there in the final moments, even Dougal had been hundreds of feet below Luke when he hit the water.

Daniel was barely an arm's length away as the last touches of colour faded, his chest stopped its ragged lurching as lungs struggled for air and finally, his body slumped.

Keir let go of Daniel's hair, letting his head fall passively back against the alter. His eyes were as soulless as the statues of the angels watching over the scene—no spark, no light.

The rustle of cloth was as loud as a gunshot in the silence it left. Keir rose to full height and faced Luke.

'He that doeth wrong shall receive for the wrong which he hath done.'

'Avenge not yourselves, but rather give place unto wrath, for it is written, "vengeance is mine, I will repay," saith the lord,' retorted Luke, stone-faced.

Keir's mouth tweaked into a thin smile.

'I never thought anything from my theology lectures ever penetrated the stubborn disdain you always had for them.'

'Don't sound so surprised Keir, underestimating me is practically a pastime for you,' Luke shifted, positioning himself between the priest and his friends, 'and for the record it was you I had issues with, never your lectures.'

Luke's eyes flickered towards the gun still in Keir's hand. He had left Luke in some tight situations but the Priest's attitude towards Luke had always been more of irritation than outright malice. But then again, Luke had never seen him kill a man either and something about the way Keir held himself made him uneasy.

'But is it not the responsibility of the church and the clergy to do Gods will? To be his eyes, his ears, his hands.' Keir's own hand relaxed on the pistol's grip and he moved his finger out from the trigger guard, resting it on the slide. 'Besides, not to speak for the Almighty, but I think even a benevolent God would agree Mr Montrose deserved to reap what he had sown.'

Keir glanced indifferently at Daniel's body, the sight of the man he had gunned down having no effect of the priest's stony demeanour.

'Yes, that well-known addendum to the sixth commandment,' said Evelyn sarcastically, 'and Moses said unto the people, thou shall not kill... unless they've been a complete prick in which case, crack on.'

'Quite.' Keir glared at her.

He turned away from them and walked the few short paces to the alter, ignoring the body slumped against it. He rounded the platform and stood square to the cloth-covered stone that sat at its centre. If it weren't for Daniel, dead at the foot of the alter, Keir looked for all the world like he was about to deliver a sermon. The closest Luke had ever seen to glee swept across Keir's face as he pulled the cloth away and cast it aside.

Compared to the majesty of the alabaster

carvings, or the innate power commanded by the gothic chapel, the stone on the alter seemed unremarkable.

'Remarkable,' breathed Keir, 'Thirty-two monarchs have been crowned sitting on a seven hundred year old lie. The foundation of an institution has been nothing but pretence.'

Keir's hand moved towards the stone, stopping a hair's breadth from its surface as if some invisible shield lay over it.

'Rather fitting don't you think?' Keir lifted his head and smirked.

'Twenty-nine,' said Luke dryly. 'Mary II was crowned on an imitation and Edward's V and VIII were never crowned.'

Campbell coughed, 'nerd.'

Luke ignored him and took a wary step towards the alter.

'Why are you here?' he asked raising the tip of the sword slightly, not outright threatening but enough. 'And don't try and tell me you had a change of heart, we both know you don't have one.'

'The relationship between Crown and the Catholic Church has long been a tender thread,' he started to wrap the stone gently back into the shroud that had covered it. 'The reformation, the glorious revolution, the act of settlement. The church, in its wisdom, believed it best that its involvement in Edward's deception and the concealment of one of the most important symbols of the Crown's sovereignty over Scotland didn't come to light. 700 years of treason isn't something that would be forgiven lightly.'

The last glimpse of the stone disappeared beneath the shroud.

'In short Luke, I came for the stone, saving you three was merely collateral.'

Luke wiped his brow with the back of his wrist, scrunching his eyes shut as he tried to hold off the adrenaline leaving his system.

'I mean Keir, why now, why not just come after the stone from the start?' Luke threw his arm back down.

Keir strode across the chapel, his robes billowing behind him. He brushed past Luke and stopped at the iron gate. He stooped to pick up the dull brass bullet casing that had lodged nearly into a crack between the flagstones.

'Plausible deniability,' he said, rising back to full height and slipping the casing into a hidden pocket inside his robes, 'should things get as messy as I suspected they would.'

He turned and walked back to the stone. Luke's hand tightened on the sword as the priest moved back past him.

'You see as difficult a situation it would be should the part the church had to play in the stone's history be discovered, cold-blooded murder is something we would rather avoid.'

'Tell that to the Cathars.' Keir ignored him and rounded the alter.

'Then why not get the stone before all of this?' Evelyn exploded from behind Luke. 'Why wait for Daniel to kill John, to try and kill us?'

'Repeatedly,' added Campbell quietly.

Keir sighed and rested his arms on the table. He looked tired. Luke had never seen the priest as an old man, had never seen him as much more than a holy thorn in his side. But there in the flickering light of the candles, Keir actually looked almost human.

'We tried; we knew it was only a matter of time before someone outside the church uncovered the truth.' He looked pointedly at Luke. 'Thomas de Balmerino wrote of the deception while he was Abbot of Scone, Wishart and Beaton of its hiding, but it became clear we were missing some rather crucial details and quite frankly, we assumed if we couldn't find it no one could, that was until John came to me with what he had found...'

'John came to you for help?' Evelyn interrupted him.

'John came to me looking for Mr Knight,' corrected Keir, 'and I pointed him in a different direction.'

'Straight into a bullet,' spat Evelyn.

Keir gritted his teeth and hissed back, 'that wasn't my intention. I won't deny I was going to use him to find the stone but I underestimated

Daniel Montrose.'

Genuine remorse crept into his voice.

'The Lord knows Luke's moral self-righteousness would have gotten him killed if his mouth didn't manage it first, but John, I thought, would be safe with Daniel, at least until I could retrieve the stone from them.'

Evelyn stayed silent, her eyes burnt like torched spirit. She walked slowly to the edge of the chapel, to where the sabre lay discarded, the cold steel still stained with Daniel's blood.

'Do not repay evil with evil, that's what the bible says, doesn't it?' Evelyn turned and weighed the sabre in her hand then swung the curved tip towards Keir. 'I suggest you leave before God decides to test my faith.'

Keir stayed silent, he dropped his eyes from Evelyn and bowed to retrieve the wrapped stone from the alter.

A metallic clang rung though the chapel as the blade of a sword appeared atop the stone a few inches below Keir's face.

He studied his reflection in the polished steel for a moment and sighed.

'Luke, Luke, Luke,' Keir said, practically shouting the last. 'The stone belongs to the church, you have no right to stop me taking it to its rightful place.'

Luke's arm was as rigid as the sword, he kept the blade pressed firmly against the stone.

'The stone belongs to the people Keir, *you* have no right to take it to some dusty Vatican archive a thousand miles from where it belongs.'

Luke relaxed his arm, tilting his wrist up and bringing the sword's blunted tip to the white square of the priest's collar and forcing him to take a step back.

'It'll take more than a blunted sword to stop me from taking that stone Luke.'

Keir pressed forward as much as the sword would allow without choking him, keen not to let the stone out of reach.

Luke smiled and held the sword firm.

'Funny, he said the same thing.' Luke nodded at Daniel's cold, colourless body that was still slumped at the foot of the alter.

Keir looked quickly away from the body.

His faced hardened as he hissed.

'I'm taking the stone Luke.'

'Not if I stop you Keir.'

'You and whose army?'

A second blade appeared at Keir's throat. Evelyn pressed the very not blunt edge of the sabre against Keir's pulse.

'This one,' she said, grinning viciously.

Keir's head snapped towards the click of a slide being pulled back, making the sharp steel sabre bite into his neck, leaving a thin red line.

'Not so much an army,' Campbell stood from where he retrieved his Glock from Daniel's body and trained the barrel on Keir, 'more of a bunch of hapless misfits.'

Keir seethed but kept still, save deepening the cut to his neck.

'I told you I didn't want to see you harmed Luke,' the thin veins in Keir's temples popped as he hissed at Luke. The priest's glare was sharper than the blade at his neck and cut deep into Luke. 'But that was when you were still useful to me. Should that change you will find my benevolence painfully short lived.'

Keir flinched, sucking air though his teeth as Evelyn pressed the sabre into the thin cut it had already made.

'So much for the virtue of charity,' said Luke. He let the tip of the sword fall away from Keir's throat and waved for Evelyn to do the same. The sabre was more reluctant to move but dropped to Evelyn's side, tension flowing out of Keir's muscles as it did so.

The priest regained himself and stalked around the alter. He paused close to Luke, not so much face to face since the top of Luke's head barely met Keir's chin but the priest stood in a way that Luke was all but isolated by his imposing form despite Evelyn and Campbell being only a few steps away. Keir leaned further over Luke, blocking off most of what little light still remained.

'It's a brave man that makes an enemy of God Luke, but it's a fool that makes an enemy of the

Church.'

Luke didn't back down from the priest, instead for all the world he appeared to rise to Keir's height, presence of will making up for the difference in stature.

'If being a friend of the people makes me an enemy of God, so be it,' Luke stepped closer to Keir and whispered, 'and if you're the worst the Church can throw at me, then I'm offended.'

Luke stared into Keir's cold blue eyes as he walked slowly backwards until he was flanked by Evelyn and Campbell.

For a heartbeat it looked as though Keir would rush forward and make good his threats but instead black robes flapped as he turned and walked swiftly through the iron gate and the chapel door beyond.

Luke breathed a sigh of relief and rushed over to the alter. He reached towards the cloth that wrapped the stone but his hand froze in the air.

'What's wrong?' asked Evelyn.

'Nothing, just...' Luke let his hand rest on the clothed stone, '...The Stone of Destiny, it's inspired wars and revolutions, songs, poems, movies. It was at the centre of a suffragette bombing, concealed during the war with secret maps drawn to its hiding place, taken home by students who loved their country, broken in two and buried in a Kentish field. And all that time, all that the stone symbolised and inspired.'

Luke couldn't contain his laugh. 'No one inspired by that lump of rock knew that it was nothing but a seven hundred year old up your's to the King.'

Whether it was the absurd truth in what Luke had said, or hysteria from the traumas of the past few days they would never know but as Luke laughed Evelyn and Campbell joined him until it echoed though the tiny Chapel.

Luke regained his composure and slid the stone towards the edge of the alter. He grunted in pain as he strained to lift its weight and the wound across his chest burned anew.

Evelyn moved in to take some of the weight and together the two of them manoeuvred the stone towards the chapel door.

'What now?' asked Evelyn as they struggled with the stone.

Luke's face twisted with the pain in across his chest.

'Now we get this stone out of here until we figure out what to do with it. It won't be long before the press Daniel arranged arrive and either find Corban unconscious in the grounds or wonder where the charming man of the hour is and come looking.'

As if on cue blue lights shone through the tall windows, dancing across the walls accompanied by muffled but serious voices outside.

'Looks like out the front isn't an option,' panic edged into Campbell's voice. 'How did they get here so fast, response times aren't that good.'

'I would wager we have our friendly neighbourhood priest to thank for that.' Luke cursed and guided Evelyn to set the stone onto the floor and walked to the centre of the chapel. He picked up the broadsword and slotted the tip into a gap between the stone floor and a squared slab that lay at its centre.

'What are you doing?'

'This is a mortuary chapel,' said Luke carefully pressing his weight onto the sword. 'It would have been used by the family at Scone…'

'Not the time Luke,' Campbell snapped.

Luke frowned at him but relented. 'Fair enough, the point is there's a vault below, a crypt, there will be stairs leading back outside.'

The slab shifted up, Luke grabbed the edge that protruded and strained to lift it up revealing a dark, damp room below.

'There's always a back door.'

The voices outside sounded closer to the door and feet in heavy boots trudged towards the chapel.

'Time to go,' said Luke as he helped Evelyn drop down into the vault below.

Luke sat on the edge of the hole, swung his legs over the edge and dragged the stone towards him. He turned to Campbell who still stood by the metal gate, looking at Daniel's body and the lights flashing through the windows.

'Joining us?' Campbell shook his head slowly.

'Someone needs to explain what the hell happened here, plus as far as the police are concerned you two are still persons of interest. If I don't clear up this mess you and Evelyn will be in a heap of trouble.'

Luke got up from the hole and held his hand out to Campbell who took it and shook it firmly. 'It's been a hell of an adventure.'

'Aye, that it has.'

Luke pulled the detective into an embrace and clapped him on the back with his free hand.

'Don't think you'll be rid of me this easy,' said Luke. He released Campbell and strode back to the hole, dropping his legs back into the opening. 'I promise a less life-or-death adventure next time.'

Campbell smirked and called after him, 'I told you Luke, some of us like the danger.'

Luke gave a joking salute then dropped through the hole, dragging the stone with a after him with a grunt.

Campbell had only moments to shift the slab back into place, concealing Luke and Evelyn's escape, before the door to the chapel rocked with the long arm of the law trying to break through. Campbell turned just as the door burst open.

'DS Edward Campbell,' shouted Campbell holding up his badge as a flood of armed police poured into the chapel.

A tall, wiry, dark-haired officer led the charge

into the small space. He stopped in front of Campbell, taking a moment to register the badge.

'DI Simon Nicholas,' the detective inspector looked around the room at the swords lying on the floor, the blood splattered effigies and at Daniel's body lying against the alter. 'What the hell happened in here?'

Campbell smirked and tucked his badge back inside his jacket. 'Trust me Sir, you wouldn't believe me if I told you.'

❊ ❊ ❊

Daniel was met by a storm of flash bulbs on leaving the chapel. Unfortunately, he would have been hard pressed to enjoy the grand moment he had planned from the black vinyl bodybag his corpse lay in. Crime always did garner more interest than history or politics ever did and the collected media being held back by the police lines was more than even Daniel's wildest dreams could have imagined. Journalists and cameras all baying for a snippet of the story of the decade. In the end he got his wish in a way, Daniel would be remembered for a long time, after-all its the infamous that have their place in history etched deep into the public memory and when the headlines broke in the early hours of the morning, infamy is what he would have.

Luke and Evelyn watched the trails of blue lights of emergency vehicles still swarming the grounds of the Palace of Scone as they drifted gently along the River Tay towards the coast.

'You know he's going to kill you for stealing another boat,' Evelyn teased as she took a seat beside Luke at the boat's helm.

'Borrowed, I borrowed another boat and I left a note. Anyway, what Campbell doesn't know won't hurt him, or rather he can't hurt me for.'

Evelyn giggled softly. Her hand drifted over the stone at Luke's feet. He hadn't let the bundle leave his side for a second. He wasn't going to lose it again.

'What happens to it now?' asked Evelyn.

Luke glanced down at her. Even in the dark her eyes burned with the intense blue of a raging ocean. The Stone of Destiny, whose destiny though?

'What would you do with it?'

Evelyn smiled absently and sang softly into the night.

'o ghalghad a' Chlach, 'S gur coma leam i 'n Cearrara,

An Calasraid no 'n Calbhaigh, Cho fad' 's a tha i 'n Albainn.'

She looked up at Luke when he said nothing and saw the deep confused frown on his face.

'It's a poem by Donald Macintyre, about the stone being brought home. *"My brave Stone, I don't care whether it's in Kerrera, Callendar or Calvay. As long as it's in, Steep, rugged Scotland."'* She let her hand rest atop the stone, 'it's what John wanted.'

Luke put a hand on her shoulder and gave a reassuring squeeze.

'It belongs to Scotland, to the people, but…'

'But no one can ever know it's been returned or someone like Daniel could use it for their own ends. So, what do we do?'

Luke looked thoughtfully into the distance before shrugging. 'We give it to the people without them knowing.'

It was Evelyn's turn to frown. 'You sound like you have a plan?'

'I might have an idea.'

'I'm guessing it's not entirely legal.'

Luke's grin was all the confirmation Evelyn needed that her suspicion was correct. She shook her head at him then stood and leaned against the railing that topped the gunwale.

Cold wind blew her hair as she closed her eyes and felt the bite of the breeze on her face.

'How do we go back to normal after this?' she said after a long silence. 'After all this, what? You go back to the university and adventuring around the world. And I try and figure out what normal even is anymore.'

'I doubt I have anything to go back to, not at the university anyway, Keir will have seen to that by now.' A hint of bitterness touched Luke's voice but disappeared as quickly as it came. 'Although just before I left I heard a rumour about the lost grave of Edward the Martyr. I might check it out and see if I can pull a Richard the III and find him in a carpark.'

Luke watched Evelyn's head bow, some of the light falling from those burning eyes. He cut the boat's engine and joined Evelyn staring into their reflections in the dark water.

'You know, I always thought normal was overrated,' said Luke, 'so if you want my advice don't go back to it.'

Evelyn scoffed, 'and do what instead, go hunting lost treasures and thwart evil plots with you?'

'Why not?' said Luke.

Evelyn snapped her head towards him and raised her eyebrow. 'Are you serious?'

'Sure,' said Luke, a wide smile spreading across his face.

'I warn you though it's not all swash buckling and glory, it's muddy, thankless and more often than not you end up running for your life. Plus, you have to put up with me,' Luke added with a grin. He turned to face Evelyn fully, 'so what do you think?'

'Edward the Martyr you say?' Evelyn beamed at him through the dark night. 'I think we have a train to catch.'

EPILOGUE

3 months later

It didn't feel like they had won, not really. Campell flipped the thick manila file closed and tossed it back into the open desk drawer. He leant back in his chair and stretched the tension out of his spine, unsure if the creaking was the chair or his back. The months since Scone had taken their toll. Daniel's part in the murder of John Crawford wasn't hard to prove. His arguments with John and the communication with Corban and Dougal had taken the digital forensics team less than a day to uncover and the contents were damning. The messages on Daniel's phone lead a trail to John's body, not to mention practically storyboarding Daniel's crimes, complete with a cast and crew. There was enough evidence to keep them all in some sorry forgotten cell for a lifetime. Unfortunately, only Corban was charged. Daniel and Dougal would never answer for what they did, after all, it's quite hard to prosecute corpses.

Funnily enough Daniel and Dougal's deaths would too go unpunished. Investigations into the deaths dried up soon after they started and were swiftly lost in a dark corner of a filing cabinet. Campbell had expected to have a tough time explaining everything that had happened and turning attention away from Luke and Evelyn, not to mention the stone. But there turned out to be little appetite to pursue the matters. No doubt Keir had some hand in enquires being quietly forgotten and any mention of the Stone of Destiny being left out of the official reports. Probably the only helpful thing the priest had done since they had crossed his path.

Everything was fading into the past; Luke and Evelyn were free and absolved of sin. Although, from what little he'd heard of them, it would be forgiven to think the pair were still on the run.

Campbell had gotten a few scant updates on their exploits, once or twice in the form of police reports. Nothing ever mentioning them by name but when you hear of CCTV catching two people running through the battlefield of Bannockburn memorial carrying spades, well, it didn't take a detective.

The door at the far end of the office creaked open as a short, dark-haired detective slipped into the room.

DS Clary Angel. A position had recently opened making way for the young Sergeant's transfer from the Met. There were a few things Campbell had expected to come from the aftermath of their adventure to find the stone and stop Daniel. A prolonged enquiry, disciplinary proceedings, and a likely suspension. But not a promotion. Although he had to admit, Detective Inspector Edward Campbell had a nice ring to it.

'Morning Angel, what have we got.'

The detective smiled and handed a folder to Campbell.

'Break in at Kelvingrove boss.'

Campbell's hand stopped on the folder and he frowned, puzzled.

'Robbery isn't our remit Angel, uniforms can handle it.' He moved to hand back the file but Clary pushed it back into his hand.

'Not a robbery sir, nothing was taken.'

'Still doesn't explain why you're bringing it to me.'

'Nothing was taken, but something was left.'

She opened the file in Campbell's hand to reveal a small square of paper with a handwritten note.

'It was in an envelope addressed to you tucked into the frame of an oil portrait of Robert Burns,' DS Angel laughed. 'Either they were trying to get your attention or they're the worst thieves I've ever seen. Almost every alarm between their entry point and the portrait was tripped.'

Campbell wasn't listening anymore, his eyes were scanning the note, just two short lines.

Sometimes history is set in stone, sometimes it's

only buried beneath the ground and all we need do is dig it up.

Nothing is ever truly lost, things turn up as surely as the break O'day glints in the East.

'Does it mean anything to you?'

Campbell read the lines over and over. Something was staring him in the face but he couldn't see. He shook his head slowly.

'Funny, that last line,' said Clary looking over the page. 'It's like the Burns' poem, "At Bannockburn the English lay,– The Scots they were nae far away, But waited for the break o' day, that glinted in the east."'

'What's wrong with some simple directions?' Campbell said under his breath. 'I'm really getting tired of…' he trailed off and snapped his head up at Clary.

'Did you say Bannockburn?'

AUTHOR'S NOTE

They say never to let the truth get in the way of a good story, but more often than not the real historical detail is far more exciting and unbelievable than any work of fiction. It's because of this that the historical details and backgrounds of Set In Stone are based on published historical sources, modern archaeological and historical publications, and are accurate as far as possible. This being said, some minor details have been altered or invented as was required by the story. For example, to the best of my knowledge there is no hidden chamber beneath Wallace's well, similarly both the tunnel between Glasgow High Court and the Tollbooth, and the basement room at Inchmurrin Castle are documented only in rumour, anecdote, and some in person observation.

I would love to go through every point in Set In Stone and talk about the historical fact and any creative liberties I have taken, however this would end up being a book in its own right and

I simply don't have the space to do that here. So, while I have used history as a foundation and a starting point, despite Luke's penchant for giving history lessons, Set In Stone is a work of fiction not a textbook. If reading this book can inspire an interest in researching the wild and wonderous history of Britain I would be overjoyed, but its main purpose is to entertain, and I hope this admission does not diminish that for anyone.

Acknowledgements

I will be forever grateful to my friends and family who encouraged and supported me through the, at times, difficult journey that brought Set In Stone to life. Without their (mostly) unwavering patience you would not be reading this today.

Thanks, are also most certainly due to my brilliant Editor Natalie Angus without whom you would likely need the Rosetta Stone to decipher this book.

My friends at Clashing Steel, without you all Luke's fights would be far less exciting.

Finally, to all of you, the readers who gave Luke Knight a chance and joined in his adventure, especially those who read the early drafts: Jodie Pinnell, Kerry Randall, Stephanie Campbell (many drinks are owed). I first wrote Set In Stone just for myself, but I couldn't be happier to share it with all of you.

ABOUT THE AUTHOR

Sam L. Randall

Sam was born and raised in the heart of the West Country, surrounded by some of the richest historical landscape in the world. After completing a degree in Archaeology and Anthropology he went on to work in both research and commercial archaeology.

When he's not writing, Sam is diving headfirst (sometimes literally) into history, whether that be in the field or competing in archery and historic fencing.

Email: samlrandallauthor@outlook.com
Instagram: @sam_l_author
TikTok: @sam.l.author

www.ingramcontent.com/pod-product-compliance
Ingram Content Group UK Ltd.
Pitfield, Milton Keynes, MK11 3LW, UK
UKHW020636290125
4342UKWH00045B/652